T0278159

Book 2
Supercharge Your Body and Brain Power

TALKING ABOUT
ADOLESCENCE

How to Navigate Through Adolescence
Successfully and Have a Happy Life

Eichin Chang-Lim, OD, MS, MA

Adolescence is a border between childhood and adulthood.
Like all borders, it's teeming with energy and fraught with danger.
~ Mary Pipher

Reviewed and edited by Lora L. Erickson PhD,
LCPC, LMHC-QS, LPC

ISBN: 979-8-35095-992-5 (print)
ISBN: 979-8-35095-993-2 (eBook)

AUTHOR'S NOTE

Have you ever wondered why you sometimes feel like a kid and sometimes like an adult? Why do you have mood swings, growth spurts, and weird dreams? Why do you suddenly care more about what others think of you and how you fit in? The answer is simple: As an adolescent, you're in one of the most exciting and transformative periods of your life, where you'll experience rapid changes in both your body and brain. They are changing and developing rapidly, making you smarter, stronger, and more capable every day. But they also need your help to reach their full potential. You must feed them with knowledge and challenge them with new experiences, skills, and goals. You need to protect them from harm, stress, and bad habits.

You will learn how to do all that and more in this book. You will discover how your body and brain work, what they need, and how they affect your thoughts, feelings, and actions. You will get practical tips and advice on coping with these challenges and making the best decisions for yourself.

With *Supercharge Your Body and Brain Power*, you'll better understand how your body and brain work together and how you can optimize their growth and take control of your health and well-being. You'll learn practical strategies for staying healthy, managing stress, and building resilience during this critical time. So, if you're ready to take charge of your health and well-being and embark on a journey of self-discovery and personal growth, optimizing your physical and brain development in this crucial period, this book is for you.

Each book under the umbrella of the *Taking About Adolescence* series is a standalone book. These books are written in a conversational style and use a PowerPoint format to keep readers engaged and to provide relevant knowledge—knowledge that can be a powerful tool when you need it. For adolescents, these books serve as handbooks or guidebooks. Every chapter begins with one or more thought-provoking quotations, followed by a box, **Questions for You to Ponder**, and ends with another box, **Chapter Reflections**. Please take a moment to contemplate those questions. Doing so will help you solidify what you have learned in greater depth!

You may also find superscripts (small numbers just above the text line) after some sentences or paragraphs, which tell you the sources of the information. You may find the detailed data and report under the **References for Each Chapter** section in the later part of this book. The author recommends you focus on the text and skip the superscripted numbers during your first read for smooth reading. You can always dive into the depth of the contents in that specific passage later.

For a deeper understanding of each chapter's material, please check out the **Appendices** section after going through the text. You can also find vast amount of information in the **More References and Relevant Resources** section to better understand certain subjects that pique your interest.

These books aim to equip adolescent readers with the knowledge to make sound decisions at a crossroads. Even if you perceive that you have no challenges in life, this knowledge may help you understand or help your friends who are going through a tough time. My deepest desire is for all of you, teens and young adults, to become successful, thriving adults and have a happy life. YOU are the future pillars of society and the leading players in the ever-changing world.

Although *Talking About Adolescence* is written for teens and young adults, parents, guardians, therapists, and educators will also find it enlightening. They can use it as a reference or resource when interacting with adolescents. Also, adults can use it as an icebreaker to open the door to healthy dialogue about topics that have until recently been taboo.

PROFESSIONAL DISCLAIMER

The author does not endorse any sites, products, or advertisements presented in this book or associated with any sites or links. The author has no financial affiliations with or financial interests in any of the products presented or associated with any sites or links mentioned or referenced in this book. The author and editor have done their best to ensure the accuracy and authenticity of the information. However, due to the complexity of and rapid advances in the understanding of the human mind, the field of mental health, and health care, the author and editor cannot be held accountable or assume liability for any information that is outdated or inaccurate. This book and any reference sites, links, or advertisements are not substitutes for mental health or health care advice. If you have questions or concerns about your or your loved ones' mental health, you should always contact your primary physician or mental health professional.

Last but not least, I want to mention that all the links and images included in this manuscript are to serve as references and resources for the readers, and we have credited the content to the originators. We sincerely appreciate the creators and speakers associated with these links for the valuable information they provide. We have no intention of violating the copyrights. If you are the creator or speaker of any links and do not want your product or presentation to be included in this book, please inform us, and we will remove it upon request without delay.

CONTENTS

Author's Note v

Professional Disclaimer vii

Part 1

Your Exciting Journey from Childhood to Adulthood

Chapter 1: How Does the Journey Begin?. 3

Chapter 2: Your Amazing Body is Transforming 11

Chapter 3: Secondary Sex Characteristics. 16

Chapter 4: The Primary Sexual Characteristics 22

Part 2

Your Precious Brain is Developing

Chapter 5: An Overview of Our Remarkable Brain 31

Chapter 6: Your Growing Brain is Reorganizing 44

Chapter 7: How to Take Advantage of Dual Systems in the
Developing Brain. 49

Chapter 8: Plasticity, Prime Time,
and a Second Window of Opportunity 60

Chapter 9: Why Addiction is a Thief to Your Brain Power 64

Part 3

How to Nurture and Supercharge Your Developing Brain and Body

Chapter 10: The Classical Developmental Theories
and Dual Systems 97

Chapter 11: What is Executive Function?. 103

Chapter 12: How to Optimize Your Executive Function............111

Chapter 13: How to Support Your Mental Health and
Optimize Your Brain Development 133

Chapter 14: How Not to Let Childhood Trauma Interfere
With Your Brain Development...................................187

Chapter 15: Transformation through the Confidence in Yourself.. 230

You are Empowered: Transformation through Knowledge
and Action 252

Appendices 255

References for Each Chapter......................................275

Additional References and Relevant Resources....................317

Acknowledgements 371

About the Author 373

About the Reviewer and Editor 375

About This Series..377

Part 1

YOUR EXCITING JOURNEY FROM CHILDHOOD TO ADULTHOOD

The process of transitioning from childhood to adulthood has many names: sexual maturation, puberty, reproductive development, adolescence, menarche, and adrenarche. You may have heard of and even used some of them.

In this book, let's speak of the process as a journey. That's really what it is, right? An exciting, scary, wonderful, sometimes challenging, journey. I like to refer to you as an "adolescent" and this period as "adolescence."

Some refer to this process as "a caterpillar transforming into a butterfly." Although it could at times feel unpleasant and uncomfortable, the outcome is stunning. Adolescence also serves as a reminder that change is a natural part of life. Understanding that things will change is part of growing up.

With that being said, are you ready to embark on this journey? Let's go!

Chapter 1

HOW DOES THE JOURNEY BEGIN?

Puberty was rough. But I learned that it's important to embrace your flaws and imperfections, because they make you who you are.

~ *Demi Lovato*

Questions for You to Ponder

As you read through this chapter, please consider the following questions:

- What does the famous quote "Knowledge is power" mean to you?

- What things in your life stress you out the most at this moment? Is it about your schoolwork or your relationship with family members? Or something else?

- What does the term "puberty" mean to you? Good or bad?

- What is your reaction when adults remark that you are in puberty?

Introduction

During adolescence, your understanding of the world is thrown into chaos, thanks to rapid physical, sexual, and emotional changes. Adjusting to all these changes can be exciting, confusing, disheartening, and stressful. On top of all these, you're expected to keep up with academic demands and adults' expectations.

No wonder some people regard adolescence as one of the most thrilling, yet challenging, times of life.

The Initiation of Adolescence

Entering puberty is marked as the beginning of adolescence. The American Psychological Association defines *puberty* as "the stage of development when the genital organs reach maturity, and secondary sex characteristics begin to appear, signaling the start of adolescence."

You may say, "Hey, wait a minute. I didn't sign up for this initiation." I know that! You are right! None of us asked to be born. Getting on the train for this journey is not like joining a club. Your body automatically proceeds to the changes. In fact, your body has undergone the transformation even before you notice it. There are a few things to be noted:

- Physical and sexual maturation occurring during puberty is due to the increase in gonadal hormone. Everyone goes through puberty and begins the journey of adolescence at their own pace and timing.

- You might be tempted to compare your puberty changes with those of your friends. Please be aware that no two people have the exact same experiences during puberty. Please ask your parents, a trusted adult, or school nurse if you have any questions or concerns about your body changes.

- The onset of puberty and the initiation of adolescence depends on several factors, such as genes, gender, nutrition, and environment. After researching and reading, I have found the age of pubertal onset ranges from 8 to 14 years for females and 10 to 16 for males. You may find some variations in different reports.

- Researchers also reported that pubertal onset starts earlier now than in the 1970s. There is no definite explanation for that. However, social scientists are studying the implications that might result from individuals experiencing puberty at an earlier age.[1, 2, 3]

Stages of Adolescence

As mentioned earlier, adolescence is a journey. You are a unique individual. However, your growth along this journey may be influenced by outside factors, like your family, neighborhood environment, culture, faith, and the media. Based on the collective characteristics of physical, biological, intellectual, behavioral, emotional, and social developments, researchers suggest three phases along this journey: early, middle, and late adolescence/young adulthood.

Early Adolescence (10 to 14 Years)

In this phase, you are somewhere between fifth grade and junior high school.

During this time, you may be asking yourself, "Am I normal?"

- Your body is changing rapidly as puberty begins. You may feel overwhelmed, awkward, self-conscious, and insecure about your appearance.[4]

- You may become anxious and wonder whether your peers are judging you.

- You want privacy. You don't want anyone else in your bedroom. If you share a bedroom with your siblings, you don't want anyone to get near your desk. You guard your phone so that no one can listen to your phone conversations or see your text messages.

- You want a sense of independence and can be annoyed by the adults treating you like a child and constantly asking your whereabouts or nagging about little things when you think it's absolutely unnecessary.

- You want to hang out with your peers, those you call your close friends, to share your secrets and stories. It's much more fun with your buddies than with your family!

- You feel it is *super* important that you fit in with your peer group.

- You may start arguing with your parents more frequently and doubt your parents' opinions. You might Google whatever your parents say, intending to find faults.

- You may be plain rude to your parents without concern for their feelings, especially when they seem to disagree with you about everything: your music, the TV shows you watch, the amount of time you spend on social media, or how you dress.

- You get moody and act out your emotions more than you intend to. You might feel overly sensitive or become easily agitated.

Middle Adolescence (14 to 17 Years)

Most of you are attending high school at this stage. You may be asking yourself, "Who am I?" and try to discover your strengths and interests during this time.

- The puberty-related changes continue. Some of you may become interested in romantic relationships, exploring sex and sexuality.

- Intellectual thinking becomes important to you.

- You may have difficulty controlling your impulses and handling peer pressure. Because of that, you may make inappropriate or unwise decisions that you might regret later. (We will talk about the reasons and remedies for this in later chapters. Don't feel awful if you've made poor decisions. Think about how to avoid making the same mistake next time, though).

- The tension between you and your parents or immediate adults may intensify because you strive to be independent.

- At this stage, you may be even more self-conscious about your appearance. Concerns about sexual attractiveness and popularity can be an important matter. Some of you may become a loner and sink into constant self-doubt and depression. (We will talk more about this later, so hang in there for now).

- You may alternate between being overly self-confident, with high expectations, and feeling self-doubt with intense insecurity.

- You may have feelings of passion and love for someone special during this time. You might even be fearful of showing them your true feelings. This can consume you and affect your concentration at school and at home. You probably share your secret with your close friends.

- You grow greater awareness in moral reasoning, and intellectual gain becomes important.

- You may advance your ideals, select your role models, and search for spirituality.

- You may begin thinking about your future.

Those who intend to go to college are often stressed with grades. To boost your college application, you may be registering for advanced placement (AP) classes, taking the ACT and SAT, joining extracurricular activities, etc. All of these can generate tremendous pressure on you. Deciding on a major or field of study can be challenging. Working with your high school counselor is essential.

Some of you may join the military and set long-term goals. Additionally, for those who plan to enter the workforce after high school, you may take ROP (Regional Occupational Program) classes and contemplate your future career. You may do part-time jobs and consult with your school counselor for guidance or check out the free online career tests at https://www.truity.com.

Yes, finding what you like to do and your occupational direction can be overwhelming. At this time, you may even feel the burden and worries of becoming financially independent.

- Some may drop out of school due to unforeseen circumstances or engage in risky behaviors.
- Some youth in foster care may face an age-out dilemma and need support. For support and resources on transitioning to independence, learning about opportunities for educational advancement, and participating in job training programs, please check out local Foster Care Transition Programs, the Annie E. Casey Foundation, and the National Foster Youth Institute (NFYI).

  https://www.aecf.org/resources/fostering-youth-transitions-2023

  https://nfyi.org/

Late Adolescence/Young Adulthood (18 to 25 years or beyond)

You may continue with your academic pursuits or enter the job market at this stage. The lingering questions can remain: "Where am I going?" Or, "Am I heading in the right direction?" Therefore, you focus more on the future based on your hopes and ideals.

- Most of you have fully grown, physically and biologically.
- You may become more comfortable with your body and sexual feelings.

- You gain a stronger sense of your own individuality/identity and establish your values.

- You have better impulse control and judge risks vs. rewards more accurately. You are more stable emotionally and gain the ability to delay gratification.

- Some may have a stable romantic relationship. You gain confidence in tender and sensual love. However, some may put the steady, intimate relationship on the back burner until the completion of graduate/professional school or until their income reaches a certain level.

- You probably move away from your parents but reestablish an adult relationship with them. You might consider your parents' advice and respect their perspective more.

- You may take more time to examine your inner experiences and increase concerns for others. You are likely to pay more attention to social and cultural issues.

Erikson's Fifth Stage of Psychosocial Development

In his psychosocial developmental theory, German American psychologist Erik Erikson lists the entire adolescent period as Stage 5.[5] He titled this stage "Identity vs. Role Confusion."

You learn from your past experiences by exploring your independence, experimenting with different roles, grasping societal expectations, and reflecting on your strengths and goals to develop a unique sense of self and identity. The fundamental virtue evolving through adolescence is fidelity.

It is not uncommon for university students to change their major in the first two years. Also, job-hopping is common during the early stages of a career, especially among younger generations. However, you may suffer from "role confusion" if you find yourself:

- Constantly feel restless, lost, or confused about your place in life
- Uncomfortable in many social situations and often avoid a social life
- Uncertain about your aspirations and sexuality
- Feel inadequate and unable to form a stable friendship or close relationship

If you or someone you care about is struggling with role confusion or identity issues, I encourage you to talk to a mental health professional. It is not something to be ashamed of, and it is never too late to get help. We are all human!

Chapter Reflections

1. Considering this chapter's content, is there someone you have read about or encountered who handled the transition from adolescence to adulthood well? What sticks out in your mind about their success?

2. Going deeper, what is one way you envision your transition to adulthood with hope and positivity about your future? What special skills, mindset, or talents will get you there?

3. How can you see yourself supporting an adolescent once you are an adult—with the knowledge and support you received or wish you would have receive

Chapter 2

YOUR AMAZING BODY IS TRANSFORMING

Most of what I've written songs about are things that come out of the confusing emotional, spiritual and psychological period of time when you're going through puberty.

~ Ian Anderson

Questions for You to Ponder

As you read through this chapter, please consider the following questions:

1. How well do you know this body that you inhabit? I understand this question is broad. Please take a moment to contemplate it, then move on to the following few questions.

2. How has your body served you well so far in life?

3. What part of your body are you most grateful for?

4. How do you currently show love and care for your body?

Introduction

Puberty may stir your sexual curiosity and desires. It is completely normal. I love watching nature shows on Netflix. When the time comes, almost all living things on earth will display their unique tactics for attracting and finding a mate, like flaunting their feathers or singing with special mating calls. It is part of nature's design.

I don't recall my parents ever talking to my brothers and me about the birds and the bees or relationships. I assume my brothers found out from pornographic magazines during recess in the boy's restroom in junior high, whereas I only learned about sex later. However, I obtained my sex education by reading R-rated romantic novels from my aunt's bookshelf when I was around ten years old; no solid idea, just imagination. Many years later, it occurred to me that learning about sex through graphic novels or pornography was not such a cool idea. Those commercially produced, profit-driven products embed a wealth of misinformation, misguidance, and misconceptions. They could skew a person's perceptions and are not in the best interest of consumers.

Your initial experience with sexual awareness may be entirely different than mine. Take a few minutes to think about it. Please remember that you are a unique individual. There is nobody else like you, and everyone develops at their own pace. Try not to compare yourself to your peers or to Photoshopped images of people you see in magazines or on social media or TV. I know it's hard not to take a quick glance at those bulging body parts, and it's even more difficult to avoid comparing yourself to what you see. But trust me: size is not essential. Many images you have seen on the magazine have been Photoshopped or altered. You cannot always trust what you see.

If you have any questions about your health and development, please talk to your parents, school nurse, or another trusted adult with qualifications.[1]

Blame it on the Hormones

Glands in the endocrine system create hormones, which are chemical messengers. They travel through the bloodstream to different parts of the body and help regulate various bodily functions such as growth and development, metabolism, mood, and sexual function.[2]

All of the endocrine glands in your body have been developing and working together since you were in your mother's womb. During puberty, four major endocrine glands produce hormones that play significant roles in your transformation from a child to an adult.

Endocrine glands are not easily visible, like your eyes and nose. The idea of endocrine glands and hormones may seem abstract to you. They are like the behind-the-scenes stage coordinators. You hardly see them in a magnificent play. Still, they are the ones to make sure the entire production can run smoothly, and all the actors and actresses on stage perform according to the time and sequence of a screenplay:

- Hypothalamus: It secretes gonadotropin-releasing hormone (GnRH) to regulate Luteinizing hormone (LH) and follicle-stimulating hormone (FSH) production in the pituitary gland.

- Pituitary gland: When GnRH reaches the pituitary gland, it triggers the release of puberty hormones—adrenocorticotrophic hormone (ACTH), LH, and FSH—into the bloodstreams.

- Ovaries: They are mostly only found in women, although ovaries can also be found in intersex or trans people. Ovaries have contained eggs since birth. The FSH and LH stimulate the ovaries to produce estrogen, testosterone, and progesterone. All these hormones regulate the menstrual cycle and prepare the body to support a pregnancy.

- Testes: They are mostly found in men, although testes can also be found in intersex or trans people. The testes increase secretion of testosterone and produce sperm.

All humans can have estrogen and testosterone, just in different amounts. Hormones can affect moods in several ways. Generally, the two hormones that significantly impact mood in women are estrogen and progesterone. Around the onset of puberty, the ovaries begin releasing estrogen and progesterone in coordination with each menstrual cycle, causing hormone levels to rise, fall, and spike throughout the month. If you notice your mood swings throughout the month, now you know why. So don't be alarmed by the change.

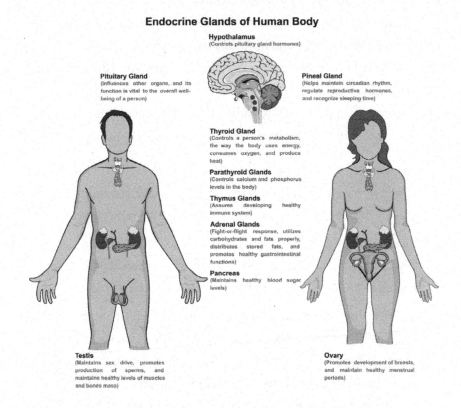

Endocrine Glands of Human Body for male and female.
Vector Contributor – udaix via Shutterstock

Chapter Reflections

1. As you pause to consider what you read in this chapter, what is one new piece of information that you could share with a friend to combat the misinformation that sometimes exists?

2. Consider, too, how you were taught about puberty and your changing body. What sources have you relied on?

3. How has the media you access affected your perception of your body and physical changes?

Chapter 3

SECONDARY SEX CHARACTERISTICS

Puberty is a difficult and awkward time for most people. I certainly had my share of pimples and uncertainty. But it's a time of growth and learning about yourself and who you want to be.

~ Emma Watson

Questions for You to Ponder

As you read through this chapter, please consider the following questions:

1. How is puberty typically portrayed in the media?

2. Has any imposition from an older generation affected your anticipation or experience of puberty?

3. What do you wish you knew about puberty before you experienced it?

4. How can you support someone else concerning your answer to #3 above?

Introduction

The different amount of estrogen and testosterone causes the development of secondary sex characteristics and physical maturation. The secondary sex characteristics are not involved in reproduction (having a baby).

Everyone has different reactions and emotions when they first notice the signs of secondary sex characteristics. Some may feel embarrassed, self-conscious, confused, or even scared. Some may feel excited about the changes and view them as a sign of growing up.

The truth is that these changes are normal, and everyone goes through them at their own pace.

Changes in Sexes

- Pubescent growth spurt. The increased growth hormone secretion promotes rapid bone elongation and muscle development, resulting in height and weight gain.

- Hair grows under the arms and around the genitals. At first, it is soft like baby hair and only in a small area, but it darkens and becomes coarser and spreads.

- The body sweats more. The adrenal glands produce hormones to cause the increase of armpit sweating and body odor. Don't get offended if someone near you suggests you take a shower or use deodorant/antiperspirant. Take the hint! Nothing personal.

- Acne and pimples. Overactive sebaceous (oil-producing) glands and sweat glands blocking the skin ducts (clogging the skin pores) are the leading causes of acne. You may have acne on your face, upper back, or chest. According to research, acne affects the majority of adolescents. Talk to your primary care physician if the number of acne scars bothers you. They may recommend certain facial washes or lotions specifically for acne. They may also refer you to a dermatologist.

- Besides the physical changes, you may grow greater sexual interests.

Common Changes with Males

The male sex hormone, testosterone, secreted from the male gonads (testes), is accountable for developing the male reproductive organs and secondary sexual characteristics specifically. The secondary sexual characteristics include:

- Your shoulders broaden, and the upper body becomes muscular with increased muscle mass and strength.

- Hair sprouts on the face and chest, or even on the thighs and stomach, besides under the arms and the pubic area.

- You may notice the enlargement in the scrotum and testes. Later, your penis grows in length and then in width. You will start to get erections. (Just a quick reminder: Your sexual function is unrelated to your penis size, and the flaccid penis does not indicate the size when erect).

- The testes constantly produce sperm; therefore, you can ejaculate sperm (cum) out of the penis.

- The automatic erection and ejaculation during sleep is called nocturnal emissions. Some refer to them as "wet dreams." Nocturnal emissions are a completely normal part of growing up, and you cannot prevent them from happening.

- Your voice may crack and lower in pitch because of the increase in the size of your larynx, or voice box. The enlarged voice box appears as a protrusion in the throat area; we call it the Adam's apple.

Common Changes with Females

The estrogen secreted by the ovaries affects the development of female reproductive tissues and initiates the secondary sexual characteristics. The secondary female sexual characteristics are as follows:

- Your hips may become rounded, and you might notice an increase in body fat composition below the waist.

- As your breast buds begin to develop at the start of puberty, the breasts and nipples elevate, and the areola (the dark area of skin around the nipple) increases in size. It takes several years for the breasts to fully develop. At that point, your breasts will become rounded, and only the nipples will be raised.

- The onset of menstruation (menarche) usually occurs two years after the appearance of breast buds and pubic hair. You may experience abdominal cramping or pain, which is normal. If the menstrual cramps are severe, talk to your primary physician about the options.

- You may notice clear or whitish, mucous-like vaginal secretions. This is related to the different phases of fertility across the person's cycle. Most of the time, this is normal. If it causes you discomfort, don't be shy, talk to your primary physician.

- If you are interested in shaving your legs and armpits, be sure not to share a razor with anyone to avoid the spread of bacteria and skin infections.

- Please check out the following resource about period:

  ○ Menstrupedia. (2020). *Hello periods (English) - The complete guide to periods for girls* [Video]. YouTube. https://www.youtube.com/watch?v=qUNTtn1WPEw

- Wash Institute. (2017). *Animation film menstrual hygiene* [Video]. YouTube. https://www.youtube.com/watch?v=W-CGhmKHWbo

Please remember, no question is too silly or embarrassing regarding puberty. Have open communication with your school nurse or a trusted adult who can guide you to find trustworthy resources to help you navigate this critical phase of your life.

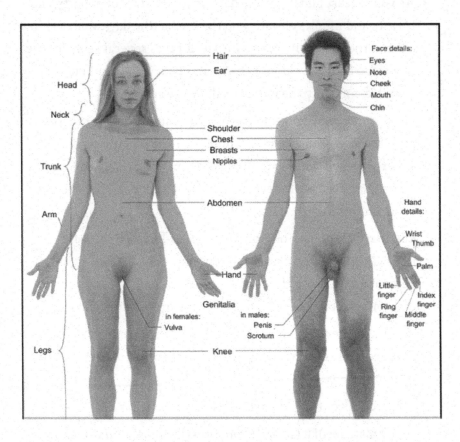

Secondary Sex Characteristics: Image credit: Dr. Mikael Häggström
https://www.linkedin.com/in/drhaggstrom/

Chapter Reflections

1. As you ponder this chapter's content, what is one area that you wish to learn more about? What is a wise, healthy, and safe way to learn more about sex characteristics?

2. Puberty is often viewed with a degree of secrecy or even shame. What do you think is the reason for this?

3. As you read about puberty beginning earlier today than in years past, do you think the onset of puberty may change in the future?

Chapter 4

THE PRIMARY SEXUAL CHARACTERISTICS

Puberty can be a really tough time for kids, but it's also a time when you discover who you are and what you're passionate about. It's a time to be curious and explore the world around you.

~ Bill Nye

Once you get over that peak of puberty, you hit a nice stride.

~ Claire Danes

Questions for You to Ponder

As you read through this chapter, please consider the following questions:

1. Do you consider human beings as more alike or different, especially regarding the sexes?

2. Do you see yourself having children as you envision your future? Consider making a pros-and-cons list!

3. What do your sexual and gender identities mean to you?

Introduction

The differences between males and females have intrigued people since the beginning of humankind. You can find literature and artwork from ancient to modern times that depict the two sexes, as well as cultures that have long held that multiple genders exist (e.g. Two-Spirit-Native American, the Hijra in India, the Sekrata in Madagascar, etc.). Scientists have spent many years studying the biological and physiological characteristics of males and females—especially their reproductive systems. Additionally, intersex people have also been studied; nearly two percent of all babies are born intersex worldwide.[1]

You may have heard the terms *sex* and *gender* and wondered about their differences. Can they be interchanged during a conversation? Let's take a moment to gain proper information about them. According to the Council of Europe, based on the World Health Organization summary[2]

> *Sex* refers to "the different biological and physiological characteristics of males and females, such as reproductive organs, chromosomes, hormones, etc."
>
> *Gender* refers to "the socially constructed characteristics of women and men – such as norms, roles and relationships of and between groups of women and men. It varies from society to society and can be changed. The concept of gender includes five important elements: relational, hierarchical, historical, contextual, and institutional."

When we talk about the primary sexual characteristics, we mainly talk about the sex organs involved in reproduction. In everyday language, reproduction means "making babies" or "becoming parents." With reproduction, the human population grows, and humanity continues.

Male Reproductive Organs

As your testes, penis, and scrotum grow and enlarge, you have your first ejaculation of semen. Male sex organs include the scrotum, testes, epididymis, vas deferens, prostate, seminal vesicles, urethra, and penis.

Instead of boring you to death with a long explanation and text, I encourage you to watch the following video. Who knows, you might actually be entertained while you're learning something new.

Click the link: https://www.youtube.com/watch?v=-XQcnO4iX_U

CrashCourse. (2015). *Reproductive system, Part 2 - Male reproductive system: Crash course anatomy & physiology #41.*

Female Reproductive Organs

About 400,00 immature female gametes have been stored in the ovaries since birth, but only 500 of them will become mature eggs. With the growth of the uterus and sex hormones in puberty, females will typically experience the first menstrual period, or menarche. From there, the ovaries usually release an egg, called an ovum, every 28 to 35 days, depending on the individual. This process is known as ovulation.

Female sex organs include the ovaries, fallopian tubes, uterus, cervix, vaginal canal, Bartholin's and Skenes glands, vagina, clitoris, and clitoral hood.

Here's a link to an informative little video that will explain how it all works. I bet some of you haven't seen this one on YouTube!

Go to this link:

Reproductive System, Part 1 - Female Reproductive System: Crash Course A&P #40. Click the link: https://www.youtube.com/watch?v=RFDatCchpus

CrashCourse. (2015). *Reproductive system, Part 1 - Female reproductive system: Crash course anatomy & physiology #40.*

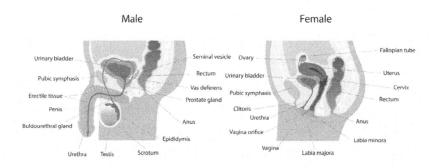

Male and female Reproductive Systems in the Median Section:
Vector Contributor Nostagrams via Shutterstock

The Initiation of Pregnancy

The moment a young male has his first ejaculation and a young female begins her first menstrual cycle, they have the potential to reproduce. Like all living things in the animal kingdom, becoming reproductive means breeding and producing babies!

Every ejaculation holds 200 million to 500 million sperm. If one sperm can successfully meet with an egg, a zygote can develop, and the stages of pregnancy may get underway. But how does a sperm find an egg to hook up with? Let's watch the following fascinating video.

CrashCourse. (2015). *Reproductive system, Part 4: Pregnancy & development: Crash course anatomy & physiology #43.* https://www.youtube.com/watch?v=BtsSbZ85yiQ

It explains how the body changes from the moment a sperm finds and fertilizes an egg, through nine months of pregnancy to labor.

Parenthood

Dear teens, I want to remind you that as you go through puberty and experience the changes that come with it, your body becomes capable of producing a baby. This is an incredible responsibility, and it's essential to remember that pregnancy can happen before you're mentally and financially prepared to care for a child.

Let's take some time to chat about something super important: having a baby before you're truly ready. We understand that life can throw curveballs, but knowing how this decision, intentionally or unintentionally, can shake things up is crucial. Your teenage years are like a treasure chest full of adventures waiting to be unlocked. It's time to explore, discover, and chase your dreams with unbridled enthusiasm. Having a baby too early can feel like putting a giant pause button on your youthful spirit. You may even feel as though your boundless adolescent joy has been pilfered.

Imagine you're juggling late-night feedings, diaper changes, and homework. It's a challenging ride, and it might make it tougher to keep your dreams on track. Can you picture it? Balancing high school with a crying, hungry baby? It's a lot to handle, right?

And then there's the emotional side. Weighty decisions, like whether or not to have an abortion, place a child for adoption, or parent can be difficult. We want to remind you that nobody's perfect, and sometimes mistakes happen. But here's the uplifting part: if you've found yourself in the world of teen pregnancy, don't beat yourself up. Life is full of twists and turns; we're all learning along the way. Chin up! You have the strength to turn things around and strive for a bright future for you and your baby. Remember, there is always time to chase those dreams and make your mark on the world. Life may throw you a few challenges, but you have what it takes to rise above them. Keep pushing forward, and your future will shine even brighter!

Nevertheless, do all you can to avoid the predicament of teen pregnancy. A firm grasp of your biological and physiological development can help you make wise decisions ahead of time or when encountering a formidable situation.

Again and again, please remember that while your body is capable of making a baby, that doesn't mean you're ready for parenthood. Take the time to educate yourself about safe sex, birth control, and other ways to prevent unintended pregnancies. Your future is bright, and I want to encourage you to make choices that will help you achieve all your goals and dreams.

You may want to talk to your parents, school nurse, or family physician about how to avoid teenage pregnancy. I understand the subjects can be awkward and embarrassing. But, by equipping yourself with knowledge, you may help your good friends or even yourself someday.

FERTILIZATION

Spermatozoon

Ovum

Fertilization is the union of an ovum and a spermatozoon. When a sperm contacts the surface of an egg, it initiates metabolic reactions within the egg that trigger the onset of embryonic development. Vector Contributor: SVETLANA VERBINSKAYA via Shuttersock.

Chapter Reflections

1. As you reflect on the content of this chapter, what did you find most impactful when it comes to reproduction?

2. What do you think about the spontaneous or impulsive sexual activities depicted on TV, social media, in films, or in a romantic novel after reading this chapter?

3. Consider someone you know who became a teen parent. How did things go for them regarding their educational and professional pursuits?

4. What values or beliefs do you hold that may shape your perspectives on sexual activity?

Part 2

YOUR PRECIOUS BRAIN IS DEVELOPING

We spend so much time looking in the mirror and paying attention to our appearance and hair, but we seldom think about that thing hiding beneath our scalp: the brain. Understandably, we neglect it because we don't see it. Our brain controls our whole being, from breathing to playing sports. It even plays a vital role when we are watching TV or sleeping. Some people regard the brain as the boss of the body.

Some scientists and developmental psychologists used to assume that our brain was fully grown in the first few years of life and that the structure and size were relatively stable by early teens. Hormones had taken the blame for much of what goes off-kilter in adolescence. However, with the advancement of technology and the use of functional magnetic resonance imaging (fMRI), neuroscientists discovered that the myelination would not fully complete until 25 years old and a significant portion of our brain, the prefrontal lobe, does not fully mature until 23 to 25 years of age or even beyond.[1, 2, 3] This finding ignited scientists' vast interest in studying adolescent brain growth relative to typical mood swings, risk-seeking behavior, and impulsivity in the second decade of a person's life.

The discord between parents and teens is mostly due to the fact that developing brains don't work in the same manner as fully developed ones. Adults can typically think with the frontal lobe, the rational part associated with good decision-making and impulse control. Adolescents, however, process information with the amygdala, the brain's emotional area, and the reward-sensitive region.

We talked about the initiation of puberty and biological changes in the first four chapters. Scientists still don't know for sure how the timing of puberty and sexual maturation is associated with the growth spurt of the brain during adolescence. It's an exciting field of study. Maybe some of you will someday study neuroscience, developmental psychology, pediatrics, or related fields.

We will discuss the brain's development in Part 2 in detail, especially the work in progress of the adolescent's brain! I will use the scenario of building a magnificent, thriving metropolis in *Minecraft* to parallel your brain's development from the day you were formed in your mother's womb to around age 25.

I am sure you will enjoy learning about how your precious brain diligently works night and day during this period.

Let's explore the journey with fun!

(Note: *Minecraft* is a 3D sandbox game. It is not just about building structures or anything with Lego blocks in different environments on a computer. It is also a game that allows players to create and explore their virtual worlds in a 3D sandbox environment on a computer or other devices. If you don't play *Minecraft*, no worries. You will likely get the idea as we go through the chapters.)

Chapter **5**

AN OVERVIEW OF OUR REMARKABLE BRAIN

The human brain has 100 billion neurons, each neuron connected to 10 thousand other neurons. Sitting on your shoulders is the most complicated object in the known universe.

~ Michio Kaku

Questions for You to Ponder

As you read through this chapter, please consider the following questions:

1. How often do you consider what your brain has done for you?
2. What is one new activity you'd like to try to improve your brain health?
3. What activities do you want to reduce or eliminate to care for your brain properly?

The Development of the Human Brain

Considering how remarkable our brains are. Anatomically and structurally, all human brains are very much alike, regardless of race and personal background.

Once the egg and sperm meet, the teensy-weensy embryo grows at lightning speed in nine months. By the time a baby is born, the human brain encompasses 100 billion cells; around 250,000 brain cells are generated every minute on average inside the mother's womb.[1] Isn't that amazing, just to think about how long it will take you to count from 1 to 250,000?

Also, it is mind-blowing that the cells are well differentiated at birth in typically developed infants; they know their role. For instance, some are responsible for keeping breath and heartbeat rhythmic, and some are for body movement, etc. And they coordinate so harmoniously, like a conductor directing various instruments to play a symphony so brilliantly.

In 2012, neuroscientist Suzana Herculano-Houzel[2] argued that our brain only contains about 86 billion neurons (cells) versus 100 billion cells as previously proposed. Either way, the number of neurons encased inside our skull is still phenomenal, don't you think so?

With the advance of neuroimaging in recent years, neuroscientists affirmed that the human prefrontal lobe—the executive decision-making center—continues to grow and mature from birth until around 25 years old or even later. In other words, the prefrontal lobe is not fully mature until in the mid-20s or beyond.[3, 4]

- All parts of our brain have existed since birth, but they are not equally mature. In general, the human brain matures from the bottom up and inside out.[5, 6, 7]

- According to one study, adolescents have less white matter (myelin) in the frontal lobes of their brains than adults, but this quantity increases as adolescents mature.[8]

- Emotional recognition studies using functional magnetic resonance imaging (fMRI) show that the adolescent lower brain is more activated than in an adult brain, but the prefrontal lobe is less activated.

- The cerebrum lies at the top of the brain and contains the largest portion of brain mass. The cerebrum comprises the subcortical structures and the cerebral cortex.

In the following sections, the anatomy and significant functions of the human cerebrum will be roughly listed from the bottom up and inside out, from the oldest and most primitive brain for basic survival to the youngest brain for making rational decisions, understanding the world, and achieving the ultimate goal.[9]

Before diving into the rest of chapter, I am excited to share this cool site with you: an interactive brain model from The Society for Neuroscience. Click this link and check it out. Learn all the brain structures by clicking the drop-down list in the upper left-hand corner: https://www.brainfacts.org/3d-brain#intro=true

Credit: The Society for Neuroscience. (2017). *The interactive brain model*. Brainfacts.org.

The Subcortical Structure

Subcortical refers to the structures in the region below the cerebral cortex.

Old Brain (Hindbrain or Reptilian Brain)

- Medulla: controls heart rate and breathing, digestive functions, blood pressure
- Pons: helps regulate several automatic functions, like sleeping and eating
- Reticular formation: a network inside the brainstem, essential for arousal
- Cerebellum: coordinates fine motor movement, timing, and nonverbal learning

- Thalamus: receives and relays sensory information as a "sensory switchboard"

Limbic System (The Mammalian Brain)

- Hypothalamus: involved with essential living functions, like sleep, and helps regulate the endocrine system
- Amygdala: involved in emotions, memory consolidation, and defensive responses to external threats. In short, it is responsible for fear and reward.
- Hippocampus: responsible for learning and event memory
- Basal ganglia: responsible for planning, motivation and controlling movement
- Pituitary gland: the master gland, which plays a significant role in monitoring the body's endocrine system
- Cingulate gyrus is the gateway to the limbic system from the cerebral cortex.

To learn more about limbic system, please check out the following link:

https://www.brainfacts.org/3d-brain#intro=false&focus=Brain-limbic_system (Copyright © Society for Neuroscience, 2017)

LIMBIC SYSTEM

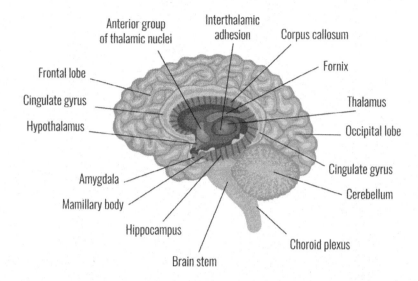

Different areas of limbic system
Vector Contributor: Macrovectormage via Shutterstock

Cerebral Cortex

The human cerebral cortex is regarded as the most well-developed, in comparison to other animals.

- The cerebral cortex is the cerebrum's outermost layer of neural tissue.
- It consists of six layers of nerve cells (neurons).
- The cerebral cortex appears wrinkled (convoluted). The deep grooves are known as *sulci*; the elevated bulges are called *gyri*.

Lobes of the Brain

The sulci and gyri divide the cerebral cortex into four distinct lobes: frontal, parietal, temporal, and occipital. The lobes are able to communicate with one another and other brain regions to enhance their primary functions.

- Occipital lobe: It is located at the rear of the brain and is responsible for visual processing, such as color, motion, and orientation perception. It is also accountable for object and facial recognition.

- Temporal lobe: It is the second-largest lobe of the cerebral cortex. The temporal lobe processes auditory information to understand sound and speech. It is also associated with memory, emotion, and language formation.

- Parietal lobe: It is positioned between the frontal and occipital lobe, above the temporal lobe. The parietal lobe processes sense of touch and various sensations, like pressure, taste, and temperature. It also helps our body to establish spatial relationships with our environments.

- Frontal lobe: It is the largest brain structure and the slowest part of the brain to mature; it continues to develop until a person's mid-twenties or even beyond. It is located behind the forehead, at the front of the brain, and is vulnerable to injuries. The frontal lobe primarily involves "higher" cognitive and behavioral functions, like thinking, organizing, problem-solving, decision-making, impulse control, emotional control, attention, language production, and short-term memory. The frontal lobe is also associated with our highest intellectual capabilities and is where our personalities are reserved.

The front part of the frontal lobe is called the prefrontal cortex. It is best known for the highest-level cognitive functioning, also called executive functioning. The prefrontal cortex helps you set, plan, and accomplish goals. I mentioned that our brain develops from back to front; therefore, the prefrontal cortex is the last area to fully develop and mature. Several mental illnesses can negatively impact this part of the brain (e.g., Major Depressive Disorder, Intermittent Explosive Disorder, Post Traumatic Stress Disorder, and more).

I will share more later about how to help your brain—especially the prefrontal cortex in the frontal lobe—achieve its greatest potential in the rest of the book. Read on!

Gray Matter and White Matter [10,11,12]

The human brain is made up of two kinds of matter: the nerve cell bodies (gray matter), which process sensation, control voluntary movement, and enable speech, learning and cognition, and the axons (white matter), which connect cells to each other and project to the rest of the body.

Summary of Gray Matter

- Gray matter, also known as substantia grisea, is the outermost layer of the brain and spinal cord, responsible for processing sensation, controlling voluntary movement, and enabling speech, learning, and cognition.

- It is abundant in the cerebellum, cerebrum, and brain stem, and forms a butterfly-shaped portion of the central spinal cord.

- The cerebellum has the highest concentration of neuronal cells, while other areas, like the basal ganglia, are also covered by gray matter.

- The brain's gray matter processes information and releases new information through axon signaling, making it crucial for daily functioning.

Summary of White Matter

- White matter, or substantia alba, is a vast system of neural connections in the brain, consisting of bundles of axons coated with myelin.

- These axons, which can be up to three feet long, are the longest projections of brain cells and carry signals.

- White matter forms various fiber collections, including projection, association, and commissural fibers, which are crucial for higher brain functions.

- The frontal regions of the brain have the highest degree of connectivity, with an abundance of white matter.

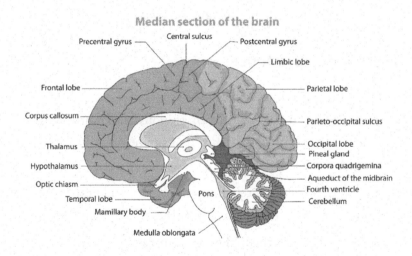

The Brain, Median section of the brain
Vector Contributor: NatthapongSachan via Shutterstock

Are you confused yet? Don't worry. It may take a few reads to grasp the nature of our amazing brain. Let me clarify this for you by comparing the brain to the game *Minecraft*. The analogy isn't perfect, but it will help you to envision the development of your precious brain.

The Overview on Your Developing Brain vs. The World of *Minecraft*

In the *Minecraft* scenario, the capital city symbolizes your frontal lobe. Let's name the capital city as Wondamento. There is Capitol building in Wondamento as the frontal lobe. And the robust executive operational unit inside the Capitol is designated as your prefrontal cortex. The entire state is like your whole brain. The goal is to provide all the resources for building an effective, powerful Capitol with the most advanced technologies and communication gear for the best benefit of the citizens in this metropolis. We need a robust defense system to protect the whole state city from enemies seeking to invade, seize the resources, destroy the transportation system, and deplete the power of the capital.

The analogy continues with different parts of the brain being compared to different cities in the state. For example, amygdala in the limbic system (in the subcortical) is compared to a recreational and entertaining district in the central state. The neural connections (myelination) are compared to transportation systems such as roads, paths, and superhighways connecting cities and supplying resources and material to establish the capital.

The prefrontal cortex is compared to the very front part of the frontal lobe and is last to fully develop. Executive functions continue to improve via life experience.

Your Developing Brain	The World of *Minecraft*
Your neurosystem develops during the fetus stage	Finding seeds and establishing villages on a vast plain to build a state
Learning many basic skills and language during your childhood	Creating farms and mines to supply food and resources to the villagers. Also building houses and schools to make cites
Establishing healthy habits during your early age	Building defensive systems, like military bases
The entire brain: developing from bottom up and from center out	The entire state: building from south to north and center out
Different parts of the brain	**Different cities in the state**
Limbic system	Pleasure district: the fun zone, a recreational area like a vibrant district with games, parties, and emotional adventures.
Amygdala in the limbic system (in the subcortical). It is key to processing strong emotions like fear, pleasure, and reward-related information.	A head of security monitors the pleasure district and activates sirens when he detects potential danger. Furthermore, in an exciting setting, it is easy to become restless and expect rewards.
The frontal lobe	**The capital city (Wondamento)**
The prefrontal cortex: the very front part of the frontal lobe and the last to fully develop. Executive functions continue to improve via life experiences and practicing good habits.	The "command and control" unit inside the Capitol building in the center of Wondamento. Its setup, equipment, and networking devices continue to update and upgrade.

The neural connections (myelination: the insulation on axons) communicate among different brain parts and enhance the cerebral cortex's growth, especially the frontal lobe.	Cities are upgrading their transportation systems, enhancing the flow of information and resources from local to other cities and capital, thereby establishing a smoother and faster transportation system.
The gray matter, the nerve cell bodies, which process sensation, control voluntary movement, and enable speech, learning and cognition,	The town center, like city halls, libraries, and crafting tables, is where information is processed, decisions are made, and plans are formulated.
The white matter, the long, white cables called axons, bundled together, connect cells to each other and project to the rest of the body like information superhighways zipping around the brain.	The redstone circuits, minecart tracks, and even teleportation portals that let information and resources flow between cities. It delivers the resources and instructions to the right places.
The effects of drugs, alcohol, and bad habits on your brain: molecular, biochemical, structural, and functional changes leading to reduced myelinations and brain volume/size, impaired executive function, and lower IQ.	The consequences of enemies' attacks include bombing the cities, killing civilians, damaging transportation systems, and destroying the structures.
Best defense system to fight temptations and addictions to ensure frontal lobe's optimal growth: self-regulation (self-control)	Guard against enemy invasions and protect the entire metropolis by building robust military bases and strong local police forces.

Suppose you're interested in building cities and a capital resembling our brain's development with *Minecraft*. In that case, you can use the following steps as a reference. It may take a long time, so you have to be patient. You can also simplify the steps as much as you like.

Note: Before you start the game, be sure to communicate with your parents.

If you're not a fan of *Minecraft*, there are no problems.

The Blueprint of Building a Magnificent Metropolitan City in *Minecraft*

The biome is a vast barren plain with a small hill at the northern end by a coastline. The goal is to build a metropolis with a powerful capital on the northern hill at the present time.

The steps are as follows:

- Find seeds to make the land beautiful and habitable.
- Build some villages in the southern part of the plain and have villagers living there.
- Create farms to supply food.
- Create mines to provide resources like iron, stone, and coal.
- Create a system of roads and transportation to develop the city and transport the resources from south to north.
- Start building defensive systems, like a military base and navy vessels, by the coast.
- Build a recreational and entertaining district at the center of the map as the city develops for citizens to gather and have fun.
- Continue to make houses, schools, a religious center, and other buildings from the center out, south to north.
- Continue to gather material and upgrade the transportation system to move the resources to the north for building the capital.

The end design will be a magnificent, thriving capital city/ Wondamento with a powerful Capitol building in the northern part of the city. The Capitol has one highest command center, the commander in chief. All are filled with high-tech equipment, the necessities, and security resources to make executive decisions and secure the Capitol and the cities in the state.

Chapter Reflections

1. How has this chapter changed your perspective and understanding of your brain?

2. How did the *Minecraft* analogy help you understand how your brain develops, even if you don't actually play it?

3. How do you intend to use your newfound knowledge to modify how you approach brain health?

Chapter 6

YOUR GROWING BRAIN IS REORGANIZING

Most of us [grown up] have had that experience—at around puberty—of realising that, despite whatever efforts we put into our chosen sports, we will become at best competent.

~ Will Self

Questions for You to Ponder

As you read through this chapter, please consider the following questions:

1. When you first glance at the chapter title, "Your Growing Brain is Reorganizing," what image comes to mind?

2. Is there a skill you were good at but digressed because of lack of practice, like a musical instrument, language, or sports?

3. What skills have you improved in the last few years through consistent practice?

Introduction

During childhood, your body isn't the only thing that grows; your brain does too. You have learned to walk, to run; you learned your ABCs, simple math, and so much more. For the longest time, the general assumption was that the most critical years of brain development were from birth to around five or six years old. Once we pass the critical period, our brain remains relatively the same throughout life. However, in recent longitudinal MRI studies, scientists have confirmed that the second surge of neuronal growth happens before or around the onset of puberty—a thickening of the gray matter. After that, the brain undergoes a dynamic "rewiring" or reorganization until around the middle of a person's third decade. This reorganization involves synaptic pruning and myelination. I will explain the fancy terms: synaptic pruning and myelination soon. They are not as complicated as they appeared, I promise you.

Minecraft Scenario

In the *Minecraft* scenario, the small villages grow into cities in the first 10 to 12 years. Mines, farms, schools, and a religious center are created. Much more foliage appears, and the forest grows on the plain. Buildings are established from south to north along simple rough roads. The outer structure of the capital (Wondamento) has formed on the northern hill, yet its surrounding area is a jumble of trees and bushes.

In order to ship all of the necessary material and valuable resources to the capital and move stuff in and out of the Capitol building efficiently, we must clean up the terrain, get rid of weeds, bushes, and trim trees to build an effective transit system and well-established roads. Besides the roads and paths around the cities, we construct superhighways and railroads, moving around with *Minecarts*, from south to north. Public transportation hubs will enhance efficient travel. The goal is to complete a fully functional capital city, containing government buildings with super-executive power, in a marvelous metropolis by the year 25.

Synaptic Pruning

Our brains continually grow during childhood and reach their maximum size around 12 years old for girls and 14 years old for boys. In other words, "the brain reaches its biggest size in early adolescence," according to the National Institute of Mental Health.[1]

- Synapses are the brain's communication hubs and are essential for maturation, learning, and memory.

- Synaptic pruning is also called dendritic pruning or neural pruning.

- In botany, pruning is trimming branches from plants (such as trees and bushes) to improve their future growth and health and make the area appear more presentable.

- During the teenage years, our brain gets rid of those connections that weren't used, and it prunes back automatically.

- Synaptic pruning is part of brain maturation; it takes place automatically and naturally.

- The process of eliminating (cutting away) the weak, unused, excess neural connection is to specialize the brain. It removes roughly half of all synapses during pruning, so our brains can focus energy and resources on the connections that are used most.

- The pruning process and reorganization of cortical circuits— communications among different parts of the brain—occur in adolescence and continue to the mid-20s or beyond.

- The pruning occurs in an experience-dependent way.

- The removal of unused, unnecessary connections is considered a valuable process. It helps to improve neural circuits and enhance network proficiency.

- The pruning process is part of cognitive functioning maturation during adolescence.

- (Cognitive functioning maturation means the higher ability to understand the world around you.)

- Pruning applies the use-it-or-lose-it principle. That means if you don't practice a skill, your brain will automatically get rid of that part of the circuits/connections. Consider this when you are thinking about throwing in the towel too soon on a new, difficult task or skill!

- Another side of pruning is that you can activate certain circuits to keep them alive during adolescence. For example, you can stimulate and strengthen neural connections by learning to play a new musical instrument, read classical literature, play sports, or learn a new language.

In the *Minecraft* scenario, think of it as trimming bushes and removing junk to construct paths, streets, and highways to improve connections between towns. The end goal is to efficiently deliver valuable resources to the Capitol so that a strong "command and control" unit can be constructed there.

Myelination

Another major event involved in brain reorganization starting in early adolescence is myelin formation, also called myelination.

- Neurons, the cell bodies in the gray matter, communicate with each other by sending signals down the axons.

- Myelination is the process of wrapping myelin around the axons.

- Myelin is a fatty substance that electronically insulates nerve fibers, the axons. It's protective!

- The myelination increases the white matter, which allows the neurons to send information and communicate with each other thousands of times faster.

- Myelination also optimizes brain connections and speeds up neural transmission between various brain areas.

- According to neuroscientists, myelination proceeds from inferior to superior brain areas and back to front.

- In the *Minecraft* scenario, you can envision the construction of a super-highway from south to north and from the center out.

The Results of Brain Reorganization

The remodeling of the brain initiated in early adolescence is essential. The synaptic pruning and myelination make the adolescent brain more efficient, balanced, and integrated. The more the integrated brain increases learning capacity and processes information faster, the more it enhances cognitive development through adolescence.

Chapter Reflections

1. Do you find the information on the neuroscience of the brain in this chapter overwhelming? Or is it too abstract? That's okay. What concept was the easiest for you to grasp and retain?

2. How about the most difficult one?

3. Pruning applies the use-it-or-lose-it principle. Can you find an example in your life that confirms this principle?

Chapter 7

HOW TO TAKE ADVANTAGE OF DUAL SYSTEMS IN THE DEVELOPING BRAIN

The limbic system explodes during puberty, but the prefrontal cortex keeps maturing for another 10 years.

~ Robin Marantz Henig

Questions for You to Ponder

As you read through this chapter, please consider the following questions:

1. What is the first thing that comes to mind when you think of the word "dual"?

2. Have you seen your thought process or understanding of the world around you change from year to year?

3. What do you hope or envision you will be like once your brain is fully developed (e.g., a character trait you hope to develop or a person you want to be in various aspects of your life)?

What is the Dual System?

- Some experts also referred to the dual system as an *imbalance model.*

- The *dual system* refers to the emotional/reward processing system of the subcortical region and the emotional regulation/executive functioning system of the prefrontal cortex.

- The imbalance model implies uneven maturation in the two regions mentioned above: the emotional/reward processing system (subcortical region) matures much earlier than the emotional regulation/executive functioning system (the prefrontal area) during adolescence.

Minecraft Scenario

In the *Minecraft* scenario, the cities develop from the south to the northern hill, where the capital is located. The freeways and railroads are under construction to provide material and resources to the capital. Amid building the executive department in the capital to make the whole metropolitan area run smoothly and effectively, the downtown area at the center of the map has become the recreational and entertaining district, where citizens gather for fun. The environment and lighthearted atmosphere excite the people. They are eager for instant enjoyment and rewards, become rowdy, and sometimes run into trouble.

Without the completion of the capital, the recreational and entertaining district plays an essential role in affecting citizens' lives. How can the energetic people in the recreational and entertaining district be trained to become valuable inhabitants and learn self-control?

The Implications of the Dual System and Imbalance Model

In Chapter 5, we learned about the limbic system in the subcortical region and the prefrontal cortex in the front-most part of the frontal lobes. Shall we review these two systems again?[1, 2]

The Limbic System

The limbic system is situated deep inside the cerebrum. It contains a group of structures and is associated with many functions. The limbic system is most commonly related to emotional expression.

- The limbic system is well developed, even in early adolescence.
- The active limbic system accounts for adolescents' wild mood swings, uncontrollable rages on some days, and impulsive tendencies.
- The amygdala is part of the limbic system. It has been associated with fearful and anxious emotions, emotional memories, and reward system.
- The cingulate gyrus is the gateway to the limbic system from the cerebral cortex.

LIMBIC SYSTEM

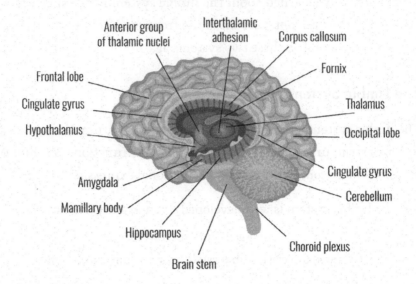

Different areas of limbic system
Vector Contributor: Macrovectormage via Shutterstock

The 3-D view of the limbic system with an interactive brain model (Copyright © Society for Neuroscience, 2017).

https://www.brainfacts.
org/3d-brain#intro=false&focus=Brain-limbic_system

The Prefrontal Cortex

Please bear with me if you're sick of hearing about your still-maturing prefrontal cortex. I'm definitely not trying to offend or annoy you. Everyone has to experience these growing pains, including adults.

- The prefrontal cortex is crucial for evaluating risk, exercising sound judgment, doing logical planning, regulating emotions, and controlling impulsive behaviors. Most neuroscientists agree that the prefrontal cortex is not fully mature until a person reaches their mid-20s.

- It doesn't mean that children or adolescents have no functional prefrontal cortices. As myelination proceeds from the back of the brain to the front, the neural connections from the limbic system to the prefrontal cortex have not entirely grown. In other words, the primary portion of the brain that provides complex decision-making still cannot communicate efficiently with the part of the brain that controls emotional arousal and reward cravings in adolescence.

- The 3-D view of the prefrontal cortex with an interactive brain model (Copyright © Society for Neuroscience, 2017).

  https://www.brainfacts.org/3d-brain#intro=false&focus=Brain-cerebral_hemisphere-frontal_lobe-prefrontal_cortex

Don't get discouraged. As you're reading this text at this very moment, your brain is diligently building connections to strengthen your prefrontal cortex. Give yourself a high five!

The Reward System

- The reward system plays a vital role in survival. For example, eating fulfills your hunger. The gratifying and memorable sensation is rewarding, making you want to do it repeatedly when you're hungry.

- The primary reward pathways and structures are in the subcortical area, such as the dopamine reward pathway, ventral striatal reward regions, nucleus accumbens, mesocorticolimbic dopamine (DA) system, etc. They are fully developed in early adolescence.

- The striatum is the crucial structure of the reward system. The striatum is very responsive. It releases dopamine when you do something and find it rewarding.

- The reward-sensitive area of the brain matures as the self-regulatory region of the brain, the prefrontal cortex, is still not fully connected, creating an imbalance situation in adolescence. In other words, the network to regulate the hyperactive reward system and the integration between different areas of the brain are still works in progress.

- The exaggerated reactivity in the reward system accounts for the adolescents' affinity for sensation-seeking, risk-taking, impulsiveness, and being prone to emotional arousal for a moment of pleasurable feelings and excitement. The immediate gratification frequently overpowers any concerns about severe long-term consequences. (In other words, at that high arousal moment, your reward system desires instant pleasure, takes control of your rational thinking, and logic goes out the window. Those moments would explain the high percentage of teens engaged in unprotected sexual activities or horrendous car accidents).

- Reactivity within the reward system is amplified while an adolescent is with peers. Most of the time, a teen can exercise good judgment and make rational decisions when alone, even in a challenging situation. However, with friends around and under social pressure, teens are impulsively drawn to risky activities—things like reckless driving, unprotected sex, binge drinking, and drug abuse—often to gain acceptance or approval from their peers.

- Although the research has documented the dual systems and imbalance model existing across various countries and cultures, the reward sensitivity differs from individual to individual.

- Some adolescents demonstrate better short-term vs. long-term reward assessment than others, such as risk control, delayed gratification, and emotional regulation.

- Research shows that poor sleep increases the risk-raising effect when under stress.

- Your brain is a work in progress. You can enhance the neural connection between the subcortical region and the prefrontal cortex by practicing saying "no" when under peer pressure to do something you know you shouldn't. This will help your frontal lobe mature more quickly.

- Train yourself to pause, take a deep breath, count to ten or even more, and allow yourself to evaluate the situation before reacting. With practice, it will get easier if you mindfully remind yourself to stop and think for a moment instead of responding emotionally. You can also try to step away from the situation you are in, even just outside or in a different room, for a few moments, in order to give your brain the time it needs to make a more calculated decision.

How to Take Advantage of the Dual System

Adolescents' sensation-seeking, risk-taking, and independence-craving are not behavior or emotional problems. They are a natural part of human development and civilization evolution. How can you take advantage of this challenging growing period?[3]

- As you learn about your developing brain and the increase in connectivity between different regions during this critical period, you should feel encouraged because you have a marvelous opportunity to construct your own identity and work toward your dreams and goals.

- You can take advantage of the sensation-seeking and reward-sensitive propensity by pushing yourself to take scary but not-harmful challenges, like joining a debate or public speech team, trying out for the school play, or learning to play a musical instrument. Do something positive and constructive. Challenge yourself by stepping out of your comfort zone and into the discomfort zone! Often, where there is discomfort, there is a possibility for growth. However, please also assess whether you feel a sense of psychological safety.

- You can find rewarding activities to gain a sense of accomplishment, like joining a local junior Lions Club, signing up as a volunteer in the local hospital, doing beach cleaning, or other community services.

The skills you develop, experiences, and difficulties you meet and conquer during adolescence will help you flourish and benefit you for the rest of your life. Remember the "use it or lose it" rule? The more you practice a wholesome skill or hobby, the stronger your brain's connection becomes. Otherwise, the neurons will be trimmed away automatically.

Make Safety Your Priority

Based on a recent CDC report, the leading causes of death among adolescents from 15 to 19 years old are accidents, homicide, and suicide. The CDC (2022) also reported that about seven to eight teens died due to motor vehicle crashes daily, and hundreds more were injured.[4] However, some studies have reported the firearm injuries became the leading cause of death among U.S. children and adolescents since 2020.[5, 6, 7, 8]

The Factors Put Teen Drivers at Risk

Teen motor vehicle accidents and fatal crashes are often preventable if you grasp the risk factors and think twice before handling the wheels. The risk factors are inexperience, nighttime and weekend driving, not using seat belts, distracted driving from texting or talking on the phone, speeding, drinking alcohol, and using drugs/substances.[9] (CDC, 2022).

Other Safety Questions

Let me ask you a few questions about safety. It's best to think about these things before entering a dangerous situation. The better you plan for them in advance, the more likely you will use wise judgment when under pressure or confronting an unexpected circumstance.

- Do you notice you become bolder, wilder, and louder when with friends? Think ahead of time about how to remain cool when your friends provoke you, push you, or try to influence you to do something you know you shouldn't—things like driving too fast, not using your seatbelt, using alcohol or drugs at a party, having casual, unprotected sex, joining a violent gang, etc.

- Do you wear a helmet when riding a bike, motorcycle, or all-terrain vehicle? How can you protect yourself from unintentional injuries while participating in sports?

- Do you practice safe sex if you decide to have sex with someone? Think about it. Is this the right time? Is this person the right person for you? What's your intention for having sex with this person? Is it worth it to get sexually transmitted diseases and suffer the pain? Is it worth facing the dilemma of having the burden of a baby while you are not ready?

- Most adolescent homicides are unintentional killings in a moment of rage. Do you have a strategy for controlling your impulsive acts when you're provoked and angry? Learn to take a deep breath, count to ten, and walk away, even if someone punches you in the face. Walking away does not mean you're a coward. Instead, it's a heroic act! You know better. Is it worth going to jail, wearing a hideous inmate uniform, and sitting in a tiny, stinky cell for years just because of a spurt of uncontrolled emotion?

- How can you get out of a dangerous or uncomfortable situation? What would you do if someone pressured you to try drugs, binge drink, use a firearm, or join a gang? Before a party or gathering, you must decide whether it's a good idea to attend it or plan ahead with your parents or older sibling to pick you up upon notice, no questions are asked. Sometimes, skipping a gathering because you feel in your gut that something is not right can save you much hassle or even your life.

- Last but not least, do you get enough sleep and eat healthily? The study has discovered that teenagers need 8–10 hours of sleep per day, including naps, in order to think clearly and function optimally. Lack of adequate sleep can muddle your mind and affect your prudent judgment. Healthy food is also essential for your developing brain's maturity.

- According to the CDC's Web-based Injury Statistics Query and Reporting System, unintentional injury was the number one leading cause of death between 10 and 24 years old in 2020.[10, 11, 12]

- Homicide was the fourth-leading cause in the age group 10–14 and the second-leading cause in ages 15–24.

- Please keep in mind that the use of a firearm can result in unintended harm and homicide. Please be prudent, never get involved in gangs, and steer away from violent activity. Your life and future are priceless. Do not waste it away!

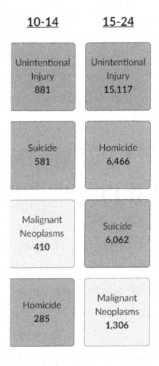

10-14	15-24
Unintentional Injury 881	Unintentional Injury 15,117
Suicide 581	Homicide 6,466
Malignant Neoplasms 410	Suicide 6,062
Homicide 285	Malignant Neoplasms 1,306

Chapter Reflections

1. Have you lost a friend or peer at your school to an early and tragic death? How do you remember them today?

2. What is one thing you'd like to start doing differently to protect yourself during this time of your life?

3. What is one thing you'd like to stop doing to protect yourself from unnecessary harm?

4. Have you designed (written down, typed out, spoken aloud with a trusted person) a safety plan in advance before encountering any dangerous situation that may cause harm? Talk to a trusted adult if you need help.

Chapter 8

PLASTICITY, PRIME TIME, AND A SECOND WINDOW OF OPPORTUNITY

To me, "Garden of Delete" is a way of describing the idea that good things can bloom out of a negative situation. All the traumatic experiences I had during puberty, ugly memories and ugly thoughts in general can yield something good, like a record or whatever.

~ Oneohtrix Point Never (OPN)

Questions for You to Ponder

As you read through this chapter, please consider the following questions:

1. What do you think of when you hear the word "plastic?"

2. What does "a second window of opportunity" mean to you?

3. Do you perceive yourself intellectually at the "prime time" of learning and growth?

4. What area of your life (academically or outside of school) have you noticed "getting better" now compared with twelve months ago?

Introduction

The word *plasticity* may suggest something stiff and rigidly formed to you. However, the American Psychological Association defines *neural plasticity* as "the ability of the nervous system to change in response to experience or environmental stimulation." Or think of plasticity in this way: Your brain is like a fresh sponge, able to take in knowledge and experiences from your surroundings, modify its structure, and function accordingly.

Neural plasticity is also known as neuroplasticity, brain plasticity, or synaptic plasticity.

Minecraft Scenario

In the *Minecraft* scenario, you may notice during the rapid construction stage that some streets or buildings that are out of place interfere with the beauty of the metropolis. Also, they disturb the transportation system used to ship materials and resources smoothly to the capital to set up a striving government to meet the needs and interests of the citizens.

Based on your evaluation and current environmental condition, you realize this is the prime time to make adjustments and changes. You have the flexibility to make your metropolitan area incredible if you take action.

Adolescence is the Prime Time to Learn

- During adolescence, your brain is continuously under reconstruction, consolidation, and maturation through pruning and myelination. Neuroplasticity offers your brain the capacity to change and adapt.

- Because of the plasticity, your brain is fully moldable/malleable. You can pick up new skills faster, and the environmental influences can have lasting effects on your cortical circuitry. Remember the use-it-or-lose-it principle!

- You may be surprised how the experiences of visiting museums, exploring nature, reading autobiographies, and volunteer work during your teen years benefit you for the rest of your life.

- Even neuroplasticity exists throughout a person's life. Based on years of study, neuroscientist Dr. Daphna Shohamy affirms that teens' brains are particularly wired to learn.[1] They can absorb information and memorize material faster and develop talents easier.[2]

Adolescence is the Prime Time to Establish Good Habits

- The first window of opportunity is the first few years of life. Neuroscientists regard adolescence as the "Second Window of Opportunity," or "Age of Opportunity," because of fast brain development and its plasticity.[3, 4, 5]

- Not only is the brain able to learn things faster, but the plasticity and neural circuitry give you the opportunity to get rid of bad habits and establish good ones for life. This takes repeated efforts. You can do it!

- Good habits might include planning things ahead of time, exercising self-regulation, delayed gratification, etc.

- Through practice, the desirable behaviors become habits quicker and easier in the second decade of a person's life. The good habits help you excel and propel you to succeed in life.

- This is also a great time to learn good manners and be kind to others.

- Research from the University of Pennsylvania suggests:
  - There is a distinct pattern of brain development that occurs in different regions of the brain.
  - Because the parts of the brain that support cognitive, social, and emotional activities appear to be more plastic or open to change, adaptation, and remodeling than other brain regions.[6]
  - Adolescents continue to be sensitive to their socioeconomic settings. Not everything is a matter of will or choice in your life—we get that!

Chapter Reflections

1. Is there something you want to change to improve your life that is within your control?

2. What good habits or matters do you want to keep doing or improve?

3. In what areas do you feel empowered or appliable to your life after learning the concept of neuroplasticity?

Chapter 9

WHY ADDICTION IS A THIEF TO YOUR BRAIN POWER

It's like having a second chance at life. ... Seeing everything with clarity, gratitude; it's unbelievable. I feel so good. And to have these little blessings is the icing on the cake.

~ Ronnie Wood

Happiness is not to be found at the bottom of a bottle or from the tip of a needle; it is not to be found amidst a cloud of smoke or within a sugar-coated pill. If you look for it in these places, you will find naught but despair.
~Wayne Gerard Trotman, British filmmaker and composer

...I see the lights in their eyes come on and they get through the terrible part of addiction and the detox and they're able to live a normal life as long as they do a certain amount of work every day
~ Matthew Perry, Friends, Lovers, and the Big Terrible Thing

Questions for You to Ponder

As you read through this chapter, please consider the following questions:

1. What kind of image jumps into your mind when you hear the word "addiction"?
2. What knowledge do you possess regarding addiction based on the media, from school or family members?
3. Do you believe that addiction is a matter of personal preference or choice?

Introduction

Plasticity helps adolescents learn information faster and adapt to environmental changes more quickly. It's a marvelous thing! Don't you think so?

However, during the brain-reorganizing, reward-sensitive period, when young minds are prone to novelty-seeking and risk-taking, neural plasticity acts as a double-edged sword. It helps you learn good stuff faster and easier, but the faster and easier learning capability has negative implications regarding bad things. It makes a person more vulnerable to detrimental substance or bad habits influences and susceptible to addictions, like drugs or unhealthy behaviors. Instant pleasure can overpower sound judgment and hide unfavorable long-term consequences. Without stepping on the brakes, a person can see addiction take control of their life and spiral down. No wonder some experts regard addiction as a Trojan horse—a giant horse that appeared harmless but had powerful, destructive force—for the brain, health, and life.

Minecraft Scenario

In the *Minecraft* scenario, the capital and the metropolis are diligently under construction based on your original blueprint. Along the way, you have made some adjustments according to what you have learned in the past. Everything is looking good, except the defense system is still not at its best.

The executive command center in the capital has not been well established. Navy troops, air force, and army are still in training. The enemy takes advantage of the vulnerability. At first, some impostors mingle with the entertainers in the central recreational center as friends to steal valuable information and resources. The pretenders arouse everyone's excitement to gain the citizens' trust, while sneakily damaging the local streets and highways. Then, the mobs raid the city, and the spies bury landmines to destroy the railroads, weakening the transportation system to further disrupt the Capitol building's construction. In the end, the enemy intends to send a missile to damage the Capitol's command quarter unless you create an anti-missile defense in time.

How can you strengthen your defensive power to protect the metropolis from the enemy's sly raid? Do you have strategies to reverse the detrimental situation and rebuild the capital and other cities after the enemy's malicious attack?

What is Addiction?

Merriam-Webster defines *addiction* as a "compulsive, chronic, physiological or psychological need for a habit-forming substance, behavior, or activity having harmful physical, psychological, or social effects and typically causing well-defined symptoms (such as anxiety, irritability, tremors, or nausea) upon withdrawal or abstinence"; it is "a strong inclination to do, use, or indulge in something repeatedly."

The primary reasons for preteen and teen drug use are curiosity, peer pressure, the desire to be accepted and fit in with friends, or for a moment of escape. But during the reward-sensitive period, many of them can't stop once they experience the "high." In addition, underlying and untreated mental illness is often a strong contributor towards the propensity of addiction.

Dopamine (DA) is a neurotransmitter and plays a crucial role in reward and movement regulation in the brain. The release of DA is responsible for motivating our actions and repeating pleasurable experiences. It reinforces the act of taking the drug and becoming addicted.

- Addiction is a psychological and/or physical dependence on and craving for a particular substance or behavior to experience a "high" beyond self-control.
- Addiction is chronic brain dysfunction involving reward, motivation, and memory systems.
- Addiction displays a compulsive or obsessive desire to seek reward and immediate satisfaction, without concern for the negative consequences.
- The younger a person is involved in harmful behavior or addiction, the more challenging it is to get rid of it, and the more damaging it is to a person's life in the long run.

The most common substance abuse disorders include, but are not limited to, the use of cannabinoids, nicotine, opioids, cocaine, amphetamines, and alcohol.

The most common behavioral addictions are the internet, sex, shopping, video games, and gambling.

We will focus on substance abuse disorders/drug addiction in this chapter.

Youth Substance Abuse in the USA

According to the National Center for Drug Abuse Statistics' (NCDAS) 2022 report:[1]

- 70% of users who try an illegal drug before age 13 develop a substance abuse disorder within the next seven years compared to 27% of those who try an illegal drug after age 17.

- 47% of young people use an illegal drug by the time they graduate from high school; other users within the last 30 days include:

  o 5% of 8th graders

  o 20% of 10th graders

  o 24% of 12th graders

- 90% of addictions start in the teenage years.

- 1 in 6 teens has used a prescription drug to get high or change their mood.

- One person dies every 19 minutes from a drug overdose in the United States, according to the National Institute on Alcohol Abuse and Alcoholism (2023).[2] 443,000 American adolescents from 12 to 17 years old suffer from an alcohol use disorder.

- Substance abuse may gravely impair your body, and you may have to live with the consequences for the rest of your life. Furthermore, addiction is strongly tied to poverty, which may be transgenerational (passed down from generation to generation). A member of a household who is addicted tends to affect the following generation and may continue to live in an undesirable situation, below the standard of living that you want for yourself.[3]

Gateway Drug Theory

- The gateway drug theory is also known as the gateway drug hypothesis. It is the idea that certain drug use, apparently harmless (soft) initially, acts as a gateway and sequentially progresses to more harmful (harder) drugs.

- The gateway drug theory is derived from decades of observation established via longitudinal studies and statistical probability.

- The neurobiological impact of substance use during the vulnerable adolescent brain development period sets the stage and serves as a gateway for future substance abuse and addiction.

- Gateway drug use alters neuropathways in the brain and increases the risk of advancing to other illicit drugs and long-term addiction.

- The most common gateway drugs are said to be tobacco, alcohol, and marijuana. But any drug can act as a gateway drug.

- Based on the gateway drug theory, no amount of substance use is safe for adolescents and young adults.

- Do you really want to open that gate and let the thief or predator in? Once it's open, it's very hard to lock it again.

The Risks of Substance Use in Adolescents

- It affects physical and mental health, especially brain development.

- It promotes risky behaviors, such as dangerous driving and unprotected sex.

- Injecting drugs put an individual at immediate risk for hepatitis B, hepatitis C, HIV, and AIDS.

- Drugs use puts youth at risk of overdose.

- According to the CDC (2020) report, compared to other students, students who report using prescription drugs without a doctor's prescription are more likely to be the victims of physical or sexual dating violence.[4]

- According to research, the earlier people start using drugs, the more likely they are to develop major health issues and dampen their future.[5]

- A teen's brain is still developing, which increases their chances of attempting drugs or continuing to use them. Drugs used during this development phase may trigger brain alterations with severe and long-term adverse effects.[6]

- Drug use is associated with the experience of violence, mental health issues, and suicide risks.

- The younger a teen experiences alcohol and drugs, the greater the chance of becoming addicted later in life.

- Adolescent drug use affects learning and memory due to alteration of neural connections.

- Addiction takes a toll on finances and is strongly associated with poverty in life.

- It contributes to adult mental illness and health problems, such as heart diseases, high blood pressure, sleeping disorders, negatively impacting the general quality of life.

- Taking drugs during pregnancy can cause birth defects or affect fetal brain growth, leading to developmental disabilities later. Taking drugs during breastfeeding is harmful to an infant's overall growth.[7]

Potential Drug-Specific Consequences Caused by Adolescent Drug Exposure

Studies have shown that drug exposure during adolescence has drug-specific neural, behavioral, and cognitive effects. The neurotoxicity and alterations in neurocircuitry damage the prefrontal cortex, impair cognitive, and behavioral performance, and activate neuroin-flammation.[8, 9 ,10]

In short, the negative consequences of chronic and prolonged substance abuse increase the risk of psychiatric disorders, and affect learning and memory processes.

Note: *Polydrug usage* means intaking more than one drug or type of drug at the same time. Mixing more than one drug, including over-the-counter or prescribed medications, can have unpredictable effects. Polydrug use is hazardous and can be deadly!

Let's look at the most commonly used drugs among adolescents.

Marijuana

- Marijuana has been evidence of classification as a gateway drug. Its chemical, delta-9-tetrahydrocannabinol (THC), is responsible for the strong psychoactive effects of cannabis.

- Initial marijuana experience often happens during adolescence.

- Marijuana usage in adolescence leads to structural and functional changes in the brain.

- THC can prime the brain for enhanced responses to other drugs.

- Street names for marijuana include Aunt Mary, BC Bud, Blunts, Boom, Budder, Chronic, Dope, Gangster, Ganja, Grass, Hash, Herb, Honeycomb, Hydro, Indo, Joint, Keef, Kif, Mary Jane (MJ), Mota, Pot, Purp, Reefer, Rosin, Shatter, Sinsemilla, Skunk, Smoke, Trees, Weed, Yerba, etc.

- Marijuana can be introduced to the body through various routes, like inhaling, eating, drinking, or vaping.

- Marijuana is frequently used with other drugs, like alcohol, which can cause hazardous damage to the neural system and body.

- Concentrates or "dabs" have high concentrations of THC, sometimes blended with toxic chemicals. It can cause severe harm to a user's health.

- A cheap alternative to marijuana is a synthetic cannabinoid, street named K2 or Spice. It can cause a life-threatening condition.

- Several studies have discovered links between cannabis usage and pulmonary, cardiovascular, gastrointestinal, and endocrine function, as well as body mass index (BMI) and sleep. More research is needed at this time to determine the impact of cannabis usage on physical health, particularly among adolescent samples.[11]

- Marijuana users had considerably higher amounts of metals like lead and cadmium in their blood and urine, according to researchers.[12]

- THC exposure during pregnancy changes the placental and fetal epigenome, resulting to neurobehavioral problems such as autism spectrum disorder. This research reveals that prenatal THC exposure may have an impact on child's life-long health outcomes.[13]

- In conclusion, here are the negative impacts of teen marijuana usage.[14, 15, 16] Marijuana can:

  O Alter the structure of dendrites and synapses in the brain, causing the reduction in the myelination of frontal-temporal regions.

  O Increase the risk of mental health issues like depression, anxiety, and psychosis. It has been reported that marijuana usage may be associated with schizophrenia.

  O Impair memory and learning, thereby lowering IQ.

○ Reduce thinking and problem-solving ability and coordination.

○ Dysregulation in dopamine pathway

○ Change gene expression

○ Increase the risk of drug abuse

○ A licensed physician should keep an eye on your marijuana use if it is for medical purposes. There is a distinction between the medical use of marijuana and its recreational use. Risk factors are involved in the intake of marijuana during adolescence, while the brain is rapidly developing and the neural connection is vulnerable to alteration and insult.

Nicotine[17]

· The use of e-tobacco or vaping, along with flavored tobacco, has become popular in the youth population due to unethical marketing. That is a real concern for public health.

· Adolescent nicotine exposure affects the brain's long-term molecular, biochemical, and functional changes.

· Studies have shown that nicotine use in adolescence interferes with myelinization (the neural connection between brain areas) and affects white matter integrity.

○ Nicotine changes the structure of dendrites and synapses in prefrontal cortex and nucleus accumbens

○ It increases anxiety and novelty seeking, even if it may feel relaxing in the moment.

○ It reduces learning ability and increase memory impairments

· The use of tobacco or nicotine serves as a gateway to other drug abuse.

- Exposure to nicotine during adolescence may result in addiction that persists into adulthood. It can lead to chronic cigarette smoking and its adverse health consequences, like lung cancer, emphysema, etc.

- Several studies have documented the negative consequences of using electronic cigarettes on the physical and mental development of teenagers and young adults.[18]

- E-cigarettes are a rising tobacco product with health risks. Cognitive deterioration may result from vascular and blood-brain barrier disorders. Non-nicotinic e-cigarette aerosol may affect immunological and endothelial cells. E-cigarettes may induce neurovascular damage because nicotine counteracts non-nicotinic pro-inflammatory effects.[19, 20]

- Researchers are investigating the effects of combining e-cigarettes and alcohol on the blood-brain barrier, which can lead to neurological damage and cognitive decline. The NIH-funded study aims to identify potential biomarkers for clinical use and understand the specific injuries caused by this combination. It also seeks to identify biomarkers for detecting blood-brain barrier injury in substance users.[21]

- Vaping can lead to:[22,23,24,25]

  o Cognitive maladjustments such as poor learning and academic performance

  o Increased aggressive and impulsive behavior

  o Poor sleep quality

  o Attention deficits

  o Decreased memory and slowed thinking

  o Increased depression and suicidal thoughts

It should also be noted that e-cigarette usage alone can damage the blood-brain barrier and induce brain inflammation.

Opioids

- Opioids and their receptors are traditionally used to treat pain and related disorders.

- Adolescent opioid abuse can result in organ and brain alterations, leading to addiction and triggering the development of psychiatric disorders later in life.

- Opioids prescribed by a licensed health care professional to relieve pain are legal, such as hydrocodone (e.g., Vicodin®); oxycodone (e.g., OxyContin®); oxymorphone; morphine (Kadian®, Avinza®); codeine; and fentanyl.

- Illegal opioids include heroin and fentanyl.

- Opioid misuse and overdose occur when a person uses heroin or misuses prescription pain relievers. Historically, these have sometimes been over-prescribed, increasing the temptations and opportunities for individuals to misuse them.

- Heroin may have many street names, such as Big H, Black Tar, Chiva, Hell Dust, Horse, Negra, Smack, and Thunder.

- Heroin can be in powder form or as a black sticky substance.

- Heroin can be smoked, sniffed, snorted, and injected.

- The risks of injecting heroin include collapsed veins and exposure to HIV or hepatitis C.

- To reinforce the above statement, research has reported that teen opioid abuse and HIV are interrelated problems. By facing these problems head on, we can make sure that young people are safe and work to end the drug crisis among young people.[26]

- Aside from relieving pain, the short-term opioids' harmful health effects are extreme drowsiness, constipation, nausea, vomiting, confusion, and reduced breathing rate or stopped breathing.

- Fentanyl is another type of opioid similar to morphine. It is 50 times stronger than heroin. It is easy to get and often results in overdose and death. Oftentimes, people do not know that fentanyl is in a drug that they are using, causing unintentional overdoses.

- Over a million Americans have died of drug overdoses since 2000, mostly from opioids. The crisis has been driven mainly by synthetic opioids, and Mexico has become a significant supply source.[27]

- In August 2022, the Drug Enforcement Administration (DEA) warned about brightly-colored candy like fentanyl, labeled "rainbow fentanyl." The drug cartels sell the highly addictive and potentially deadly fentanyl to attract children and young people.[28]

- The DEA lab has revealed the following frightening facts and warnings (2022):[29]

  o Six out of every ten fake pills contain at least 2 mg of fentanyl, a potentially lethal dose.

  o Drug traffickers use fake pills to exploit the opioid crisis and prescription drug misuse.

  o In 2021, 107,622 people died by drug poisoning in the United States.

  o Criminal drug networks mass-produce fake pills and falsely market them as legitimate prescription pills to deceive the American public.

  o Fake pills are easy to purchase, widely available, and often sold on social media and e-commerce platforms, making them available to anyone with a smartphone.

  o Fake pills often contain fentanyl or methamphetamine and can be deadly.

- Many counterfeit pills resemble prescription opioids such as oxycodone (Oxycontin®, Percocet®); hydrocodone (Vicodin®); alprazolam (Xanax®); or stimulants such as amphetamines (Adderall®).

- In 2022, DEA seized over 50.6 million fake pills, often laced with fentanyl.

- DEA warns that pills purchased outside a licensed pharmacy are illegal, dangerous, and potentially lethal.

• Prolonged use or misuse of opioids can cause insomnia, muscle pain, and heart and lung infections.

• Opioid overdose can cause slowed breathing and hypoxia. Hypoxia—lack of oxygen reaching the brain—can lead to coma, permanent brain damage, or death.

• Overdose deaths from heroin and other opioids have increased in recent years, especially in adolescents and young adults.[30, 31]

• To avoid opioid misuse:

- Always follow the doctor's instructions and read the directions before taking medicine, even over-the-counter medication.

- Never take pills that are not prescribed for you.

- Do not share medications with anyone, not even your family members or friends.

- Do not take opioids to get high or escape. Opioids are highly addictive and can be very hard to get off.

Cocaine [32, 33]

• Cocaine is a stimulant. It can come in powder (cocaine or coke) and rock (crack) forms. It is commonly taken by smoking, snorting, or injecting it into the blood vessels.

- Drug dealers can mix a variety of dangerous substances as filler to cut costs. The filler can cause severe damage to your brain and health.

- Cocaine affects the central nervous system. The neurotoxicity of cocaine can cause neuroplasticity dysfunctions in the nucleus accumbens, change dopamine brain activity, reduce striatal gray matter, and cause brain cells to age quickly and die.[34,35,36,37]

- The above sentence describes various negative impacts of cocaine's neurotoxicity on the brain, particularly in the nucleus accumbens, a region crucial for reward processing and motivation. Here's a breakdown of the effects mentioned:

  o Neurotoxicity refers to the ability of a substance to damage the nervous system, including brain cells.

  o Neuroplasticity Dysfunctions: Disruption of the brain's natural ability to adapt and change its structure and function in response to experiences.

  o Reduced Striatal Gray Matter: The striatum, located near the nucleus accumbens, regulates movement and plays a role in reward processing. Gray matter reduction indicates loss of nerve cells and connections in this area.

  o Accelerated Cell Aging and Death: Cocaine exposure can damage and prematurely age brain cells, leading to their death.

- The most common short-term effects are euphoria, high energy, and alertness; some users become aggressive and violent. The health risks are sensitivity to light, sound, and touch, paranoia, nausea, upset stomach, high blood pressure (from constricted blood vessels), elevated body temperature, rapid or irregular heartbeats, heart attack, stroke, and seizures.

- Long-term cocaine use can cause nose bleeding, loss of smell/ olfactory function, respiratory and lungs diseases (bronchitis and pneumonia), digestive system problems, weakened immune system, irregular heartbeat, severe paranoia, anxiety, depression, hallucinations, seizure disorders, Parkinson's disease (movement disorders), intracerebral hemorrhage (internal brain bleeding), impaired memory and decision-making ability, and death by overdose.

- In short, there are two primary reasons that cocaine use harms your brain cells and affects your cognitive ability:

  ○ One, it disrupts your brain cells' communications/ connections with an excess of dopamine, which causes neurons to die off.

  ○ Two, cocaine's effect of constricting blood vessels fails to provide adequate blood and oxygen to the brain cells.

- The good news is that the study indicates that cocaine-induced cognitive impairment can be reversible after one year of complete abstinence; however, the earlier age of cocaine initiation seems to hinder the recovery process.[38]

- First, DON'T TRY IT!

- If you have tried it, STOP IMMEDIATELY.

- It's never too late to GET HELP!

Amphetamines/Methamphetamine (MA)

- Both amphetamines and methamphetamine are central nervous stimulant drugs. Some scientists refer to them as psychostimulant drugs.

- A licensed doctor may prescribe them as medication to treat attention-deficit hyperactivity disorder (ADHD), narcolepsy, or to suppress appetite. They may include Adderall®, Concerta®, Dexedrine®, Focalin®, Metadate®, Methylin®, Ritalin®, or Vyvanse®.

- Amphetamines and methamphetamine have been used illegally as a study aid or to get high. The street names are Ecstasy, Molly, MDMA, Bennies, Black Beauties, Crank, Ice, Speed, Uppers, up, Chalk, Christmas tree, Crystal, Meth, Rock, louee, goey, whiz, rack, etc.

- Methamphetamine is more potent than amphetamines and causes more damage to your central nervous system if you use it repeatedly without a licensed doctor's supervision.

- Adolescent exposure to amphetamines and methamphetamine can influence the central nervous system's neuronal circuits. Studies have shown that usage has reduced the frontal cortex's gray matter and interfered with neuron communications. It is negatively linked to short-term memory performance, impulsivity, verbal learning, and reduced IQ.

- "Meth" can be swallowed (tablet), injected (crank), snorted, smoked (crystallized methamphetamine hydrochloride, "ice" or rock), or inhaled. The powder form is referred to as speed. Methamphetamine can be clear or a variety of colors.

  o Dealers may package them in aluminum foil ("foils"), plastic bags, or small balloons to sell illegally.

  o Amphetamines can destroy gray matter in the brain, change dopamine receptors, and alter brain functions.

  o Its short-term effects on the body are similar to cocaine: increased body temperature, pale skin, insomnia, decreased appetite, more active and talkative, repetitive movement, jaw clamping/teeth grinding, panic attacks, physical exhaustion, prone to injury, sweating, headaches, blurred vision, enlarged pupils, dry mouth, hot flashes, dizziness, increased blood pressure and heartbeat leading to stroke, heart attack, and heart failure.

- Long-term abuse can be addictive and cause psychosis-like paranoia, anxiety, hallucination, violence/aggression, unpredictable behaviors, mood swings, digestive upset, malnutrition, weight loss, prone to infections, increased heart rate, elevated blood pressure, inability to keep up with personal responsibility (work/school/home), loss of interest in previous hobbies and activities, depression, and suicidal tendencies.

- Use of methamphetamine can cause severe tooth decay, tooth loss, and gum disease, a condition often called "meth mouth."

- Overdose can be fatal from strokes, heart failure, and seizures. Signs of overdose can be hyperactivity, sweating, rapid breathing or a feeling that you can't breathe, difficulty passing urine, shaking/trembling/spasms, chest pain, pounding heart, raised temperature, body chills, disorientation, severe headache, vomiting, paranoia, delusions, agitation, irritability, anxiousness or psychotic behavior, or convulsions.[39]

- Amphetamines can cause birth defects when taken during pregnancy and are harmful to infants during breastfeeding.

Alcohol

- Even though the legal drinking age is 21 in the USA, alcohol use is prevalent in adolescents younger than 21 years old—especially high schoolers or first-year students in college.

- Alcohol is a psychoactive substance; it is neurotoxic to the developing brain.

- MRI studies of adolescents with alcohol use disorders show disruption in myelination and alteration in connectivity between frontal and limbic regions. They also reveal smaller gray matter volume in several brain regions, such as the frontal, parietal, and temporal cortices, as well as limbic regions such as the hippocampus and the cerebellum.

- Research has found that alcohol use in adolescence has a gateway effect, which leads to subsequent use of other illicit substances and possible long-term addiction.

- Examining data from a nationally representative sample of 2,835 US 12th graders, a research article published in *Journal of School Health* by Barry et al. (2016) revealed the following:[40] (1) Alcohol was the most commonly used substance. (2) Alcohol was initiated earliest. (3) Alcohol was the first substance widely used in the progression of substance use. (4) The delay of alcohol initiation reduced the lifetime illicit drug usage.

- According to the *Monitoring the Future* national survey in 2016, in the United States, the prevalence of alcohol drinking in adolescents was 21%, 42%, and 58% for 8th, 10th, and 12th graders, respectively. Binge drinking rates were 5%, 16%, and 24% in corresponding grades.[41]

- The short-term adverse effects of alcohol abuse include school dropout, strained relationships with family and others, injury, loss of life due to severe accidents, and risk of co-occurring alcohol use disorder and other drug use disorders.[42, 43]

- Binge drinking has a severe impact on the brain in the short term and long term.[44, 45]

- For youth, binge drinking is approximately three drinks for girls and three to five drinks for boys (depending on weight) in about two hours, to reach 0.08 blood alcohol concentration.[46]

- Please keep in mind there is no safe level of alcohol!

- In summary, alcohol use in adolescents:[47]
  - ○ Reduces volume in prefrontal cortex, corpus callosum, and hippocampus
  - ○ Increases anxiety and depression
  - ○ Increases risky decision-making, learning memory deficiency
  - ○ Increases subsequent abuse of other drugs
  - ○ Increases alcohol dependence
- According to the National Institute on Alcohol Abuse and Alcoholism (NIAAA), 1 in 10 children lives in a home with a parent who has a drinking problem.[48, 49] If you are one of those children, you may experience alcohol at an early age. But you do not have to inherit the problem and mess up your life. Help is available. Get help!

I strongly encourage you to check out the following links. Learning about alcohol's effects on health and treatments can empower you! You may find an opportunity to help your friends or sibling.

- National Institute on Alcohol Abuse and Alcoholism. (2021). *Treatment for alcohol problems: Finding and getting help.*

  https://www.niaaa.nih.gov/publications/brochures-and-fact-sheets/treatment-alcohol-problems-finding-and-getting-help
- National Institute on Alcohol Abuse and Alcoholism (NIAAA). (n. d.) *Alcohol's Effects on health.* https://www.niaaa.nih.gov/alcohols-effects-health

Anabolic Androgenic Steroids (AAS)

Besides the commonly abused drugs mentioned previously, anabolic androgenic steroids (AAS) have been used illicitly among adolescent males most commonly to build muscle mass and maintain strength. It can alter many brain regions and impair the immune system.

Substance Abuse During Pregnancy

Studies have shown that substance exposure during pregnancy may adversely affect the infant's mental and cognitive development.[50,51,52,53,54]

Substance	Long Term Effects
Tobacco/Nicotine	behavior problems, including ADHD
Marijuana	impairments in attention, visual perceptual abilities, behavior problems, including delinquent behavior
Alcohol	poor physical growth, lower intelligence, attention problems, and academic underachievement
Cocaine	lower intelligence, impairments in attention, language, and executive functions (organization, memory, time management, self-control), as well as emotional and behavioral problems
Opioid	attention, memory, and behavior problems (including hyperactivity)

Table source: Samaritan Neuropsychology. (2020). *How do drugs affect a baby's development during pregnancy?*

https://www.samhealth.org/about-samaritan/news-search/2020/06/08/how-do-drugs-affect-babys-development-during-pregnancy

How Does Addiction Hijack Your Brain?

Substance addiction changes brain chemistry by quickly boosting dopamine, a neurotransmitter required for pleasure and motivation. These spikes are more potent and linger longer (like super-fireworks) than the pleasure they usually represent. Chronic exposure to these surges alters a person's typical hierarchy (daily happiness, such as enjoying sports with friends) by dulling the dopamine system's reactivity to everyday occurrences.[55]

In other words, addiction alters the brain by interfering with dopamine, the "feel-good" neurotransmitter. It's like a super-intense light show, making regular delights appear dull.

It's like your brain gets stuck in this loop, chasing the next megablast, even if it means ignoring school, friends, or your health. It's a maze, and addiction is the cunning monster lurking around every corner.

But here's the good news: you're not trapped! Even after getting lost in the maze, you can find your way out. Addiction is a serious issue, but it doesn't have to define you. Remember, you're not just a character in the maze; you're the hero with the potential to escape and build a brighter future.

How Not to Let Drugs and Alcohol Take Over Your Good Judgment

It's not news that drug cartels and dealers are doing all they can to lure youngsters into the drug world and get them hooked. They are everywhere: by the campus gate, in the popular youth cafe, in fast food restaurants; some even infiltrate the school campuses and the internet via popular social media platforms. They're looking for long-term customers. Drug dealing is a lucrative business to them! They don't care about your brain, health, or future.

They pretend to be your friend, then drag you down. The drug dealers are like wolves in sheep's clothing, waiting for their prey. All they care about is MONEY, MONEY, MONEY. It can be tempting to fall for their games. However, you may find yourself like a fly or little insect falling into a spider web, and it will be hard to escape. The money you spend on drugs fuels the drug trafficker's power, resulting in homicides, arms dealing, human trafficking, and expanding criminal organizations worldwide.

So, how can you be wise and defeat their tricks and traps? I am confident that you can outsmart them!

- First, don't give the drug dealers a chance. Be alert to their tricks and traps. Do not allow anyone to pressure, persuade, or manipulate you to try drugs or alcohol, even if you think they're your good friend. Turn around and stay away as fast as you can. The bottom line is: do not allow any substance or alcohol into your system. Guard your gate; do not let them sneak in. (Remember the gateway drug theory?)

- Second, if you've already tried drugs or alcohol, shut the gate and resist the temptation. Be brave and say "NO!" to the thief who wants to steal your money and brain power.

- Last, if you are on the slippery slope of addiction, please get help immediately. Don't hesitate. Addiction can make you feel lonely, depressed, anxious and scared at times, but you don't have to deal with your addiction alone. You have made mistakes, but you are not a bad person. Don't feel ashamed. Don't look back; look forward.

According to research, illegal drug use causes adverse health and psychological consequences and is associated with self-reported poor life satisfaction and poor self-rated health in young people.[56] Addiction often leads to a low quality of life and long-term poverty. Terrifyingly, fatal overdoses involving stimulants and fentanyl in the United States rose from 0.6% in 2010 to 32.3% in 2021.[57]

I don't believe that you would want to be a self-imposed prisoner, dependent on illegal drugs, and living a miserable life or death. Your life can be bright and full of joy!

Get Help! Recovery is Possible! There is Hope!

According to Dr. Nora D. Volkow, director of the National Institute on Drug Abuse, "Drug addiction is a brain disease that can be treated."

We've discussed the many ways that drugs can harm or even kill you. Now, let's take a look at the many avenues and options you can consider as a way to get on the road to recovery.

- The Substance Abuse and Mental Health Service's (SAMHSA) National Helpline is a free, confidential, 24/7, 365-day-a-year treatment referral and information service (in English and Spanish) for individuals and families facing mental and/or substance use disorders.
  - ○ SAMHSA's National Helpline:
    https://www.samhsa.gov/find-help/national-helpline
    Call: 1-800-662-HELP (4357)
  - ○ National Council on Alcoholism and Drug Dependence, Inc. (NCADD) –
    Call: 1-800-NCA-CALL (622-2255)
- According to the NIAAA, 1 in 10 children lives in a home with a parent who has a drinking problem. If you are dealing with a difficult situation like this call for help.
  - ○ National Association for Children of Alcoholics – 1-888-554-COAS (2627)
- National Drug Helpline: (844) 289-0879
- If you believe you or someone with you may be experiencing a drug overdose, call 911 immediately.
- According to National Institute on Drug Abuse, "Nearly 92,000 people died of drug overdoses in 2020."

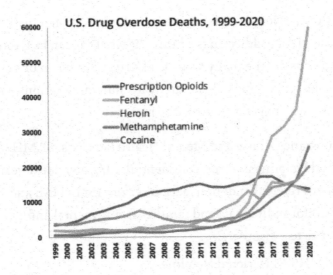

Source: https://nida.nih.gov/sites/default/files/nida_23_cj.pdf

- These resources may help you on the road to recovery and prevent relapse:
    - The Partnership for Drug-free Kids: drugfree.org/
      Call: 1-855-DRUG-FREE (378-4373)
    - LifeRing: www.lifering.org/
    - SMART Recovery: www.smartrecovery.org/
    - Narcotics Anonymous: www.na.org/
- The Jed Foundation: https://jedfoundation.org/

Closing Thoughts: Insights from Matthew Perry on Addiction and Recovery

As we wrap up this chapter, I am compelled to share some of Matthew Perry's uplifting words. Known worldwide for his portrayal of Chandler Bing on the iconic television series "Friends," Matthew Perry's journey with addiction touched the hearts of many, mine included. His untimely departure left a void in the entertainment world, but his legacy of honesty and resilience continues to inspire.

While Matthew Perry may not have directed his words specifically toward adolescent audiences, his reflections on addiction and recovery offer invaluable wisdom for all. Here are some quotes that echo both caution and hope, from various fields of addiction recovery, urging young minds to steer clear of the dangers of substance abuse. They reflect common sentiments in addiction recovery programs, counseling sessions, and motivational speeches.

"Addiction doesn't care if you're young, successful, or famous. It can happen to anyone, and it can take everything from you if you let it."

"I wasted so many years of my life chasing a high that was never worth it. Don't make the same mistake I did. There's nothing glamorous about addiction."

"Drugs and alcohol might seem like an escape, but they only trap you in a cycle of pain and despair. You deserve better than that."

"Don't let peer pressure or curiosity lead you down a path you'll regret. The temporary high isn't worth the long-term consequences."

"It takes strength and courage to say no to drugs and alcohol, but it's worth it. Your future self will thank you."

"If you're struggling with addiction, know that you're not alone. There is help available, and recovery is possible. Reach out and take that first step towards a better life."

"The hardest part of overcoming addiction is admitting you have a problem. But once you do, you can start rebuilding your life one day at a time."

"Don't let addiction define who you are. You are so much more than your struggles. Believe in yourself and your ability to overcome."

"Find healthy ways to cope with stress and difficult emotions. Drugs and alcohol only offer temporary relief, but they come with a high price."

"Your life is precious, and you have the power to shape your own destiny. Don't let addiction rob you of your potential. Choose life, choose recovery."

While these quotes may not be directly from Matthew Perry, they reflect the essence of his journey and can serve as inspirational reminders for adolescents to steer clear of substance abuse.

Chapter Reflections

1. What do you think people would get into substances for, besides peer pressure?

2. What is one move or decision you can make to avoid substances?

3. What quote about addiction from the closing thoughts section that stood out to you the most? Do you plan to share any of these quotes with anyone?

4. Why is it important to get help early to treat addiction or bad habits?

Recap for Part 2

Your Developing Brain	The World of *Minecraft*
The entire brain: developing from bottom up and from center out	The entire metropolis: building from south to north and center out
Different parts of the brain	Different cities in the metropolis
The neural connections (myelination): communicate among different brain parts and enhance the cerebral cortex's growth, especially the frontal lobe.	The transportation system: roads, paths, and superhighways connecting cities and supplying resources and material to establish the capital.
The frontal lobe	The capital city (Wondamento)
The prefrontal cortex: the very front part of the frontal lobe and the last to fully develop. Executive functions continue to improve via life experiences and practicing good habits.	The "Command and Control" unit inside the capitol building in the center of Wondamento. Its setup, equipment, and networking devices continue to update and upgrade
The effects of drugs, alcohol, and bad habits on your brain: molecular, biochemical, structural, and functional changes leading to reduced myelinations and brain volume/size, impaired executive function, and lower IQ.	The consequences of enemies' attacks include bombing the cities, killing civilians, damaging transportation systems, and destroying the structures.
Best defense system to fight temptations and addictions to ensure frontal lobe's optimal growth: self-regulation (self-control)	Guard against enemy invasions and protect the entire metropolis by building robust military bases and strong local police forces.

I trust you have a good grasp of how your brain grows and develops by now. Your goal is to establish healthy myelinations (neural connections) through all brain regions and central nerve systems—especially the links to the frontal cortex. Even though our brain neurons can continue to learn and build new connections throughout our lives (unless it is badly abused), adolescence is the prime time for your brain to learn and advance. You want to take advantage of this precious time to learn self-regulation skills and to nurture your brain—particularly the prefrontal cortex, the ultimate control center.

In the *Minecraft* scenario, you have defeated the enemies' invasions, the mobs' raids. The defense department has set up military bases in various regions and police departments in every city to strengthen the metropolis's security. By building outward, the residential, commercial, and industrial zones have been constructed nicely with different skyscrapers, heights, and looks. The roads, pathways, and superhighways have connected to and around the capital and every other city. The capitol is a more extensive, gaudier building made of fancy materials like terra-cotta and glass, with statues and fountains in front of it. The surrounding area has three other government buildings to enhance the capital's effective leadership power.

The capitol is the planning and control center of the metropolis. To optimize its executive function and productivity, you continue to fine-tune the internal designs and improve communication instruments and necessary networking gears. The improvement of the capitol and metropolis is an ongoing and enduring process.

I understand the analogy of *Minecraft* is not perfect. I hope it helps you picture the evolution of your brain during adolescence. Please see the Appendices section for further information about your brain's development during this vital period of your life.

Last but not least, this is a reminder that your brain is still under construction, especially your prefrontal cortex, which continues vigorously developing until your mid-twenties. It does not stop advancing afterward; it just slows down the pace. Just like in *Minecraft*, the more you practice and experience new things, the stronger your brain-cities become and the better your connections get. So keep exploring, building, and learning—your brain is a masterpiece in the making!

Part 2 Reflections

1. In what area do you better understand your brain development after reading Part 2 of this book with the analogy of *Minecraft*, even if you do not play *Minecraft*?

2. Please consider the following statement: "Starting to use drugs and alcohol earlier in adolescence raises the risk of becoming addicted later on and may make treatment more difficult."

   a. With your understanding of brain development, can you explain the reason(s) of the above statement in your own words?

   b. Why is it crucial to get treatment for addiction or unhealthy habits as soon as possible?

Part 3

HOW TO NURTURE AND SUPERCHARGE YOUR DEVELOPING BRAIN AND BODY

Adolescence is a period of rapid changes. Between the ages of 12 and 17, for example, a parent ages as much as 20 years.

~ Al Bernstein

Get ready to be inspired as we delve into the fascinating analogy between a flower's growth and a human's development from conception to adolescence.

Imagine a tiny seed buried deep in the soil, gradually sprouting and blooming into a magnificent flower. Similarly, a baby grows inside a womb, and is born, learning to walk and run before reaching adolescence, the cusp of adulthood.

In the following chapter, we'll explore how to optimize your unique journey. You're full of potential; I am here to help you embrace it. So, let's make the most of your body's and brain's transformation during this incredible time of your life.

Together, we'll discover how to withstand life's storms, face traumas head-on, and nurture your executive function. So, come along on this exciting adventure, and let's make your second and third decades the best they can be!

Chapter **10**

THE CLASSICAL DEVELOPMENTAL THEORIES AND DUAL SYSTEMS

The principal goal of education in the schools should be creating men and women who are capable of doing new things, not simply repeating what other generations have done; men and women who are creative, inventive, and discoverers, who can be critical and verify, and not accept, everything they are offered.

~ *Jean Piaget*

Questions for You to Ponder

As you read through this chapter, please consider the following questions:

1. Imagine if you were a flower; what would it be? What is your favorite flower?

2. When did you first learn about where babies come from?

3. And, who did you learn it from?

Flower Analogy

A life begins to grow from a tiny seed buried deep in the soil. It takes time, patience, and a nurturing environment for the seed to sprout from the ground. Soon enough, a small green stem emerges from the earth, stretching upwards towards the sun. With each passing day, the stem grows taller and stronger, its leaves unfurling and soaking up the warmth of the sun's rays. Slowly but surely, a tiny bud appears at the top of the stem, waiting patiently to bloom.

After nine months in the womb, a baby is born. During childhood, you are like a young, tender shoot, with growth potential. The developmental process is already embedded in you but requires the right conditions to flourish. As you grow and gain knowledge, you become like the stem of the flower, reaching upwards and seeking to establish your place in the world.

As you enter adolescence, you are like a flower bud, with your full potential and unique beauty still hidden within you. During this time, you require the most care and support as you navigate the challenges of growing up and figuring out who you are.

The Classical Developmental Theories and Dual Systems

According to Piaget's developmental stages, adolescents transition from the concrete operational stage (7 to 11 years old) into the formal operational stage (12 years old and over). The beginning of the formal operational stage roughly coincides with the initiation of puberty. I want to emphasize that this is just a generalized timeline; every individual progresses at their own pace. Everyone is different![1]

The characteristics of the formal operational stage are:[2]

- You can deal with abstract scenarios. Things don't have to be tangible for you!

- You can reason through hypothetical problems with many possible solutions and consequences.

- You begin to consider relevant moral, ethical, social, political, and philosophical issues that need theoretical and logical reasoning.

- You can think self-reflectively, which indicates the development of metacognitive skills: thinking about thinking.

- Based on Erikson's fifth stage of psychological development, it is the time when an adolescent struggles to discover the "self" and establish an identity.[3]

- The classical cognitive and psychological developments may correlate with the contemporary neuroscientists' findings in dual-system brain development through advanced neuroimaging technology, like fMRI.[4, 5]

    o Risk-seeking and self-regulation both increased from pre-adolescence, around the same time as the beginning of puberty (biologically), the formal operational stage (cognitively), and brain reorganization (neurologically).

    o Sensation-seeking peaked during late adolescence and declined afterward.

- Self-regulation increased steadily, but slower, and lagged behind sensation-seeking until it caught up in young adulthood and plateaued around the mid-20s.

- There are other cognitive-developmental theories. Vygotsky's social-cultural developmental theory is a famous one regularly equated with Piaget's. I don't want to bore you with all the theories' details, so I decided not to include them in this book. However, the following table may help you get a grasp of the two main theories.

- Comparison and contrast of Piaget and Vygotsky's developmental theories.[6, 7, 8]

Aspect	Piaget's Theory	Vygotsky's Theory
Focus	Individual construction of knowledge through interaction with the environment	Social and cultural influences on individual development
Key Concepts	Stages of cognitive development; assimilation and accommodation; schema; equilibration	Zone of proximal development; sociocultural mediation; cultural tools; private speech
Role of Language	Supports cognitive development; language acquisition reflects cognitive development	Essential tool for cognitive development; language and thought are intertwined
Learning Process	Active exploration and discovery of the environment; constructivism	Social interaction and collaboration with more knowledgeable others; scaffolding
Teacher's Role	Facilitator; encourages exploration and discovery	Collaborator; provides support and guidance
View of Development	Discontinuous and stage-like; qualitative changes	Continuous and gradual; quantitative changes
Criticisms	Underestimated the role of social and cultural factors in development; stage theory is too rigid	Overemphasized the role of social and cultural factors in development; vague on the mechanisms of cognitive development

Note: This table is not exhaustive and is only meant to provide a brief comparison of Piaget's and Vygotsky's theories.

Roles of the Prefrontal Cortex

We have discussed how the prefrontal cortex served as the "Command and Control" unit inside the capitol building. Let's review it.[9, 10, 11, 12]

- The prefrontal cortex is located at the very front part of the frontal lobe.

- It accounts for over 10% of the brain's volume.

- It is the slowest part of the brain to mature.

- It continues to generate and prune neural connections until the mid-20s.

- It receives input from various brain regions to process information, coordinate, adjust, and adapt accordingly.

- It plays a significant role in personality development.

- The prefrontal cortex is best known for "executive function" in the cognitive domain.

- The prefrontal cortex is responsible for many important functions such as decision-making, planning, and working memory. These are all skills that are important for teens and young adults as they navigate the challenges of growing up.

- The prefrontal cortex does not stop maturing and developing after the mid-20s. While the bulk of structural changes in the prefrontal cortex occur during adolescence and early adulthood, research has shown that the prefrontal cortex undergoes further changes throughout adulthood, including changes in synaptic connections, neural plasticity, and myelination.

- The prefrontal context can be affected by different factors such as stress and aging.

- In other words, although the prefrontal cortex may reach a level of maturity in structure and function by the mid-20s, it continues to undergo subtle changes and refinements throughout adulthood. Therefore, it's important to continue engaging in activities that promote brain health and cognitive function throughout life.

Chapter Reflections

1. Which theory were you more drawn to—Piaget or Vygotsky? Why? (If you feel the concepts of these theories are difficult to understand or digest, it's OK. Don't be too hard on yourself).

2. Have you noticed that your prefrontal cortex is maturing in your decision-making today compared to one or two years ago?

3. What is one activity that you are doing currently or would like to start that would enhance your brain's growth or health?

Chapter 11

WHAT IS EXECUTIVE FUNCTION?

Adolescence represents an inner emotional upheaval, a struggle between the eternal human wish to cling to the past and the equally powerful wish to get on with the future.

~ *Louise J. Kaplan*

Questions for You to Ponder

As you read through this chapter, please consider the following questions:

1. What does executive functioning mean to you if you have heard of this term? Take a moment and verbalize it if you would.

2. What do you think "acting on impulse" has anything to do with executive functioning?

3. Can you think of a time when you were about to act on impulse but stopped yourself from doing it and avoided trouble? (If you do, high five! Give yourself a pat on the back).

Flower Analogy

Have you ever wondered how your brain manages all the different things you do every day? For example, which classroom do you need to go to for your English class? What items would you want to pick for your lunch in the cafeteria if you had the choice? What would you like to wear to your good friend's birthday party? Of course, you have learned that the primary player is your prefrontal cortex. Now, let's use the growth of a flower to explain the concept of executive function in a simple way.

Just like a flower needs certain conditions to grow, such as sunlight, water, and nutrients, our lives need certain skills to function effectively. These skills are called *executive functions*.

Imagine that the roots of a flower represent the foundation of our executive function. Just as the roots anchor and nourish the flower, our executive function skills give us the foundation to manage our thoughts, actions, and emotions. The stem of the flower can represent our ability to set and work towards goals, just as the stem supports the growth of the flower towards the sun.

The flower leaves represent our ability to sustain our attention and focus, just as the leaves use sunlight to nourish the plant. Finally, the blossoming of the flower can represent our ability to adapt to new situations and solve problems, just as the flower blooms and adapts to its environment.

Like a healthy root is important for other parts of the plant, our executive function skills also require certain conditions to develop a robust prefrontal cortex and effective communication to other brain areas.

What is Executive Function?[1,2,3,4,5,6,7,8,9,10]

Executive function (EF), or executive functioning, sounds like a fancy term. It may not offer a clue to its meaning at first glance. Or, it may give you the image of a stern CEO dressed in expensive suits giving a speech or giving directions in an important board meeting. Since this term is frequently associated with the prefrontal cortex and brain development, let's get acquainted with it.

The definition of *executive functions* in the American Psychological Association (APA) dictionary:

> Higher level cognitive processes of planning, decision-making, problem-solving, action sequencing, task assignment and organization, effortful and persistent goal pursuit, inhibition of competing impulses, flexibility in goal selection, and goal-conflict resolution. These often involve the use of language, judgment, abstraction and concept formation, and logic and reasoning. They are frequently associated with neural networks that include the frontal lobe, particularly the prefrontal cortex.

In other words, executive function refers to the mental processes that allow individuals to plan, organize, regulate their behavior and emotions, and solve problems effectively. Developing executive function is essential for success in academics, career, and personal relationships.

Therefore, EF is considered a collective range of "higher" intellectual functioning skills within the command-and-control process. It serves as the director and management system of the brain. The executive functions can be trained and practiced.

Let's break it down. Executive functions include:

- Impulse control and delaying gratification: managing intense emotions and inhibiting unimportant and inappropriate sensations and behaviors. For example, you focus on your class assignment first before going to a party or watching your favorite TikTok creator.

- Making conscious and complex decisions according to an individual's motivations and socially appropriate decisions to initiate

105

appropriate behaviors. For example, instead of joining your friends to tease someone, you come forward as an upstander.

- Evaluating and balancing short-term rewards with long-term goals. For example, instead of impulsively purchasing a petty item you don't need just because it's on sale, you deposit that money into your savings account for an essential item you need later, like an impressive and appropriate outfit for an important job interview.

- Anticipating events in the environment and predicting how one's behaviors will influence the future (assessing and foreseeing the consequences of one's actions). For example, you have learned that your SAT score will affect your college application; therefore, you have determined to study hard for it.

- Regulating attention by selective attention; ignoring unimportant events and focusing on the task at hand for achieving the predetermined goal. For example, instead of scrolling Instagram and doing homework simultaneously, you turn off all the social media notifications and your cell phone and concentrate on completing your task to boost your chance of earning a good grade.

- Considering multiple streams of information upon facing complex and challenging information while solving a problem or performing a task. For example, before you start a term assignment, you thoroughly research the subjects, fully understand the information and have an organized outline.

- Determining the priority and proper sequencing when facing multiple tasks. For example, on Saturday morning, you must mow the lawn, clean your room, and get ready for a friend's party. You lay out the priorities and complete all the tasks one by one, on time.

- Adjusting and shifting behavior when situations change. For example, you have planned an outdoor birthday party, but the weather does not cooperate. Instead of feeling frustrated and upset, you rearrange the party to be indoors and have a good time.

- Formation and retention of long-term memories. For example, you have established a system, like a notebook or to-do list, to help you remember things you have learned or need to do.

- Coordinating and adjusting complex behaviors based on the memories. For example, you use diaries or journals to remember mistakes you have made or things you have done right for future reference.

- Expressing one's and understanding others' emotions to have empathy. For example, you cultivate your listening skills and make efforts to understand others' situations without being judgmental or jumping into quick conclusions.

- Executive functions contribute to the complex attitudes and choices that form an individual's personality. For example, you make efforts to improve yourself and want to be the best version of yourself every day.

To sum up, the eight categories of executive functions are impulse control, emotional control, flexible thinking, working memory, self-monitoring, planning and prioritizing, task initiation, and organization.[11]

It is essential to point out that executive functions develop and evolve throughout a person's lifetime. In other words, one can improve executive functions with practice. In his recent article, Dr. J. S. Ablon stated[12]

EF skills improve with practice, and the research shows the more practice, the better. Also, like many other skills, if you don't keep practicing, you likely will lose the skills you may have gained. In other words, when it comes to EF skills, it is "use it or lose it."

Executive Function Skills are like Air Traffic Control System[13]

The Center on the Developing Child at Harvard University published a serial of articles about executive function. It reinforces the concept of executive function and self-control from different angle. The key points are:

- When it comes to the brain, being able to hold on to and use information, focus thoughts, block out distractions, and switch gears is like an airport having a very good air traffic control system that can handle dozens of planes coming and going on multiple runways.
- Scientists call these skills executive function and self-regulation.
- They are skills that depend on three types of brain function: working memory, mental flexibility, and self-control.
- Children don't start out with these skills, but they have the ability to learn them.
- Through the teen years and into early adulthood, all these skills continue to grow and progress with the brain's continual development and maturing, especially the prefrontal lobe.

Why are Executive Function Skills Important Throughout Life?

As you develop executive function and self-regulation/self-control skills, you will experience lifelong benefits and be a contributing member of the society.[14]

- School Achievement: Executive function skills help you remember and follow multi-step directions, avoid distractions, control impulsive responses, adapt when rules change, keep trying to solve problems, and handle long-term assignments. For society as a whole, the result is a more educated community that can handle the problems of the 21st century.

- Positive Behaviors: Executive functions help you learn how to work as a team, be a leader, make decisions, work toward goals, think critically, be flexible, and be aware of your own feelings as well as those of others. For society as a whole, the result is more stable neighborhoods, less crime, and closer ties between people.

- Good Health: Executive function skills help you make better decisions about what to eat and how much to exercise. They also help you fight pressure to take risks, try drugs, or have sex without protection or considering its consequence, and they make you more aware of your own and your friends' safety. When we have good brain function, our bodies and ways of dealing with stress are ready. The result is a healthier community, a more productive workforce, and lower health care costs for society as a whole.

- Work Success: Executive function skills improve your chances of career and economic success because they help you be more organized, solve problems that need planning, and be ready to adapt to changing situations. For society as a whole, having a creative, skilled, and flexible workforce leads to more functionality.

Be mindful of practicing your executive function. Your brain will appreciate you for that!

Remember, while refining and honing your executive function, you enhance the connections between different areas of your brain and nurture the growth of your prefrontal lobe. The result? A smarter, more capable you! You are building a successful future and a fulfilling life! Doesn't that sound fantastic to you? Of course, your pursuit of excellence is unstoppable, and your boundless potential knows no limits. Keep reaching for the stars!

Chapter Reflections

1. Research has shown that executive functioning may be improved with practice. What practice may you begin to use to increase your executive functioning skills?

2. What is a current habit or activity you are engaged in that may hinder the development of your executive functioning and brain development?

3. Who might you turn to for support to create stronger executive functioning habits?

Chapter 12

HOW TO OPTIMIZE YOUR EXECUTIVE FUNCTION

Well, I had this little notion—I started writing when I was eleven, writing poetry. I was passionately addicted to it; it was my great refuge through adolescence.

~ Harry Mathews

All our dreams can come true, if we have the courage to pursue them.

~ Walt Disney

Questions for You to Ponder

As you read through this chapter, please consider the following questions:

1. Have you ever envisioned and prepared for the possible scenarios before an event, like a party or concert? What would you do if the party got rowdy, substances and drinks were tossed around, and you were pressured to join the crowd to do something you didn't feel comfortable doing? How do you handle the situation?

2. What is your most common instant response when you make a mistake?

3. What method would you use to reflect on the mistake you have made? Will you write it in your journal? Talk to a trusted adult about it? Or, just forget it and pretend it never happened? Making excuses for the mistake?

4. What seems fairer—a harsh, critical response to oneself or a compassionate one?

Flower Analogy

Like flower buds, adolescents need time and patience to bloom and fully develop. This process can be messy, with twists and turns along the way. Still, it ultimately leads to the emergence of a fully formed and unique individual. As Chapter One mentions, transitioning from childhood to adulthood takes about 15 years (from 10 to 25).

As the flower bud continues to reach towards the sky, basking in the sun's light, its root continues to soak up the nourishment of the earth. It gradually spreads its petals, inviting bees and butterflies to come and pollinate it, ensuring its continued growth and survival. Providing the environment for an adolescent's optimal growth is critical during this time, especially neurologically.

Like a flower that needs sunlight, water, and nutrients to grow, an adolescent's brain needs a healthy environment, nutritious food, and good habits to develop executive function optimally. Strategically, a healthy lifestyle and good habits can be trained and practiced.

The Three Main Executive Function in Adolescence

We discussed executive function as a set of cognitive skills in the previous chapter. These abilities are in charge of organizing, planning, starting, and carrying out complicated behaviors. The executive function is essential for managing everyday chores, setting objectives, prioritizing, problem solving, regulating emotions, and adapting to changing environments. The executive function comprises three major areas:

1. Working memory: The ability to retain information in the mind for a brief length of time while it is processed.

2. Inhibition: The ability to control inappropriate reactions and urges.

3. Cognitive flexibility: It is also called mental flexibility. The ability to shift between tasks or views and adapt to new or changing circumstances.

I want to specifically address the value of practicing "inhibition." Inhibition is also known as *inhibitory control, self-control, self-regulation,* or *self-regulatory behavior.* Inhibition is like stepping on the brake when you see a yellow light instead of stepping on the throttle and going through the red light. It is an essential skill for teens and young adults to master. With this skill, you will avoid stepping into a landmine or falling into a trap during your adolescent journey and suffering in life. You will gain the courage or feel comfortable to say NO to the temptations or resist the pressure of drugs, unsafe sex, unplanned parenthood, sexually transmitted diseases, gangs, violence, unsafe driving, unfavorable situations, potential crime activities, etc.

Studies have shown that people with better inhibitory control tend to be wealthier, healthier, and less likely to be charged with crimes. The researchers found the following steps to accelerate the maturity of inhibitory control: [1, 2, 3]

- Envision the situation and prepare for an impulsive response before the circumstances arise. For example, what would it look like for you to halt your sexual urge before jumping to the back of a car seat?
- Plan to take the right actions before an event, like a party or a friend's gathering.
  For example, how exactly do you say NO when your friends press you to try drugs, alcohol, gang activities, or something else you don't feel right doing?
- Reflect on your past blunders or others' mistakes, and see these as opportunities to try something more effective, healthier, or wiser.

The Brain Development and Executive Function Skills are Mutually Enhanced[4,5,6,7,8,9]

- The prefrontal cortex, a brain region responsible for executive functions, undergoes significant changes during adolescence, with continued maturation until the mid-20s. This development leads to improvements in planning, decision-making, impulse control, and working memory.

- Research has shown that there is a positive relationship between improved executive function and brain development during adolescence.

- Several studies have found that better executive function is associated with increased activation in the prefrontal cortex, indicating that the maturation of this brain region is critical for the development of executive functions.

- Furthermore, training in executive function has been shown to lead to structural changes in the prefrontal cortex, suggesting that the brain is adaptable and responsive to environmental influences. Remember the plasticity of our brains!

- As the brain matures and structures responsible for executive functions become more efficient, individuals can enhance their ability to plan, organize, and regulate their behavior towards goal-directed activities.

In conclusion, improved executive function is associated with brain development during adolescence. As the brain matures, and structures responsible for executive functions become more efficient, individuals can enhance their ability to plan, organize, and regulate their behavior towards goal-directed activities.

How to Train and Optimize Your Executive Function

We, adults, depend on executive functions and emotional regulation daily. We learn from our experiences to make the best judgments and decisions. To manage our behaviors, we must regulate our emotions, such as feeling overwhelmed, frustrated, angry, sad, and happy. Self-control is connecting our thoughts and feelings before actions; it is a skill that can be learned and will be valuable for the rest of everyone's life!

Just as a flower needs certain conditions to grow well, our executive function skills also require certain conditions to develop and function properly.

Practice Self-Control to Avoid Saying or Doing the Wrong Thing

Aim to avoid making rushed decisions or acting reactively (we get that this is not always possible). We have mentioned self-regulation in the previous section. It is worth reviewing because it is a valuable skill to acquire. This skill will benefit you for the rest of your life!

- Train yourself to pause, take a deep breath, and think before acting on it.
- Resist impulsive actions or responses (again, take a deep breath and count to 10 or 20 or more). Try this breath work skill: Take a very deep inhale through the nose, then top it off through the nose with about 5% more breath, and then exhale loudly out through the mouth—this is a fast, effective way to engage the parasympathetic nervous system.
- Consider and respect the rules and laws.
- Consider the consequences of your actions.
- Hold fast and fix your eyes on your goals.
- If you can't or don't want to decide on the spot, tell the others that you need more time to think about it without feeling bad. One of my favorite lines is "I need to talk with my pillow tonight." (It shows you have a good brain and you can think independently.)
- Giving yourself time to stay calm and think over your options can help you make a better decision. To calm your rambling mind, consider drinking a glass of cold water (without containing any alcohol) and taking a cold shower.

Plan Ahead and Write Down Step by Step Before Engaging a Task or an Event

When you plan ahead, it can help reduce anxiety. You can also benefit from developing planning and organization skills, such as breaking down tasks into smaller steps, using checklists, and setting goals. This can help you better manage your time and prioritize tasks.

- Think ahead and envision what possible situations you may encounter and how to avoid uncomfortable interactions. Rehearse and write it down on paper or in your phone as a reminder.

- Tell yourself that it is a brave act to say "no" and walk away whenever you don't feel right in a situation.

- Before heading out with friends or attending a party, let your parents or older siblings know your whereabouts and when you need to be picked up. Keep your location turned on! (I know you crave independence, but your safety is essential!)

- Determine when you will and will not get into a car with a group of friends. (Think ahead so you will not be swayed by peer pressure.)

Practice Organization Skills

- Use a calendar and daily planner to organize and prioritize your homework, assignments, due dates, chores, and daily activities. (Your parents, teachers, and even the CEO of a company need to do that as well. I do it too).

- Create checklists, and estimate how long each task will take.

- Use watches or alarms to keep yourself on schedule. (Many of us have to do that every day).

Focus on the Task at hand,
and Avoid Interruptions or Distractions

- Consider studying in the library if you are a student. Turn your phone off and leave it where you can't reach it easily. Avoid logging in to social media on the computer while working on a project. Turn off notifications on all social media.

- Organize your workspace/study space. Cut clutter. Research has shown that a cluttered living space increases your stress level, affects your concentration, and delays you from doing important tasks.[10]

Practice Self-Reflection

- Writing in a journal or diary. (Your author preferred a notebook and a pen. I know you probably think it's old-fashioned, so last century, but it works well, steering away from screens). Some ideas to include are:

  O Write about events or activities that make you feel good about yourself (give yourself a pat on the back), even for something as minor as letting someone go ahead of you in line at McDonald's, or riding a bike in the local park to destress.

  O Any events that trigger your emotions.

  O Any little thing you are grateful for, like a tiny flower by the sidewalk that made you smile. Please check out the free app: *365 Gratitude Journal*.

  O Your dreams, your goals.

  O You can even keep it simple—three feelings that visited you that day. This helps you to remember all feelings are fleeting and temporary, even the enjoyable ones, and especially the difficult ones.

Always Put Forth Your Best Effort

- Hold steadfast to your goal.
- Persist through challenges; see challenges as adventures and opportunities. This is called a growth-oriented mindset.
- Accept failure as a learning experience; feel your disappointment and frustration, write them down on your journal, then bounce back.

Get Adequate Sleep and Rest

- 8–10 hours for teenagers aged 13–18—to improve your executive functions.
- A study by the American Psychological Association found that sleep deprivation can significantly impact emotional well-being. After analyzing data from 154 studies involving 5,715 participants, it was discovered that sleep deprivation reduces positive emotions and increases anxiety symptoms. Even short periods of sleep loss can dramatically affect mood and emotional responses.[11]
- Following a 20- to 30-minute rigorous study session, a quick three- to five-minute break is recommended. These mental pauses save adolescents from feeling overwhelmed and provide opportunities for contemplation, happiness, and interpersonal relationships on a hectic academic day. They are also an essential part of the learning process.

Neuroscientist Leonardo Cohen and his colleagues argued that adding breaks to the learning process is just as important as practicing a new skill. These pauses help to condense and consolidate memories associated with the practiced content.[12]

Practice Mindfulness[13,14,15,16]

- Use mindfulness to calm your mind and have some quiet time every day.

  - Mindfulness and meditation practices have been shown to improve attention, working memory, and cognitive flexibility in adolescents.

  - Meditation has been shown to stimulate neuroplasticity in the brain, potentially promoting structural growth in the hippocampus, a crucial memory region.

  - It also reduces stress, boosting memory performance by mitigating stress hormones.

  - Mindfulness practices have been shown to enhance working memory capacity. Long-term meditation practice can lead to increased cortical thickness, particularly in regions related to attention, interoception, and sensory processing. These practices involve focusing attention on the present moment, and can be taught through structured programs or apps.

  - Mindfulness has been proven to improve negative emotions, enhance attention, and strengthen executive functions. There are good free apps like *Insight Timers*, *Smiling Mind*, or *UCLA Mindful* for meditation.

  - A study from the University of Utah shows that people with addictions can be helped by practicing mindfulness meditation, which can lead to a healthy altered state of consciousness.

○ In short, mindfulness training can provide a natural, non-substance-induced high.

Eat a Healthy Diet

- Have balance and nutritious diet.

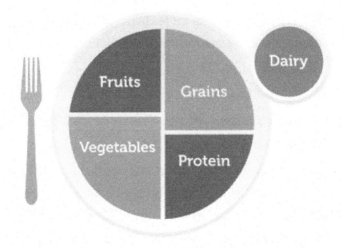

USDA. (2022). *My plate*. https://www.myplate.gov/

- Eat food contains Omega-3 fatty acids, particular Docosahexaenoic acid (DHA).

  ○ A study that was published in *European Child and Adolescent Psychiatry* found that diets higher in docosahexaenoic acid (DHA) may improve attention-requiring activities, while diets higher in alpha-linolenic acid (ALA) may lessen impulsive behaviors in adolescents who are otherwise healthy.[17]

- The three main omega-3 fatty acids are alpha-linolenic acid (ALA), eicosapentaenoic acid (EPA), and docosahexaenoic acid

(DHA). ALA is found mainly in plant oils such as flaxseed, soybean, and canola oils. DHA and EPA are found in fish and other seafood. Krill oils also contain DHA and EPA.

- Teens who consume walnuts daily show improvements in their cognitive development and psychological maturity.[18, 19]

  o Adding walnuts to adolescents' diets for 100 days resulted in improvements in attention function, and regular consumption of walnuts was associated with behavioral changes in adolescents diagnosed with ADHD. The researchers also saw an increase in fluid intelligence in those individuals who consumed walnuts daily.

  o Consuming walnuts daily may help teenage cognitive development and psychological maturation.

- A new study has discovered a link between ultra-processed food diets and an increased risk of depression.[20, 21]

  o According to the study, those who consume more than 30% of their daily diet as ultra-processed food have a much higher risk of depression, even after controlling for characteristics like smoking, lower education, income, and physical exercise.

Exercise Regularly

- Regular exercise has been shown to improve executive function in adolescents.

- Engaging in activities that require coordination, balance, and concentration can be especially beneficial.

- Exercise can enhance attentional control, which is a part of inhibitory control, especially with adolescent girls.[22]

- Exercise can help relieve depression and anxiety, among a variety of mental health conditions. Research suggests that exercise may be more effective than medication and counseling, especially for mild anxiety and depression.[23]

• Neural synaptic maturation happens faster when the muscle media contracts during exercise. The study provides new information about how exercise may improve hippocampal function by controlling astrocyte growth and shaping neurons' activity into a network.[24]

• Regular exercise promotes brain health and cognitive function by stimulating neurogenesis, increasing mood-regulating neurotransmitters, and improving cognitive functions.[25]

• Even simple stretching is beneficial to one's body and mind, as it reduces the allostatic load on the brain (stress bearing).

Key facts:

○ Aerobic Exercise and Brain Volume: Running or aerobic exercise regularly increases the hippocampus and preserves brain matter, improving spatial memory and cognitive function.

○ Regular exercise improves sleep quality, which helps the brain consolidate memories and remove toxins.

○ Exercise and Stress Reduction: Exercise raises norepinephrine and endorphin levels, which reduce stress and elevate your mood.

In a nutshell, regular exercise has substantial effects on our brain and neurological system, with significant impacts for our overall health and quality of life.

Limit Screen Time

• Excessive screen time has been linked to reduced executive function in adolescents.

- A report from *Trends in Cognitive Sciences* stated that social media algorithms aim to increase user engagement to increase the company's advertising income. Consequently, it accentuates the biases inherent in human social learning processes, resulting in disinformation and division.[26]

- Monitor and aim to limit your use of electronic devices and engage in other activities, such as reading, playing sports or cardboard games, or socializing, which can improve executive function, enhance your brain's development, and improve your intelligence and IQ.[27]

- A study suggests that the negative effects of late-night media use are associated with poor sleep quality, and insufficient sleeping time leads to daytime exhaustion among adolescents.[28]

- Adolescents' habits of using social media could hinder their brain development.[29, 30]

- Push notifications are increasingly associated with decreased productivity, poor concentration, and more significant distractions at work and in the classroom. Turning off all notifications is preferable because you don't need them to control your attention and daily life. Adjust these on your phone![31]

Read Good Books

- There are countless benefits of reading a good book:

  o Reading requires imagination, critical thinking, and word processing. Reading strengthens and expands your brain like an exercise.

  o Reading expands your knowledge and viewpoints. You discover new places, civilizations, and eras. This broadens your worldview and increases your understanding of many subjects.

○ Reading improves vocabulary and language: Reading increases vocabulary and this improves your writing and speech.

○ Reading improves concentration: Reading needs focus in a distracted environment. Reading improves concentration, which helps with learning and other duties.

○ Reading boosts creativity. You visualize the story as you read. This inventive method inspires creativity and encourages out-of-the-box thinking.

○ Reading good books stimulates your mind, as if exercise strengthens your muscles.

○ Reading regularly lets you enjoy wonderful stories, learn new things, and exercise your brain. Reading increases your knowledge, language abilities, creativity, and brainpower. It also makes you well-rounded and open-minded.

Grab a book, immerse yourself in its pages, and let your brain grow and thrive with every word you read!

• 25 essential middle school reads from the second decade of 21st century recommended by educators:

Tutt, P. (2022). *25 essential middle school reads from the last decade.* (The Second Decade of the 21st Century.) Edutopia. https://www.edutopia.org/article/25-essential-middle-school-reads-from-the-last-decade?utm_content=link-pos1&utm_source=edu-legacy&utm_medium=email&utm_campaign=weekly-2022-12-07

Book Title	Author	Genre
The Hate U Give	Angie Thomas	Contemporary Fiction
Stamped: Racism, Antiracism, and You: A Remix of the National Book Award-Winning Stamped From the Beginning	Dr. Ibram X. Kendi and Jason Reynolds	Nonfiction/Social Justice
Refugee	Alan Gratz	Historical Fiction
The Fault in Our Stars	John Green	Contemporary Fiction
Dear Martin	Nic Stone	Contemporary Fiction
Starfish	Lisa Fipps	Contemporary Fiction
Ghost Boys	Jewell Parker Rhodes	Historical Fiction
The 57 Bus: A True Story of Two Teenagers and the Crime That Changed Their Lives	Dashka Slater	Nonfiction/Social Justice
Hidden Figures	Margot Lee Shetterly	Nonfiction/Biography
Counting by 7s	Holly Goldberg Sloan	Contemporary Fiction
When Stars Are Scattered	Victoria Jamieson and Omar Mohamed	Graphic Novel/ Biography
The Benefits of Being an Octopus	Ann Braden	Contemporary Fiction
Orbiting Jupiter	Gary D. Schmidt	Contemporary Fiction
Harbor Me	Jacqueline Woodson	Contemporary Fiction
The Thing About Jellyfish	Ali Benjamin	Contemporary Fiction

Book Title	Author	Genre
Born a Crime: Stories From a South African Childhood	Trevor Noah	Memoir
Front Desk	Kelly Yang	Contemporary Fiction
Wonder	R. J. Palacio	Contemporary Fiction
Insignificant Events in the Life of a Cactus	Dusti Bowling	Contemporary Fiction
El Deafo	Cece Bell	Graphic Novel/ Autobiography
The War That Saved My Life	Kimberly Brubaker Bradley	Historical Fiction
Fish in a Tree	Lynda Mullaly Hunt	Contemporary Fiction
The Midnight Library	Matt Haig	Fantasy
Maybe He Just Likes You	Barbara Dee	Contemporary Fiction
The Land of Forgotten Girls	Erin Entrada Kelly	Contemporary Fiction

- 25 essential high school reads from the second decade of 21st century recommended by educators:

Tutt, P. (2022). *25 essential high school reads from the last decade.* (The Second Decade of the 21st Century.) Edutopia.

https://www.edutopia.org/article/25-essential-high-school-reads-last-decade

Book Title	Author	Genre
The Hate U Give	Angie Thomas	Young Adult, Contemporary
Educated: A Memoir	Tara Westover	Memoir, Autobiography
Dear Martin	Nic Stone	Young Adult, Contemporary
The Poet X	Elizabeth Acevedo	Young Adult, Poetry
Long Way Down	Jason Reynolds	Young Adult, Contemporary
Refugee	Alan Gratz	Young Adult, Historical
Homegoing	Yaa Gyasi	Historical, Literary
Firekeeper's Daughter	Angeline Boulley	Young Adult, Mystery
All The Light We Cannot See	Anthony Doerr	Historical, War
Beartown	Fredrik Backman	Fiction, Sports
I Am Not Your Perfect Mexican Daughter	Erika Sánchez	Young Adult, Contemporary
Just Mercy: A Story of Justice and Redemption	Bryan Stevenson	Memoir, Social Justice
Patron Saints of Nothing	Randy Ribay	Young Adult, Mystery
The Invention of Wings	Sue Monk Kidd	Historical, Literary
The Midnight Library	Matt Haig	Fiction, Fantasy
The Nickel Boys	Colson Whitehead	Fiction, Historical

Book Title	Author	Genre
The Sun Does Shine: How I Found Life and Freedom on Death Row	Anthony Ray Hinton	Memoir, Social Justice
The Tattooist of Auschwitz	Heather Morris	Historical, Fiction
Born a Crime: Stories from a South African Childhood	Trevor Noah	Memoir, Autobiography
I Am Malala: The Girl Who Stood Up for Education	Malala Yousafzai	Memoir, Biography
The Marrow Thieves	Cherie Dimaline	Young Adult, Dystopian
Aristotle and Dante Discover the Secrets of the Universe	Benjamin Alire Sáenz	Young Adult, Contemporary
Sing, Unburied, Sing: A Novel	Jesmyn Ward	Fiction, Literary
The 57 Bus: A True Story of Two Teenagers and the Crime That Changed Their Lives	Dashka Slater	Young Adult, Nonfiction
The Anthropocene Reviewed: Essays on a Human-Centered Planet	John Green	Essays, Nonfiction

O Please note that the genres listed are general categorizations, and some books may fall into multiple genres.

Cultivate Transcendent Thanking[32]

A longitudinal study spanning five years and involving 65 youths aged 14-18 years, examined through fMRI brain scans, delves into the concept of "transcendent thinking" among teenagers. It posits that this cognitive process holds significant power over adolescent brain development.

- Transcendent Thinking: Transcendent thinking rise above immediate social situations, delving into broader implications. It involves analyzing situations for:
  - Deeper meaning
  - Historical context
  - Civic significance
  - Underlying ideas
- Key Findings:
  - Transcendent thinking enhances collaboration between critical brain networks essential for focus and reflection.
  - These networks include the default mode network (internal reflection) and the executive control network (focused thinking).
  - Adolescents who engage in transcendent thinking exhibit increased brain network coordination over time, correlating with positive developmental outcomes in young adulthood, such as enhanced identity and improved relationships.
  - Educational approaches that encourage the exploration of complex issues are suggested to benefit adolescents' cognitive and emotional development.
  - Importantly, these findings hold irrespective of factors like IQ, ethnicity, and socioeconomic background.

- In Summary:

○ This study underscores the potential advantages of educational strategies that stimulate teenagers to grapple with complex social and personal issues. By nurturing transcendent thinking, we can positively influence adolescents' brain development and overall well-being.

○ Engaging in transcendent thinking leads to heightened brain connectivity, contributing to favorable developmental outcomes in young adulthood, including stronger identity formation and healthier relationships.

Executive Function Skills Enhanced with Practice

Please remember that executive function skills improve with practice. The more practice, the better, and they'll become valuable habits for life. It is "use it or lose it."[33]

Some executive function skills may develop faster than others, and some may require more attention and intentional practice to develop fully.

If you find yourself struggling with any area of executive functions, ask to meet with your teacher or school counselor to troubleshoot the problem and work on it. Please don't give up. The sooner and more frequently you sharpen your EF skills, the more confident you will be.

Practicing your EF skills also helps your brain connect and develop in the prefrontal area faster. Ultimately, this improves your IQ and makes you smarter and more productive.

No one is born with perfect EF; all EF skills take practice.

Chapter Reflections

1. What was the last book that you read for pleasure?

2. What book(s) stuck out to pique your interest from the lists shared?

3. If you read one of these books, who would you ask to be a partner to read along and discuss along the way?

4. Have you developed a plan to supercharge your executive functioning after reading this chapter? Who will you ask for support on this journey?

5. Is there any news you heard recently that inspired your transcendent thinking? For example, did you consider or discuss the event's deeper meaning with your classmates or other adults? Is there a historical context involved?

Chapter 13

HOW TO SUPPORT YOUR MENTAL HEALTH AND OPTIMIZE YOUR BRAIN DEVELOPMENT

I found that, with depression, one of the most important things you could realize is that you're not alone. Depression never discriminates. Took me a long time to realize it but the key is to not be afraid to open up.

~ Dwayne "The Rock" Johnson

The capacity to care, share, listen, value, and be empathetic develops from being cared for, shared with, listened to, valued, and nurtured.

~ Dr. Bruce Perry

Questions for You to Ponder

As you read through this chapter, please consider the following questions:

1. When someone mentions "mental illness," what comes to your mind? Where do you get the impression of mental illness? From social media? Or movies? Or from other adults?

2. Do you think a person who has a mental illness appears or acts differently from others? Do you think you can tell someone they have a mental illness immediately? Why?

3. What do you think is the reason that mental health may not be viewed in the same way as physical health by many people?

Flower Analogy

Just like a raging gust in a storm can cause damage to a flower, mental illness can impact an adolescent's life. The wind may buffet the flower, tearing at its petals and threatening to uproot it from the ground. Storms can be scary, unpredictable, and overwhelming, like mental illness, for many teens and young adults. It can affect how they feel, think, and act, making it difficult to navigate daily life. It can affect how the brain develops, causing the adolescent to feel sad, anxious, or disconnected from the world around them. They may struggle with school, relationships, or just getting through the day.

Getting help from trusted adults or peers can be like preparing for a storm by seeking shelter or creating a safety kit. Research has demonstrated that social support plays a crucial role in fostering resilience. It can help create a safe and supportive environment that empowers adolescents to manage their mental health. With support, the adolescents learn to dig deep, hold onto the things that anchor them, give them strength, and resist the pull of the wind. Adolescents can learn to manage their symptoms, become more robust, and develop more resilience on the other side, just like a flower can bloom again after suffering damage from a storm. They've weathered the storm and come out the other side, ready to face whatever challenges come their way.

Mental illnesses are invisible wounds. They are painful but treatable, and a full recovery is possible. Don't give up hope; brighter days are ahead.

Adolescence Mental Health Overview

Adolescents are vulnerable to mental health issues because of ongoing brain development and rapid physical, emotional, and social changes. Many mental illnesses emerge during adolescence, such as schizophrenia, anxiety, depression, bipolar disorder, and eating disorders.[1]

- 50% of all lifetime mental illness cases begin by age 14, and 75% by age 24.[2, 3]

- 37% of students, age 14 and older, with a mental health problem, drop out of school—the highest dropout rate of any disability group.[4]

- 70% of those within state and local juvenile justice systems have a mental illness.[5]

- Mental illness can take several forms and have varying degrees of severity, ranging from no obvious sign to mild, moderate, and severe impairment.[6]

- Youth mental health may have worsened due to the acute stress caused by prolonged COVID-19 pandemic.[7, 8, 9, 10]

- Mental illness is real and painful, although invisible. No one must bear the pain alone. Do not let stigma stop you from seeking help.

- As Dwayne "The Rock" Johnson said, mental illness does not discriminate. It can affect anyone, regardless of age, gender, ethnicity, or social background.

- Having a mental health condition is not your fault at all! Never blame yourself.

- We should work on our mental health in the same way that we work on our physical fitness.

- A mental illness is not something to be embarrassed about. Physical and mental wellness are equally important. We can tell others when we have headaches or stomachaches; why can't we tell them when we're depressed or anxious?

- The youth groups at higher risk of mental illness and suicide attempts are lesbians, gays, bisexual youth, and racial minorities. They need community and society's support.[11]

- LGBTQ people are twice as likely as the general population to suffer from a mental health issue, such as severe depression or generalized anxiety disorder.[12]

- Transgender people are approximately four times as likely than cisgender people (those whose gender identity aligns with their biological sex) to have a mental health problem, and 12 times more likely to attempt suicide than the general population.[13]

- A study found that children from families with histories of alcohol and substance abuse can experience numerous problems, even as young as 9–10 years old, including psychopathology and mental disorders.[14, 15]

- Eating disorders can develop in children as young as 8 years old.[16]

- Students who experience bullying are at increased risk for depression, anxiety, sleep difficulties, lower academic achievement, and dropping out of school.[17]

- Students who are both targets of bullying and engage in bullying behavior are at greater risk for both mental health and behavior problems than students who only bully or are only bullied.[18]

- In a controlled study, the targets of bullying were up to six times more likely to self-harm. If you are being bullied or witness bullies, please report to someone that you trust, like your parent, teacher, school counselor or director. Being bullied is not your fault. Please do not be victimized silently. You bravely reporting the bullying instances may help other students avoid a similar situation.[19]

- According to research results, young people who experience cyberbullying may experience depressed symptoms. However, by boosting self-efficacy and improving parental communication, their mental health can be enhanced. (Note: Self-efficacy is having self-confidence and focusing on believing that you can perform tasks and succeed).[20]

- Adolescents and young adults in the United States are experiencing a mental health crisis, particularly among girls and young women. The rise of digital media may have contributed to this problem through various factors, such as peer comparisons, fear of missing out (FOMO), "Thinspiration," etc.

- A person's mental health and body image can be negatively impacted by excessive use of social media. Research found that social media users are more likely to be self-critical and inclined to undergo cosmetic operations, according to a study of 238 young Australian women. Over half (54%) consider it a potential future treatment option. The findings stress the need to promote positive, realistic body images in mainstream media. However, less than 40% of women reported being content with their bodies after surgery, demonstrating the need to encourage a healthy and realistic body image.[21]

- Adolescent depression rates have risen in tandem with the use of digital media. The percentage of worsening mental health corresponds to the number of hours a day spent on social media.[22]

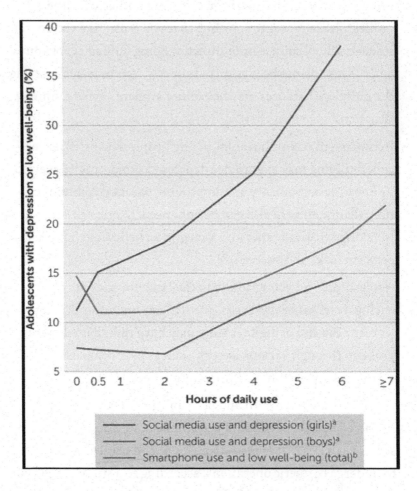

See this image and copyright information in PMC:
https://pubmed.ncbi.nlm.nih.gov/36101887/

- Almost 95% of 13- to 17-year-olds say they use social media, and more than one-third say they use it "almost constantly." The U.S. Surgeon General has warned that social media could negatively impact young people's mental health. There is mounting evidence that social media use can detrimentally impact adolescents' mental health. Harmful content, trouble sleeping, and decreased physical activity are among the significant issues.[23]

- Mental illness can be treated. Don't let the stigma stop you from getting help. Talk to your parents or trusted guardian, school counselor, or health-care provider.

- Since the National Institute of Mental Health (NIH) mandated in 2016 that fundamental research must incorporate sex as a biological component, researchers have been exploring the progress in understanding gender variations in mood disorders.

A study conducted by the College of Science at Virginia Tech reveals significant findings:[24]

  O Women are twice as likely as men to develop depression and anxiety disorders, with an earlier onset and more cumulative episodes throughout their lives.

  O Due to differences in symptom presentation, men may be underdiagnosed with major depressive disorder, as they frequently exhibit externalized symptoms such as aggression, violence, or co-occurring substance or alcohol use disorder.

- With therapy, medication, and support, most individuals with mental illness can continue to perform well in their daily tasks and live productive lives. Some mental illnesses do not need medication at all for effective treatment. Therapy alone can be sufficient! The key is to get help!

- There are widespread misconceptions about mental health that impact the general population. Gaining knowledge and the truth about mental health is essential for everyone. It is never too late to learn accurate information and the truth!

The following mental health myths and facts are taken from the U.S. Department of Health & Human Services website:

https://www.mentalhealth.gov/basics/mental-health-myths-facts

Myth: Mental health issues can't affect me.

Fact: Mental health issues can affect anyone.

Myth: Children don't experience mental health issues.

Fact: Very young children may show early warning signs of mental health concerns, even infants (e.g., anaclitic depression or infantile depression is real).

Myth: People with mental health conditions are violent.

Fact: Most people with mental health conditions are no more likely to be violent than anyone else. In fact, they are more likely to be the victim of a violent crime than the perpetrator!

Myth: People with mental health needs, even those managing their mental health conditions, cannot tolerate the stress of holding down a job.

Fact: People with mental health conditions can be just as productive as other employees, especially when they have support and can manage their condition.

Myth: Mental health issues result from personality weaknesses or character flaws, and people can "snap out of it" if they try hard enough.

Fact: Mental health conditions have nothing to do with being lazy or weak; many people need help getting better. Many factors, such as biological factors, life experiences, or family history, contribute to mental health conditions.

Myth: There is no hope for people with mental health issues. Once a friend or family member develops a mental health condition, they will never recover.

Fact: Studies show that people with mental health conditions get better, and many are on the path to recovery. Recovery refers to the process by which people can live, work, learn, and participate fully in their communities.

Myth: Therapy and self-help are a waste of time. Why bother when you can take a pill?

Fact: The treatment for mental health conditions varies depending on the individual and could include medication, therapy, or both. Many individuals do best when working with a support system during healing and recovery. In addition, some medications can have undesirable side effects.

Myth: I can't do anything for someone with a mental health issue.

Fact: Friends and loved ones can make a big difference.

Myth: It is impossible to prevent a mental health condition.

Fact: Prevention of mental, emotional, and behavioral disorders focuses on addressing known risk factors, such as reducing exposure to trauma that can affect the chances that children, youth, and young adults will develop mental health conditions. Promoting a person's social-emotional well-being leads to the following:

○ Higher overall productivity

○ Better educational outcomes

○ Lower crime rates

○ Stronger economies

○ Improved quality of life

○ Increased lifespan

○ Improved family life

Adolescence Mental Illness Prevalence and Relevant Statistics

- An estimated 49.5% of adolescents aged 13–18 had any mental disorder.[25] Access to support and diagnostics likely means that this number is on the low side.

- Of adolescents with any mental disorder, an estimated 22.2% had a severe impairment. Diagnostic and Statistical Manual of Mental Disorders, Edition 5, (DSM-5)-based criteria were used to determine impairment level. [26]

- According to the CDC's Web-based Injury Statistics Query and Reporting System, suicide was the second leading cause in the age group 10–14 and the third leading cause in the age group 15–24 in 2020 in the U.S.[27]

- Annual prevalence of serious thoughts of suicide in high-risk populations:[28]

  - Youth Populations

    - Young adults aged 18–25: 13%
    - High school students: 22%
    - LGBTQ youth: 45%

- In the year 2020:[29]

  Among U.S. adolescents (aged 12–17):

  - 1 in 6 experienced a major depressive episode (MDE)
  - 3 million had serious thoughts of suicide
  - 31% increase in mental health-related emergency department visits

  Among U.S. young adults (aged 18–25):

  - 1 in 3 experienced a mental illness
  - 1 in 10 experienced a serious mental illness
  - 3.8 million had serious thoughts of suicide

- The World Health Organization reported in March 2022 that the COVID-19 pandemic had caused a 25% increase in the prevalence of anxiety and depressive disorders globally.[30]

- 1 in 6 (17%) U.S. youth aged 6–17 experience a mental health disorder each year.[31]

- After excluding hospitalizations related to pregnancy and birth, depressive disorders are the most prevalent reason for hospitalization among Americans under the age of 18.[32]

What is Mental Health

Mental health includes mental wellness, a state of well-being in which the individual realizes his or her own abilities, can cope with the normal stresses of life, can work productively, and is able to make a contribution to his or her community. Mental health includes emotional, psychological, and social well-being.

Just as being physically fit doesn't guarantee you'll never get sick or injured, mental health isn't about being happy all the time or the absence of mental illness. Just like you might fracture your ankle while playing sports and need medical attention, seeking help for mental health doesn't mean you are weak. It means you are aware of your needs and taking proactive steps to address them. It is normal to experience a full range of human emotions.

Taking care of your mental health is as crucial as taking care of your physical health. Mental well-being involves being able to cope with everyday stress, making a positive impact on your community, and striving to be the best version of yourself. It's about recognizing and understanding your emotions, whether it's feeling depressed, anxious, overwhelmed, or having thoughts of self-harm. Opening up honestly and seeking help without hesitation are signs of strength and self-awareness.

Remember, mental health is an essential part of your overall well-being and your ability to thrive in life. Just as one can prioritize physical fitness, it's important to give equal attention and care to your mental well-being. By taking care of your mental health, you equip yourself with the resilience, strength, and skills needed to navigate life's challenges and seize opportunities for growth and happiness. Furthermore, mental and physical health are closely linked; they cannot be fully separated from one another.

What is Mental Illness

Mental illnesses go beyond temporary feelings of sadness or stress. They are characterized by persistent symptoms that affect how you feel, think, act, and react to your surroundings and the world on a deeper level. These symptoms can be intense and significantly impact behavior and various aspects of life. Functional impairment is a critical diagnostic component.

Let me elaborate on the above message. When someone experiences a mental illness, it's not just a passing phase or a fleeting emotion. It's an ongoing condition that can disrupt your everyday life and make it difficult to engage in regular activities. For example, relationships with family and friends may be strained due to mood, behavior, or social withdrawal changes. Schoolwork may become challenging because of difficulties concentrating, remembering information, or managing troubled emotions. Sleep patterns can be disrupted, leading to difficulties falling asleep or staying asleep, which in turn affects energy levels and overall well-being. Eating habits may change, resulting in either loss of appetite or overeating.

Symptoms can significantly impact a young person's ability to function and enjoy daily life. You may feel overwhelmed, and even the simplest tasks can drain your motivation and energy. It's essential to recognize that mental health disorders are not a result of personal weakness or character flaws but genuine medical conditions requiring attention and treatment timely.

Common Mental Health Warning Signs

The National Institute of Mental Health lists the following warning signs for children and adolescents. If you experience these signs and symptoms or notice your friends or loved ones display these signs, reach out to adults or professionals for help.[33, 34, 35]

- Lose interest in activities that they used to enjoy
- Have low energy
- Have difficulty sleeping or eating
- Excessive exercise, diet, and/or binge eating
- Have frequent outbursts or are intensely irritable much of the time
- Talk about irrational fears or worries often
- Experience frequent stomachaches or headaches with no apparent medical cause
- Constantly moving and cannot sit quietly (except when they are watching videos or playing video games)
- Sleep too much or too little, have frequent nightmares, or seem sleepy during the day
- Struggle academically or have experienced a recent decline in grades
- Repeat actions or check things many times out of fear that something terrible may happen
- Spend more and more time alone and avoid social activities with friends or family
- Engage in self-harm behaviors (such as cutting or burning their skin)
- Smoke, drink alcohol, or use drugs
- Engage in risky or destructive behavior alone or with friends
- Have thoughts of suicide
- Have periods of highly elevated energy and activity and require much less sleep than usual
- Stated that they think someone is trying to control their mind or that they hear things that other people cannot hear

Major Adolescent Mental Illness

Adolescence is a time filled with various challenges and unexpected events that can sometimes feel overwhelming. The stress of school, relationships, and unforeseen circumstances like the COVID-19 pandemic or the loss of a loved one can take a toll on your well-being. It's important to remember that experiencing occasional down moments is normal, but it's equally important to bounce back and take care of your mental health. We will discuss four of the common adolescent mental illnesses here: anxiety disorders, depression, eating disorders, and substance use disorders.

Anxiety Disorders[36]

- Anxiety disorders are the most common mental illness affecting adolescents.

- Anxiety disorders are more than just isolated symptoms of distress; they impede a person's ability to go about their daily life. Remember that functional impairment piece from earlier in the chapter?

- Because there are many types of anxiety disorders, it is essential to consult a mental health professional if you have concerns about developing this mental health problem.

- Anxiety disorders can be classified as phobias, panic disorders, social anxiety disorders, or generalized anxiety disorders.

- It is crucial to seek professional therapy for any conditions mentioned above, especially for adolescents.

Signs & Symptoms of Generalized Anxiety Disorder

- A feeling of restlessness or nervousness

- Difficulty concentrating
- Ill-tempered and irritable
- Lack of energy and being quickly tired
- Headaches, muscle aches, stomachaches, or other unexplained pain and aches
- Feelings of being on edge or wound up
- Difficulty falling or staying asleep
- Difficulty taking control of anxious sensations or perceptions
- Frequent sweating, nausea, or diarrhea

Signs & Symptoms of Panic Attacks

During a panic attack, a person may experience:

- Shortness of breath
- Sweating
- Trembling
- Tingling
- Feelings of impending doom or danger or dying
- Feeling out of control
- Rapid heartbeat or chest pain
- Chills or hot flashes
- Nausea

Some people may describe the episode of panic attack as if the sky is falling, the room's four walls are closing in, or the house is on fire. The sensation of being crashed into or that the heat is ready to scorch them to death is as immediate, even if they are in a safe place. Once the panic attack is over, the person may frequently worry that another attack is threatening.

Anxiety and panic attacks are very treatable. It is essential to seek a professional's help to design strategies to overcome them.

Depression[37, 38, 39, 40]

- Depression is the second most common mental illness in young people.
- Clinical depression is also known as major depression or major depressive disorder. It is a severe form of depression.
- 3% of 15–19-year-olds around the world have depression, which is likely a significant underestimate given the reality of barriers in accessing care and appropriate diagnostics.
- In 2020, about 13% of 12–17-year-olds in the United States had a major episode of depression.
- In the U.S., 9% of young people, or 2.2 million, were dealing with severe major depression in 2020.
- Depression disorder is characterized by repeated, severe periods of dreary mood, negative thoughts, and a lack of motivation.
- Teenagers and young people who are depressed often feel hopeless, alone, drained, or numb.
- In addition, in children and adolescents, depression does not always include low mood; irritability is a common symptom instead.
- Depression can affect a person's school attendance (frequent absence or tardiness), difficult getting along with others, and poor performance in general.
- In recent years, due to COVID-19, prolonged lockdowns have created isolation and deepened symptoms of depression for some adolescents.

- A research report indicates that females who begin puberty before their peers are at a higher risk of developing adolescent depression.[41]

- Depression can be a severe condition. If left untreated, depression can persist into adulthood and/or lead to issues with substance abuse and thoughts of suicide.

Common Signs of Depression[42, 43, 44]

- Changes in sleep or appetite
- Irritability
- Lack of concentration (unable to focus on the tasks)
- Loss of energy and motivation
- Lack of interest in activities or friendships
- Hopelessness and emotionlessness
- Physical aches, pains, and general illnesses
- Suicidal thoughts
- When you notice someone may have suicidal thoughts, it's okay to talk about suicide[45]
- It is critical to learn about suicide prevention for yourself and your loved ones

Please check out the following link: National Institute of Mental Health (NIMH): *Suicide prevention*. https://www.nimh.nih.gov/health/topics/suicide-prevention

Eating Disorders

Introduction

- Eating disorders can develop in children as young as 8 years of age. Or even earlier, such as Pica.

- An eating disorder is a serious mental health condition that can lead to severe health complications.

- People with eating disorders experience maladaptive thoughts about eating, food, weight, appearance, nutrition and health. These thoughts may lead to dangerous behaviors with severe and life-threatening consequences.

- An eating disorder is a serious medical illness that can lead to many severe and dangerous problems, such as nutritional deficiencies, systemic health issues, and death. In fact, eating disorders are the mostly deadly of all mental illnesses.

- According to the National Eating Disorders Association (NEDA), at least 30 million people in the United States have an eating disorder, and 13% of women and 7% of men will experience an eating disorder at some point in their lives.

- Eating disorders often develop during adolescence and early adulthood, with the majority of cases appearing between the ages of 12 and 25.[46]

- In a survey conducted by NEDA, 62% of teenage girls reported feeling insecure about their appearance, and 35% said they had engaged in disordered eating behaviors such as skipping meals, fasting, or vomiting.

- Among college students, 20% of women and 10% of men reported having an eating disorder, according to a study published in the Journal of American College Health.

- Anorexia nervosa has a death rate of up to 10%, according to the National Institute of Mental Health.

- It's important to note that these statistics are just a snapshot of the prevalence of eating disorders in teens and young adults. Many people struggle with these illnesses in silence, and there is still a lot of stigma and misinformation surrounding eating disorders that can make it difficult for individuals to seek help. If you or someone you know is struggling with an eating disorder, it's important to reach out to a medical or mental health professional for support.

- Eating disorders can develop for many reasons, such as stress, trauma, low self-esteem, peer pressure, social media influence, or unrealistic beauty standards. They can cause people to have an unhealthy relationship with food and their body image, and lead to serious physical and emotional problems.

- Adverse Childhood Experiences (ACEs) increase the risks for eating disorders in youth.[47, 48, 49]

- Some common types of eating disorders are anorexia nervosa, bulimia nervosa, and binge eating disorder.

  o Anorexia nervosa is when someone restricts their food intake to the point of starvation, or vomits their food, and has a distorted perception of their weight and shape. They are grossly underweight and malnourished. Teens who are struggling with anorexia will often deny hunger, refuse to eat, and often exercise to the point of exhaustion, or purge their limited caloric intake.[50]

  o Bulimia nervosa is when someone binge eats large amounts of food in a short period of time, and then purges it by vomiting, using laxatives, or exercising excessively. Individuals with bulimia nervosa are often of average weight or can even be overweight.

○ Binge eating disorder (BED) is when someone eats excessively large portions of food over a short period of time without purging. They feel out of control, guilty, self-disgust, depression, shame afterwards.

• Eating disorders can affect anyone, regardless of age, gender, race, or background. They can start at any time in life, but often begin in adolescence or young adulthood. They can be triggered by major life changes, such as puberty, moving to a new place, starting a new school or job, or breaking up with someone.

• If you think you or someone you know might have an eating disorder, please don't hesitate to seek help. Eating disorders are treatable, and recovery is possible. You are not alone, and you deserve to be healthy and happy.

• There are many resources available online and offline to support you. You can also talk to a trusted adult, such as a parent, teacher, counselor, or doctor. They can help you find professional help and treatment options that suit your needs.

• Remember that you are beautiful, unique, and valuable just the way you are. You don't need to change yourself to fit someone else's expectations or standards. You don't have to imitate or emulate others. You have so much potential and talent to offer the world. Don't let an eating disorder take that away from you.

Please keep in mind that the facts and figures presented above were culled from various research publications and websites. Some statements may look repetitive and redundant because they are important enough to repeat. I cannot emphasize enough the importance of recognizing the features and severity of eating disorders for yourself and your loved ones.

Again, eating disorders can be fatal but treatable. The sooner you get help, the easier it is to recover.[51, 52, 53, 54, 55, 56]

Disordered Eating

- Recognizing "disordered eating" behaviors is essential because most eating disorders start with disordered eating. Therefore, "disordered eating" behaviors are the red flags for developing eating disorders, even if they appear insignificant and harmless initially.
- Disordered eating involves irregular and unhealthy eating behaviors that can harm one's mental and physical health.
- Seven warning signs indicate the behaviors can lead to a full-blown eating disorder.

  o Skipping meals, fasting, obsessively counting calories, or restricting certain food groups
  o Obsessively checking their weight
  o Avoiding social events that involve food
  o Expressing negative body image thoughts
  o Engaging in excessive exercise routines or extreme exercising
  o Unhealthy behaviors like binge eating and purging behaviors, including induced vomiting or using laxatives
  o Showing signs of anxiety or depression

- If you or someone you know is struggling with disordered eating, don't hesitate to reach out for help.
- Early intervention is the key. The earlier treatment, the easier it is to gain full recovery before the conditions deteriorate.
- Recovery is possible with the right treatment and support. Remember, you are not alone.

The Umbrella Indication for Signs
and Symptoms of an Eating Disorder[57, 58, 59, 60, 61]

- The mind is excessively preoccupied with food, calories, weight, and body shape. (Looking at the mirror, stepping on the scale, and calculating the calorie intake several times daily.)
- Avoiding or restricting certain foods or food groups
- Eating very little or very much in a short time
- Overwhelmed by the feeling guilty, ashamed, or out of control after eating
- Using vomiting, laxatives, exercise, or other methods to reduce calories
- Having a distorted perception of your weight and shape

  Let me share a quote from Dennis Quaid, an American actor, to illustrate this point: "I'd look in the mirror and still see a 180-lb. guy even though I was 138 pounds."

- Extreme mood swings and struggle with mental well-being
- Noticeable fluctuations in weight, both up and down
- Stomach cramps and other non-specific gastrointestinal complaints (constipation, acid reflux, etc.)
- Irregular menstruation—missing periods or only having a period while on hormonal contraceptives (this is not considered a "true" period)
- Difficulties concentrating. Mind fog throughout the day
- Abnormal laboratory findings (anemia, low thyroid and hormone levels, low potassium, low white and red blood cell counts)
- Dizziness, primarily upon standing
- Fainting/convulsions spell
- Feeling cold all the time

- Sleep problems (maybe due to an empty stomach at night)
- Cuts and calluses across the top of finger joints (a result of inducing vomiting)
- Dental problems include enamel erosion, cavities, discolored teeth, tooth/gum sensitivity, and bad breath
- Dry skin and brittle nails
- Thin hair. Hair that falls off easily and appears bald
- Swelling around the area of salivary glands
- Fine hair on the body (lanugo)
- Loss of muscle mass, muscle weakness
- Yellow skin (in the context of eating large amounts of carrots)
- Cold, mottled hands and feet or swelling of feet
- Poor wound healing from impaired immune functioning

Signs and Symptoms of Anorexia Nervosa[62]

I want to specifically address the symptoms of anorexia nervosa. Compared to other mental disorders, anorexia nervosa has an exceedingly high death rate (mortality). Medical complications associated with malnutrition pose a mortality risk for anorexic individuals. Suicide is the second highest cause of death for anorexia nervosa patients.

- Symptoms of anorexia nervosa (signs that someone may have the condition):
    - Eating very little or exercising excessively
    - Being extremely thin
    - Obsession with being thin and refusing to maintain a healthy weight
    - Strong fear of gaining weight

○ Having a distorted view of one's body shape and weight

○ Not realizing or ignoring the seriousness of being underweight

- Health consequences of anorexia nervosa (serious health problems that can happen over time):

  ○ Weak bones that can easily break (osteopenia or osteoporosis)

  ○ Mild form of anemia (low red blood cell count)

  ○ Loss of muscle mass and weakness

  ○ Fragile hair and nails

  ○ Dry and yellowish skin

  ○ Growth of fine hair all over the body to keep warm (lanugo)

  ○ Severe difficulty with bowel movements (constipation)

  ○ Low blood pressure

  ○ Slow breathing and pulse rate

  ○ Damage to the structure and function of the heart

  ○ Feeling constantly cold due to low body temperature and insufficient body fat

  ○ Being constantly tired and lacking energy

  ○ Problems with fertility (ability to have children)

  ○ Damage to the brain

  ○ Failure of multiple organs in the body

If you or anyone you know is suffering from anorexia nervosa, please talk to trusted adults or your family doctor and get treatment as soon as possible!

Social Media Impact Adolescents Body Image and Eating Disorders[63, 64, 65, 66, 67, 68]

The advances in smartphones and photography apps have made it easy to manipulate photos. With Photoshop, it is possible to make a picture of an 80-year-old lady look like an 18-year-old gorgeous young girl or someone who looks 50 pounds lighter in a swimming suit with an hourglass body shape and slender figure. Almost all celebrities' images in magazines or on social media have been modified with minor retouching, heavy editing, or manipulation with filters. Virtually all the time, what you see is not real, especially with their heavy makeup and AI techniques. They are fake!

- Body image is an individual's subjective perception of their body, regardless of how it actually appears. Body image is a complicated construct that includes thoughts, feelings, assessments, and behaviors about one's own body. Body image misperception is widespread in the general population. It is a key component of several major disorders, including body dysmorphic disorder, anorexia nervosa, and bulimia nervosa.

- According to a national survey, 69% of parents believe that social media filters negatively impact their children's body image.[69]

- "A child's feelings about their body can affect their mental health," said Dr. Erin McTiernan, a pediatric psychologist at Nationwide Children's Hospital.[70]

- A study suggests that social media (SM) may exacerbate body image concerns and influence adolescent girls' mental health by promoting peer comparisons and increasing focus on one's own appearance. In other words, this study presents a developmental-sociocultural framework for adolescent girls' body image concerns, depressive symptoms, and disordered eating.[71, 72]

Substance Use Disorders

We have discussed the detrimental effects of addiction in Chapter 9. Addiction is not just a bad habit—it's a disorder that affects your brain and mental health. During adolescence, it is normal to be more likely to take risks, which sometimes means trying drugs or alcohol. But for some people, it's not just a phase or experiment. Many teens and young adults get addicted during their rapid brain development and vulnerable period and develop substance use disorders.[73, 74, 75]

There are different types of substance use disorders, depending on the drug someone uses. The symptoms of a substance use disorder can also be similar to those of other mental health disorders. It's essential to know that substance use and mental health issues like depression and anxiety often happen together. We call this a co-occurring disorder, or comorbidity. If someone is struggling with depression, for example, they're about twice as likely to develop a substance use disorder.

Common Signs of Substance Use Disorder in Adolescents [76, 77]

- Withdrawal from family or friends
- Sudden changes in behavior
- Engaging in riskier behaviors such as sex, fighting, or driving while intoxicated
- Developing a high tolerance to drugs and alcohol
- Experiencing withdrawal symptoms when not intoxicated or high
- Believing that they require a substance to operate properly

Studies About Cannabis Use Related to Mental Health

Due to recent changes in policy trends, cannabis has become one of the most consumed psychoactive substances worldwide. A few studies published recently are worth sharing with teens, young adults, even grownups. Yes, knowledge is power.[78]

- Researchers at the National Institute on Drug Abuse and Mental Health Services in Denmark found that young men with cannabis use disorder are at a higher risk of developing schizophrenia, a severe psychotic disorder. The study analyzed data from over six million people in Denmark, finding a stronger association between cannabis use disorder and schizophrenia.[79, 80]

- A video lecture by Dr. Diana Martinez at the Department of Psychiatry in Columbia University Medical Center titled *Does Cannabis Use Cause Psychiatric Disorders?* In her lecture, she illustrated the following key points (taking directly from her slides):

  o Cannabis use is prevalent among patients with psychiatric disorders.

  o Its use might lead to the development of a mental illness.

  o Cannabis use combined with a risk for a psychotic disorder is associated with:

  - Earlier onset
  - Worse prognosis
  - Greater likelihood of schizophrenia

  o There is an association between cannabis use and social anxiety disorder.

  o There is an association between heavy use and suicidal thoughts and suicide completion.

  o Suicide risk is not specific to cannabis over other drugs.

○ Be concerned about suicidal impulses in patients with heavy drug use.

▶ Martinez, D. (2021). *Does cannabis use cause psychiatric disorders?* [Video]. YouTube, https://psychopharmacologyinstitute.com/section/cannabis-and-psychosis-2614-5102?utm_medium=YouTube&utm_source=YouTube&utm_campaign=4602

▶ Neuroscience News. (2023). *Cannabis use disorder linked to increased schizophrenia risk in* males. [Video]. YouTube. https://www.youtube.com/watch?v=wysGWln_i1A&t=56s

Alcohol Use Disorders and Mental Health

A study intends to explain why those with anxiety or mood disorders are at greater risk of developing an alcohol use disorder.

• Anxiety and mood disorders together are called internalizing disorders (INTD). INTD commonly co-occurs ("comorbid") with alcohol use disorders (AUD). It has been reported that using alcohol excessively to cope with INTD symptoms is, at best, a partial explanation for the high comorbidity rates observed. People with anxiety and major depressive disorders experience more alcohol-related symptoms than those without, even at the same drinking levels.[81]

How Mental Illness Affects Brain Development and Executive Function

We have mentioned that an adolescent's brain is vulnerable while it is developing. Any insult or stress, like mental illness (depression, anxiety, eating disorders, substance use, etc.), can affect its optimal development. It is crucial to recognize that genetic predisposition, environmental stressors, family substance abuse history, and insufficient support can all influence the likelihood and severity of mental illness in teenagers and brain development.

Depressions and Anxiety

- An adolescent who is experiencing mental health issues may be less motivated and struggle with cognitive activities like planning and making decisions.[82]

- Before diving into the subject of social media, I want to clarify my point. As mentioned in Chapter 5 of Book 1, *Talking About Adolescence*, I am not against social media or internet usage. In fact, I am a strong supporter of online learning. The increased risk of depression and anxiety symptoms related to social media depends not just on the frequency and duration of use but also on how a person uses it. The key is to use social media wisely and take control of it rather than allowing it to consume you or drive you to addiction. If you use it wisely, social media may be associated with positive mental health and well-being.

  With that said, how might increased social media usage and frequent social media checking affect adolescent brain development? Adolescent brains may grow more sensitive when they anticipate social rewards and penalties. The findings show how social media use can have significant and long-term effects on brain development.[83]

- Having a mental illness can slow the formation of the hippocampus, which is responsible for consolidating memory.[84, 85]

- Adolescents with mental health disorders are especially vulnerable to social isolation, discrimination, stigma (which influences their willingness to seek care), educational challenges, risk-taking behaviors, physical illness, and human rights violations. All these factors affect their executive function growth.[86]

- A study further confirmed that depression has been linked to a decrease in hippocampal volume, a region important for memory and emotional regulation.[87]

- Mental illnesses can affect the connectivity and communication between different brain regions. For instance, disruptions in the connectivity between the prefrontal cortex and the limbic system, which is involved in emotional processing, have been observed in individuals with anxiety disorders. These alterations in connectivity can impact emotional regulation and contribute to the symptoms experienced by adolescents.[88]

Eating Disorders [89, 90, 91, 92, 93, 94, 95, 96]

Scientists, doctors, and psychologists are learning more about how eating disorders like anorexia, bulimia, and binge eating disorder affect our brain. Although there's still much to discover, it's clear that these disorders can harm the nervous system, which includes the brain and nerves. Here's what research has found:

- Eating disorders can disrupt the behavior of neurotransmitters, which are chemicals that help transmit signals between nerves.

- Adolescents with eating disorders may have a higher risk of experiencing neurological symptoms in early adulthood.

- Certain parts of the brain can undergo structural changes and show abnormal activity during states of anorexia.

- Reduced heart rate in eating disorder patients may deprive the brain of oxygen.

- Nerve-related conditions such as seizures, disordered thinking, and strange sensations in the hands or feet can occur.

- The brain regions involved in the reward system may have a weakened response.

- The overall size of the brain, including both gray and white matter, may shrink.

- Eating disorders can negatively affect the emotional centers of the brain, leading to depression, irritability, and isolation.

- Difficulties may arise in thinking, switching tasks, and setting priorities.

- Learning about the impact of eating disorders on brain development can be concerning and scary, but there is hope. Many scientists believe that some of the neural damage caused by eating disorders can be reversed if intervened on time. Health organizations, like the Mayo Clinic and the National Institutes of Health, hold varying opinions. Still, all agree that damage reversal is possible, at least some of the time. The key is to receive treatment!

  o Factors that affect the amount of damage reversed include the duration and severity of the eating disorder. Someone who seeks treatment and recovery early may have more success in reversing neural damages compared to someone who has struggled with anorexia or bulimia for many years.

  o It's important to note that the type of eating disorder does not influence the level of disruption to the brain or the potential for damage reversal.

  o Please remember, there is hope for healing and recovery. With the right treatment and support, you can overcome the challenges and regain your well-being.

  o Adolescent eating disorder treatment involves different levels of care, depending on the severity of the disorder.

  o Treatment may include group, family, or individual therapy, medical and psychiatric care, medication, and nutritional counseling.

○ Various therapies, such as cognitive behavior therapy, strength-focused therapy, etc., help adolescents regulate their emotions, challenge their thoughts, and receive support.

○ Treatment should be provided by experts in adolescent development and eating disorders. This requires specialized care. Hospitalization may be necessary in some cases.

You don't have to face it alone. Seek help from healthcare professionals who can guide you on your path to recovery.

Substance Addiction

• Results show that marijuana abuse may be linked to a short-term decrease in verbal learning ability and a long-term decline in recognizing emotions, paying attention, and controlling impulses.

• A systematic review published in the scientific journal *Addiction* has discovered that cannabis abuse leads to acute cognitive impairments that may continue beyond the period of intoxication. It can have a considerable impact on users' daily lives. The study found that cannabis intoxication leads to small to moderate cognitive impairments in areas including [97, 98]

○ Problems concentrating, especially when the time is needed to complete a mental task

○ Difficulties remembering and learning through reading and listening

○ Difficulties in making proper decisions

○ Suppressing inappropriate responses

○ Difficulties in remember or following what one reads in a text or hears in a conversation

- Researchers found that consuming one to two alcoholic beverages every day can reduce brain volume. Additionally, the total volume lost increased as alcohol consumption increased. Although this study is not explicitly addressed to adolescents, it applies to this age group.[99]

Overcoming the Stigma of Mental Illness

What is Mental Health Stigma?

Stigma is the term for disparaging, undervaluing, and humiliating someone due to their traits or qualities. The adverse effects of stigma can result in social exclusion, rejection, marginalization, discrimination, etc., for a person.

According to researchers, stigma is an individual's primary barrier to seeking help. The stigma and shame associated with mental illness prevent most teenagers from getting the support or treatment they need.[100, 101, 102, 103, 104]

Sources of Stigma[105, 106]

- Personal/self-stigma
- Stigma among family and friends
- Stigma in public and society
- Stigma in the workplace
- Employment stigma

Steps for Coping with Stigma for Those Who Experience Mental Illness[107, 108]

- Get treatment.

- Resist letting stigma create self-doubt and shame.

- Avoid isolating yourself.

- Refrain from equating yourself with your illness.

- Join a support group, such as the National Alliance on Mental Illness (NAMI), which offers local programs and internet resources for individual and family. The NAMI Family Support Group is a support group for family members, significant others, and friends of people suffering from mental illnesses. [109]

- Get help at school. Talk to the school counselor or school nurse for a referral or other resources.

- Open discussions, share personal stories, and debunk myths and stereotypes.

- Speak out against stigma. Empower yourself and empower others! About half of teens have mental health difficulties, especially after the recent COVID-19 pandemic. You know you are not alone. Consider how to gain support from school teachers and administrators and form a mental health support program in school. You can inspire and encourage others facing similar conditions and educate the public about mental illness.

Strategies for Mental Illness-Free Individuals to Promote De-stigmatization[110, 111]

- Encourage your friends to develop empathy by helping them understand that mental illnesses are real medical conditions and not a result of personal weakness or character flaws.

- Foster a supportive and inclusive environment in schools by organizing mental health support groups or clubs where students can share their experiences, offer support, and promote understanding.

- Encourage friends to reach out to peers who may be struggling with mental health issues, offering support, and showing empathy.

- Celebrate individuals who have overcome mental health challenges or made significant contributions despite their mental illnesses, showcasing them as role models.

- Collaborate with mental health advocacy organizations to provide resources, guest speakers, or workshops on mental health awareness and reducing stigma.

- Speak out against stigmatizing messages about mental illness on social media. Sharing on social media and educating yourself and others about mental health by responding to misconceptions or damaging comments with facts and personal experiences.

Strategies to Reduce Mental Distress

Adolescence can be a challenging time, and it's important for adolescents to have healthy coping mechanisms to manage mental stress. Here are some strategies that can help:[112, 113, 114, 115]

Practice Self-Care

- Engage in activities that bring joy and relaxation, such as hobbies, reading, listening to music, dancing, yoga, etc.

- Spend time in nature. Being around nature is linked to reduce stress and have lasting mental health benefits.

   O The study shows that walking in nature decreases amygdala activation, suggesting it can prevent mental strain and potentially disease. This could influence urban planning to create green spaces and adapt urban environments for better mental health.[116]

○ A study examines how green exercise (GE) and virtual green exercise (VGE) affect psychological reactions during self-paced walking through brain processes. The study has 30 participants in two experimental and one control condition. GE had the most impact, whereas VGE induced happy feelings and somewhat redirected attention. Increased frontal and parietal connections and theta activity may explain brain processes.[117]
Note: Experts believe theta waves (activity) are essential for processing information and making memories.

○ According to a study by an interdisciplinary Cornell team, spending as little as 10 minutes in nature can help college students feel happier and reduce the consequences of both physical and mental stress. This evaluation also presents time-dose and activity-type evidence for programs seeking to employ time in nature as a stress and mental health strain prevention tool.[118, 119]

• Getting enough sleep and having a good sleep routine

○ The American Academy of Sleep Medicine (AASM) recommends regular sleep for adults and teens, with adults needing 7–9 hours and teens 8–10 hours, respectively, for optimal health and executive functioning.[120]

○ A survey by AASM reveals that video games and social media are significant disruptors impacting children's and teens' sleep schedules.[121]

○ Sleep is essential for cognitive functions such as attention, learning, and memory, as well as sustaining optimal brain function and physical health. Adequate sleep supports healthy cognitive and psychosocial development and is required for appropriate brain growth. Sleep may alter brain shape and function, according to research, offering unique knowledge of the need for regular sleep to obtain a healthy brain and cognitive development.[122, 123]

○ Lack of sleep significantly impacts cognitive and psychological development, leading to chronic health issues, poor decision-making, emotional and behavioral control, and coping with change. Early-life sleep disturbances trigger mental ailments like anxiety disorders, depression, and cognitive impairment, with persistent effects lasting over time.[124, 125, 126, 127, 128]

○ Sleep issues can influence mental health. Mental health conditions can also worsen sleep problems. Sleep deprivation can lead to psychological problems. Because of the circular relationship between sleep habits and mental health, you must consult a doctor if you are experiencing difficulty getting or staying asleep. Please do not put it off![129]

○ Consider composing short, mental A–Z lists when you're having trouble falling or staying asleep. This allows your brain to focus on something unimportant, minimizing the rushing thoughts that might keep you awake at night. Lists can include animals, food, or cities in the United States and even worldwide.

• Eating regularly and having nutritious meals: The human brain needs all the required nutrients for proper development and continued structure; just like a car needs a good fuel grade and appropriate energy input to run smoothly, a plant needs a proper environment and condition to grow healthy and strong, or a building needs a steady foundation and good-quality construction blocks.[130, 131, 132]

• Engaging in regular exercise.[133]

○ A study examined the viability of 10 weeks of group exercise programs delivered by the student health service to students with mental health issues twice a week for 60 minutes. The results showed that this intervention was feasible and beneficial for participants' mental health and physical fitness. Oftentimes, working out in the morning is best as is exposure to sunlight in the morning and early afternoon; this helps to support your circadian rhythm. (Note: *Circadian rhythm* is any periodic variation in physiological or behavioral activity that repeats at approximately 24-hour intervals, such as the sleep-wake cycle, defined by the *APA Dictionary of Psychology*.)

   ○ Alternatively, you can team up with your friends to design a workout plan to boost your mental and physical health.

- Avoid excess caffeine which can increase feelings of anxiety and agitation. Limit caffeine after 12pm.

- Avoid illegal drugs, alcohol, and tobacco. We have discussed this subject extensively in Chapter 9. Please review it or share it with your family and friends if needed.

Build a Support Network

- Seek support from trusted friends, family members, or mentors who can provide a listening ear and offer guidance.

- Consider joining support groups or online communities where you can connect with peers who may be going through similar experiences.

Develop Healthy Coping Skills

- Practice mindfulness and relaxation techniques, such as deep breathing exercises, progressive muscle relaxation, meditation, or yoga, to help manage stress and promote emotional well-being.

- Evidence suggests the following benefits of meditation and yoga:[134, 135, 136, 137]

  ○ Meditation can stimulate changes in the brain, or neuroplasticity, which may promote structural growth in the hippocampus, a crucial memory region.

  ○ Long-term meditation has been found to increase frontal volumes of gray matter.

  ○ Meditation also contributes to stress reduction by mitigating the negative effects of stress hormones on the brain, thereby indirectly enhancing memory performance.

  ○ Mindfulness practices have been demonstrated to improve working memory capacity, a crucial cognitive function.

  ○ Yoga has been recommended as an adjunct therapy for anxiety and history of trauma.[138]

- Express yourself through creative outlets like writing, drawing, dancing, stage performances, photographing, or playing an instrument as a way to process emotions.

- Guided imagery can also be a useful and effective tool to help stressed students cope with academic, social, and other stressors. Visualizations can help you calm down, detach from what's stressing you, and reduce your body's stress response.[139, 140]

Set Realistic Goals and Manage Time

- Break tasks into smaller, manageable steps to avoid feeling overwhelmed.

- Prioritize tasks, create schedules, and practice good time management to reduce stress related to academic or personal responsibilities. Don't hesitate to talk to your academic adviser for help in the area if needed, if you have access to one. These skills will benefit you for the rest of your life!

- Rehearse in advance and practice situations which cause stress.
- Try Time Management Apps.

  Lauretta, A. (2023). *Best time management apps*. Verywell Mind. https://www.verywellmind.com/ best-time-management-apps-5116817

Engage in Positive Activities

- Participate in activities that promote positive psychology principles and pleasant emotions, such as volunteering, community service, helping others, or engaging in acts of kindness.
- Find activities that promote a sense of accomplishment and boost self-esteem, such as pursuing interests or learning new skills.

Have a Sense of Spirituality[141, 142]

- Spirituality can refer to traditional religious practices based on faith in a higher power. It can also refer to a more profound sense of connection with others, nature, the earth, and the universe.
- According to research, incorporating religion or spirituality in one's life can encourage transcendence (a sense of greatness, uplift, and enlightenment) in physical and mental health.
- Healthy individuals with higher spirituality and religiousness report a higher health-related quality of life and well-being.
- During trying and uncertain times, such as a pandemic, a sense of higher power and the spiritual system can provide comfort and support.
- Spirituality and positive psychology complement one another.

- Spirituality may promote successful interventions for substance misuse or eating problems.
- Through psychological therapies on forgiveness, gratitude, and meaning-making, spirituality helps adolescents with childhood trauma have higher levels of resilience and less depression.

Limit Stressful Triggers Where Possible

- Identify situations or environments that contribute to stress and try to minimize exposure to them if possible. Please know that we understand you cannot always escape a difficult home life as a youth!
- Set boundaries with technology and social media to create a healthy balance and reduce comparison-induced stress or unnecessary gossip.
  - According to the researchers, a self-limited approach to regulating social media use, such as setting a timer for a certain amount of time per day (e.g., 30 or 60 minutes), could be more practicable than total abstinence and can be an effective intervention against the escalating mental health issues that young adults are experiencing.[143] We realize and affirm that social media is an important part of many young peoples' lives and would never advocate for the total removal of this, unless you want or need to!

Practice Deep Breathing Techniques to Reduce Stress and Anxiety

- Focus on your breathing. It can help to concentrate on breathing slowly in and out while counting.
- An easy breathing method is called a box relaxation technique.

○ Box breathing, also known as square or four-square breathing, is a relaxation technique that involves taking slow, deep breaths in a specific pattern:

○ You deeply inhale through your nose while mentally counting to four. Hold your breath for four seconds. Exhale slowly through your mouth while counting to four in your head. Hold your breath for four seconds. Repeat the pattern of inhaling for a count of four, holding for a count of four, exhaling for a count of four, and holding for a count of four for several minutes or until you feel relaxed.

• Some people find it helpful to imagine tracing the shape of a square or a box with their breath. You can also change the counting to suit your needs. Some people prefer to inhale for six counts and exhale for eight, for example.

Box breathing can be helpful in coping with stress, anxiety, and other challenging emotions, such as facing a critical examination, preparing for a public speech, or an important event. It can also be used to improve focus and concentration.

Practice Grounding Techniques

Grounding techniques can help you feel more in control when you encounter panic attacks, high anxiety, or help a friend amid the same.

They're especially useful if you experience dissociation (feeling disconnected from reality) during panic or anxiety. You can do this simple grounding technique by following these steps:

1. Place both feet firmly on the ground.

2. Say the current date and time.

3. Take slow, deep breaths. You can focus on breathing by consciously inhaling through the nose and exhaling through the mouth. You can also enhance the breathing exercises by placing

175

your hands on your abdomen and feeling it move up and down with each breath.

4. Say what you can see in your surroundings and describe items around you in detail.

5. Use the 5,4,3,2,1 grounding techniques to stay present and focus on the present moment: Name five things you can see, four things you can touch, three things you can hear, two things you can smell, and one thing you can taste (or think about one thing you like about yourself).

6. Remind yourself that you are in a safe place right now.

Seek Professional Help

• If stress becomes overwhelming or begins to interfere with daily life, it's important to reach out to a mental health professional who can provide guidance and support.

Remember, everyone copes with stress differently, so it's essential to find strategies that work best for you. It's okay to ask for help when needed, and prioritizing your mental well-being is crucial. You deserve support and care as you navigate through the challenges of adolescence. There are some free mental health resources available in many states, and we will share some of these at the end of this chapter.

Note: Words of caution. Mental illness is nothing to be ashamed of, as mentioned before. But please don't share your mental distress with strangers or people you just met in person or on the internet/social media. Devious people, like bullies or even traffickers, may use the information to trap you or take advantage of you later.

The Urgency of Getting Help

- The National Institute of Mental Health (NIMH) emphasizes that the earlier a youth with symptoms of a mental disorder begins treatment, the greater the likelihood of successfully achieving full recovery. Early intervention can prevent a child or adolescent from developing more severe, long-lasting problems as they grow.[144]

- The World Health Organization (WHO) also stresses adolescent mental health issues to prevent long-lasting effects. It states that if left untreated, mental disorders can impact an individual's well-being and hinder their ability to lead a fulfilling and successful adult life.[145]

- Research confirms that untreated mental illness that starts in childhood or adolescence can lead to lower educational aspirations and poorer employment outcomes. That increases the risk of ending up in low-skilled, undesirable jobs and having a lower quality of life due to poverty.[146, 147]

Remember, if you experience mental distress, seeking help for mental health concerns is essential. Getting support early on can improve your chances of achieving your goals, having a brighter future, and enjoying a higher quality of life. Don't hesitate to reach out to a trusted adult, school counselor, or mental health professional who can guide you toward the help you deserve. You're not alone, and there are people who genuinely want to support you on your journey to better mental health and enjoy a fulfilling and productive life.

More Words of Encouragement

You know the saying, "When life gives you lemons, make lemonade"? When life gets tough, you have the strength to turn it around. Like making lemonade from lemons, you can overcome mental illness and regain confidence. Challenges may seem overwhelming, but they're opportunities for growth. Asking for help is a brave step. Trusted adults and professionals can support you, provide coping strategies, and lend an ear. You can develop resilience, which is not a personality trait—it is a developmental process. Like adding sugar and water to lemons, you can add protective factors and self-care to your life. With time and proper support, you can regain strength and confidence.

Remember, mental illness doesn't define you. It may be part of your journey, but it does not determine your worth or future. Embrace the process and celebrate progress. It may take time, but believe in yourself— your author does! When life gives you lemons (mental illness), make lemonade. Reach out for help, regain strength, and keep moving forward. I am confident you will not let your mental dilemma or unhealthy habits disrupt your optimal brain development. You're strong, and a bright future awaits. Keep going, and believe in your incredible strength.

Inspirational Recovery Books for High Schoolers

Book Title	Author	Genre	Brief Description	Addiction Focus
All the Bright Places	Jennifer Niven	Young Adult Fiction	Two teens, one dealing with loss and the other with suicidal thoughts, find solace in their connection	Indirect - depression
Tweak: The Living Watercolor	Nic Sheff	Memoir	A man chronicles his battle with methamphetamine addiction and his journey to recovery	Yes
The Perks of Being a Wallflower	Stephen Chbosky	Coming-of-Age Fiction	A shy freshman with anxiety finds friendship and acceptance with a group of seniors	Indirect - depression, self-harm
Dry	Augusten Burroughs	Memoir	A humorous and frank look at one man's experience with alcoholism	Yes
Start Here: Every Day	Eleanor Henderson	Young Adult Fiction	A nameless soul experiences life from a variety of perspectives, including those of people struggling with addiction and other challenges	Indirect - various mental health issues

Get Help Now for
Mental Health and Emergency

In The USA

- Get immediate help if emergency: Call 911

- Office of Population Affairs. (2023). *Mental health resources.*

  https://opa.hhs.gov/adolescent-health/mental-health-adolescents/
  mental-health-resources

  This website provides abundant information about adolescent
  mental health screenings and treatments.

- Substance Abuse and Mental Health Services Administration
  (SAMHSA). (2023).

  Website: Resources for families coping with mental and substance
  use disorders.

  https://www.samhsa.gov/families This website have many resources
  to help individual or families find support and treatments. This
  website also provides Language Assistance from many countries
  besides English and Spanish.

  You can also call SAMHSA's National Helpline at 1-800-662-
  HELP (4357) for free, confidential, 24/7, 365-day-a-year treatment
  referral and information service in English and Spanish.

  Or TTY: 1-800-487-4889

  Or text your zip code to 435748 (HELP4U)

  Or use FindTreatment.gov to get help.

- If you or anyone you know is going through a suicidal crisis or
  emotional distress, reach out for help!

O 988 Suicide and Crisis Lifeline⬚: Call or text 988 (for English or Spanish) to be connected to trained counselors in the National Suicide Prevention Lifeline network.

O For TTY users, use your preferred relay service or dial 711 then 988.

O The Lifeline network includes trained counselors from over 200 crisis centers who will listen, provide support, and connect you to resources.

O Lifeline Chat⬚ also connects you to counselors for emotional support and other services via web chat.

O Crisis Text Line: Text SIGNS to 741741 for 24/7, anonymous, free crisis counseling.

• For self-harm: Website: https://www.crisistextline.org/topics/self-harm/#what-is-self-harm-1 Crisis Text Line: Text 741741

This confidential, free text line serves anyone in the US 24/7, connecting you with a trained crisis counselor.

• National Alliance on Mental Health (NAMI)

https://www.nami.org/About-Mental-Illness/Common-with-Mental-Illness/Self-harm Call: 1-800-950-NAME

Text "NAMI" to 741741

• LGBT National Hotline: Call 1-888-843-4564

With hours Monday through Saturday, the LGBT National Hotline provides one-to-one peer support and a confidential, safe space for anyone to discuss issues with coming out, gender or sexual identity, relationship concerns, bullying, self-harm, and more.

• The Trevor Project: Call 1-866-488-7386 or Text "START" to 678678

With phone, chat, and text options, The Trevor Project is a national organization providing 24/7 crisis intervention to LGBTQ young people.

   o NAMI Helpline: 1-800-950-NAMI (6264)

The NAMI HelpLine: https://www.nami.org/help is a nationwide peer-support service, *not* a crisis line. Still, it does provide information, resource referrals, and community support if you or someone you know are living with a mental health condition.

- Suicide Prevention Resource Center. (2023). *All Resources Related to Strategic Planning.* https://sprc.org/effective-prevention/strategic-planning/

- In some states, there may be professional mental health services available to you at low or no cost. Check out this program in Colorado for instance: https://www.imattercolorado.org/?utm_source=google&utm_medium=geo&utm_campaign=ymh_fy24_eng&utm_content=search

- Check out this program in Illinois: https://www.womenrisechicago.org/

In New Zealand

- Call or Text 1737 at any time to talk with a trained counsellor

In Australia

- Website: https://au.reachout.com/mental-health-issues/suicide
- Or: https://au.reachout.com/urgent-help
- Call Lifeline: 13-11-14
- https://au.reachout.com/mental-health-issues/self-harm

- https://au.reachout.com/articles/
  how-to-help-a-friend-who-self-harms

In the UK

- Website: https://www.mind.org.uk/need-urgent-help/
  using-this-tool/
- Call 1-800-SUICIDE (1-800-784-2433)
- Website:

  https://www.mind.org.uk/information-support/types-of-mental-health-problems/self-harm /for-friends-and-family/

  Or: https://www.mind.org.uk/information-support/types-of-mental-health-problems/self-harm /helping-yourself-now/

- National Self-Harm Network (NSHN)

  https://nshn.co.uk/ is a survivor-led online support forum for people who self-harm, and their friends and families.

In India

- **Lifeline Foundation**

  Hotline: +91-33-2474-4704

  Hotline: +91-33-2474-5886

  Hotline: 2474-5255

In Japan

- Childline Japan: open from 4 p.m. to 9 p.m. for all children and young people in Japan who are in distress, in crisis, or at risk of suicide.

  Tel: 0120-99-7777

- Inochi no Denwa Suicide Hotline: offers emotional support and assistance to people in Japan who are in distress, in crisis, or at risk of suicide.

  Tel: 03-6634-2556

- Website: https://telljp.com/lifeline/

  TELL Lifeline provides emotional support to people all across Japan who are in distress and may be at risk. It opens 9 a.m. – 11 p.m. every day.

  Tel: 03-5774-0992

In China

- Beijing Suicide Research and Prevention Center Hotline (free)

  Hotline: 0800-810-1117

  Hotline: Mobile/IP/extension users: 010-8295-1332

- Lifeline: Hotline: 400-821-1215
- Lifeline Yanji Hotline: (0433)-273-9595

In Taiwan

- Taiwan Suicide Prevention Center Hotline: 0800-788-995
- Website: https://www.tsos.org.tw/

In the Philippines

- Manila Lifeline Centre Hotline: (02)-8969191
- Hotline: Mobile phone: 0917-854-9191

For the Rest of the Countries around the World

- Click the link, choose your country, and call the number.
- Website: https://www.suicidestop.com/call_a_hotline.html
- Find support at Befrienders Worldwide
- Website: https://help.befrienders.org/

Get Help Now for Eating Disorders

In the USA

- If it's an emergency, call 911.
- Contact the National Eating Disorder Association (NEDA) Helpline for support, resources, and treatment options for yourself or a loved one struggling with an eating disorder. Helpline volunteers are trained to help you find the support and information you need. Reach out today!

  You can always leave a message on the helpline if it is unavailable, and they will promptly return your call or message.

  - Website: https://www.nationaleatingdisorders.org/help-support/contact-helpline
  - Call: (800) 931-2237

    Monday–Thursday 11 a.m.–9 p.m. ET

    Friday 11 a.m.–5 p.m. ET

    Translation services are available on the phone.

  - Text: (800) 931-2237

    Monday–Thursday 3 p.m.–6 p.m. ET

    Friday 1 p.m.–5 p.m. ET

    Standard text messaging rates may apply.

- Crisis Text Line

  If you are in a crisis and need help immediately, text "NEDA" to 741741 to be connected with a trained volunteer at Crisis Text Line.

  Crisis Text Line provides free, 24/7 support via text message to individuals struggling with mental health issues, including eating disorders, or experiencing crisis situations.

In the UK

- If you or someone you know needs help for an eating disorder, please get in touch with your GP first.
- Beat, the Nation Eating Disorders Charity, can also help. They have helplines and online support groups to give people a place to feel listened to and supported.

  https://www.beateatingdisorders.org.uk/
- Help and support for people affected by eating disorders:
  - Website: https://www.leedsandyorkpft.nhs.uk/our-services/ connect-west-yorkshire -adult-eating-disorders-service/ help-support-people-affected-eating-disorders/
  - Adults call: 0808-801-0677
  - Youth call: Youthline 0808-801-0711

  Their helplines are open 365 days a year from 3 p.m. to 10 p.m.
- Find out more about Beat at www.beateatingdisorders

For the Rest of the Countries Around the World

- Click the link, choose your country, and call the number to get a referral for a clinic specializing in eating disorders.

  Website: https://www.suicidestop.com/call_a_hotline.html

Chapter Reflections

1. In this chapter, we mentioned that feeling distressed is normal occasionally. The main thing is to identify the source of stress and find ways to reduce it or get help. Take a moment to think: What have you done lately to take care of yourself physically and mentally? Can you write them down?

2. Have you tried the deep breathing techniques? How about closing your eyes and trying it now? Let your lungs fill with air like a balloon, and slowly breathe it out.

3. Do you have a pre-thought-out plan to help yourself or your friend as the urge to self-harm comes to mind? Such as talking to a trusted adult for help or calling the helpline? Do you have the helpline information handy?

4. Have you practiced saying "no" in front of a mirror in rehearsal when encountering situations like being pressured to take drugs or alcohol or something you do not feel comfortable doing?

Chapter 14

HOW NOT TO LET CHILDHOOD TRAUMA INTERFERE WITH YOUR BRAIN DEVELOPMENT

Trauma robs you of the feeling that you are in charge of yourself... The challenge of recovery is to reestablish ownership of your body and your mind— of yourself. This means feeling free to know what you know and to feel what you feel without becoming overwhelmed, enraged, ashamed, or collapsed. In order to regain control over yourself, you need to revisit the trauma.

~ Dr. Bessel van der Kolk, The Body Keeps the Score

Until recently, this bidirectional communication between body and mind was largely ignored by Western science, even as it had long been central to traditional healing practices in many other parts of the world, notably in India and China. Today it is transforming our understanding of trauma and recovery.

~ Dr. Bessel van der Kolk, The Body Keeps the Score

We are healed of a suffering only by expressing it to the full.

~ Marcel Proust

Questions for You to Ponder

As you read through this chapter, please consider the following questions:

1. What is the earliest memory you have of your childhood? Did you remember it through a photo, an item, or something else?

2. If your teacher wants you to write a story about your childhood, what will you write about?

3. You may have heard that some celebrities or famous people, such as Charlize Theron, Gerald Ford, or Oprah Winfrey, have experienced and overcome adverse childhood trauma and strived to live a fulfilling life. What do you think might be possible? Please check out the following link to learn about their traumatic experience.

Blair, (2023). *10 celebrities who overcame brutal childhood trauma.* https://www.shared. com/10-celebrities-who-overcame-brutal-childhood-trauma/

Flower Analogy

Just as a flower requires the right conditions to flourish, so does an adolescent's brain need the proper conditions to develop normally. Occasionally, however, things can impede this development, such as insects that can damage the stem and leaves of a bud; poor soil drainage, or fungal infections that can hurt the roots.

When a child experiences trauma, it's never their fault. But it can be like an insect or fungus that comes along and damages the flower. Trauma can affect the brain's development, causing the adolescent to feel anxious, stressed, depressed, to self-blame, or have nightmares.

They may have difficulty learning, staying focused, making friends, or dealing with emotions.

But just like a flower can recover from insect damage or fungus infection with the proper care, an adolescent can recover from trauma with help and support. It may take time and patience, but it is possible to heal and thrive. Getting help can be like giving the roots new soil with fertilizer or spraying the stem and leaves with insecticide. It helps to create a safe and nurturing environment that supports the adolescent's growth and development. This could mean talking to a counselor, therapist, or trusted adult and finding healthy ways to cope with the effects of trauma.

It's crucial to keep in mind that an adolescent can recover and fully develop as the flower regains its strength to grow after suffering damage from earlier poor condition. With the proper care and support, adolescents can learn to manage the effects of trauma and emerge more robust and resilient on the other side.

So, if you have ever faced traumatic experiences or know someone who has, remember that it's okay to ask for help. Some people care and want to support you on your journey to healing. Together, we can help each other grow and bloom, just like a flower that withstands unfavorable conditions and becomes more substantial and beautiful.

What are Adverse Childhood Experiences (ACEs)

Many potentially stressful incidents that happened to a person while they were a child or a teenager are called adverse childhood experiences (ACEs).[1] ACEs can take on a variety of shapes and be imposed by diverse individuals in various contexts and environments. The National Institute of Mental Health defined *childhood trauma* as "The experience of an event by a child that is emotionally painful or distressful, which often results in lasting mental and physical effects."

The National Conference of State Legislature[2] stated, "Adverse childhood experiences (ACEs) are potentially traumatic events that occur before a child reaches the age of 18. Such experiences can interfere with a person's health, opportunities and stability throughout his or her lifetime—and can even affect future generations." This is known as epigenetic trauma.

What Are the Major Categories of ACEs?

The eight primary categories of ACEs are:[3, 4]

- physical abuse
- emotional abuse
- sexual abuse
- household mental illness
- household substance use
- domestic household violence
- incarcerated household member(s)
- parental separation or divorce

The recently added categories are:[5]

- exposure to community violence (ECV)
- economic hardship in childhood (EHC)
- bullying
- absence/death of a parent or significant others
- discrimination

Make an appointment to see your primary doctor or a mental health professional if you are unsure whether you have experienced ACEs or other trauma in the past. They will evaluate your situation, provide an

ACE score to predict how the trauma may negatively impact you, and help you design an intervention plan to achieve your optimal well-being.

Image Source: National Conference of State Legislature. https://www.ncsl.org/health/adverse-childhood-experiences

The Prevalence of Childhood Trauma

I am listing several reports about the prevalence of ACEs from various sources so you can see how common they are among us. When you are standing in line at McDonald's or sitting in the classroom, the chance of someone suffering an ACE is high. So, be kind. You never know what others are going through at the moment.

- According CDC, about 61% of adults surveyed across 25 states reported they had experienced at least one type of ACE before age 18, and nearly 1 in 6 reported they had experienced four or more types of ACEs.[6]

- A cross-sectional survey was conducted across 23 states in the US from 2011 to 2014 to study the prevalence of ACEs based on eight categories. The survey results revealed that 61.55% of 214,157 respondents had at least one ACE, and 24.64% experienced three or more ACEs.[7]

- A recent survey across 34 states studied the same eight domains of ACEs. The data showed that 57.8% of 211,376 respondents reported at least one ACE, and 21.5% experienced three or more ACEs.[8]

- According to a recent research article, in the United States, 54% of adolescents aged 12 to 17 years old have experienced at least one ACE, and 28% encountered two or more ACEs.[9]

Toxic Stress vs. Healthy Stress

Many of us have faced stressful situations, like studying for an important exam, facing a sports competition, or standing on the podium to give a speech. Not all stress is harmful. Healthy stress helps us grow and enhance our executive function; this is sometimes called eustress. However, when a child experiences repeated trauma and chronic stress, this can be referred to as distress or "toxic stress."[10, 11]

A table comparing and contrasting healthy stress and toxic stress, along with their effects on an individual physically and psychologically in the short and long term:[12]

	Healthy Stress/ Eustress	Toxic Stress/ Distress
Description	Temporary, manageable stress	Ongoing, overwhelming stress
Example	Juggling tasks with confidence	Endless piles of tasks or repeated trauma without relief
Physical Effects	Increased alertness, energy	Fatigue, headaches, weakened immune system

	Healthy Stress/ Eustress	Toxic Stress/ Distress
Psychological Effects	Motivation, growth, learning new skills	Anxiety, irritability, difficulty concentrating
Short-term Impact	Enhances performance, builds resilience	Difficulty focusing, mood swings, sleep problems
Long-term Impact	Promotes personal development	Increased risk of mental and physical health issues

It's important to note that the effects of stress can vary from person to person, and the impact of toxic stress may be more severe and long-lasting compared to healthy stress. Seeking support from trusted adults, like a school counselor, and professionals can help in managing and reducing the impact of toxic stress.

How Toxic Stress Causes Complex-Post Traumatic Stress Disorder (C-PTSD)

Imagine your brain as a complex computer that helps you process and make sense of the world around you. Like a computer, your brain has different parts that work together to help you think, feel, and react to different situations, as we have mentioned in Part 2.

When you experience a traumatic event, like ongoing abuse, neglect, or other extremely distressing experiences, it can overwhelm your brain's ability to cope with and process that stress. This is what we call *toxic stress* or *distress*. It's like a computer system that gets overloaded with too much information or tasks and starts to malfunction. Toxic stress can significantly impact your brain and how it functions and behaves. It can affect your ability to feel safe, trust others, and regulate emotions. It's like a computer system having trouble managing its tasks, causing errors, glitches, crashes, and freezing.

Over time, when distress continues without relief or support, it can lead to a condition called *complex post-traumatic stress disorder* (C-PTSD). C-PTSD is similar to post-traumatic stress disorder (PTSD), though C-PTSD is not currently a formal diagnosis. Still, it's more complex because it involves ongoing or repeated traumatic experiences. C-PTSD can affect various aspects of your life. It can cause difficulties with managing emotions, staying focused, causing dissociation, having difficulty forming healthy relationships, and even impacting your self-esteem. It's like the computer system is experiencing ongoing glitches and errors, making it harder to do its job properly, even shutting down entirely.[13, 14, 15]

- Remember that C-PTSD is not your fault, and it does not indicate that you are defective.

- It's a normal reaction to prolonged and severe stress.

- Because of the continuing or repetitive trauma involved, C-PTSD presents as a more complex and long-lasting illness than PTSD.

- Just as a computer might need specialized technicians to fix its complex issues, C-PTSD often requires the help of mental health professionals who specialize in trauma.

  They can provide support, guidance, and strategies to help your brain heal and manage C-PTSD due to the effects of toxic stress.

- Assume you or someone you know suffers from toxic stress or C-PTSD symptoms. Seeking help and support is vital to coping, healing, and living a healthier and happier life.

Comparing and Contrasting PTSD and C-PTSD

- Please note that the differences and similarities between PTSD and C-PTSD are not absolute. This table is intended to give you a general understanding. All trauma needs specialist care, and the diagnosis is classified as a severe mental disorder. If you have experienced any forms of trauma in the past or recently, you must seek professional assessments and treatments.

	PTSD (Post-Traumatic Stress Disorder)	C-PTSD (Complex Post-Traumatic Stress Disorder)
Description	A diagnosis resulting from a single traumatic event	A more complex condition resulting from ongoing or repeated trauma
Causes	One-time traumatic event (e.g., accident, assault, natural disaster)	Ongoing or repeated trauma (e.g., abuse, neglect, violence)
Signs/Symptoms	Flashbacks, nightmares, avoidance of reminders, hyperarousal	Flashbacks, nightmares, emotional dysregulation, difficulties staying focused and with relationships, experiences dissociation
Impact	Affects daily functioning, sense of self, and overall well-being	Impacts overall quality of life and sense of self
Treatment	Therapy (such as TF-CBT, PET, CPT, EMDR, etc.) and support	Specialized therapy for trauma (e.g., trauma-focused therapy)

How Childhood Trauma Affects Brain Development and Executive Function

ACEs can affect the brain's development and executive function if no intervention occurs.[16, 17, 18, 19, 20, 21, 22, 23, 24, 25]

- Adverse Childhood Experiences (ACEs) can have a significant effect on brain development during adolescence. According to the Centers for Disease Control and Prevention (CDC), toxic stress from ACEs can negatively impact brain development and affect how the body responds to stress. [26]

- ACEs can alter the structure and function of various brain regions, including the prefrontal cortex, amygdala, and hippocampus.[27]

- Here are five significant hindrances of brain development during adolescence if an individual suffers Adverse Childhood Experience/Childhood trauma: [28]

  o Reduced gray matter volume in the prefrontal cortex

  o Smaller posterior cerebral and cerebellar gray matter volumes

  o Reduced hippocampal volume

  o Reduced white matter integrity

  o Reduced connectivity between the amygdala and prefrontal cortex

  o Increased activity in the amygdala

- The prefrontal cortex, which is responsible for executive function and impulse control, may be particularly affected by ACEs. Chronic stress can lead to reduced activity in this region, which can result in difficulties with decision-making, planning, and regulating emotions.

- ACEs can also impact the development of the amygdala, which is involved in processing emotions and responding to threats. Exposure to ACEs can lead to an overactive amygdala, which can result in heightened anxiety, hypervigilance, and a heightened stress response.

- ACEs can impact the development of the hippocampus, which is involved in memory formation and learning. Chronic stress can lead to reduced activity in this region, which can result in memory and learning difficulties.

- Researchers have discovered a worrisome link between alexithymia (difficulty understanding and articulating/expressing emotions) and numerous types of child abuse.[29, 30]

- Without intervention, ACEs can have a lasting impact on adolescent brain development, leading to difficulties with executive function, emotional regulation, and learning. It is important for individuals who have experienced ACEs to receive appropriate support and interventions to promote healing and mitigate the effects of trauma.[31]

- Parental drug use disorders (PDUDs) are a significant risk factor for developing youngsters' psychiatric and substance abuse problems. According to meta-analytic data, PDUDs are a substantial risk factor for youth's overall health development. Prevention and intervention are needed for parental drug use and youth psychopathology.[32, 33]

- A study found that children exposed to adverse childhood experiences (ACEs), including parental drug misuse and mental health challenges, are over twice as likely to use cannabis regularly during their teenage years.[34]

- A study reported that the prevalence based on 12 ACEs was 75.1%. The occurrence of any peer victimization (history of being bullied in any form, monthly or more often) was 24.1%. 20.6% experienced both ACEs and peer victimization. The conclusion of the research found significant cumulative effects on substance use among adolescents with a history of both ACEs and peer victimization. It means the executive function was affected when individuals suffered both ACEs and were bullied victims—their self-regulation weakened. It can serve as a reminder for the community, health care provider, or school system to pay extra attention to supporting those youngsters.[35] (Note: Childhood bullying can result in one form of ACE.)

If you have been in this situation, please do not hesitate to get help! Remember, you are valuable!

Have Hope! Heal and Recover from ACEs is Possible

Without intervention, ACEs can have a lasting impact, but it is not a life sentence if you can get support and help. While I categorize neuroplasticity, resilience, executive function, and expert advice into distinct subsections for ACE healing and recovery, as you peruse this material, you'll discover their interconnectedness and recurring themes. When you have support to strengthen one area, your brain can often toughen other areas.

Healing Power of Neuroplasticity[36, 37, 38]

We discussed the brain's plasticity in Chapter 8. Let's review it here to understand that plasticity has to do with the brain's structural changes, and that one can heal from the impact of childhood trauma. As you will recall from what we discussed earlier, an adolescent's brain is at its prime time to reorganize and develop. Therefore, it was called "a second window of opportunity."

Neuroplasticity, also known as *neural plasticity* or *brain plasticity*, is a process in which the brain undergoes adaptive structural and functional changes. A comprehensive definition is "the ability of the nervous system to change its activity in response to intrinsic or extrinsic stimuli by reorganizing its structure, functions, or connections." Other, more straightforward definitions are "the brain's ability to change in structure or function in response to experience," shortened to "the capacity of the nervous system for adaptation or regeneration after trauma."

- You need to believe in the healing potential of neuroplasticity—your brain is changeable and malleable to overcome the adverse effects of ACEs. Indeed, our brains have this incredible ability to change and heal, even if we've faced threatening and unbearable experiences in the past.

Your Powerful Brain

Our brains are like super adaptable machines. They can reorganize themselves and form new connections between different parts. It's like superhero power! When we go through difficult experiences, our brains might be affected, but here's the amazing part: we can actually rewire our brains to overcome those challenges. Positive interventions, experiences, and healthy habits can promote brain healing and rewiring. Your experiences during adolescence can shape brain development. For example, your social, emotional, and cognitive experiences can alter the structure and function of the networks subserving these domains of behavior.[39]

- Focus on your strengths. To begin, choose and name one thing you like about yourself. Use it as a springboard to move forward. Some people who have experienced childhood trauma have skewed perceptions of themselves and have difficulty liking themselves. Be brave. Make an appointment with your school psychologist or trusted teachers to help you identify your strengths.

- To harness the power of neuroplasticity, surround yourself as much as you can with positive influences and supportive people who believe in you. This creates a nurturing environment for your brain to heal and grow. Connect yourself with resources such as therapy, counseling, support groups, or mentorship programs that can assist in your healing journey.

- Write down a goal you want to achieve. For example, strive to not be tardy for one month, eat a healthy breakfast most mornings, or turn in your homework on time for a week, then a month, then the whole semester. Talk to a trusted adult to help you set realistic personal growth and recovery goals. Break down your goal into smaller, achievable steps. Celebrate your progress along the way to keep you motivated and reinforce your belief in the healing power of neuroplasticity.

- Healing through neuroplasticity may not be a simple, smooth journey. It can be bumpy or twisted. It might take time, effort, and support, but it's possible. Just like we can strengthen our muscles through exercise, we can enhance our brain pathways through positive experiences and interventions.

- You have the power within you to shape your journey. Remember, progress might not always be linear, and asking for help along the way is okay. Some professionals specialize in trauma and understand the potential of neuroplasticity. They can guide you on this path of healing and recovery.

- Have hope! Believe in yourself. Do not hesitate to ask for help.

Even if you have experienced trauma or an emotional, physical, or mental injury, there is always hope that you can recover. This ability, known as neuroplasticity, is discussed in a number of excellent publications listed in the following table.

(Note: This list of books is geared toward upper-grade high schoolers, young adults, college students, parents, and educators. The genres listed are general categorizations, and some books may encompass multiple genres.)

Book Title	Author	Genre
Born for Love: Why Empathy is Essential and Endangered	Bruce Perry	Psychology/Sociology
The Boy Who Was Raised as a Dog: And Other Stories from a Child Psychiatrist's Notebook	Bruce Perry	Psychology
The Brain that Changes Itself: Stories of Personal Triumph from the Frontiers of Brain Science	Norman Doidge	Neuroscience
The Woman Who Changed her Brain: How I Left My Learning Disability Behind	Barbara Arrowsmith-Young	Biography/Education
Mindsight: The New Science of Personal Transformation	Daniel Siegel	Psychology/Self-help
The Whole Brain Child: 12 Revolutionary Strategies to Nurture Your Child's Developing Mind	Daniel Siegel	Parenting/Psychology
Lost in School	Ross Greene	Education/Psychology
What Happened to You? Conversations on Trauma, Resilience, and Healing	Oprah Winfrey, Bruce D. Perry	Psychology/Memoir
The Body Keeps the Score: Brain, Mind, and Body in the Healing of Trauma	Bessel van der Kolk M.D.	Psychology

Source: North American Council on Adoptable Children. (2019). (Except the last book.) https://nacac.org/resource/ the-teen-years-brain-development-and-trauma-recovery/

Healing Though Resilience

According to the National Institute on Mental Health (NIMH), the teen brain can be quite resilient. Despite the stresses and difficulties of adolescence, most adolescents mature into healthy adults. Some alterations in the brain during this crucial period of development actually promote long-term resilience and mental health.[40, 41]

- The development of resilience can happen to a person, family, community, economy, health care, or any system. We are going to focus on the individual level. Resilience is the dynamic process of adapting to and overcoming changes when facing or experiencing challenges and getting back on your feet after a threat or risk. [42]
- A person's resilience has nothing to do with intelligence level, physical stature, or ethnicity.[43]
- Resilience is about how we deal with adversity, misfortune, or frustration. It helps us survive, recover, and even thrive in the face of misfortune.[44]

Resilience Theory

According to resilience theory, there are two factors involved in the resilience theory: *assets* and *resources*. These are known as protective factors. Children and adolescents can become resilient if they are able to identify positive attributes/strengths (assets) within themselves and, critically, can take advantage of the positive available resources they have in their personal and social environments (resources).[45] Combining *assets* and *resources* gives youth personal and environmental advantages that can protect them from the harmful effects of risk factors and help them overcome negative factors that hinder their healthy development, like unhelpful behaviors, mental health conditions, or challenging habits.[46] The goal is to promote the youth's overall optimal development.

Let's use analogies to illustrate the resilience theory. Resilience theory is all about knowing and using your inner strengths and the supportive factors outside of you, and finding ways to bounce back from challenges. It's like having a superhero power that helps you overcome tough times and come out stronger.

Think of "assets" as what you possess, like the superpowers you already have or about to develop within you. These are your positive qualities and strengths that make you who you are. Just like superheroes have unique abilities, each of us has special qualities that can help us face difficulties. Some of your unique qualities may be deep inside of you waiting for you to discover and fortify.

Resources, on the other hand, are the support team that surrounds you. They are the people, places, and things in your environment that can help you in tough situations. They provide you with the tools and support you need to navigate challenges. For example, think of your friends, family, teachers, or mentors who are there to listen, guide, and support you when you're going through a tough time; you may also have a pet that serves as an emotional support. They are like your trusty sidekicks who have your back.[47, 48, 49]

Resilience Theory: Assets vs. Resources

Category	Description	Analogy	Example
Resilience Factors	The internal strengths and external supports that help individuals and communities overcome challenges and adapt to adversity.		
Assets (Internal)	Internal strengths and positive qualities that individuals or communities possess. These are inherent characteristics or abilities that can be developed over time.	Imagine a toolbox. Assets are the different tools themselves, like a hammer, screwdriver, or wrench. They represent the skills, knowledge, personality traits, and positive beliefs that a person can draw on to navigate challenges.	A student facing a difficult academic semester might have strong assets such as good study habits, time management skills, a positive attitude, and a growth mindset.
Resources (External)	External sources of support that can be accessed when needed. These can be tangible (like money or food) or intangible (like social networks or professional help).	Resources are like the things you might keep in your toolbox alongside the tools. This could include extra nails, screws, or a level. They represent the external support systems, opportunities, and services that can be used to supplement your internal assets and help you overcome difficulties.	The student's resources could include access to tutors, supportive teachers, a quiet study space at the library, or a study group with classmates.

How to Build up Your Assets

First, you recognize and build on your assets, your inner strengths. Yes, everyone is born with particular inner strengths. But it can be tough to identify them by yourself. Sometimes others can help us find these strengths. Humans are social animals!

- Work to develop a positive mindset and outlook. Developing a positive attitude and perspective can be valuable for overcoming ACEs. You can focus on your strengths and abilities rather than your weaknesses. To be clear, we are not referring to toxic positivity here.

  o Practicing gratitude: Find something for which to be thankful every day, like seeing a beautiful flower by the sidewalk, hearing a bird chirp, or whatever minute thing you have around you. A grateful thought can calm a chaotic mind like cold fountain water quenches your thirst on a hot summer day.

- Practicing mindfulness. There are times when your mind runs like an untamed wild horse. Put both your feet on the ground and take deep breaths. Use the 5-4-3-2-1 grounding techniques to stay present and focus on the present moment: Name five things you can see, four things you can touch, three things you can hear, two things you can smell, and one thing you can taste (or think about one thing you like about yourself).[50, 51]

  o Practice positive self-talk. Do you know you talk to yourself more than anyone else throughout the day? Always remember, you must speak to yourself kindly and with compassion. Stop yourself if you notice you are too critical or mean to yourself, and try to balance that unkind thought or message with another, more gentle one.

- Explore coping strategies for dealing with stress and trauma. You can write down the strategies on paper and post them on the wall where you can easily see them. Some effective coping strategies include:

  ○ Deep breathing. Deep breathing can help you cope with stress, anxiety, and other challenging emotions. It can also improve focus and concentration. Try taking a few rounds of a four-second inhale, and then a five-second exhale. You can develop your box-breathing technique through regular practice and find whatever works best for you, like more prolonged and deeper inhales and slower exhales.

  ○ Even simple yoga stretches, power walking for one minute, or dancing to your favorite music, can help you unwind and regain energy and perspective.

  ○ Have a notebook to write freely when you feel "fed up." Do not worry about grammar or wording; write whatever comes to mind. Consider using a Feelings Wheel (https://feelingswheel.com/) start in the center and then build the feelings out.

  ○ Engage in hobbies or activities that bring joy and relaxation. Use your power of creative expression to boost your mood and beat stress. Watch this short video: https://youtube.com/shorts/X1j87fN99uw?feature=share

- Developing self-awareness and self-regulation. Always work to interpret what's happening inside of you, before you attempt to do this with others!

  ○ Self-awareness is the ability to recognize and understand your own emotions, thoughts, and behaviors.

  ○ Self-regulation is the ability to manage/control those emotions, thoughts, and behaviors effectively.

Adolescents can improve self-awareness and self-regulation by practicing mindfulness, meditation, and deep breathing exercises, as we have mentioned above. These practices can help you develop emotional regulation skills, increase self-awareness, decrease stress, and become a robust strength within you, like a superpower.

How to Gain Resources

The resources are like your reliable helpers/sidekicks. They will give you a hand when you need it. Imagine a scenario: You're playing a game of dodgeball. You're on a team with your friends and you're playing against another team. You're having fun until you get hit by the ball. You feel frustrated and upset because you're out of the game. But then you remember that you have other friends on your team who can still play and win the game. Your friends are your assets because they help you feel better when you're upset. The other team is like adversity because they're trying to make you lose the game. But your friends and the environment around you are your resources because they help you win the game.

- Do not purposefully isolate yourself. Remember, you cannot play the dodgeball game by yourself. When you isolate yourself, you are not only deprived the resources, but also reduce your assets. Prolonged loneliness can harm your physical and mental health.[52, 53] Moreover, the duration of isolation has a more significant impact on symptoms like depression and anxiety than its intensity.

  o Adolescence is a unique time when brain development, self-concept creation, and mental health depend on peer interaction.[54] Studies show that teenagers are "wired to connect" and at risk of psychopathology when their interactions are interrupted due to their brain circuitry.[55,

[56] Long-term isolation and social deprivation may affect adolescents' brains and behavior.[57]

- Building and maintaining healthy relationships. Building and maintaining healthy relationships can help develop resilience. You can cultivate healthy relationships by communicating effectively, setting boundaries, and seeking support from trusted friends and family members.

- Developing a support network. Cultivating a support network is vital to overcoming ACEs. Adolescents can build a support network by connecting with community resources, such as support groups, mentorship programs, volunteer community services, and extracurricular activities. You can discover these resources by visiting the community center, local library, or chamber of commerce. You can also ask your school counselor or career director for recommendations or check out volunteer opportunity online.[58] Stepping out of your comfort zone does take courage, but you can do it!

- A study by Baumeister and Leary[59] noted that the desire to belong is human nature; belongingness is essential for cognitive and emotional processes, behavioral regulation, and physical and psychological well-being. The authors concluded that humans need frequent, positive interactions in long-term, caring relationships.

- Be sure to surround yourself with positive, supportive, and understanding people. A strong support network can provide a sense of belonging, love, and security. Avoid negative people who constantly drain your energy and waste your time.

To heal your ACEs, seeking a trusted adult's or professional's help is vital. They can evaluate your assets and resources, design an intervention program step by step, strategically guide you to overcome the adverse effects of ACEs and optimize your resiliency development. Overcoming

ACEs and developing resilience is a journey. It takes time, effort, and support. But with determination, perseverance, and a positive attitude, you can overcome challenges and build a bright and hopeful future.

Practice and Strengthen EF to Help Develop the Brain's Rewiring

In the previous chapters, we mentioned that executive function and brain development mutually enhance each other. We also went over how to optimize your executive function. Therefore, some messages in this section may be familiar and redundant. Executive function skills are paramount for your brain's rewiring and connectivity to overcome the ACEs and are beneficial for the rest of your life. They are worth repeating. Bear with me!

For Adolescents

- Improving organization and time management skills: Effective organization and time management skills are essential for success in academics and personal life. Adolescents can improve these skills by creating daily schedules, breaking down larger tasks into smaller ones, and prioritizing tasks based on importance and urgency. Using organizational tools such as planners and to-do lists can also be helpful.

- Enhancing decision-making abilities: You can improve your decision-making abilities by considering the potential outcomes of your choices, weighing the pros and cons, and seeking advice from trusted adults or peers. Curb yourself from making a rushed or impulsive decision. Practicing making informed decisions that align with your values and goals is essential.

- Improving problem-solving skills: Problem-solving skills are crucial for navigating challenging situations. You can develop these skills by identifying the problem, brainstorming possible solutions, evaluating the pros and cons of each solution, and implementing the best solution. Tackling your creativity and flexibility in problem-solving can also be beneficial.

Remember, all these skills take practice. You may make mistakes, but don't get discouraged or frustrated. What is important is to learn from the error and keep going!

For Parents, Caregivers and Educators

We, as adults, play an important role as "resources" for young people to help them build and store their "assets" and strengthen their resilience. However, there are moments when we unknowingly cause our children suffering. I am speaking from my own parental experiences!

Growing up in an Asian family, my parents were controlling and believed in physical discipline. Sometimes, the disciplines were severe and painful. My parents were firmly convinced that was the only way to be good parents. When I became a parent, I was confused and lacked confidence in my parenting skills. I did take parenting classes when my kids were young, but from time to time, my parents' controlling manner sneaked up on me unconsciously. I spoke to my kids unkindly, harshly, and demandingly. That caused many conflicts with my kids.

My kids and I went to eight sections of therapy together when they were in high school to resolve some conflicts, tensions, and painful issues. That was one of the best decisions I have made in my journey of parenthood. I am trying to say here that you should not beat yourself up if you notice you have unknowingly made some parenting mistakes. We are all humans! If needed, it is valuable to seek a reputable therapist and have family therapy during their adolescent years. It's never too late to do the right thing.

Note: Dr. Erickson inserted the following comment into the text while she reviews the manuscript.

"My childhood was marked by adults with untreated mental illness, socioeconomic instability, and substance abuse, significantly impacting my young mental health. I fostered resilience through positive relationships with educators and extended family. As a parent, I've prioritized creating a functional, healthy home for my children, navigating potential family strain with intentionality."

The following are suggestions to help your youngster grow and strive. No matter what you do, do it with care and love. Be patient. Each person develops at their own pace and in their own way.

- Promote a safe and nurturing environment. A safe and nurturing environment is critical for the healthy development of executive function in children who have experienced ACEs. Providing a predictable and stable home environment can help children feel secure and reduce their stress levels. Consider your tone with your kids. Treat interactions with your children with an attitude of curiosity and warmth rather than punitively or dismissively. Positive reinforcement is the most effective and efficient way to shape behavior; punishment is the least effective and efficient way. Ask for help from extended family or the community if that is attainable and doable.

- Build strong relationships: Building strong relationships with caring adults, such as parents, foster parents, teachers, youth group leaders in your spiritual community, and mentors, can help children who have experienced ACEs develop resilience and improve their executive function. These relationships can provide emotional support, guidance, and positive role models.

- Encourage healthy behaviors: Encouraging healthy behaviors, such as regular exercise, healthy eating, and adequate sleep, can help children improve their executive function. Normalize seeing therapy for support.

Note: The following comment was inserted by Dr. Erickson while she reviewed the manuscript:

"My experience working with children and adolescents suggests that family involvement, especially for parents, in treatment is often essential. This collaborative approach can significantly reduce stress and promote optimal brain development for all members. Additionally, model emotional regulation to your children, as well as apologizing when you mess up!"

- Teach problem-solving skills: Teaching children problem-solving skills can help them develop their executive function. Encouraging children to think through problems, make decisions, and consider the consequences of their actions can help them build critical thinking skills and improve their executive function. At times, adults need to refrain from making decision for them. Sometimes, parents in some cultures try to force their ideals and aspirations upon their children. Your children did not ask to be born, and they are autonomous beings.

- Provide cognitive training: Cognitive training, such as memory exercises and attention training, can help children with ACEs improve their executive function. These types of activities can improve working memory, attention control, and other cognitive skills that are important for executive function.

Overall, it is important to remind adolescents that developing executive function skills takes time and effort, and it is okay to make mistakes and learn from them. Please refrain from setting unrealistic expectations or put pressure on them. Encouraging them to practice these skills regularly and seek support when needed can help them overcome the challenges they may face.

Support Youths Living in Violent Neighborhoods or Foster Care

- A study published in *Developmental Psychology* found that children living in violent neighborhoods exhibit increased amygdala reactivity, indicating increased stress sensitivity to threats. This can affect their mental health, socioemotional and executive functioning.[60]

  - O The research involved functional MRI scans of 708 children and teens.

  - O The result demonstrates that supportive parental relationships can act as a buffer against the negative influences of environmental stressors.

  - O Nurturing adults can protect against these adverse effects, reducing exposure to community violence and its impact on the brain.

  - O The youngsters need to be aware of the dangers of violent involvement and learn to resist the pressure of joining a gang through supportive adults' guidance.

  - O The study highlights the crucial role of parental support in fostering resilience among youth facing neighborhood adversity.

  - O While nurturing parents and adults can mitigate some effects of neighborhood violence, broader policy efforts are necessary to address the root causes of community disadvantage and violence exposure. Policymakers must prioritize addressing and tackling these important challenges.

- A relatively high percentage of youths in foster care experience childhood trauma and unstable living environments; in fact, they face some of the highest rates in the U.S. for PTSD diagnoses.

According to the report from the White House, there were more than 391,000 American children and youth living in foster care in May 2023.[61]

○ I applaud foster parents and families for providing care and love to these wounded children.

○ If your friend is in foster care, be supportive and kind to them. Your kindness means a ton to them.

○ Teachers can provide a sense of safety and support to help them develop resilience.[62]

○ Please check out the following heartfelt middle grade books about kids in foster care:|
Taylor, M. (2023). *16 heartfelt middle grade books about kids in foster care.*
https://imaginationsoup.net/chapter-books-kids-foster-care/

Book Title	Author	Genre
Fighting Words	Kimberly Brubaker Bradley	Fiction, Middle Grade, Foster Care
Tune It Out	Jamie Sumner	Fiction, Middle Grade, Sensory Processing Disorder
All the Impossible Things	Lindsay Lackey	Fiction, Middle Grade, Foster Care
When Friendship Followed Me Home	Paul Griffin	Fiction, Middle Grade, Foster Care
Extraordinary Birds	Sandy Stark-McGinnis	Fiction, Middle Grade, Foster Care
Planet Earth is Blue	Nicole Panteleakos	Fiction, Middle Grade, Autism, Foster Care

Book Title	Author	Genre
Three Pennies	Melanie Crowder	Fiction, Middle Grade, Foster Care
The Great Gilly Hopkins	Katherine Paterson	Fiction, Middle Grade, Foster Care
Wish	Barbara O'Connor	Fiction, Middle Grade, Foster Care
Something Like Home	Andrea Beatriz Arango	Fiction, Middle Grade, Foster Care
Forever or a Long, Long Time	Caela Carter	Fiction, Middle Grade, Foster Care
Peas and Carrots	Tanita S. Davis	Fiction, Middle Grade, Foster Care
Greetings From Witness Protection	Jake Burt	Fiction, Middle Grade, Witness Protection
Orbiting Jupiter	Gary D. Schmidt	Fiction, Middle Grade, Foster Care
One for the Murphys	Lynda Mullaly Hunt	Fiction, Middle Grade, Foster Care
Primer	Jennifer Muro and Thomas Krajewski	Graphic Novel, Middle Grade, Foster Care
The Boy on the Porch	Sharon Creech	Fiction, Middle Grade, Foster Care
Pictures of Hollis Woods	Patricia Reilly Giff	Fiction, Middle Grade, Foster Care
Anne of Green Gables	L.M. Montgomery	Fiction, Middle Grade, Foster Care

Book Title	Author	Genre
The Season of Styx Malone	Kekla Magoon	Fiction, Middle Grade, Foster Care

The Role of Physical Health in Developing Resilience and Executive Function

Practicing self-care is essential during the years when your whole being is rapidly changing. Taking care of yourself mentally and physically can make a big difference. Engaging in activities that bring you joy, practicing mindfulness or relaxation techniques, and making sure you're getting enough rest and exercise are vital. These healthy habits provide a solid foundation for your brain's healing and optimal development.

- Adolescents who have experienced ACEs may struggle with physical health issues, such as obesity, chronic illnesses, eating disorder, and sleep disorders. It is important to recognize the link between physical health and resilience and the role of exercise, nutrition, and sleep in developing executive function.

- Regular exercise has been shown to improve cognitive function, memory, and attention and reduce symptoms of depression and anxiety. Physical activities such as sports, dancing, yoga, or martial arts can improve both your physical and mental health.[63, 64, 65, 66, 67, 68, 69]

- Proper nutrition is also essential for physical and cognitive development. Eating a balanced diet with sufficient protein, fruits, and vegetables can help maintain a healthy weight, reduce inflammation, and provide the necessary nutrients for brain development. Remember, your brain works diligently, day and night, even when you are daydreaming or sleeping.

- Furthermore, sleep is crucial for maintaining executive function and regulating emotions.

The National Institute of Mental Health cited a study that shows how the sleep hormone melatonin functions differently in adolescents than in infants and adults. Melatonin levels remain elevated later at night and decline later in the morning during adolescence, which may explain why adolescents may stay up late and have difficulty rising early. Many adolescents don't get enough sleep, making it difficult to concentrate, control their impulses, and perform well in school. A decent night's sleep is beneficial for mental health.

Chronic sleep deprivation can impair attention, memory, and decision-making abilities. Adolescents should aim for 8–10 hours of sleep per night and should establish a regular sleep schedule to maintain a healthy sleep pattern.[70, 71]

In conclusion, physical health plays a significant role in developing resilience and executive function. Healthy lifestyle habits, such as exercise, nutrition, and sleep, can help adolescents with ACEs improve their physical and mental health and, ultimately, their ability to cope with adversity.

Healing Through Therapeutic Interventions

Trauma-Focused Cognitive-Behavioral Therapy (TF-CBT)[72, 73, 74]

- Effective treatment for children who have experienced sexual abuse, domestic violence, or other traumas.
- Reduces symptoms of PTSD, C-PTSD, anxiety, and depression.
- Addresses behavioral difficulties.
- Evidence-based approach with strong research support.

Parent-Child Interaction Therapy (PCIT)[75, 76]

- Specifically beneficial for foster and adopted children and their families.

- It focuses on enhancing the relationship between foster/adopted children and their caregivers.

- It lessens behavioral problems.

- It promotes positive interactions and communication.

Please remember that the interventions listed above are for your information and reference. They are to encourage and help children facing challenging experiences realize that help is available. Intervention methods have been extensively studied and proven to make a positive difference in people's lives. Don't hesitate to contact caring adults, counselors, or mental health professionals to obtain thorough evaluations and explore therapeutic options and planned interventions. Find the support you need. You're not alone, and there is hope for healing and growth.

The Possible Reasons for a Person to Deny the Traumas

Facing trauma can be an incredibly difficult and overwhelming experience. It is natural to want to avoid or suppress the pain and discomfort associated with it. However, trying to cope with trauma alone and ignoring the pain it has caused is not a sustainable solution. It is like carrying a bag of rotten potatoes: the weight will eventually become too much to bear, and the potatoes will start to rot and deteriorate. The longer we carry the bag, the heavier it gets. The weight of the bag can make it difficult to walk, breathe, and think clearly. The rotten potatoes can leak and smell, making us feel dreary and uncomfortable.

There can be several reasons why a person may deny or minimize their Adverse Childhood Experiences (ACEs).

- Survival mechanism: Denial is a survival mechanism that helps the person cope with overwhelming emotions and memories that could be too painful to confront. Denying or minimizing the impact of ACEs may be an unconscious way of coping with painful experiences.

- Shame and guilt: The person may feel ashamed and guilty about what happened and may believe they are responsible for what happened to them and blamed on themselves. Denial can be a way to avoid feeling these haunting emotions.

- Religious teachings: Religious faith sometimes instills in a person's mind to honor thy father and mother. People may feel shame and guilt for sharing their parents' (or other respected elders') wrongdoings with others.

- Fear of repercussions: The person may fear that if they acknowledge the trauma, they will be re-traumatized or punished in some way, either by the perpetrator or by others.

- Lack of awareness: The person may not know what they experienced was traumatic. They may have normalized the experience or minimized the impact of the trauma. They might think these abusive behaviors are normal or happen to everyone else. Denial can stem from a lack of understanding that ACEs are not typical or healthy experiences.

- Brainwashing: The adults or abusers make a person believe they are doing the right thing for them because they "love you!" They brainwash the person into believing that physical discipline or abusive/harsh measures are meant to help them become a good person and have a successful life.

- Cultural and social factors: Some cultures and social groups stigmatize or invalidate trauma experiences, making it difficult for individuals to acknowledge and process their traumatic experiences.

- Limited support system: A person's denial of ACEs can also be influenced by a lack of support or validation from their immediate social circles. Suppose they haven't received acknowledgment or empathy from others. In that case, they may question the significance of their experiences or feel isolated in their perspective.

Please remember that no matter what happens, it is never your fault! When we ignore our trauma, it doesn't just go away. It continues to fester and grow beneath the surface, negatively affecting our thoughts, feelings, and behaviors. It thrives in the isolation of your mind. Denial of childhood trauma can hinder a person from receiving support, treatment, and broad healthy development, including optimal brain development, ultimately preventing a person from experiencing a joyful and fulfilling life.

A better way to cope with trauma is to acknowledge what happened and how it affected you, and to seek professional help if needed. There are many healthy ways of dealing with trauma, such as accepting support from trusted friends, family members, or other people who have gone through similar experiences or finding the right help from a therapist, counselor, or support group specializing in trauma recovery. Seeking professional service and support can help you heal and move forward and live a productive and fulfilling life. It can also break the transgenerational trauma cycle.

It is essential for adults, educators, and caregivers to approach conversations about ACEs with empathy, forbearance, and respect. Children are to be believed. It is very damaging when their trauma is not acknowledged; it can even be re-traumatizing to them when they are not regarded. Encouraging open communication, providing education about adverse childhood experiences (ACEs) and their effects, and creating a secure and supportive environment help individuals feel more at ease sharing, acknowledging, and discussing their experiences.

Draw Strength and Inspiration from the Banyan Tree's Story[77]

I was shocked and saddened by the devastating news of the Maui wildfires in early August 2023. My heart ached for the residents of Lahaina and the majestic Banyan tree that had graced the town for over 150 years.

In 2017, my family and I vacationed on Maui, and we lingered in Lahaina to marvel at the historical buildings and Banyan's ancient beauty. The tree provided shade and beauty to locals and tourists, with its massive branches reaching out like arms.

Doubt, like a shroud of despair, settled over the hearts of many, casting shadows of uncertainty over the tree's fate after the ferocious fire. Some people voiced concerns that the charred tree would never recover for its severe burned. But then I learned that there was still hope. A group of brave and kind volunteers had dedicated themselves to saving the tree. They gave it water, nutrients, care, and love, hoping it would recover from the harrowing damage.

On September 19, an inspiring news report in *HAWAI'I Magazine* announced: "After just over a month since the blazing fires, new clusters of green leaves have begun sprouting on its massive branches." This news brought tears of joy to my eyes. It was a testament to the resilience of nature and the human spirit. I was reminded of the profound resilience woven into the very fabric of our existence—the enduring partnership between humanity and nature. It is a testament to the invincible spirit of life itself, despite the incomprehensible devastation that had occurred in Lahaina and the heart-rending trials that endured.

Please click the following link to read this story. Allow it to serve as a reminder that lives, bound inextricably together, possess a boundless capacity for renewal and revival. In the face of adversity, in the crucible of despair, hope blooms brighter and more splendid than ever.

Allen, K. (2023, September 19). "The Lahaina Banyan tree: New leaves have sprouted" *HAWAI'I Magazine.* https://www. hawaiimagazine.com/a-ray-of-hope-the-lahaina-banyan-tree/

Get Help Now!

For Child Maltreatment

If you or a child you know is being abused, get help and support!

- In the USA: https://childhelphotline.org/

  Childhelp: https://www.childhelp.org/contact/ with 24/7 support

  Call 1-800-4-A-Child or 1-800-422-4453

- In Canada: Kids Help Phone with 24/7 support

  Call 1-800-668-6868

- Call Child Protective Services. You can find the number for each state on the Child Welfare Information Gateway.

  https://childhelphotline.org

- National Domestic Violence Hotline with 24/7 support

  Call 1-800-799-SAFE (7233)

For Sexual Abuse

Please remember: whatever happened is not your fault. You do not need to bear the pain, carry the burden, or suffer the agony alone. Trained professionals can help you with strategies, like solution-focused techniques, trauma-informed cognitive-behavioral therapies, or any specific therapy deemed most appropriate for you. Recovering from the nightmares is possible.

- In the USA, get help 24/7: call 1-800-656-HOPE (4673)

  https://www.rainn.org/about-sexual-assault

  Online resources for survivors: https://www.nsvrc.org/

- In Canada, call 613-763-5332 | Toll-free 866-239-0558

  https://www.voicefound.ca/

- South Asia

  o If you are in a South Asian country, you can contact UNICEF (United Nations Children's Fund) via the following link to get help:

  https://www.unicef.org/rosa/contact-us

  https://www.unicef.org/rosa/

  o United Nations Children's Fund | Regional Office for South Asia (ROSA)

  P.O. Box 5815, Lekhnath Marg

  Kathmandu, Nepal

  Tel: +977-1-4417082

  Fax: +977-1-4418466

  Email: rosa@unicef.org

  o Speak out through social media:

  Facebook: https://www.unicef.org/rosa/www.facebook.com/unicefsouthasia

  X/Twitter: https://twitter.com/UNICEFROSA

  @UNICEFROSA

- For Various Matters in All Countries around the World

  o Clink on this link: https://findahelpline.com/

    Scroll down the page and find "Helplines by country." Please click on the region where you are and then find your country.

For Stop Bullying

- If you or someone you know is being bullied, please act now!

  Click the link https://www.stopbullying.gov/resources/get-help-now for detail information:

  o To talk to someone in English now: Call 1-800-273-8255 (TALK)

  o For Spanish speakers: Call 1-888-628-9454

  o For deaf/hard of hearing: Call 1-800-799-4889

- No Bully: website https://nobully.org/resources/

  o HELP HOTLINE: 1-866-488-7386

- The Help Chat Line: https://www.stompoutbullying.org/helpchat

- Find support at Befrienders Worldwide: https://help.befrienders.org/

- To report cyberbullying on social media, please click on the link:

  Cyberbullying Research Center. (n.d.) *Report cyberbullying: Social media apps, gaming and online platforms.* https://cyberbullying.org/report.

For Families in Times of Needs

The mission of Boys Town is to save children and heal families. This organization supports parents, teens, and families in crisis or need.

- Hotline: 1.800.448.3000

- Link: https://www.boystown.org/hotline/Pages/default.aspx
- Text: VOICE to 20121
- The speech- and hearing-impaired can email at: hotline@boystown.org

The Boys Town National Hotline is open 24 hours a day, 365 days a year, and is staffed by specially trained Boys Town counselors. Spanish-speaking counselors and translation services for more than 100 languages also are available 24 hours a day.

Resources Provided to Support for Youth in Foster Care Facing Aging Out.

Please remember that you are valuable, precious and resilient. Take advantage of the following resources for a bright future!

These resources offer valuable support and assistance for youth aging out of foster care:

- **National Foster Youth Institute (NFYI)**: NFYI provides resources, advocacy, and leadership development opportunities for foster youth, empowering them to become involved in advocacy efforts. National Foster Youth Institute

- **The Trevor Project**: Specifically serving LGBTQ youth, The Trevor Project offers crisis intervention and suicide prevention services, recognizing the unique challenges faced by this population, including a high number of foster youths. The Trevor Project

- **Chafee Foster Care Independence Program**: This program provides funding to states for initiatives that help foster youth transition to adulthood, offering support in areas like education, employment, housing, and financial literacy. Chafee Foster Care Independence Program

- **Your Local Department of Child Services**: Local departments can connect youth with resources specific to their area, offering personalized support tailored to individual needs.

- **Annie E. Casey Foundation**: This foundation offers resources on the impacts of aging out of foster care and provides support for youth in transition, helping them navigate challenges and build successful futures. Ensuring the Future of At-Risk Youth - The Annie E. Casey Foundation (aecf.org), https://www.aecf.org/

- **Administration for Children and Families**: This agency provides information on educational and training vouchers, independent living programs, and various resources to support youth transitioning from foster care.

- **Aging Out Institute**: Features a database of organizations and programs focused on helping youth age out of foster care successfully, offering a centralized resource for finding support.

- **Foster Care Transition Toolkit**: A resource from the U.S. Department of Education, this toolkit aims to inspire and support youth in foster care to pursue college and career opportunities, providing guidance and resources for their transition.

- **FosterClub**: This national network provides resources, support, and advocacy for current and former foster youth, offering a community where youth can connect, access resources, and find support. FosterClub

- **Youth.gov**: Offers resources and information for youth transitioning out of foster care, including links to federal programs and services, providing valuable guidance and support during the transition process. https://youth.gov/youth-topics/transition-age-youth

- **National Resource Center for Youth Services (NRCYS)**: Provides training, resources, and support for professionals working with youth in foster care, offering resources for youth transitioning out of care and those who work with them. https://outreach.ou.edu/News/the-national-resource-center-for-youth-services-nrcys

- **National Foster Care & Adoption Directory**: Provides state-by-state resources for foster care and adoption, including information on agencies, support services, and advocacy organizations, helping youth access local resources and support. https://www.childwelfare.gov/resources/states-territories-tribes/nfcad/

- **Covenant House**: Offers housing and support services for homeless and at-risk youth, including those aging out of foster care, providing shelter, education, job training, and other resources to help them succeed. https://www.covenanthouse.org/

- **Casey Family Programs**: Works to improve the foster care system and support youth in care, providing resources, research, and advocacy to help improve outcomes for youth aging out of foster care. **Casey Family Programs**

- **211**: A national helpline that connects individuals with resources and services in their local area, offering assistance to youth aging out of foster care by connecting them with support services in their community.

- **Local Social Services Agencies**: Contacting local social services agencies or departments of child and family services can also provide information on available resources and support services for youth aging out of foster care, offering tailored support based on individual needs and circumstances.

- **Forever Family**: https://www.foreverfamily.org/

For General Support and Information about Trauma

- The National Child Traumatic Stress Network https://www.nctsn.org/

- National Alliance on Mental Illness (NAMI). *Trauma.*
  https://www.nami.org/Support-Education/Justice-Library/
  Trauma?categoryname=YouthAndYoungAdults

You are not alone on your journey to heal from ACEs. It can be challenging, but building a brighter future is possible. This chapter has tools and resources to help you navigate your experiences and start thriving. I believe in you and your strength to overcome challenges, present or past. Let's apply this knowledge and resources together and create a path toward a bright future.

Chapter Reflections

1. You have learned about the two main components of resilience: assets and resources. Take a moment to write down all your inner strengths. Believe in yourself; you have your strengths! Yes, you do. And YOU CAN! If you have difficulty identifying it, ask a "trusted" adult.

2. Who can you ask for support from if you feel like hitting rock bottom now? Or have you encountered traumatic experiences during your childhood and felt overwhelmed? If you prefer to talk with a stranger, please remember that helplines are available in the "Get Help Now" section. (Note: The stranger must be in a credible professional setting or someone you know and trust. They cannot be the ones you just met on social media, in a cafe, or at the mall.)

3. Can you identify the important elements of the Banyan tree's survival and revival with the **resilience theory** after reading the following article?

In this article about the Lahaina Banyan tree, it was noted that after the deadly fire, "While a number of volunteers immediately began to help rehabilitate the tree by airing out its soil, treating it with a nutrient-rich compost and making sure it was getting watered daily, there was still no way to know for sure if the historic banyan tree was going to make it... However, life finds a way. After just over a month since the blazing fires, new clusters of green leaves have begun sprouting on its massive branches..."

Allen, K. (2023, September 19). *The Lahaina Banyan tree: New leaves have sprouted.* HAWAIʻI Magazine. https://www.hawaiimagazine. com/a-ray-of-hope-the-lahaina-banyan-tree/

Chapter 15

TRANSFORMATION THROUGH THE CONFIDENCE IN YOURSELF

Everything negative—pressure, challenges—is all an opportunity for me to rise.

~ Kobe Bryant

Empathy is seeing with the eyes of another, listening with the ears of another, and feeling with the heart of another.

~ Alfred Adler

There are two kinds of light: the glow that illuminates, and the glare that obscures.

~ James Thurber

Questions for You to Ponder

As you read through this chapter, please consider the following questions:

1. Confidence can seem daunting. Sometimes it helps to think about one thing you are confident about. What would that be for you?
2. Who in your life has a healthy confidence level you would like to emulate?
3. Are there moments when you feel most confident (e.g., what activity boosts this for you, or who are you around when you feel most confident)?

Flower Analogy

You are like a flower, growing and changing through the seasons. Flowers benefit from the warmth of the sun's rays and the drizzling raindrops. They have also endured the trials of the cold winter, the spring storms, and the summer heat. As a flower, adolescents undergo a transformative journey from childhood to adulthood. Circumstances arise through this lengthy expedition, with countless ups and downs, yet you progress step by step, day by day.

You have nurtured your roots and stretched your stem. You have developed your buds and petals. As the journey advances, you learn from your experiences and gain knowledge, skills, wisdom, and strength. You embrace this journey and let your vigorous spirit flourish with confidence and resilience!

Growth Mindset

Sometimes, the stress from schoolwork and the noises from adults and the media may make you doubt yourself. Adolescence is the turning point of your life—a major transition. Some of you are diligently working toward adulthood. Some may get sidetracked, and perhaps for reasons not in your control. Whatever your situation, this is an excellent opportunity to redefine yourself, steer in the right direction, find your passions, and set your goals. It is fantastic to get the reassurance that "the teen brain is resilient."[1] Confidence can be learned and enhanced through practice!

No matter how bleak things may look, you can move forward and become a confident young adult with a meaningful life. Let's learn the growth mindset to fortify your confidence!

What is a Growth Mindset?[2, 3, 4]

- A growth mindset is the belief that your abilities, skills, and intelligence can be improved and developed through effort, feedback, learning, and hard work.

- You embrace challenges, setbacks, and mistakes as opportunities to learn and grow.

- You understand that effort, persistence, and dedication are essential for personal growth and success.

- A growth mindset is the opposite of a fixed mindset, which is the belief that you are born with a certain intelligence or ability and cannot change it.

Understand the Neuroscience Behind the Growth Mindset

Let's dive into the neuroscience behind the growth mindset, and how it can empower us to achieve remarkable results. Brace yourselves for an enlightening fact about the advancement of human civilization.[5, 6]

The Power of Dopamine

Have you ever wondered why some activities seem to make time fly by, while others seem to drag on forever? The answer lies in a chemical in your brain called dopamine.

In Part 2, we discussed the effects of dopamine. Let's review it. Dopamine is like a reward system that makes you feel good when you do something enjoyable or satisfying. But dopamine also affects how you perceive time and effort. Let me elaborate further: think of dopamine as a happy cheer from your brain. When you engage in enjoyable activities such as playing a game or completing a challenging task, your brain releases dopamine. This cheer motivates you to keep going! However, dopamine also acts like a time warper. When you're having fun and getting those happy cheers, time seems to fly by, and effort feels less daunting.

When you do something complicated or boring, like studying or exercising, you might think of the reward that comes after, like getting a good grade or a fit body. This can motivate you to keep going but also make you feel less enjoyable while doing the activity. That's because your brain separates dopamine from the reward and only releases it when you achieve the final result. As a result, your brain may delay the release of dopamine until you reach the desired outcome, such as a good grade or a toned body. This makes the activity seem like a prolonged drag and more challenging than it really is.

- Dopamine, a brain chemical, influences our perception of time.

- When we engage in activities driven by the anticipation of rewards, dopamine comes into play.

- Interestingly, this extends our perception of time, making the experience feel longer.

- However, as the external reward is delayed until the end, the neural circuits for dopamine and the activity start to dissociate.

- Consequently, we begin to experience diminishing pleasure while engaging in the activity itself.

Enter the Growth Mindset

What if you could enjoy the activity itself, not just the reward or end results? What if you could feel good while studying or exercising, not just wait until after or for the reward? That's what a growth mindset can do for you. A growth mindset is the belief that you can improve your skills and abilities through effort and learning. People with growth mindsets perform better because they focus on the process, not the outcome. They see challenges as rewarding opportunities to grow and learn, not as obstacles to avoid.

- The growth mindset is the key to exceptional performance and personal development.

- Individuals with a growth mindset focus on the effort invested in a task, rather than solely on the end result.

- Here is the exciting part: All of us can cultivate a growth mindset by accessing the rewards of effort and action!

Unleashing the Power of Effort

How can you develop a growth mindset? By changing how you think about effort and action. Instead of seeing your efforts as painful or boring, see them as purposeful and intentional. This might sound hard, but it is possible. You have a part of your brain that can create your own rewards from within. You can activate this part by telling yourself that what you are doing is enjoyable and meaningful, even if it is hard or uncomfortable. You can also celebrate your progress and achievements along the way, not just at the end. How you talk to yourself matters!

- Developing a growth mindset involves activating the prefrontal component of the mesolimbic circuit in our brains.

- This may sound challenging, but it's the gateway to transforming effort into a source of joy and fulfillment.

- Even when facing physical discomfort during activities like exercising or studying, we can train our minds to perceive effort as enjoyable. Tell yourself that you are becoming stronger and smarter. Say it out loud to yourself for an extra boost here.

Relying on the Internal Reward System

You can boost your dopamine levels while doing the activity, not just after. This will make you feel happier and more motivated while doing it. It will also make the activity seem shorter and easier than it really is. This is the power of a growth mindset. It can help you achieve anything you set your mind to, and you can enjoy the journey along the way.

- Rather than relying on external sources of dopamine to kick-start your motivation, you can tap into our internally generated reward system.

- This ancient brain (limbic system) has been part of the human mind for countless generations.

- Cultivating the ability to derive pleasure from exerting effort and embracing challenges is one of the mechanisms our ancestors used to advance human civilization. Think for a moment about all the people who came before you, whose names you may never know, to create the wonder that is you!

Let's harness the power of neuroscience and cultivate a growth mindset. Embrace effort and action, finding joy in the process of growth. By activating your internal reward system, you'll unlock boundless motivation and the ability to thrive in any endeavor. Remember, the journey itself holds immense value and brings forth a sense of satisfaction and accomplishment. You've got this!

Growth Mindset vs. Fix Mindset

I will use tables to illustrate the difference between growth and fixed mindsets.[7]

	Growth Mindset	Fixed Mindset
Response to Challenges	Embraces challenges as opportunities for learning and growth.	Avoids challenges, doubts potential for improvement.
Response to Setbacks	Sees setbacks as opportunities to learn and improve.	Gets discouraged by setbacks, tends to give up easily.
Response to Mistakes	Acknowledges mistakes as part of the learning process and uses them for growth.	Internalizes mistakes, leading to negative self-perception.
Approach to Effort	Believes that effort leads to improvement and success.	Believes abilities are fixed, sees little value in effort.
Seeking Help and Feedback	Actively seeks strategies, help, and feedback to overcome obstacles.	Avoids seeking help, may perceive it as a sign of weakness.

The following are some examples and scenarios of a growth mindset vs. a fix mindset in action.

	Growth Mindset	Fixed Mindset
Response to Math Test Problem	"This is a challenging problem, but I can try to figure it out. I can use the strategies that I learned in class. I can ask for help if I need it."	"I'm bad at math. I can't do this. I should just skip it. I hate this."
Response to Missed Soccer Goal	"I made a mistake, but I can learn from it. I can practice more. I can ask for feedback from my coach or teammates."	"I'm a terrible player. I always mess up. I should just quit."
Response to Grammatical Error in Language Learning	"I made an error, but I can correct it. I can study more. I can practice with native speakers."	"I'm not good at languages. I can't speak this language. I should just stop trying."

The Benefit of Having a Growth Mindset

- The mindset of "I CAN" help you embrace new challenges, find your passion and succeed in various aspects of life, including academic performance and future career success.[8]

- "I CAN" mindset improvement your capabilities and strengthen your brain networks associated with persistence. [9]

- It increases your resiliency development potential. You can bounce back stronger from setbacks and view them as temporary hurdles rather than cement walls.

- It builds up your learning skills. Embracing challenges helps you develop new skills and expand your knowledge to tackle more complex tasks.

- It boosts your confidence. You create a strong belief in yourself by believing in your ability to learn and grow.

- It provides you with greater motivation. Seeing effort as a path to mastery keeps you driven and enthusiastic.

- It helps you to achieve your short- and long-term goals by overcoming challenges and learning from mistakes instead of giving up halfway.

- It builds your inner strength – your assets, which is an essential element of resilience.

- It also makes you happier to know that you do have the potential.

A study found that teenagers with a "growth mindset" – who believe they can learn and improve, tend to have brains better wired for sticking with challenges.[10] That's pretty awesome, right?

- Here's the exciting part: the study also showed that YOU can develop this growth mindset! By believing in yourself and your ability to learn, you can set yourself up for success.

- Remember, you grow and achieve your dreams by facing challenges and not giving up. This research is like a roadmap, showing you that your brain is on board for the journey as long as you have the right mindset. So, keep pushing yourself, keep learning, and never stop believing in yourself!

How to Cultivate Growth Mindset

To cultivate your growth mindset, first, you must convince yourself that the present agony will increase dopamine release later. Remember that all feelings and emotions come and go—nothing is permanent. You must also convince yourself that you are doing it willingly because you enjoy it and will become a better person while working on it. This mindset is different from thinking about the prize or praise that will come after you have completed the task. The growth mindset allows you to link dopamine release with discomfort and effort while you are in the midst of work. One of the most powerful and vital functions of dopamine in human biology is facilitating access to pleasure via the effort component of our dopaminergic circuitry. Learning to get a dopamine rush from working hard gives us a natural high that may keep us energized, motivated, and focused on the task at hand.

Let's apply neuroscience principles to build your growth mindset![11, 12]

Embrace Challenges and Difficulties

- Step out of your comfort zone and view challenges as opportunities to grow and learn something new. Consider saying this out loud to yourself. Thoughts are powerful, and spoken words only reinforce that power.
- Don't avoid difficult situations or give up easily.
- Try different strategies and approaches to solve the obstacle.
- Let's remember Albert Einstein's timeless quotes:
  - O *In the middle of difficulty lies opportunity*
  - O *Genius is 1% talent and 99% percent hard work*

  You can even post these quotes on your desk or phone screen as inspiration.

Believe in Your Ability to Learn

- Believe in your ability to learn and progress, no matter what your present level of knowledge or skill is. The best, most lasting progress is often slow, steady, and incremental.
- Welcome the learning process, and pursue new challenges and experiences.

Focus on the Process

- Concentrate on learning and progress rather than the ultimate outcome. A grade is temporary and likely will not matter much in a few years. Your understanding of the content can be forever.

- Celebrate gradual progress toward goals and minor successes rather than the end result. Tell others about your progress along the way.

- Recognize your accomplishments, no matter how large or small, and use them as motivators to keep improving.

Learn from Failure

- Consider the failure to be a chance to learn and grow.

- Learn from your mistakes and weaknesses, viewing them as learning opportunities rather than setbacks. Take notes on your mistakes or careless oversights as a reminder to avoid making the same errors.

- It is okay to feel discouraged, frustrated, or depressed; sit with these hard feelings for a bit. Then, examine and analyze your failures and draw valuable lessons from them.

Emphasize Effort

- Highlight the significance of effort over natural talent or ability. This is what makes the difference in the long run!

- Refrain from concentrating on the result.

- Focus on the process and the advancement.

- Appreciate the effort and perseverance that you and others put into accomplishing something.

- Celebrate effort. Some of the best physicians and well-known scientists I know today were not straight "A" students.

Accept Feedback with a Positive, Solution-Oriented Attitude

- Open yourself up to thoughtful, critical feedback. Use it as constructive information to help you grow and perform better next time rather than becoming discouraged or defensive. Remember to take a deep breath before reacting when you feel that defensiveness rising inside of you.
- Ask for advice and critical feedback from those that you trust, who can help you improve your skills and abilities; use their feedback to progress and develop.
- You can maintain an optimistic outlook and healthy attitude even when encountering trials or failures. Nothing is forever, not even a failure!

Set Realistic and Specific Goals with a Plan for Yourself

- Define and write down your specific and realistic short- and long-term goals.
- Break them down into smaller, actionable steps to track your progress.
- Celebrate your achievements and reward yourself for reaching your milestones along the way.

Learn from Others

- Find role models or mentors who have achieved similar goals you have in mind or overcame similar obstacles.

- Learn from their accomplishments and experiences.

- Ask them for suggestions or guidance on enhancing your skills and abilities if the circumstance allows.

- Do not compare yourself to others or be envious of their accomplishments. Instead, you can applaud and respect their abilities and achievements and ask them for advice or tips on how they did it.

Encourage Others

- Encourage and assist others as they make efforts to learn and progress. This compassion and encouragement for others will fuel you too!

Surround Yourself with Growth-Oriented People

- Find friends and mentors who can motivate and encourage one another's growth rather than those who are negative and punitive towards you.

Practice Perseverance

- Be persistent and hold steadfast even when you encounter what seems like insurmountable obstacles or setbacks. Believe your efforts will pay off, even if it takes longer and is more challenging than expected.

- Let me share with you one more of Einstein's quotes, which I treasure greatly: *It's not that I'm so smart; it's just that I stay with problems longer.*

Adopt a Positive Inner Dialogue

- We all face negative self-talk at times. Aim to counterbalance that with uplifting and empowering thoughts that support your potential and growth. Speak these out loud!
- Avoid fixed mindset phrases like "I can't do this," "I'm not good at this," "I am not smart enough," or "I don't have good genes." Instead, use growth mindset phrases like "I can learn how to do this" or "I can improve at this with practice" or "I don't have to do this perfectly" or "I am not just trying, I am doing!" or "I shall overcome my family's caste system mentality."
- Acknowledge your negative thoughts, but don't let them tell the whole story. They don't have to stop you from trying new things or pursuing your dreams and goals.

Apply Growth Mindset to Build Confidence

Applying the growth mindset to build confidence is a great way to improve your self-esteem and achieve your goals. Here are some steps you can take to do that.

Steps for Building Confidence in Yourself[13, 14, 15, 16, 17, 18]

- Start your day with a positive affirmation upon awakening.
  - Tell yourself something like, "I can learn and grow today," "I can overcome any challenge I face today," "I will stay calm whatever life's challenges throwing at me today," "I'm

getting closer to achieve my goals today," or "I will not let any frustration doubt my self-value," or "I am only good," or "Because I am good, I will do good."

○ Remember, speak to yourself kindly and positively. You talk to yourself more than anyone else each day. You deserve compassion!

○ When the negative self-dialogue comes, refuse to believe it. Counterbalance a negative self-thought with a positive one.

• If you believe in a higher power, you may pray and ask God or the universe for wisdom, strength, and guidance throughout the day.

○ Being spiritual does not mean you are weak or superstitious; it is your belief system. It helps you stay grounded.

• Practice self-love. To be confident, you need to love yourself first.

○ Have a healthy, regular routine in exercising, healthy eating and sleeping.

○ Nurturing your body and brain to function optimally so you can have a sense of being in control.

• Work to stand up tall or sit straight with good posture—this oozes confidence to yourself, and those around you. Remind yourself to relax and smile too!

○ Amy Cuddy, a social psychologist, suggested learning how to act confidently can increase your confidence levels. Power posturing, or standing in a confident posture, can boost your confidence.

○ Change your physiology. Your body language can have an impact on both your state of mind and your level of confidence. Take on a posture that exudes self-assurance by standing up straight, smiling, and making eye contact. Take a few slow, deep breaths and try to relax your muscles.

Make gestures and movements that convey the energy and enthusiasm you feel.[19]

- Post positive affirmations to yourself, like inspirational quotes from famous people, your past successes, or anything that makes you feel good about yourself. You can post motivational messages where you can easily see them, like on the wall near your computer or even on your smartphone screen wall. Simple words like "YES, I CAN DO IT!" Dry erase markers work great on mirrors, and they are easy to clean off when you want to change the message.

- Take an inventory of yourself and generate a list of your strengths and growth areas. Honestly knowing yourself, accepting who you are, and giving yourself room to grow are important steps in building confidence.

  O Appreciate your strengths and accept your limitations.

  O Don't be harsh or judgmental with yourself. You are a human being, full of dignity and worth.

  O Treat yourself like a good friend would, with kindness and respect.

- Value your strengths. Are you loyal, accountable, a self-starter, a good organizer, a strong leader?

  O Write down your strengths as motivators, and intentionally use them as a springboard to move forward. Writing things down solidifies the reality of them!

- Remind yourself of the strengths and qualities you have when facing challenges or setbacks.

- Just like your brain is primed to ready to learn, you can also *unlearn* undesirable habits, like substance or behavioral addictions, poor impulse control and anger, tardiness, etc. Get professional help if needed, and if possible.

- Bad habits will deter you from feeling good about yourself. It's never too late to do it right. Again, don't hesitate to ask for help to get back on the right track.

- You have learned about your remarkable developing brain, which is still a work in progress. You can challenge your brain and develop high-value skills and knowledge that you want to excel in, like classical or contemporary literature, photography, writing, public speaking, painting, culinary arts, drama, web design, video editing, sports, etc.

  - Visit places like museums and immerse yourself in art, culture, and history. In some cities, these are free or there are free days to visit.

  - Visit your local library or find good books online, like memoirs, autobiographies, or famous literature, to gain inspiration. Librarians often love to help you find what you are passionate about!

- Find and explore your passion and purpose, push yourself to learn and grow. Psychologists agree that for those who are the best in their field, passion is the biggest factor in their success.[20]

- Engage with like-minded, positive people whenever you can. Steer away from people who drag you down and make you miserable. It is healthy to have boundaries.

- Aim to be open-minded for helpful, constructive advice or feedback for growth; avoid personalizing destructive or meaningless comments that may sway you and affect your self-worth.[21]

  - Avoid any toxic relationships that will drag you down.

  - Remember, your self-worth is not based on other people's opinions.

- Take regular breaks from social media. A study has found that social media can negatively impact youngsters' self-esteem.[22]

○ You do not need to seek validation from your social media's "likes" or "thumbs ups," or the number of friends or followers.

○ Avoid meaningless social media engagement that waste your time and energy.

○ You may discover that regular time away from social media helps you break the pattern of comparing yourself to others, and gives you more time to focus on the things that are truly matters to you and make you happy.

○ Please understand that social networks are a means of communicating information, ideas, and lifestyles. But some messages on social media can hurt young users' social behavior and can result in craving the validation of others.

○ Please remember that social media developers aim to make money for their wealth, and they do not have your best interests in mind. Please don't fall into their traps. You are in charge, and should not allow others to control you.

- Use positive visualization to build confidence.[23]

  ○ You can focus on envisioning your dreams, goals, and the steps you take to achieve them by having visuals around you in your room, your locker, and even in your phone. Find inspirational images as your phone or computer screen saver.

  ○ Hold tight to your dreams and goals. Remind yourself that who you are now is already very good, and you are also in the process of becoming the person you aspire to be 5, 10, 20, or even 30 years from now.

  ○ To minimize negative thoughts, don't rush them away. Allow them to sit, but not stay. Invite additional thoughts of yourself as having already succeeded and reached your goals victoriously.

- No one is perfect; everyone has flaws and makes mistakes. Be compassionate toward others and yourself. Forgive yourself. Forgive others too, as much as you safely can. We understand that forgiveness is not easy, and not always possible for everyone.

  ○ There is no need to beat yourself up if you make mistakes or make a fool of yourself occasionally. It's okay to laugh at yourself and shrug it off.

  ○ See your mistake as a learning opportunity to grow and better yourself. Your mistake will never be your whole story.

  ○ Be open-minded and nonjudgmental of others.

  ○ Avoid holding a grudge—it usually only hurts you and wastes your precious energy.

  ○ Establish clear boundaries to distance oneself from relationships that are abusive or destructive.

- Learn self-control/self-regulation. When facing something irritating, like negative remarks or criticism, or provocative comments, take a deep breath, count to ten, and stay calm. Not overreacting, or reacting instantly without thinking will show your confidence as well. You don't have to attend every conflict that you are invited to.

  ○ I invite you to watch this short clip of how Steve Jobs paused before answering seemingly provocative or insulting questions. By the way, this is one of my favorite video clips. I play this clip in my head whenever I feel my blood boiling from an attack or insult. It helps me avoid uncomfortable situations. Staying calm is a sign of confidence and power.

    https://www.youtube.com/watch?v=oeqPrUmVz-o

    (Field, J. (2016). *Steve Jobs insult response* - Highest quality [Video]. YouTube. https://www.youtube.com/watch?v=oeqPrUmVz-o)

- Practice saying "NO" firmly and diplomatically. That way, you won't feel pressured to do something you don't feel comfortable doing. Boundaries are necessary and a sign of maturity.
  - Hold your ground without being swayed by others' opinions or pressure.
- Celebrate your progress or little wins. Give yourself credit, even something small. Write it down in your journal or tell someone, even a pet!
- Intentionally learn and improve your ability to recognize, manage, and understand emotions. Ask yourself, "How am I feeling?" "Why do I feel this way?" Use a Feelings Wheel if needed.
  - This includes the ability to recognize and interpret your own emotions and those of other people. Always start with yourself though.
- Practice being grateful and let your gratitude show. It helps you feel good about yourself and boosts your confidence.
  - Make it a habit to appreciate yourself every day. Smile at yourself in the mirror.
  - Practice appreciating the little things—the way your dog greets you, or how your cat purrs, your favorite coffee drink, good music, etc.
  - Express your gratitude through words or actions toward others. A simple "thank you" can mean a lot for both your own heart and others.
- Practice random acts of kindness daily, which can boost your self-esteem, happiness, and confidence.
- When negative thoughts creep in, review those affirmations you stuck all over the place.

  Like having a growth mindset, confidence can be built through practice. Practice, practice, and practice to develop confidence.

Please remember that developing a growth mindset and building confidence is a journey. Be patient and allow room for mistakes and setbacks; it's all part of learning and growing. You must believe you have the power to change your mind and your life. You have the potential to achieve anything you set your mind to and unlock endless possibilities with dedication, effort, and a positive attitude.

Get Help Now!

If your addiction (substance or behavioral) or mental conditions (anxiety, depression, etc.) get in the way of being confident, get help NOW! Yes, YOU CAN set your precious life on the right track. You are not alone!

- SAMHSA National Helpline: Call 1-800-662-HELP (4357)

  Operated 24/7, the Substance Abuse and Mental Health Services Administration (SAMHSA) National Helpline provides information and referrals if you or a loved one are facing mental health and/or substance use issues. The confidential service does not provide counseling, but can direct you to helpful resources, treatment facilities, and support groups in your area.

- Affirmation apps: you do not need to get every apps. Find one that fit your most needs.

  Johansson, A. (n.d.). *10 uplifting positive affirmation apps*. Life Hack. https://www.lifehack.org/788171/best-positive-affirmation-apps

Chapter Reflections

1. Do you find the element of growth mindset in Kobe Bryant's quote: "Everything negative—pressure, challenges—is all an opportunity for me to rise"? How will you use this quote as inspiration when you feel frustrated and defeated?

2. You learned about the importance of setting limits and boundaries in this chapter, as setting boundaries is a sign of maturity. What boundaries do you know you need to put in your life now? Can you think of a situation where you must firmly say "no" to yourself or to others?

3. In your opinion, what are the difference between being confident and being arrogant?

4. The chapter says you can focus on envisioning your dreams and goals. What is your dream three years from now? How about five years or ten years from now? (Remember, Walt Disney once said, "If you can dream it, you can do it!")

YOU ARE EMPOWERED: TRANSFORMATION THROUGH KNOWLEDGE AND ACTION

Knowledge with action converts adversity into prosperity.
~ A.P.J. Abdul Kalam

Knowing is not enough; we must apply. Willing is not enough; we must do.
~ Johann Wolfgang von Goethe

Flower Analogy

One day, you will reach the end of your adolescent journey, like petals on the verge of opening to radiate their beauty and fragrance. You are prepared to share your gifts and talents with others.

As a flower matures and poises to bloom, you continue to evolve and discover your passions and unique, vibrant essence. You are a flower about to fulfill its potential and blossom into a magnificent human being. You have prepared yourself for this moment! You are unleashing your potential with courage and resilience. You are maturing into a responsible and resolute adult.

You are about to make a positive difference in your life and the lives of those around you.

You are ready to conquer the world's challenges.

You are a flower that deserves admiration and appreciation as you enter adulthood and strive for a bright future.

Dear adolescents, embrace this journey while you are still on it, and let your courageous spirit shine with resilience, confidence, and action!

Congratulations!

Congratulations on completing Book 2 of the *Talking about Adolescence* series: *Supercharge Your Body and Brain Power*! Take a moment to appreciate your accomplishment and give yourself a well-deserved pat on the back! The knowledge and insights you've gained from this book will empower you to understand the marvelous transformation happening within your body and brain every single minute and every single day, even as you sleep.

As you delved into the pages of this book, I hope you felt the thrill of discovery, realizing just how fascinating and wondrous your body and brain genuinely are. From the incredible processes shaping your growth to the intricate maturation happening within you, this journey of self-discovery is both awe-inspiring and exhilarating. The information you've absorbed is not just valuable for the present moment but can serve as a lifelong guide. Consider keeping this book as your trusty handbook, always within reach whenever you need a refresher or a deeper understanding of the amazing workings of your body and brain.

I extend my gratitude to the parents, teachers, caregivers, and guardians who have provided this book to you. Their investment in your knowledge and growth is truly commendable. I hope that this book not only provides you with valuable insights but also acts as a catalyst for meaningful discussions with your peers, friends, or fellow students.

For additional enlightenment, I invite you to explore the Appendices section, where you can gain further insights into each chapter. We (author and editor) have carefully curated and checked all the links for your convenience, but if, by chance, you encounter any broken links, please accept our sincere apologies.

Embrace this journey of self-discovery, marvel at the wonders of your body and brain, and remember that knowledge is the key to unlocking your true potential. Keep exploring, keep learning, and put your knowledge into action.

Let the world witness the incredible growth and transformation that lie within you!

APPENDICES

Part 1
Your Exciting Journey from Childhood to Adulthood

Chapter 3: Secondary Sex Characteristics

Glamour. (2016). *This is your period in 2 minutes* [Video]. YouTube.

https://www.youtube.com/watch?v=WOi2Bwvp6hw&t=40s.

Gupta, A. (2016). *A taboo-free way to talk about periods* [Video]. YouTube. Ted Talk.

https://www.youtube.com/watch?v=OaGEM-Rms48

Menstrupedia. (2020). *Hello periods (English) - The complete guide to periods for girls* [Video]. YouTube.

https://www.youtube.com/watch?v=qUNTtn1WPEw

Part 2
Your Precious Brain is Developing

Odell, S. (2022). *What sex ed doesn't tell you about your brain* [Video]. YouTube. Ted-Ed.

https://www.youtube.com/watch?v=deNGkzUlhZU

UNICEF Innocenti. (2019). *The adolescent brain: A second window of opportunity.*

    https://www.youtube.com/watch?v=-1FRco3Bjyk

Chapter 5: An Overview of Our Remarkable Brain

Additional information for understanding your brain--I strongly encourage you to check out the following videos:

- The Psych Show. (2017). *How to learn major parts of the brain quickly: Learn how the brain works in 5 minutes using only your hands* [Video]. YouTube. https://www.youtube.com/watch?v=FczvTGluHKM

- CrashCourse. (2014). *Meet your master - Getting to know your brain* [Video]. YouTube. https://www.youtube.com/watch?v=vHrmiy4W9Co

- National Geographic. (2017). *Brain 101* [Video]. YouTube. https://www.youtube.com/watch?v=pRFXSjkpKWA

- Nicolelyn. (2016). *AP psychology—the human brain* [Video]. YouTube. https://www.youtube.com/watch?v=d4Hym5TekUE

- Neuroscientifically Challenged. (2020). *2-Minute neuroscience: Cerebral cortex* [Video]. YouTube. https://www.youtube.com/watch?v=7TK1LpjV5bI

- Neuroscientifically Challenged. (2019). *2-Minute neuroscience: Prefrontal cortex* [Video]. YouTube. https://www.youtube.com/watch?v=i47_jiCsBMs

- The Science of Psychotherapy. (2016). *The prefrontal cortex in 60 seconds* [Video]. YouTube. https://www.youtube.com/watch?v=X5-HdloZ3VA

- The last video is for an upper grader or someone interested in learning more about the part of the brain under the cerebral cortex—the subcortical cerebrum. I assume this video's content is made for students preparing for the Medical College Admission Test (MCAT). Khan Academy. (2014, April 24). *Subcortical cerebrum.* https://www.youtube.com/watch?v=A_2f3onF3S8

Chapter 6: Your Growing Brain is Reorganizing

Short Videos for Further Understanding the Information

Must watch: I strongly recommend that you watch Dr. Siegel's video.

- Siegel, D. (2018). *The adolescent brain* [Video]. YouTube.

  O https://www.youtube.com/watch?v=0O1u5OEc5eY

- Optional short videos to watch

  O OxfordSparks. (2017). *Brain development in teenagers* [Video]. YouTube. https://www.youtube.com/watch?v=dISmdb5zfiQ

  O ExpandED Schools. (2014). *Use it or lose it: The adolescent brain* [Video]. YouTube. https://www.youtube.com/watch?v=MHs7vlcwRXY

  O A&P for Health Sciences. (2020). *Brain anatomy, Part 4: White vs. gray matter* [Video]. YouTube. https://www.youtube.com/watch?v=Zf4evd-Mjps

  O BrainFacts.org. (2018). *How neurons communicate* [Video]. YouTube. https://www.youtube.com/watch?v=hGDvvUNU-cw

  O Hellen Weinschutz Mendes, H. W. (2015). *Neurons, synapses and pruning oh my!* [Video]. YouTube. https://www.youtube.com/watch?v=1d1naM559w4

- The following video is best situated for older teens or you are interested in learning more about your brain.

  ○ Khan Academy. (2014). *Gray and white matter: Organ systems* [Video]. YouTube. https://www.youtube.com/ watch?v=ZZQzMeFoZYo

Chapter 7: How to Take Advantage of Dual Systems in the Developing Brain

- I strongly recommend this must-watch video. It conveys the essence of this chapter.

  ○ Fig.1/University of California. (2017). *Why the teenage brain has an evolutionary advantage?* [Video]. YouTube. https://www. youtube.com/watch?v=P629T0jpvDU

- The following short videos will help you further understand the Reward System of our brain:

  ○ Neuroscientifically Challenged. (2015). *2-Minute neuroscience: Limbic system* [Video]. YouTube. https://www.youtube.com/ watch?v=LNs9ruzoTmI

  ○ Neuroscientifically Challenged. (2016). *2-Minute neuroscience: Amygdala* [Video]. YouTube. https://www.youtube.com/ watch?v=JVvMSwsOXPw

  ○ Neuroscientifically Challenged. (2015). *2-Minute neuroscience: Reward system* [Video]. YouTube. https://www.youtube.com/ watch?v=f7EomTJQ2KM

  ○ Neuroscientifically Challenged. (2016). *2-minute neuroscience: Nucleus accumbens.*

  ○ [Video]. YouTube. https://www.youtube.com/ watch?v=3_zgB19TE-M o Neuroscientifically Challenged. (2016). *2-minute neuroscience: Striatum* [Video]. YouTube. https://www.youtube.com/watch?v=EEUxKFmIUiI&t=1s

o Neuroscientifically Challenged. (2018). *2-minute neuroscience: Dopamine* [Video]. YouTube. https://www.youtube.com/watch?v=Wa8_nLwQIpg

• The following video about the frontal cortex is meant for upper graders or college students. However, the content is easy to comprehend. The lecturer, Dr. Robert Sapolsky, is a professor at Stanford University.

o Wondrium. (2017). *What does the brain's frontal cortex do? (Professor Robert Sapolsky explains)* [Video]. YouTube. https://www.youtube.com/watch?v=3RRtyV_UFJ8

Chapter 8: Plasticity, Prime Time, and a Second Window of Opportunity

Short Videos for Further Understanding Plasticity

• The first is a must-watch video. It's only 3 minutes long.

o Shohamy, D. (2018). *Teenage brains: Wired to learn* [Video]. YouTube. Columbia University's Zuckerman Institute. https://www.youtube.com/watch?v=1GSvzgrBKaM

• I strongly encourage you to watch the following videos:

o Galván, A. (2013). *Insight into the teenage brain: Adriana Galván at TEDxYouth@Caltech* [Video]. YouTube. https://www.youtube.com/watch?v=LWUkW4s3XxY

O Halo Neuroscience. (2019). *The neuroscience of learning* [Video]. YouTube. https://www.youtube.com/watch?v=_nWMP68DqHE

O SciShow. (2014). *Your brain is plastic* [Video]. YouTube. https://www.youtube.com/watch?v=5KLPxDtMqe8

• The following video is a talk by Dr. Steinberg to parents and educators. You are welcome to watch if you are curious about what adults are saying about you. (Smile)!

O Steinberg, L. (2016). *Age of opportunity: Lessons from the new science of adolescence* [Video]. YouTube. Microsoft Research. https://www.youtube.com/watch?v=MKMIKdvGsKI

Chapter 9: Why is Addiction a Thief to Your Brain Power

Short Videos for Further Understanding the Information

• Bergstrom, A. L. (2022). *Infographic about the adolescent brain development.* Moving Science. https://movingscience.dk/infographic-about-the-adolescent-brain-development/

• Ask, Listen, Learn. (2020). *How marijuana affects your developing brain* [Video]. YouTube. https://www.youtube.com/watch?v=1Luw2tiMuLk

• Oasis Mental Health Applications. (2020). *Addiction: Types, causes, and solutions* (For Teens) [Video]. YouTube. https://www.youtube.com/watch?v=dsTwkX1cdCY

• Wait 21. (2013). *Understanding addiction as a disease (Wait21)* [Video]. YouTube. https://www.youtube.com/watch?v=-w8n9UOiBxE

• University of Maryland School of Medicine. (2013). *How marijuana affects the adolescent brain* [Video]. YouTube. New University of Maryland School of Medicine Research. https://www.youtube.com/watch?v=Tgp-oZ_f6Xk

- Addiction Policy Forum. (2019). *Addiction & the brain: For kids!* [Video]. YouTube. https://www.youtube.com/watch?v=sobqT_hxMwI

- SciShow. (2012). *The chemistry of addiction* [Video]. YouTube. https://www.youtube.com/watch?v=ukFjH9odsXw

- National Institute on Drug Abuse (NIDA/NIH). (2021). *What is the worst drug?* [Video]. YouTube. https://www.youtube.com/watch?v=VF-pTqFnQAw

- Neuroscientifically Challenged. (2018). *2-minute neuroscience: Dopamine* [Video]. YouTube. https://www.youtube.com/watch?v=Wa8_nLwQIpg

- AsapSCIENCE. (2014). *5 crazy ways social media Is changing your brain right now* [Video]. YouTube. https://www.youtube.com/watch?v=HffWFd_6bJo

- FreeMedEducation (2019). *Part 4: Dopamine: The molecule of addiction: Your brain on porn* [Video]. YouTube. https://www.youtube.com/watch?v=bdiMFQk_aW8

- ABC News. (2019, August 22). *Doctors believe teen's lung failure due to vaping.* https://www.youtube.com/watch?v=im4bTtQ99SY

- Poland, C. (2024). *Alcohol-related deaths are spiking. So why don't we take alcohol addiction more seriously?* AAMC https://www.aamc.org/news/alcohol-related-deaths-are-spiking-so-why-don-t-we-take-alcohol-addiction-more-seriously

- Drug Enforcement Administration (DEA). (2022). *DEA warns of brightly-colored fentanyl used to target young Americans.* https://www.dea.gov/press-releases/2022/08/30/dea-warns-brightly-colored-fentanyl-used-target-young-americans

- Buddy T. (2021). *Why addiction is considered a chronic brain disease?* Verywell mind
https://www.verywellmind.com/
addiction-is-a-chronic-brain-disease-67874

The brain is "rewired" when you become addicted.

- Gupta, S. (2012). *How addiction changes your brain* [Video]. YouTube.
https://www.youtube.com/watch?app=desktop&v=5f1nmqiHIII
- WGN News. (2022). *Understanding the effects of drugs on the brain: A look at the damage and potential for treatment* [Video]. YouTube.
https://www.youtube.com/watch?v=czweQQB1Igk
- Wait 21(2013). *Understanding addiction as a disease* [Video]. YouTube.
https://www.youtube.com/watch?v=-w8n9UOiBxE

Part 3
How to Nurture and Supercharge
Your Developing Brain and body

Chapter 10: The Classical Developmental Theories and Dual Systems

- These two videos provide a great review of what we've covered in this section.

  ○ National Institute on Drug Abuse (NIDA/NIH). (2016). *The human brain: Major structures and functions* [Video]. YouTube.
  https://www.youtube.com/watch?v=0-8PvNOdByc

○ National Institute on Drug Abuse (NIDA/NIH). (2019). *Teen brain development* [Video]. YouTube. https://www.youtube. com/watch?v=EpfnDijz2d8

• I strongly recommend the next two videos.

○ Center on the Developing Child at Harvard University. (2018). *How children and adults can build core capabilities for life* [Video]. YouTube. https://www.youtube.com/ watch?v=6NehuwDA45Q&t=14s

○ LW4K Gaming. (2021). *What is self control* [Video]. YouTube. https://www.youtube.com/watch?v=3uNHujLTa2c

Chapter 11: What is Executive Function?

• The following short videos are for strengthening executive function and self-regulation.

○ Edutopia. (2019). *Developing executive function with priority lists* [Video]. YouTube. https://www.youtube.com/watch?v=AhoXKhkQ6SE

○ Transforming Education. (2017). *Importance of self-efficacy* [Video]. YouTube. https://www.youtube.com/watch?v=VW5v6PQ5PEc&t=0s

○ Committee for Children. (2016). *Self-regulation skills: Why they are fundamental* [Video]. YouTube. https://www.youtube.com/watch?v=m4UGDaCgo_s

○ Committee for Children. (2016). *Executive-function skills: Important skills for childhood development* [Video]. YouTube. https://www.youtube.com/watch?v=FZLXggsK6oA

○ Career and Life Skills Lessons. (2020). *Social skills: Self-discipline lesson* [Video]. YouTube. https://www.youtube.com/watch?v=LeQ7ElbaFOg

○ Beech Acres. (2019). *Self-control* [Video]. YouTube. https://www.youtube.com/watch?v=esAUQW8w1Ww

○ Rishard, H. (2022). *Seeing a better world through pets* [Video]. YouTube. https://www.youtube.com/watch?v=54TG8vjJ_98

Chapter 12: How to Optimize Your Executive Function

• These two videos provide a great review of what we've covered in this section.

○ National Institute on Drug Abuse (NIDA/NIH). (2016). *The human brain: Major structures and functions* [Video]. YouTube. https://www.youtube.com/watch?v=0-8PvNOdByc

○ National Institute on Drug Abuse (NIDA/NIH). (2019). *Teen brain development* [Video]. YouTube. https://www.youtube.com/watch?v=EpfnDijz2d8

• I strongly recommend the next two videos.

○ Center on the Developing Child at Harvard University. (2018).
How children and adults can build core capabilities for life [Video]. YouTube. https://www.youtube.com/watch?v=6NehuwDA45Q&t=14s

○ LW4K Gaming. (2021). *What is self control* [Video]. YouTube. https://www.youtube.com/watch?v=3uNHujLTa2c

• Neuroscience News. (2023). *Mindfulness and memory: Unlocking cognitive potential through meditation* [Video]. YouTube.

Neuroscience News
https://www.youtube.com/watch?v=Aw8erQC8spo&t=70s

- The following short videos are for strengthening executive function and self-regulation.

  - Edutopia. (2019). *Developing executive function with priority lists* [Video]. YouTube. https://www.youtube.com/watch?v=AhoXKhkQ6SE

  - Transforming Education. (2017). *Importance of self-efficacy* [Video]. YouTube. https://www.youtube.com/watch?v=VW5v6PQ5PEc&t=0s

  - Committee for Children. (2016). *Self-regulation skills: Why they are fundamental* [Video]. YouTube. https://www.youtube.com/watch?v=m4UGDaCgo_s

  - Committee for Children. (2016). *Executive-function skills: Important skills for childhood development* [Video]. YouTube. https://www.youtube.com/watch?v=FZLXggsK6oA

  - Career and Life Skills Lessons. (2020). *Social skills: Self-discipline lesson* [Video]. YouTube. https://www.youtube.com/watch?v=LeQ7ElbaFOg

  - Beech Acres. (2019). *Self-control* [Video]. YouTube. https://www.youtube.com/watch?v=esAUQW8w1Ww

  - Rishard, H. (2022). *Seeing a better world through pets* [Video]. YouTube. https://www.youtube.com/watch?v=54TG8vjJ_98

- Center on the Developing Child. (n.d.) *6 playful activities for teens (13-17 years)*. Harvard University. https://harvardcenter.wpenginepowered.com/wp-content/uploads/2022/12/6-Playful-Activities-for-Teens-13-17-years.pdf

- Neuroscience News. (05.24.2023). *Digital dilemma: Navigating social media's impact on youth mental health* [Video]. YouTube. https://www.youtube.com/watch?v=2S-7gD6-lW8

- Neuroscience News. (2023). *Mindfulness and memory: Unlocking cognitive potential through meditation* [Video]. YouTube. https://www.youtube.com/watch?v=Aw8erQC8spo&t=63s

- Neuroscience News. (2023). *Power of beats fuels your workouts: The science of music-driven motivation* [Video]. YouTube. Neuroscience News.

- https://www.youtube.com/watch?v=ZCVo34NIlJU&t=41s

- Neuroscience News. (2024). *How adolescents transcendent thinking fosters brain growth and psychosocial development* [Video]. YouTube. https://www.youtube.com/watch?v=h8faz9I2TnU

Chapter 13: How to Overcome Your Mental Distress and Optimize Your Brain Development

- Neuroscience News. (2023). *Exploring interoception: The neuroscience of internal body signals* [Video]. YouTube. Neuroscience News. https://www.youtube.com/watch?v=rms5Io2Rzgo&t=12s

- Desautels, L. (2017). *Quick classroom exercises to combat stress: These brain breaks and focused-attention practices can help students cope with stress and trauma and focus on their learning.* Edutopia. https://www.edutopia.org/article/quick-classroom-exercises-combat-stress

- HHS Office of Population Affairs. (2023). *TPP mental health video.* https://www.youtube.com/watch?v=VVxqMiM8okg&t=1s

- Minin Sohn, S. (2024). *College student mental health statistics – 2024* https://www.collegetransitions.com/blog/college-students-mental-health-statistics/

- Worland, G. (2023). *Is someone you love suffering in silence? Here's what to do* [Video]. YouTube. https://www.youtube.com/watch?v=6483lpvZRJ4

- ABC15 Arizona. (2012). *Warning signs for anorexia.* https://www.youtube.com/watch?v=wz7lCjeoYww

- Chang-Lim, E. (2023). *Mental health matters: A teen's guide* [Video]. YouTube. https://youtu.be/_s6ZJQo2RYU

- Chang-Lim, E. (2023). *Understanding mental health in Adolescents: Expert definitions and celebrity quote* [Video]. YouTube. https://youtube.com/shorts/F1-dy3kkVto?feature=share

- Chang-Lim, E. (2023). *Understanding mental illness in adolescents: A quick guide from experts and celebrity quote* [Video]. YouTube. https://youtube.com/shorts/NB2mTPSjMiU?feature=share

- Chang-Lim, E. (2023). *7 surprising signs of adolescent depression you need to know* [Video]. YouTube.

- https://youtube.com/shorts/8GVPKPlmiyg?feature=share

- Chang-Lim, E. (2023). *How social media affects your brain: The science behind mental health* [Video]. YouTube.

- https://youtube.com/shorts/v3Oz8P7vd7o?feature=share

- Chang-Lim. (2023). *How to find your happy place: The power of creativity for boosting your mood and beating stress* [Video]. YouTube. https://youtube.com/shorts/X1j87fN99uw?feature=share

- Chang-Lim, E. (2023). *Eating disorders: Disordered eating indicates 7 red flags for potential eating disorders* [Video]. YouTube. https://youtube.com/shorts/1g92oxbpvJw?feature=share

- Chang-Lim, E. (2023). *Eating disorders: 10 shocking facts about eating disorders you need to know* [Video]. YouTube. https://www.youtube.com/shorts/ZKXhRQJsOEo

- Chang-Lim, E. (2023). *Understanding anxiety and panic attacks: Shocking statistics you need to know (Part 1/7)* [Video]. YouTube. https://youtube.com/shorts/TNToRnosLEI?feature=share

- Chang-Lim, E. (2023). *Understanding anxiety and panic attacks: The characteristics of panic attacks (Part 2/7).* [Video]. YouTube. https://youtube.com/shorts/biWCS2Sqtvk

- Chang-Lim, E. (2023). *Understanding anxiety and panic attacks: Expert tips on feeling confident amid attacks (Part 3/7)* [Video]. YouTube. https://youtube.com/shorts/ncWabChO-yI

- Chang-Lim, E. (2023). *Understanding and overcoming anxiety: Self-care tips for recovery and management after a panic attack (Part 4–7).* [Video]. YouTube. https://youtube.com/shorts/ojWmcTIg8TU?feature=share

- Chang-Lim, E. (2023). *Understanding anxiety and panic attack: Learn how to overcome panic attacks and thrive (Part 5/7)* [Video]. YouTube. https://youtube.com/shorts/ZhrgnmH-4LY?feature=share

- Chang-Lim, E. (2023). *Understanding anxiety and panic attack: 5 tips to help your friend get through panic attacks (Part 6/7)* [Video]. YouTube. https://youtube.com/shorts/IP-fdexiX6w?feature=share

- Chang-Lim, E. (2023). *Understanding anxiety and panic attack: 7 phrases to avoid as supporting a friend during panic attacks (Part 7/7).* [Video]. YouTube. https://youtube.com/shorts/odsnLgQJHNY?feature=share

- Chang-Lim, E. (2023). *Why adolescence is the most critical time in a person's Life: 10 compelling reasons and messages (Part 1)* [Video]. YouTube. https://youtu.be/WBEmLDo5JyU

- Chang-Lim, E. (2023). *Why adolescence is the most critical time in a person's life: 10 compelling reasons & messages (Part 2)* [Video]. YouTube. https://youtu.be/6itQLXLU-Bk

- Chang-Lim, E. (2023). *Mental health matters: A teen's guide* [Video]. YouTube https://youtu.be/_s6ZJQo2RYU

- Chang-Lim, E. (2023). *Understanding mental health in adolescents: Expert definitions and celebrity quote* [Video]. YouTube. https://youtu.be/dc5nEtcLS4A

- Chang-Lim, E. (2023). *Understanding mental illness in adolescents: A quick guide from experts and celebrity quote* [Video]. YouTube. https://youtu.be/JEXipXYxdE8

- Chang-Lim, E. (2023). *7 easy and fun ways to de-stress for stressed out teens* [Video]. YouTube. https://youtu.be/N-zdhHzPAjc
Chang-Lim, E. (2023). *Laugh your way to better mental health: 5 fun ways for adolescents to find laughter* [Video]. YouTube. https://youtu.be/H8iOZlFDFjI

- Chang-Lim, E. (2023). *7 shocking adolescent mental health statistics to be aware of* [Video]. YouTube. https://youtu.be/Ig4JOFFvITU

- Chang-Lim, E. (2023). *7 surprising signs of adolescent depression you need to know* [Video]. YouTube. https://youtu.be/O7UFgVUWmCs

- Chang-Lim, E. (2023). *The teen's guide to spotting anxiety: 8 Symptoms you don't want to miss* [Video]. YouTube. https://youtu.be/fOv9PvnocM4

- Chang-Lim, E. (2023). *5 tips for teens on choosing the right friends for better mental health* [Video]. YouTube. https://youtu.be/-z4SvytJhfU

- Chang-Lim, E. (2023). *Demi Lovato opens up about battling depression as a teenager* [Video]. YouTube. https://youtu.be/Dy2tZJIoFcY

- Mental Health America. (2023). *Mental health information.* https://mhanational.org/MentalHealthInfo

- Timmons, J. (2022). *A quick look at the best eating disorder apps.* Healthline. https://www.healthline.com/health/top-eating-disorder-iphone-android-apps

- Lee, V. (2020). *Eating disorders: A mental illness, not a lifestyle choice* [Video]. YouTube. TEDxMcGill. https://www.youtube.com/watch?v=CQ9KhtNrygE

- Psych2Go. (2018). *6 types of eating disorders* [Video]. YouTube. https://www.youtube.com/watch?v=0SRmccgFIs8

- *Wall Street Journal.* (2021). *How TikTok's algorithm figures you out* [Video]. YouTube. WSJ. https://www.youtube.com/watch?v=nfczi2cI6Cs&t=112s

- Wassmuth Center for Human Rights. (2020). *Be an upstander* [Video]. YouTube. https://www.youtube.com/watch?v=wyV6OFm2KxQ

- UNICEF. (2022). *Cyberbullying: What is it and how to stop it. What teens want to know about cyberbullying.* https://www.unicef.org/end-violence/how-to-stop-cyberbullying

- Lee, V. (2020). *Eating disorders: A mental illness, not a lifestyle choice* [Video]. YouTube. TEDxMcGill. https://www.youtube.com/watch?v=CQ9KhtNrygE

- National Eating Disorders Association (NEDA). (2017). *Warning signs & symptoms of an eating disorder* [Video]. YouTube. https://www.youtube.com/watch?v=nJMtReAg1DI&t=120s

- Ng, Z. J. (2024). *Meeting students' needs for emotional support.* Edutopia. https://www.edutopia.org/article/providing-students-emotional-support?utm_content=linkpos1&utm_campaign=weekly-2024-04-10&utm_medium=email&utm_source=edu-newsletter

- Ng, Z. J & Jennifer Seibyl, J. (2022). *Emotions come and go in waves. We can teach our students how to surf them.* EdSurge https://www. edsurge.com/news/2022-10-06-emotions-come-and-go-in-waves-we-can-teach-our-students-how-to-surf-them

Chapter 14: How not to Let Childhood Trauma Interfere Your Brain Development

- Sentis. (2013). *Neuroplasticity* [Video]. YouTube.
- https://www.youtube.com/watch?v=ELpfYCZa87g&t=116s
- Doveta. (2019). *Trauma and the brain* [Video]. YouTube. Trauma and the Brain © 2019 by Doveta. https://www.youtube.com/watch?v=ZLF_SEy6sdc
- Lambert, K. (2020). *Improving our neuroplasticity* [Video]. YouTube. TEDxBermuda. https://www.youtube.com/watch?v=gOJL3gjc8ak&t=67s
- Leicestershire Partnership NHS Trust. (2015). *Resilience but what is it? Here's 5 ways to build resilience* [Video]. YouTube. https://www.youtube.com/watch?v=1FDyiUEn8Vw
- Stanton, M. (2020). *Resilience & training your mind to tackle tough times* [Video]. YouTube. TEDxMillsHighSchool. https://www.youtube.com/watch?v=lnB2nQvyy10
- Chang-Lim, E. (2023). *How to find your happy place: The power of creativity for boosting your mood and beating stress.* https://youtube.com/shorts/X1j87fN99uw?feature=share
- Li, P. (May 14, 2023). *How to heal from childhood trauma.* Parenting for Brain. https://www.parentingforbrain.com/how-to-heal-from-childhood-trauma/

- Li, P. (2023). *Free therapy in the US*. Parenting for Brain https://www.parentingforbrain.com/free-therapy/

- Smith, K. (2023). *Trauma is trauma: A mental health talk with Kevin Smith* [Video]. YouTube. PEOPLE. https://www.youtube.com/watch?v=JBvc7Ny4iUk

- UK Trauma Council (UKTC). (2020). *Childhood trauma and the brain* [Video]. YouTube. https://www.youtube.com/watch?v=xYBUY1kZpf8

- van der Kolk, B. (2024). *How the body keeps the score on trauma* [Video]. YouTube. Big Think. https://www.youtube.com/watch?v=iTefkqYQz8g&t=20s

- Four Minute Books. (2022). *Body keeps the score summary (animated) — Heal from trauma using 3 science-backed techniques* [Video]. YouTube. https://www.youtube.com/watch?v=m5LoT1eK07I

- Therapy in a Nutshell. (2023). *How trauma and PTSD change the brain* [Video]. YouTube. https://www.youtube.com/watch?v=wdUR69J2u6c

- Evans, J. (2014). *Childhood trauma and abuse and its effects on the brain* [Video]. YouTube. https://www.youtube.com/watch?v=Lw4DyGs1u1I

- Mate, G. (2021). *How childhood trauma leads to addiction* [Video]. YouTube. After Skool. https://www.youtube.com/watch?v=BVg2bfqblGI

- Maricopa County School Superintendent. (2016). *Trauma and the brain* [Video]. YouTube. https://www.youtube.com/watch?v=XasCFJEH0MA

- Edutopia. (2018). *Fall-Hamilton Elementary: Transitioning to trauma-informed practices to support Learning* [Video]. YouTube. https://www.youtube.com/watch?v=iydalwamBtg&t=38s

- The National Child Traumatic Stress Network (NCTSN)

  The National Child Traumatic Stress Network (NCTSN) was created by Congress in 2000 as part of the Children's Health Act to raise the standard of care and increase access to services for children and families who experience or witness traumatic events. This unique network of frontline providers, family members, researchers, and national partners is committed to changing the course of children's lives by improving their care and moving scientific gains quickly into practice across the U.S. The NCTSN is administered by the Substance Abuse and Mental Health Services Administration (SAMHSA) and coordinated by the UCLA-Duke University National Center for Child Traumatic Stress (NCCTS).

  The NCTSN is funded by the Center for Mental Health Services (CMHS), Substance Abuse and Mental Health Services Administration (SAMHSA), U.S. Department of Health and Human Services and jointly coordinated by UCLA and Duke University.

  https://www.nctsn.org/resources

- Erickson, L. (2017). *Cross cultural investigation on resiliency and protective factors in the U.S. and Guatemala* (Doctoral dissertation). ProQuest. (1961607035)

Chapter 15: Transformation through the Confidence in Yourself

- Freethink. (2019). *The joy of being wrong* [Video]. YouTube. https://www.youtube.com/watch?v=mRXNUx4cuao&t=26s
- A 35–40-minute online course called 'I CAN' has been developed to enhance grit and self-belief among Norwegian students. The course, which aims to cultivate an 'I can' attitude and provide strategies to recall this belief in challenging situations, has shown significant improvements in grit. The course has been shown to be effective in changing attitudes towards personal capabilities and strengthening brain networks associated with

persistence. This intervention could potentially increase individuals' willingness to embrace new challenges, find passion, and succeed in various aspects of life, including academic performance. Encouraging self-efficacy, especially among students from lower socioeconomic backgrounds, can lead to improved school performance and help mitigate academic disparities.

Sigmundsson, H., & Hauge, H. (2023). I CAN intervention to increase grit and self-efficacy: A pilot study. *Brain Sciences, 14*(1), 33. https://doi.org/10.3390/brainsci14010033

- Nasser, F. (2019). *The power of intellectual humility* [Video]. YouTube. TEDxDonMills. https://www.youtube.com/watch?v=2vjXw_iFOMc
- Outcast Motivation. (2022). *Kobe Bryant's greatest speech: BEST motivation ever.* [Video]. YouTube. https://www.youtube.com/watch?v=dTRBnHtHehQ
- alpha m. (2014). *Respect! Seven steps to earn respect.* https://www.youtube.com/watch?v=8dNIXtPIiEA
- alpha m. (2016). *5 Secrets to boost your confidence: How to be more confident today!* https://www.youtube.com/watch?v=Ja9Fo2qqzWg
- Branden, N. (2014). *How to build self-esteem – The six pillars of self-esteem* [Video]. YouTube. https://www.youtube.com/watch?v=dhuabY4DmEo
- Child Mind Institute. (2021). *Understanding feelings - High school* [Video]. YouTube. https://www.youtube.com/watch?v=eTeYpQ-32JP8&list=PLnEQkAsadC1GIKEcYiz5EqNC2Dj2jZt9n&index=2
- Ea, P. (2019).*10 confidence hacks* [Video]. YouTube.
- https://www.youtube.com/watch?v=EGKZuVoHcVo
- Ea, P. (2019). *Every teenager NEEDS to hear this!* (2020) [Video]. YouTube. https://www.youtube.com/watch?v=UB7nGT3egak

REFERENCES FOR EACH CHAPTER

Part 1
Your Exciting Journey
from Childhood to Adulthood

Chapter 1: How does the Journey begin?

1.   Sawyer, S. M., Azzopardi, P. S., Wickremarathne, D., & Patton, G. C. (2018). The age of adolescence. *The Lancet Child & Adolescent Health, 2*(3), 223-228. https://doi.org/10.1016/ S2352-4642(18)30022-1 https://www.thelancet.com/journals/ lanchi/article/PIIS2352-4642%2818%2930022-1/fulltext

2.   Ghorayshi, A. (2022). Puberty starts earlier than it used to. No one knows why. *National Library of Medicine.* https://www.ncbi. nlm.nih.gov/search/research-news/16227/?utm_source=gque- ry&utm_medium=referral&utm_campaign=gquery-home

3.   Eckert-Lind, C., Busch, A. S., Petersen, J. H., Biro, F. M., Butler, G., Bräuner, E. V., & Juul, A. (2020). Worldwide secular trends in age at pubertal onset assessed by breast development among girls: A systematic review and meta-analysis. *JAMA pediatrics, 174*(4), e195881. https://doi.org/10.1001/jamapediatrics.2019.5881

4.   National Academies Press (US). (2019). *The promise of adolescence: Realizing opportunity for all youth.* https:// www.ncbi.nlm.nih.gov/books/NBK545476/

5.   Lally, M. & Valentine-French, S. (2019). *Lifespan development: A psychological perspective, second edition.* http:// dept.clcillinois.edu/psy/LifespanDevelopment.pdf

Chapter 2: Your Amazing Body Is Transforming

1. National Academies Press (US). (2019). *The promise of adolescence: Realizing opportunity for all youth.* https://www.ncbi.nlm.nih.gov/books/NBK545476/

2. Ibid., National Academies Press

Chapter 4: Primary Sexual Characteristics

1. The World Population Review. (2024). *Intersex people by country, 2024.* https://worldpopulationreview.com/country-rankings/intersex-people-by-country

2. Council of Europe. (2024). *Sex and gender.* https://www.coe.int/en/web/gender-matters/sex-and-gender

Part 2
Your Precious Brain is Developing

1. Goddings, A. L., Beltz, A., Peper, J. S., Crone, E. A., & Braams, B. R. (2019). Understanding the role of puberty in structural and functional development of the adolescent brain. *Journal of Research on Adolescence, 29*(1), 32-53.

2. Goddings, A. L., Roalf, D., Lebel, C., & Tamnes, C. K. (2021). Development of white matter microstructure and executive functions during childhood and adolescence: A review of diffusion MRI studies. *Developmental Cognitive Neuroscience, 51,* 101008. https://doi.org/10.1016/j.dcn.2021.101008

3. Jernigan, T. L., Brown, S. A., & Dowling, G. J. (2018). The adolescent brain cognitive development study. *Journal of Research on Adolescence: The Official Journal of the Society for Research on Adolescence, 28*(1), 154–156. https://doi.org/10.1111/jora.12374, https://www.ncbi.nlm.nih.gov/pmc/articles/PMC7477916/

Chapter 5: An Overview of Our Remarkable Brain

1. Study.com (2013, May 15). *Prenatal stages of brain development.* https://study.com/academy/lesson/prenatal-stages-of-brain-development.html

2.   Ted Talk. (2013). *Suzana Herculano-Houzel shrunk the human brain by 14 billion neurons — by developing a new way to count them. Video?* https://www.ted.com/speakers/suzana_herculano_houzel

3.   Kolk, S.M., Rakic, P. (2022). Development of prefrontal cortex. *Neuropsychopharmacol. 47*, 41–57. https://doi.org/10.1038/s41386-021-01137-9

4.   University of Rochester Medical Center. (n.d.). *Executive function.* https://www.urmc.rochester.edu/encyclopedia/content.aspx?ContentTypeID=1&ContentID=3051

5.   Von Stultz, J. (2010, May 23). *Adolescent brain development - Part 1* [Video]. YouTube. https://www.youtube.com/watch?v=Hl-R5vtERj8

6.   Von Stultz, J. (2010, May 23). *Adolescent brain development - Part 2* [Video]. YouTube. https://www.youtube.com/watch?v=4e1j3OXlKss

7.   Von Stultz, J. (2010, May 23). *Adolescent brain development - Part 3* [Video]. YouTube. https://www.youtube.com/watch?v=inKprzgu56g

8.   (U.S. Department of Health and Human Services. Office of Population Affairs (OPA). (n.d.). *Maturation of the Prefrontal Cortex.* https://bridges2understanding.com/maturation-of-the-prefrontal-cortex/)

9.   Carter, R. (2019). *The human brain book: An illustrated guide to its structure, function, and disorders.* (DK Human Body Guides). DK.

10. Spinal Cord Team. (2020). *Grey matter vs white matter in the brain.* https://www.spinalcord.com/blog/gray-matter-vs-white-matter-in-the-brain

11. Mercadante AA, Tadi P. (2024). *Neuroanatomy, Gray Matter.* In: StatPearls [Internet]. Treasure Island (FL): StatPearls Publishing. https://www.ncbi.nlm.nih.gov/books/NBK553239/

12. Timmler, S., & Simons, M. (2019). Grey matter myelination. *Glia, 67*(11), 2063–2070. https://doi.org/10.1002/glia.23614

Chapter 6: Your Growing Brain is Reorganizing

1.   National Institute of Mental Health. (2023). *The teen brain: 7 things to know.* https://www.nimh.nih.gov/health/publications/the-teen-brain-7-things-to-know

Chapter 7: How to Take Advantage of Dual Systems in the Developing Brain

1. National Institute of Mental Health (NIMH). (2023). *The teen brain: 7 things to know.* https://www.nimh.nih.gov/health/publications/the-teen-brain-7-things-to-know

2. Mills, K. L., Goddings, A. L., Clasen, L. S., Giedd, J. N., & Blakemore, S. J. (2014). The developmental mismatch in structural brain maturation during adolescence. *Developmental Neuroscience, 36*(3-4), 147–160. https://doi.org/10.1159/000362328

3. Casey, B.J., Getz.,S., & Galvan, A. (2008). The adolescent brain. *Developmental Review, 28,* (1), 62-77, https://doi.org/10.1016/j.dr.2007.08.003

4. Centers for Disease Control and Prevention (CDC). (2022). *Teen drivers: Get the facts.* https://www.cdc.gov/transportationsafety/teen_drivers/teendrivers_factsheet.html

5. CDC. (2023). *10 leading causes of death, United States.* https://wisqars.cdc.gov/data/lcd/home

6. Rees, C. A., Monuteaux, M. C., Steidley, I., Mannix, R., Lee, L. K., Barrett, J. T., & Fleegler, E. W. (2022). Trends and disparities in firearm fatalities in the United States, 1990-2021. *JAMA network open, 5*(11), e2244221. https://doi.org/10.1001/jamanetworkopen.2022.44221

7. Klein, B. R., Trowbridge, J., Schnell, C., & Lewis, K. (2024). Characteristics and obtainment methods of firearms used in adolescent school shootings. *JAMA pediatrics, 178*(1), 73–79. https://doi.org/10.1001/jamapediatrics.2023.5093

8. Curtin, S. C., & Garnett, M. F. (2023). Suicide and homicide death rates among youth and young adults aged 10-24: United States, 2001-2021. *NCHS data brief,* (471), 1–8.

9. Ibid., Centers for Disease Control and Prevention (CDC). (2022).

10. Ibid., CDC. (2023).

11. Ibid., Rees, C. A., Monuteaux, M. C., Steidley, I., Mannix, R., Lee, L. K., Barrett, J. T., & Fleegler, E. W. (2022)

12. Ibid., Klein, B. R., Trowbridge, J., Schnell, C., & Lewis, K. (2024).

Chapter 8: Plasticity, Prime Time, and a Second Window of Opportunity

1. Shohamy, D. (2018). *Teenage brains: Wired to learn.* https://zuckermaninstitute.columbia.edu/teenage-brains-wired-learn

2. Davidow, J. Y., Foerde, K., Galván, A., & Shohamy, D. (2016). An upside to reward sensitivity: The Hippocampus supports enhanced reinforcement learning in adolescence. *Neuron, 92*(1), 93–99. https://doi.org/10.1016/j.neuron.2016.08.031

3. UNICEF Innocenti. (2018). *The adolescent brain: A second window of opportunity* [Video]. YouTube. https://www.youtube.com/watch?v=-1FRco3Bjyk

4. UNICEF. (2018). *The adolescent brain: A second window of opportunity: Cutting edge insights for programmes and policy from eight leading adolescent brain researchers.* https://www.unicef-irc.org/article/1750-the-adolescent-brain-a-second-window-of-opportunity.html

5. Jolles, J., & Jolles, D. D. (2021). On neuroeducation: Why and how to improve neuroscientific literacy in educational professionals. *Frontiers in Psychology, 12,* 752151. https://doi.org/10.3389/fpsyg.2021.752151

6. Sydnor, V. J., Larsen, B., Seidlitz, J., Adebimpe, A., Alexander-Bloch, A. F., Bassett, D. S., Bertolero, M. A., Cieslak, M., Covitz, S., Fan, Y., Gur, R. E., Gur, R. C., Mackey, A. P., Moore, T. M., Roalf, D. R., Shinohara, R. T., & Satterthwaite, T. D. (2023). Intrinsic activity development unfolds along a sensorimotor-association cortical axis in youth. *Nature Neuroscience, 26*(4), 638–649. https://doi.org/10.1038/s41593-023-01282-y

Chapter 9: Why is Addiction a Thief to Your Brain Power

1. National Center for Drug Abuse Statistics (NCDAS). (2022). *Substance abuse and addiction statistics.* https://drugabusestatistics.org/

2. National Institute on Alcohol Abuse and Alcoholism. (2023). *Alcohol facts and statistics.* https://www.niaaa.nih.gov/alcohols-effects-health/alcohol-topics/alcohol-facts-and-statistics

3. American Addiction Centers. (2020). *The financial toll of addiction.* https://drugabuse.com/blog/financial-toll-addiction/

4.   Centers for Disease Control and Prevention (CDC). (2020). *High-risk substance use among youth.* https://www. cdc.gov/healthyyouth/substance-use/index.htm

5.   NIDA. (2020, July 13). *Drug misuse and addiction.* https://nida.nih.gov/publications/ drugs-brains-behavior-science-addiction/drug-misuse-addiction

6.   Ibid., NIDA. (2020, July 13).

7.   Samaritan Neuropsychology. (2020). *How do drugs affect a baby's development during pregnancy?* https://www. samhealth.org/about-samaritan/news-search/2020/06/08/ how-do-drugs-affect-babys-development-during-pregnancy

8.   Salmanzadeh, H., Ahmadi-Soleimani, S. M., Pachenari, N., Azadi, M., Halliwell, R.F., Rubino, T., Azizi, H. (2020). Adolescent drug exposure: A review of evidence for the development of persistent changes in brain function. *Brain Research Bulletin, 159,* 105-117. https://doi. org/10.1016/j.brainresbull.2020.01.007 https://www.science-direct.com/science/article/pii/S0361923019308809

9.   Deng, H. (2023). The brain under the influence of substances and addictive disorders: How it differs from a healthy one? In B. Halpern-Felsher (Ed.), *Encyclopedia of Child and Adolescent Health* (1st ed., pp. 231-244). Academic Press. ISBN 9780128188736. https://doi.org/10.1016/B978-0-12-818872-9.00124-2

10. Substance Abuse and Mental Health Services Administration (SAMHSA). (2023). *Mental health and substance use co-occurring disorders.* https://www.samhsa.gov/mental-health/ mental-health-substance-use-co-occurring-disorders

11. Tuvel, A. L., Winiger, E. A., & Ross, J. M. (2023). A review of the effects of adolescent cannabis use on physical health. *Child and Adolescent Psychiatric Clinics of North America, 32*(1), 85-105. https://doi.org/10.1016/j.chc.2022.07.005

12. McGraw, K. E., Nigra, A. E., Klett, J., Sobel, M., Oelsner, E. C., Navas-Acien, A., Hu, X., & Sanchez, T. R. (2023). Blood and urinary metal levels among exclusive marijuana users in NHANES (2005-2018). *Environmental Health Perspectives, 131*(8), 87019. https://doi.org/10.1289/EHP12074

13. Shorey-Kendrick, L. E., Roberts, V. H. J., D'Mello, R. J., Sullivan, E. L., Murphy, S. K., Mccarty, O. J. T., Schust, D. J., Hedges, J. C., Mitchell, A. J., Terrobias, J. J. D., Easley, C. A.,

4th, Spindel, E. R., & Lo, J. O. (2023). Prenatal delta-9-tetrahy-drocannabinol exposure is associated with changes in rhesus macaque DNA methylation enriched for autism genes. *Clinical Epigenetics*, 15(1), 104. https://doi.org/10.1186/s13148-023-01519-4

14. Scott, J. C., Slomiak, S. T., Jones, J. D., Rosen, A. F. G., Moore, T. M., & Gur, R. C. (2018). Association of cannabis with cognitive functioning in adolescents and young adults: A systematic review and meta-analysis. *JAMA psychiatry*, 75(6), 585–595. https://doi.org/10.1001/jamapsychiatry.2018.0335

15. Scheyer, A. F., Laviolette, S. R., Pelissier, A. L., & Manzoni, O. J. J. (2023). Cannabis in adolescence: Lasting cognitive alterations and underlying mechanisms. *Cannabis and Cannabinoid Research*, 8(1), 12–23. https://doi.org/10.1089/can.2022.0183

16. Dellazizzo, L., Potvin, S., Giguère, S., & Dumais, A. (2022). Evidence on the acute and residual neurocognitive effects of cannabis use in adolescents and adults: A systematic meta-review of meta-analyses. *Addiction (Abingdon, England)*, 117(7), 1857–1870. https://doi.org/10.1111/add.15764

17. Ibid., Salmanzadeh, H., Ahmadi-Soleimani, S. M., Pachenari, N., Azadi, M., Halliwell, R.F., Rubino, T., Azizi, H. (2020).

18. Tobore, T. O. (2019). On the potential harmful effects of E-Cigarettes (EC) on the developing brain: The relationship between vaping-induced oxidative stress and adolescent/young adults social maladjustment. *Journal of Adolescence, 76*. 202-209. https://doi.org/10.1016/j.adolescence.2019.09.004

19. Heldt, N. A., Seliga, A., Winfield, M., Gajghate, S., Reichenbach, N., Yu, X., Rom, S., Tenneti, A., May, D., Gregory, B. D., & Persidsky, Y. (2020). Electronic cigarette exposure disrupts blood-brain barrier integrity and promotes neuroinflammation. *Brain, Behavior, and Immunity*, 88, 363–380. https://doi.org/10.1016/j.bbi.2020.03.034

20. Heldt, N. A., Reichenbach, N., McGary, H. M., & Persidsky, Y. (2021). Effects of electronic nicotine delivery systems and cigarettes on systemic circulation and blood-brain barrier: Implications for cognitive decline. *The American Journal of Pathology, 191*(2), 243–255. https://doi.org/10.1016/j.ajpath.2020.11.007

21. Neuroscience News. (2023). *Probing E-Cig and alcohol's joint assault on the blood-brain barrier.* https://neuroscience-news.com/alcohol-vaping-blood-brain-barrier-23977

22. Ibid., Tobore, T. O. (2019).

23. Ibid., Heldt, N. A., Seliga, A., Winfield, M., Gajghate, S., Reichenbach, N., Yu, X., Rom, S., Tenneti, A., May, D., Gregory, B. D., & Persidsky, Y. (2020).

24. Ibid., Heldt, N. A., Reichenbach, N., McGary, H. M., & Persidsky, Y. (2021).

25. Ibid., Neuroscience News. (2023).

26. Lloyd, A. R., Savage, R., & Eaton, E. F. (2021). Opioid use disorder: A neglected human immunodeficiency virus risk in American adolescents. *AIDS (London, England)*, 35(14), 2237–2247. https://doi.org/10.1097/QAD.0000000000003051

27. Klobucista, C. (2022). *The U.S. opioid epidemic.* Backgrounder. https://www.cfr.org/backgrounder/us-opioid-epidemic

28. Drug Enforcement Administration (DEA). (2022). *DEA warns of brightly-colored fentanyl used to target young Americans.* https://www.dea.gov/press-releases/2022/08/30/dea-warns-brightly-colored-fentanyl-used-target-young-americans

29. Drug Enforcement Administration. (2022). *Fake pills fact sheet.* Department of Justice. https://www.dea.gov/sites/default/files/2022-12/DEA-OPCK_FactSheet_December_2022.pdf

30. Ferrantella, A., Huerta, C. T., Quinn, K., Mavarez, A. C., Quiroz, H. J., Thorson, C. M., Perez, E. A., & Sola, J. E. (2022). Risk factors associated with recent opioid-related hospitalizations in children: A nationwide analysis. *Pediatric Surgery International*, 38(6), 843–851. https://doi.org/10.1007/s00383-022-05088-0

31. Welsh, J. W., Sitar, S. I., Hunter, B. D., Godley, M. D., & Dennis, M. L. (2023). Substance use severity as a predictor for receiving medication for opioid use disorder among adolescents: An analysis of the 2019 TEDS. *Drug and Alcohol Dependence*, 246, 109850. https://doi.org/10.1016/j.drugalcdep.2023.109850

32. Ibid., Salmanzadeh, H., Ahmadi-Soleimani, S. M., Pachenari, N., Azadi, M., Halliwell, R.F., Rubino, T., Azizi, H. (2020).

33. Vonmoos, M., Hulka, L. M., Preller, K. H., Minder, F., Baumgartner, M. R., & Quednow, B. B. (2014). Cognitive impairment in cocaine users is drug-induced but partially reversible: Evidence from a longitudinal study. *Neuropsychopharmacology: Official publication of the American College of Neuropsychopharmacology*, 39(9), 2200–2210. https://doi.org/10.1038/npp.2014.71

34. Kelley, L. A. (2023). *Beyond addiction: Study targets rising cocaine use disorder.* https://neuroscience-news.com/addiction-research-cud-23238/

35. Drug Aware. (n.d.) *Frequently asked questions.* https://drugaware.com.au/get-the-facts/faqs-ask-a-question/amphetamines/#what-are-the-other-names-for-amphetamines

36. Barry, A. E., King, J., Sears, C., Harville, C., Bondoc, I., & Joseph, K. (2016). Prioritizing alcohol prevention: Establishing alcohol as the gateway drug and linking age of first drink with illicit drug use. *Journal of School Health, 86*(1), 31-38. https://onlinelibrary.wiley.com/doi/full/10.1111/josh.12351

37. Monitoring the Future national survey. (2023). https://monitoringthefuture.org/wp-content/uploads/2022/12/mtf2022.pdf

38. Centers for Disease Control and Prevention (CDC). (2020). *Teen substance use & risks.* https://www.cdc.gov/ncbddd/fasd/features/teen-substance-use.html

39. National Institute on Drug Abuse. (2022). *Monitoring the future.* https://nida.nih.gov/research-topics/trends-statistics/monitoring-future

40. Landin, J. D., & Chandler, L. J. (2023). Adolescent alcohol exposure alters threat avoidance in adulthood. *Frontiers in Behavioral Neuroscience, 16,* 1098343. https://doi.org/10.3389/fnbeh.2022.1098343

41. Tetteh-Quarshie, S., & Risher, M. L. (2023). Adolescent brain maturation and the neuropathological effects of binge drinking: A critical review. *Frontiers in Neuroscience, 16,* 1040049. https://doi.org/10.3389/fnins.2022.1040049

42. National Institute on Alcohol Abuse and Alcoholism (NIAAA). (2021). *Understanding binge drinking.* https://www.niaaa.nih.gov/publications/brochures-and-fact-sheets/binge-drinking

43. National Institute on Alcohol Abuse and Alcoholism (NIAAA). (2023). *Consequences for families in the United States.* https://www.niaaa.nih.gov/alcohols-effects-health/alcohol-topics/alcohol-facts-and-statistics/consequences-families-united-states

44. Lipari, R. N., & Van Horn, S. L. (2017). *Children living with parents who have a substance use disorder.*

https://www.samhsa.gov/data/sites/default/files/
report_3223/ShortReport-3223.html

45. Dodge, N. C., Jacobson, J. L., & Jacobson, S. W. (2019).
Effects of fetal substance exposure on offspring
substance use. *Pediatric clinics of North America, 66*(6),
1149–1161. https://doi.org/10.1016/j.pcl.2019.08.010

46. Sithisarn, T., Granger, D. T., & Bada, H. S. (2012). Consequences of
prenatal substance use. *International Journal of Adolescent Medicine
and Health, 24*(2), 105–112. https://doi.org/10.1515/ijamh.2012.016

47. Ibid., Salmanzadeh, H., Ahmadi-Soleimani, S. M., Pachenari,
N., Azadi, M., Halliwell, R.F., Rubino, T., Azizi, H. (2020).

48. Goldberg, L. R., & Gould, T. J. (2019). Multigenerational and
transgenerational effects of paternal exposure to drugs of abuse
on behavioral and neural function. *The European Journal of
Neuroscience, 50*(3), 2453–2466. https://doi.org/10.1111/ejn.14060

49. Odegaard, K. E., Pendyala, G., & Yelamanchili, S. V. (2021).
Generational effects of opioid exposure. *Encyclopedia, 1*(1),
99–114. https://doi.org/10.3390/encyclopedia1010012

50. Archie, S. R., Sifat, A. E., Zhang, Y., Villalba, H., Sharma, S.,
Nozohouri, S., & Abbruscato, T. J. (2023). Maternal e-cigarette use can disrupt postnatal blood-brain barrier (BBB)
integrity and deteriorates motor, learning and memory
function: influence of sex and age. *Fluids and Barriers of the
CNS, 20*(1), 17. https://doi.org/10.1186/s12987-023-00416-5

51. Addiction Education Society. (2023). *How does addiction take hold in the brain?* https://addictioneducationsoci-
ety.org/how-does-addiction-take-hold-in-the-brain/

52. Kang W. (2023). Illegal drug use is associated with poorer life
satisfaction and self-rated health (SRH) in young people. *Frontiers
in Psychiatry, 14*, 955626. https://doi.org/10.3389/fpsyt.2023.955626

53. Friedman, J., & Shover, C. L. (2023). Charting the fourth wave:
Geographic, temporal, race/ethnicity and demographic trends in
polysubstance fentanyl overdose deaths in the United States, 2010–
2021. *Addiction, 118*(12), 2477-2485. https://doi.org/10.1111/add.16318

54. Beheshti I. (2023). Cocaine destroys gray matter
brain cells and accelerates brain aging. *Biology, 12*(5),
752. https://doi.org/10.3390/biology12050752

55. Towers, E. B., Williams, I. L., Qillawala, E. I., & Lynch, W. J. (2023). Role of nucleus accumbens dopamine 2 receptors in motivating cocaine use in male and female rats prior to and following the development of an addiction-like phenotype. *Frontiers In Pharmacology, 14,* 1237990. https://doi.org/10.3389/fphar.2023.1237990

56. Wen, S., Aki, T., Funakoshi, T., Unuma, K., & Uemura, K. (2022). Role of mitochondrial dynamics in cocaine's neurotoxicity. *International Journal of Molecular Sciences,* 23(10), 5418. https://doi.org/10.3390/ijms23105418

57. National Institute on Drug Abuse. (n.d.). *Fact sheet.* https://nida.nih.gov/sites/default/files/factsheetsmod6_23.pdf

Part 3
How to Nurture and Supercharge Your Developing Brain and body

Chapter 10: The Classical Developmental Theories and Dual Systems

1. Lally, M. & Valentine-French, S. (2019). *Lifespan development: A psychological perspective, second edition.* P.225. http://dept.clcillinois.edu/psy/LifespanDevelopment.pdf

2. Ibid., Lally, M. & Valentine-French, S. (2019).

3. Lally, M. & Valentine-French, S. (2019). *Lifespan development: A psychological perspective, second edition.* P.233. http://dept.clcillinois.edu/psy/LifespanDevelopment.pdf

4. Shulman, E. P., Smith, A. R., Silva, K., Icenogle, G., Duell, N., Chein, J., & Steinberg, L., (2016). The dual systems model: Review, reappraisal, and reaffirmation, *Developmental Cognitive Neuroscience,* 17(C), 103-117. https://doaj.org/article/bcf2a35903f14e508a5b63149a144758

5. Steinberg, L., Icenogle, G., Shulman, E. P., Breiner, K., Chein, J., Bacchini, D., Chang, L., Chaudhary, N., Giunta, L. D., Dodge, K. A., Fanti, K. A., Lansford, J. E., Malone, P. S., Oburu, P., Pastorelli, C., Skinner, A.T., Sorbring, E., Tapanya, S., Tirado, L. M. U., ... Takash, H. M. S. (2018). Around the world, adolescence is a time

of heightened sensation seeking and immature self-regulation, *Developmental Science, 21*(2). n/a. https://doi.org/10.1111/desc.12532

6.   PsychologyWriting. (2023). *Piaget's and Vygotsky's theories of cognitive development.* https://psychologywriting.com/piagets-and-vygotskys-theories-of-cognitive-development

7.   Huang, Y. (2021). *Comparison and contrast of Piaget and Vygotsky's theories.* https://www.semanticscholar.org/paper/Comparison-and-Contrast-of-Piaget-and-Vygotsky%E2%80%99s-Huang/7f842a9eeod83b84c8abd6142680ecd1e6ab50de

8.   Goswami, U. (Ed.). (2011). *The Wiley-Blackwell handbook of childhood cognitive development* (2nd ed.). Wiley-Blackwell.

9.   Pochon, J. B., Levy, R., Fossati, P., Lehericy, S., Poline, J. B., Pillon, B., Le Bihan, D., & Dubois, B. (2002). The neural system that bridges reward and cognition in humans: An fMRI study. *Proceedings of the National Academy of Sciences of the United States of America, 99*(8), 5669–5674. https://doi.org/10.1073/pnas.082111099

10.   Markett, S., Reuter, M., Montag, C., Voigt, G., Lachmann, B., Rudorf, S., Elger, C. E., & Weber, B. (2014). Assessing the function of the fronto-parietal attention network: Insights from resting-state fMRI and the attentional network test. *Human Brain Mapping, 35*(4), 1700–1709. https://doi.org/10.1002/hbm.22285

11.   Moretto, M., Silvestri, E., Zangrossi, A., Corbetta, M., & Bertoldo, A. (2022). Unveiling whole-brain dynamics in normal aging through Hidden Markov Models. *Human Brain Mapping, 43*(3), 1129–1144. https://doi.org/10.1002/hbm.25714

12.   Friedman, N.P., Robbins, T.W. (2022). The role of prefrontal cortex in cognitive control and executive function. *Neuropsychopharmacol. 47*, 72–89. https://doi.org/10.1038/s41386-021-01132-0

Chapter 11: What is Executive Function?

1.   Brodsky, J. E., Bergson, Z., Chen, M., Hayward, E. O., Plass, J. L., & Homer, B. D. (2023). Language, ambiguity, and executive functions in adolescents' theory of mind. *Child Development, 94*(1), 202–218. https://doi.org/10.1111/cdev.13852

2.   Dawson, P., & Kessler, E. (n.d.) *Teens and executive function skills.* https://www.smartkidswithld.org/getting-help/executive-function-disorder/teens-and-executive-function-skills/

3.   Kolk, S.M., Rakic, P. (2022). Development of prefrontal cortex. *Neuropsychopharmacol. 47*, 41–57. https://doi.org/10.1038/s41386-021-01137-9

4.   Friedman, N.P., Robbins, T.W. (2022). The role of prefrontal cortex in cognitive control and executive function. *Neuropsychopharmacol. 47*, 72–89. https://doi.org/10.1038/s41386-021-01132-0

5.   University of Rochester Medical Center. (n.d.). *Executive function.* https://www.urmc.rochester.edu/encyclopedia/content.aspx?ContentTypeID=1&ContentID=3051

6.   Birt, J. (2023). *Executive function: Definition, importance and types.* https://www.indeed.com/career-advice/career-development/executive-functions

7.   Kolk, S.M., Rakic, P. (2022). Development of prefrontal cortex. *Neuropsychopharmacol. 47*, 41–57. https://doi.org/10.1038/s41386-021-01137-9

8.   Friedman, N.P., Robbins, T.W. (2022). The role of prefrontal cortex in cognitive control and executive function. *Neuropsychopharmacol. 47*, 72–89. https://doi.org/10.1038/s41386-021-01132-0

9.   University of Rochester Medical Center. (n.d.). *Executive function.* https://www.urmc.rochester.edu/encyclopedia/content.aspx?ContentTypeID=1&ContentID=3051

10.   Diamond A. (2013). Executive functions. *Annual Review of Psychology, 64*, 135–168. https://doi.org/10.1146/annurev-psych-113011-143750

11.   TeachThought Staff. (2022). *8 strategies to improve executive functions of the brain.* TeachThought. https://www.teachthought.com/learning/executive-functions/

12.   Ablon, J. S. (2022). *The best way to improve executive functioning skills.* Psychology Today. https://www.psychologytoday.com/us/blog/changeable/202201/the-best-way-improve-executive-functioning-skills

13.   Center on the Developing Child. (n.d.). *InBrief: Executive function: Skills for life and learning.* https://developingchild.harvard.edu/resources/inbrief-executive-function-skills-for-life-and-learning/

14.   Ibid., Center on the Developing Child. (n.d.).

Chapter 12: How to Optimize Your Executive Function

1. Pindus, D. M., Shigeta, T. T., Leahy, A. A., Mavilidi, M. F., Nayak, A., Marcozzi, D., Montero-Herrera, B., Abbas, Z., Hillman, C. H., & Lubans, D. R. (2023). Sex moderates the associations between physical activity intensity and attentional control in older adolescents. *Scandinavian Journal of Medicine & Science in Sports*, 10.1111/sms.14311. Advance Online Publication. https://doi.org/10.1111/sms.14311

2. Constantinidis, C., & Luna, B. (2019). Neural substrates of inhibitory control maturation in adolescence. *Trends in Neurosciences, 42*(9), 604–616. https://doi.org/10.1016/j.tins.2019.07.004

3. Kang, W., Hernández, S. P., Rahman, M. S., Voigt, K., & Malvaso, A. (2022). Inhibitory control development: A network neuroscience perspective. *Frontiers in Psychology, 13*, 651547. https://doi.org/10.3389/fpsyg.2022.651547

4. Diamond A. (2013). Executive functions. *Annual Review of Psychology, 64*, 135–168. https://doi.org/10.1146/annurev-psych-113011-143750

5. Casey, B. J., Galván, A., & Somerville, L. H. (2016). Beyond simple models of adolescence to an integrated circuit-based account: A commentary. *Developmental Cognitive Neuroscience, 17*, 128–130. https://doi.org/10.1016/j.dcn.2015.12.006

6. Vijayakumar, N., Mills, K. L., Alexander-Bloch, A., Tamnes, C. K., & Whittle, S. (2018). Structural brain development: A review of methodological approaches and best practices. *Developmental Cognitive Neuroscience, 33*, 129–148. https://doi.org/10.1016/j.dcn.2017.11.008

7. Tamnes, C. K., Herting, M. M., Goddings, A. L., Meuwese, R., Blakemore, S. J., Dahl, R. E., Güroğlu, B., Raznahan, A., Sowell, E. R., Crone, E. A., & Mills, K. L. (2017). Development of the cerebral cortex across Adolescence: A multisample study of inter-related longitudinal changes in cortical volume, surface area, and thickness. *The Journal of Neuroscience: The Official Journal of the Society for Neuroscience, 37*(12), 3402–3412. https://doi.org/10.1523/JNEUROSCI.3302-16.2017

8. van Duijvenvoorde, A. C. K., Achterberg, M., Braams, B. R., Peters, S., & Crone, E. A. (2016). Testing a dual-systems model of adolescent brain development using resting-state connectivity analyses. *NeuroImage, 124*(Pt A), 409–420. https://doi.org/10.1016/j.neuroimage.2015.04.069

9. van Duijvenvoorde, A. C. K., Whitmore, L. B., Westhoff, B., & Mills, K. L. (2022). A methodological perspective on learning in the developing brain. *NPJ Science of Learning, 7*(1), 12. https://doi.org/10.1038/s41539-022-00127-w

10. Fuller, K. (2022). *The negative impact of clutter on mental health*. Verywell Mind. https://www.verywellmind.com/decluttering-our-house-to-cleanse-our-minds-5101511

11. Palmer, C. A., Bower, J. L., Cho, K. W., Clementi, M. A., Lau, S., Oosterhoff, B., & Alfano, C. A. (2023). Sleep loss and emotion: A systematic review and meta-analysis of over 50 years of experimental research. Psychological Bulletin. Advance online publication. https://doi.org/10.1037/bul0000410

12. Buch, E. R., Claudino, L., Quentin, R., Bönstrup, M., & Cohen, L. G. (2021). Consolidation of human skill linked to waking hippocampo-neocortical replay. *Cell Reports, 35*(10), 109193. https://doi.org/10.1016/j.celrep.2021.109193

13. Neuroscience News. (2023). *Unleashing the mind: The neuroscience of meditation and its impact on memory*. https://neurosciencenews.com/memory-meditation-23414/

14. Guidotti, R., D'Andrea, A., Basti, A., Raffone, A., Pizzella, V., & Marzetti, L. (2023). Long-term and meditation-specific modulations of brain connectivity revealed through multivariate pattern analysis. *Brain Topography, 36*(3), 409–418. https://doi.org/10.1007/s10548-023-00950-3

15. Hölzel, B. K., Carmody, J., Vangel, M., Congleton, C., Yerramsetti, S. M., Gard, T., & Lazar, S. W. (2011). Mindfulness practice leads to increases in regional brain gray matter density. *Psychiatry Research, 191*(1), 36–43. https://doi.org/10.1016/j.pscychresns.2010.08.006

16. Garland, E. L., Hanley, A. W., Hudak, J., Nakamura, Y., & Froeliger, B. (2022). Mindfulness-induced endogenous theta stimulation occasions self-transcendence and inhibits addictive behavior. *Science Advances, 8*(41), eabo4455. https://doi.org/10.1126/sciadv.abo4455

17. Pinar-Martí, A., Fernández-Barrés, S., Gignac, F., Persavento, C., Delgado, A., Romaguera, D., Lázaro, I., Ros, E., López-Vicente, M., Salas-Salvadó, J., Sala-Vila, A., & Júlvez, J. (2022). Red blood cell omega-3 fatty acids and attention scores in healthy adolescents. *European Child & Adolescent Psychiatry*, Advance online publication. https://doi.org/10.1007/s00787-022-02064-w

18.   National Institutes of Health. (2022). *Omega-3 fatty acids, and in particular DHA, are associated with increased attention Scores in adolescents.* Neuroscience News https:// neurosciencenews.com/dha-attention-21539/

19.   Pinar-Martí, A., et al. (2023). Effect of walnut consumption on neuropsychological development in healthy adolescents: A multi-school randomised controlled trial. *eClinical Medicine. Part of The Lancet Discovery Science.* https://doi.org/10.1016/j. eclinm.2023.101954, https://www.thelancet.com/journals/eclinm/ article/PIIS2589-5370(23)00131-1/fulltext, https://neuroscience-news.com/thats-nuts-eating-walnuts-regularly-improves-cog-nitive-development-and-psychological-maturation-in-teens/

20.   Lane, M. M., Lotfaliany, M., Hodge, A. M., O'Neil, A., Travica, N., Jacka, F. N., Rocks, T., Machado, P., Forbes, M., Ashtree, D. N., & Marx, W. (2023). High ultra-processed food consumption is associated with elevated psychological distress as an indicator of depression in adults from the Melbourne Collaborative Cohort Study. *Journal of Affective Disorders, 335,* 57–66. Advance online publication. https://doi.org/10.1016/j.jad.2023.04.124

21.   Lane, M. M., Gamage, E., Travica, N., Dissanayaka, T., Ashtree, D. N., Gauci, S., Lotfaliany, M., O'Neil, A., Jacka, F. N., & Marx, W. (2022). Ultra-processed food consumption and mental health: A systematic review and meta-analysis of observational studies. *Nutrients, 14*(13), 2568. https://doi.org/10.3390/nu14132568)

22.   Pindus, D. M., Shigeta, T. T., Leahy, A. A., Mavilidi, M. F., Nayak, A., Marcozzi, D., Montero-Herrera, B., Abbas, Z., Hillman, C. H., & Lubans, D. R. (2023). Sex moderates the associations between physical activity intensity and attentional control in older adolescents. *Scandinavian Journal of Medicine & Science in Sports, 10.*1111/sms.14311. Advance online publication. https://doi.org/10.1111/sms.14311

23.   Singh, B., Olds, T., Curtis, R., Dumuid, D., Virgara, R., Watson, A., Szeto, K., O'Connor, E., Ferguson, T., Eglitis, E., Miatke, A., Simpson, C. E., & Maher, C. (2023). Effectiveness of physical activity interventions for improving depression, anxiety and distress: An overview of systematic reviews. *British Journal of Sports Medicine,* bjsports-2022-106195. Advance online publication. https://doi.org/10.1136/bjsports-2022-106195

24.   Lee, K. Y., Rhodes, J. S., & Saif, M. T. A. (2023). Astrocyte-mediated transduction of muscle fiber contractions synchronizes hippocampal neuronal network development. *Neuroscience, 515,* 25–36. https://doi.org/10.1016/j.neuroscience.2023.01.028

25. Neuroscience. (2023). *Exercise and the brain: The neuroscience of fitness explored.* https://neurosciencenews.com/fitness-neuroscience-23228/

26. Brady, W. J., Jackson, J. C., Lindström, B., & Crockett, M. J. (2023). Algorithm-mediated social learning in online social networks. *Trends in Cognitive Sciences.* https://doi.org/10.1016/j.tics.2023.06.008

27. Dekkers, T. J., & van Hoorn, J. (2022). Understanding problematic social media use in adolescents with attention-deficit/hyperactivity disorder (ADHD): A narrative review and clinical recommendations. *Brain Sciences, 12*(12), 1625. https://doi.org/10.3390/brainsci12121625

28. Kortesoja, L., Vainikainen, M. P., Hotulainen, R., & Merikanto, I. (2023). Late-night digital media use in relation to chronotype, sleep and tiredness on school days in adolescence. *Journal of Youth and Adolescence, 52*(2), 419–433. https://doi.org/10.1007/s10964-022-01703-4

29. Maza, M. T., Fox, K. A., Kwon, S. J., Flannery, J. E., Lindquist, K. A., Prinstein, M. J., & Telzer, E. H. (2023). Association of habitual checking behaviors on social media with longitudinal functional brain development. *JAMA Pediatrics, 177*(2), 160–167. https://doi.org/10.1001/jamapediatrics.2022.4924

30. The U.S. Surgeon General's Advisory. (2023). *Social media and youth mental health.* https://www.hhs.gov/sites/default/files/sg-youth-mental-health-social-media-advisory.pdf

31. Horwood, S. (2022). *Constant smartphone notifications tax your brain.* Neuroscience News. https://neurosciencenews.com/smartphone-notifications-cognition-22048/

32. Gotlieb, R. J. M., Yang, X. F., & Immordino-Yang, M. H. (2024). Diverse adolescents' transcendent thinking predicts young adult psychosocial outcomes via brain network development. Scientific Reports, 14, 6254. https://doi.org/10.1038/s41598-024-56800-0

33. Ablon, J. S. (2022). *The best way to improve executive functioning skills.* Psychology today. https://www.psychologytoday.com/us/blog/changeable/202201/the-best-way-improve-executive-functioning-skills

Chapter 13: How to Overcome Your Mental Distress and Optimize Your Brain Development

1. National Institute of Mental Health. (2023). *The teen brain: 7 things to know.* https://www.nimh.nih.gov/health/publications/the-teen-brain-7-things-to-know

2. National Alliance of Mental Illness (NAMI). (2023). *Mental health facts: Children & teens.* https://www.nami.org/NAMI/media/NAMI-Media/Infographics/Children-MH-Facts-NAMI.pdf

3. Mental Health First Aid. (2020). *10 surprising mental health statistics from 2020.* https://www.mentalhealthfirstaid.org/external/2020/11/10-surprising-mental-health-statistics-from-2020/

4. Ibid., National Alliance of Mental Illness (NAMI). (2023).

5. Ibid., National Alliance of Mental Illness (NAMI). (2023).

6. National Institute of Mental Health (NIMH). (2023). *Mental illness.* https://www.nimh.nih.gov/health/statistics/mental-illness

7. Berman, R. (2022, April 12). *Teen mental health in the pandemic: CDC data 'echo a cry for help'.* Medical News Today. https://www.medicalnewstoday.com/articles/teen-mental-health-in-the-pandemic-cdc-data-echo-a-cry-for-help

8. Bridge, J. A., Ruch, D. A., Sheftall, A. H., Hahm, H. C., O'Keefe, V. M., Fontanella, C. A., Brock, G., Campo, J. V., & Horowitz, L. M. (2023). Youth suicide during the first year of the COVID-19 pandemic. *Pediatrics, 151*(3), Article e2022058375. https://doi.org/10.1542/peds.2022-058375

9. de Figueiredo, C. S., Sandre, P. C., Portugal, L. C. L., Mázala-de-Oliveira, T., Chagas, L. S., Raony, I., Ferreira, E. S., Giestal-de-Araujo, E., Dos Santos, A. A., & Bomfim, P. O. (2021). COVID-19 pandemic impact on children and adolescents' mental health: Biological, environmental, and social factors. *Progress in Neuro-Psychopharmacology and Biological Psychiatry, 106*(2). https://doi.org/10.1016/j.pnpbp.2020.110171

10. Centers for Disease Control and Prevention (CDC). (2022). *New CDC data illuminate youth mental health threats during the COVID-19 pandemic.* https://www.cdc.gov/media/releases/2022/p0331-youth-mental-health-covid-19.html

11. Centers for Disease Control and Prevention (CDC). (2022). *New CDC data illuminate youth mental health threats during*

the COVID-19 pandemic. https://www.cdc.gov/media/
releases/2022/p0331-youth-mental-health-covid-19.html

12. National Alliance of Mental Illness (NAMI). (2023).
     LGBTQI. https://www.nami.org/Your-Journey/
     Identity-and-Cultural-Dimensions/LGBTQI

13. National Alliance of Mental Illness (NAMI). *Suicide.*
     https://www.nami.org/NAMI/media/NAMI-Media/
     Infographics/NAMI_Suicide_2020_FINAL.pdf

14. Lees, B., Stapinski, L. A., Teesson, M., Squeglia, L. M., Jacobus,
     J., & Mewton, L. (2021). Problems experienced by chil-
     dren from families with histories of substance misuse: An
     ABCD study®. *Drug and Alcohol Dependence, 218*, 108403.
     https://doi.org/10.1016/j.drugalcdep.2020.108403

15. Calhoun, S., Conner, E., Miller, M., & Messina, N. (2015). Improving
     the outcomes of children affected by parental substance abuse:
     A review of randomized controlled trials. *Substance Abuse and
     Rehabilitation, 6*, 15–24. https://doi.org/10.2147/SAR.S46439

16. Wall, D. (2018). *Children & young adolescent anorexia.*
     https://www.eatingdisorderhope.com/risk-groups/
     eating-disorders-adolescents/she-is-so-young

17. Centers for Disease Control and Prevention [CDC]. (2019). *Preventing
     bullying. National Center for Injury Prevention and Control.* https://
     www.cdc.gov/violenceprevention/pdf/yv/bullying-factsheet508.pdf

18. Ibid., Centers for Disease Control and Prevention [CDC]. (2019).

19. Myklestad, I., & Straiton, M. (2021). The relationship between
     self-harm and bullying behaviour: results from a popula-
     tion based study of adolescents. *BMC Public Health, 21*(1),
     524. https://doi.org/10.1186/s12889-021-10555-9

20. Maurya, C., Muhammad, T., Das, A., Fathah, A., & Dhillon,
     P. (2023). The role of self-efficacy and parental communi-
     cation in the association between cyber victimization and
     depression among adolescents and young adults: a struc-
     tural equation model. *BMC Psychiatry, 23*(1), 337.

21. Conboy, L., & Mingoia, J. (2023). Social networking site use,
     self-compassion, and attitudes towards cosmetic surgery in
     young Australian women. *Journal of Technology in Behavioral
     Science.* 1-10. https://doi.org/10.1007/s41347-023-00334-1https://

link.springer.com/article/10.1007/s41347-023-00334-1https://
neurosciencenews.com/social-media-cosmetic-surgery-23976/

22.   Twenge J. M. (2020). Increases in depression, self-harm,
       and suicide among U.S. adolescents after 2012 and links to
       technology use: Possible mechanisms. *Psychiatric Research
       and Clinical Practice*, 2(1), 19–25. https://doi.org/10.1176/
       appi.prcp.20190015 https://pubmed.ncbi.nlm.nih.
       gov/36101887/#&gid=article-figures&pid=figure-2-uid-1

23.   The U.S. Surgeon General's Advisory. (2023). *Social media
       and youth mental health.* https://www.hhs.gov/sites/default/
       files/sg-youth-mental-health-social-media-advisory.pdf

24.   National Institute of Mental Health (NIMH). *Mental illness.*
       https://www.nimh.nih.gov/health/statistics/mental-illness

25.   Hodes, G.E., & Kropp, D.R. (2023). Sex as a biological variable
       in stress and mood disorder research. *Nature Mental Health*, 1,
       453–461 (2023). https://doi.org/10.1038/s44220-023-00083-3

26.   Ibid., National Institute of Mental Health (NIMH).

27.   CDC. (2023). *10 leading causes of death, United States.*
       https://wisqars.cdc.gov/data/lcd/home

28.   National Alliance on Mental Health (NAMH). (2022). *Mental
       health by the numbers.* https://www.nami.org/mhstats

29.   Ibid., National Alliance on Mental Health (NAMH). (2022).

30.   World Health Organization (WHO). (2022, March 2) stated
       that *COVID-19 pandemic triggers 25% increase in prevalence of
       anxiety and depression worldwide.* https://www.who.int/news/
       item/02-03-2022-covid-19-pandemic-triggers-25-increase-
       in-prevalence-of-anxiety-and-depression-worldwide

31.   National Institute on Mental Illness (NAMI). (2023). *Mental
       health by the numbers.* https://www.nami.org/mhstats

32.   Ibid., National Institute on Mental Illness (NAMI). (2023).

33.   National Institute of Mental Health (NIMH). (2023). *Child
       and adolescent mental health.* https://www.nimh.nih.gov/
       health/topics/child-and-adolescent-mental-health

34.   Office of Population Affairs. (2023). *Mental health for adolescents.*
       https://opa.hhs.gov/adolescent-health/mental-health-adolescents

35.   U.S. Department of Health and Human Services, National Institute of Mental Health. (2021). *Mental illness.* https://www. nimh.nih.gov/health/statistics/mental-illness.shtml

36.   U.S. Department of Health & Human Services. (2023). *What is mental health?* SAMHSA. https://www. samhsa.gov/mental-health/anxiety-disorders

37.   U.S. Department of Health & Human Services. (2023). *Depression.* https://www.samhsa.gov/mental-health/depression

38.   National Institute of Mental Health. (2023). *Depression.* https://www.nimh.nih.gov/health/topics/depression

39.   U.S. Department of Health and Human Services, National Institute of Mental Health. (2017). *Major depression.* https:// www.nimh.nih.gov/health/statistics/major-depression

40.   National Institute of Mental Health (2023). *Major depression.* https://www.nimh.nih.gov/health/statistics/major-depression

41.   MacSweeney, N., Allardyce, J., Edmondson-Stait, A., Shen, X., Casey, H., Chan, S. W. Y., Cullen, B., Reynolds, R. M., Frangou, S., Kwong, A. S. F., Lawrie, S. M., Romaniuk, L., & Whalley, H. C. (2023). The role of brain structure in the association between pubertal timing and depression risk in an early adolescent sample (the ABCD Study®): A registered report. *Developmental Cognitive Neuroscience, 60,* 101223. https://doi.org/10.1016/j.dcn.2023.101223

42.   Bridge, J. A., Ruch, D. A., Sheftall, A. H., Hahm, H. C., O'Keefe, V. M., Fontanella, C. A., Brock, G., Campo, J. V., & Horowitz, L. M. (2023). Youth suicide during the first year of the COVID-19 pandemic. *Pediatrics, 151*(3), Article e2022058375. https://doi.org/10.1542/peds.2022-058375

43.   CDC. (2023). *10 leading causes of death, United States.* https://wisqars.cdc.gov/data/lcd/home

44.   National Institute of Mental Health (NIMH): *Suicide prevention.* https://www.nimh.nih.gov/health/topics/suicide-prevention)

45.   National Alliance on Mental Illness. (NAMI). *How to talk (and listen) to someone experiencing suicidal thoughts.* https://www.nami. org/Blogs/NAMI-Blog/September-2021/How-to-Talk-%28and-Listen%29-to-Someone-Experiencing-Suicidal-Thoughts

46.   Ward, Z. J., Rodriguez, P., Wright, D. R., Austin, S. B., & Long, M. W. (2019). Estimation of eating disorders prevalence by

age and associations with mortality in a simulated nationally representative US cohort. *JAMA Network Open, 2*(10), e1912925. https://doi.org/10.1001/jamanetworkopen.2019.12925

47. Fellinger, M., Knasmüller, P., Kocsis-Bogar, K., Wippel, A., Fragner, L., Mairhofer, D., Hochgatterer, P., & Aigner, M. (2022). Adverse childhood experiences as risk factors for recurrent admissions in young psychiatric inpatients. *Frontiers in Psychiatry, 13, 988695. https://doi.org/10.3389/fpsyt.2022.988695*

48. Shin, S., You, I. J., Jeong, M., Bae, Y., Wang, X. Y., Cawley, M. L., Han, A., & Lim, B. K. (2023). Early adversity promotes binge-like eating habits by remodeling a leptin-responsive lateral hypothalamus–brainstem pathway. *Nature Neuroscience, 26,* 79–91. https://doi.org/10.1038/s41593-022-01208-0, https://www.nature.com/articles/s41593-022-01208-0

49. Chu, J., Raney, J. H., Ganson, K. T., Wu, K., Rupanagunta, A., Testa, A., Jackson, D. B., Murray, S. B., & Nagata, J. M. (2022). Adverse childhood experiences and binge-eating disorder in early adolescents. *Journal of Eating Disorders, 10*(1), 168. https://doi.org/10.1186/s40337-022-00682-y

50. Mayo Clinic. (2018). *Anorexia nervosa.* https://www.mayoclinic.org/diseases-conditions/anorexia-nervosa/symptoms-causes/syc-20353591

51. U.S. Department of Health and Human Services, National Institute of Mental Health. (2017). *Eating disorders.* https://www.nimh.nih.gov/health/statistics/eating-disorders

52. National Eating Disorders Association (NEDA).(2022). *Help & support.* https://www.nationaleatingdisorders.org/help-support

53. Ward, Z. J., Rodriguez, P., Wright, D. R., Austin, S. B., & Long, M. W. (2019). Estimation of eating disorders prevalence by age and associations with mortality in a simulated nationally representative US cohort. *JAMA Network Open, 2*(10), e1912925. https://doi.org/10.1001/jamanetworkopen.2019.12925

54. National Institute of Mental Health. (2023). *Eating disorders.* https://www.nimh.nih.gov/health/topics/eating-disorders

55. Jacobson, R. (n.d.). *College students and eating disorders: Why the first years away from home are a perfect storm for anorexia and bulimia.* Child Mind Institute. https://childmind.org/article/eating-disorders-and-college/

56. National Institute of Mental Health. (2017). *Eating disorders.* https://www.nimh.nih.gov/health/statistics/eating-disorders.shtml

57. Mayo Clinic. (2023). *Eating disorders.* https://www.mayoclinic.org/diseases-conditions/eating-disorders/symptoms-causes/syc-20353603

58. National Eating Disorders Association (NEDA). (2022). *Warning signs and symptoms.* https://www.nationaleatingdisorders.org/warning-signs-and-symptoms

59. River Walk Recovery Center. (2023). *7 early signs of an eating disorder.* https://riverwalkrecovery.com/7-early-signs-of-an-eating-disorder/

60. National Institute of Mental Health (NIMH). (2023). *Eating disorders.* https://www.nimh.nih.gov/health/topics/eating-disorders

61. Byrd, F. (2022). *Signs of an eating disorder.* WebMD. https://www.webmd.com/mental-health/eating-disorders/signs-of-eating-disorders

62. U.S. Department of Health and Human Services, National Institute of Mental Health. (2021). *Eating disorders: About more than food.* https://www.nimh.nih.gov/health/publications/eating-disorders?utm_campaign=shareNIMH&utm_medium=Portal&utm_source=NIMHwebsite

63. Hosseini, S. A., & Padhy, R. K. (2023). *Body image distortion.* In StatPearls. StatPearls Publishing. https://www.ncbi.nlm.nih.gov/books/NBK546582/

64. Shoraka, H., Amirkafi, A., & Garrusi, B. (2019). Review of body image and some of contributing factors in Iranian population. *International Journal of Preventive Medicine, 10,* 19. https://doi.org/10.4103/ijpvm.IJPVM_293_18

65. Alleva, J. M., Sheeran, P., Webb, T. L., Martijn, C., & Miles, E. (2015). A meta-analytic review of stand-alone interventions to improve body image. *PloS One, 10*(9), e0139177. https://doi.org/10.1371/journal.pone.0139177

66. Spreckelsen, P. V., Glashouwer, K. A., Bennik, E. C., Wessel, I., & de Jong, P. J. (2018). Negative body image: Relationships with heightened disgust propensity, disgust sensitivity, and self-directed disgust. *PloS One, 13*(6), e0198532. https://doi.org/10.1371/journal.pone.0198532

67. Sadibolova, R., Ferrè, E. R., Linkenauger, S. A., & Longo, M. R. (2019). Distortions of perceived volume and length of body parts. *Cortex, A Journal Devoted to the Study of the Nervous System and Behavior, 111,* 74–86. https://doi.org/10.1016/j.cortex.2018.10.016

68. Gaudio, S., Brooks, S. J., & Riva, G. (2014). Nonvisual multisensory impairment of body perception in anorexia nervosa: A systematic review of neuropsychological studies. *PloS One, 9*(10), e110087. https://doi.org/10.1371/journal.pone.0110087

69. Neuroscience Psychology. (May 23, 2023). *Social media filters impacting children's body image.* https://neurosciencenews.com/social-media-body-image-23318/

70. Ibid., Neuroscience Psychology. (May 23, 2023).

71. Choukas-Bradley, S., Roberts, S. R., Maheux, A. J., & Nesi, J. (2022). The perfect storm: A developmental-sociocultural framework for the role of social media in adolescent girls' body image concerns and mental health. *Clinical Child and Family Psychology Review,* 25(4), 681–701. https://doi.org/10.1007/s10567-022-00404-5

72. National Eating Disorders Association. (2022). *Media & eating disorders.* https://www.nationaleatingdisorders.org/media-eating-disorders

73. Castellanos-Ryan, N., O'Leary-Barrett, M., & Conrod, P. J. (2013). Substance-use in childhood and adolescence: A brief overview of developmental processes and their clinical implications. *Journal of the Canadian Academy of Child and Adolescent Psychiatry = Journal de l'Academie canadienne de psychiatrie de l'enfant et de l'adolescent, 22*(1), 41–46.

74. Trucco, E. M., & Hartmann, S. A. (2021). Understanding the etiology of adolescent substance use through developmental perspectives. *Child Development Perspectives,* 15(4), 257–264. https://doi.org/10.1111/cdep.12426

75. Paulus M. P. (2022). Neural substrates of substance use disorders. *Current Opinion in Neurology, 35*(4), 460–466. https://doi.org/10.1097/WCO.0000000000001077

76. Substance Abuse and Mental Health Services Administration. (2023). *SAMHSA announces national survey on drug use and health (NSDUH) results detailing mental illness and substance use levels in 2021.* https://www.samhsa.gov/newsroom/press-announcements/20230104/samhsa-announces-nsduh-results-detailing-mental-illness-substance-use-levels-2021

77.   CDC. (2022). *High-risk substance use among youth.* https://
        www.cdc.gov/healthyyouth/substance-use/index.htm

78.   Dellazizzo, L., Potvin, S., Giguère, S., & Dumais, A. (2022).
        Evidence on the acute and residual neurocognitive effects
        of cannabis use in adolescents and adults: A system-
        atic meta-review of meta-analyses. *Addiction (Abingdon,
        England), 117*(7), 1857–1870. https://doi.org/10.1111/add.15764

79.   Hjorthøj, C., Compton, W., Starzer, M., Nordholm, D.,
        Einstein, E., Erlangsen, A., Nordentoft, M., Volkow, N. D.,
        & Han, B. (2023). Association between cannabis use disor-
        der and schizophrenia stronger in young males than in
        females. *Psychological Medicine,* 1–7. Advance online publi-
        cation. https://doi.org/10.1017/S0033291723000880

80.   Neuroscience News. (2023). *Cannabis use disorder linked
        to increased schizophrenia risk in males.* https://neurosci-
        encenews.com/cud-male-schizophernia-23184/

81.   Anker, J. J., Thuras, P., Shuai, R., Hogarth, L., & Kushner, M. G.
        (2023). Evidence for an alcohol-related "harm paradox" in individu-
        als with internalizing disorders: Test and replication in two inde-
        pendent community samples. *Alcoholism, Clinical and Experimental
        Research, 47*(4), 713–723. https://doi.org/10.1111/acer.15036

82.   Office of Population Affairs. (2023). *Cognitive devel-
        opment.* https://opa.hhs.gov/adolescent-health/
        adolescent-development-explained/cognitive-development

83.   Maza, M. T., Fox, K. A., Kwon, S. J., Flannery, J. E., Lindquist, K.
        A., Prinstein, M. J., & Telzer, E. H. (2023). Association of habit-
        ual checking behaviors on social media with longitudinal func-
        tional brain development. *JAMA Pediatrics, 177*(2), 160-167. https://
        doi.org/10.1001/jamapediatrics.2022.4924, https://jamanet-
        work.com/journals/jamapediatrics/article-abstract/2799812

84.   Romeo R. D. (2017). The impact of stress on the struc-
        ture of the adolescent brain: Implications for adoles-
        cent mental health. *Brain Research, 1654*(Pt B), 185–191.
        https://doi.org/10.1016/j.brainres.2016.03.021

85.   Harvard Health Publishing. (2011). *The adolescent brain:
        Beyond raging hormones.* https://www.health.harvard.edu/
        mind-and-mood/the-adolescent-brain-beyond-raging-hormones

86.   World Health Organization (WHO). (2021). *Mental health of adolescents*. https://www.who.int/news-room/fact-sheets/detail/adolescent-mental-health

87.   Zhang, F. F., Peng, W., Sweeney, J. A., Jia, Z. Y., & Gong, Q. Y. (2018). Brain structure alterations in depression: Psychoradiological evidence. *CNS Neuroscience & Therapeutics, 24*(11), 994–1003. https://doi.org/10.1111/cns.12835

88.   Kenwood, M. M., Kalin, N. H., & Barbas, H. (2022). The prefrontal cortex, pathological anxiety, and anxiety disorders. *Neuropsychopharmacology: Official Publication of the American College of Neuropsychopharmacology, 47*(1), 260–275. https://doi.org/10.1038/s41386-021-01109-z

89.   Frostad, S., & Bentz, M. (2022). Anorexia nervosa: Outpatient treatment and medical management. *World Journal of Psychiatry, 12*(4), 558–579. https://doi.org/10.5498/wjp.v12.i4.558)

90.   Chang, Y. S., Liao, F. T., Huang, L. C., & Chen, S. L. (2023). The treatment experience of anorexia nervosa in adolescents from healthcare professionals' perspective: A qualitative study. *International Journal of Environmental Research and Public Health, 20*(1), 794. https://doi.org/10.3390/ijerph20010794

91.   Eating Disorder Hope. (n.d.). *Eating disorders among adolescents*. https://www.eatingdisorderhope.com/risk-groups/eating-disorders-adolescents

92.   Zagorski, N. (2023). *APA releases updated guideline for treating eating disorders*. https://doi.org/10.1176/appi.pn.2023.02.2.8, https://psychnews.psychiatryonline.org/doi/10.1176/appi.pn.2023.02.2.8

93.   Mayo Clinic. (n.d.). *Eating disorder treatment: Know your options*. https://www.mayoclinic.org/diseases-conditions/eating-disorders/in-depth/eating-disorder-treatment/art-20046234

94.   Myrvang, A. D., Vangberg, T. R., Linnman, C., Stedal, K., Rø, Ø., Endestad, T., Rosenvinge, J. H., & Aslaksen, P. M. (2021). Altered functional connectivity in adolescent anorexia nervosa is related to age and cortical thickness. *BMC Psychiatry, 21*(1), 490. https://doi.org/10.1186/s12888-021-03497-4

95.   The Emily Program. (n.d.). *How eating disorders affect the neurobiology of the brain*. https://emilyprogram.com/blog/how-eating-disorders-affect-the-neurobiology-of-the-brain/

96.   Olivo, G., Gaudio, S., & Schiöth, H. B. (2019). Brain and cognitive development in adolescents with anorexia nervosa: A systematic review of fMRI studies. *Nutrients, 11*(8), 1907. https://doi.org/10.3390/nu11081907

97.   Dellazizzo, L., Potvin, S., Giguère, S., & Dumais, A. (2022). Evidence on the acute and residual neurocognitive effects of cannabis use in adolescents and adults: A systematic meta-review of meta-analyses. *Addiction (Abingdon, England), 117*(7), 1857–1870. https://doi.org/10.1111/add.15764

98.   Ren, W., & Fishbein, D. (2023). Prospective, longitudinal study to isolate the impacts of marijuana use on neurocognitive functioning in adolescents. *Frontiers in Psychiatry, 14*, 1048791. https://doi.org/10.3389/fpsyt.2023.1048791

99.   Daviet, R., Aydogan, G., Jagannathan, K., Spilka, N., Koellinger, P. D., Kranzler, H. R., Nave, G., & Wetherill, R. R. (2022). Associations between alcohol consumption and gray and white matter volumes in the UK Biobank. *Nature Communications, 13*, 1175

100. Gronholm, P. C., Thornicroft, G., Laurens, K. R., & Evans-Lacko, S. (2017). Conditional disclosure on pathways to care: Coping preferences of young people at risk of psychosis. *Qualitative Health Research, 27*(12), 1842-1855.

101. Sheikhan, N. Y., Henderson, J. L., Halsall, T., Daley, M., Brownell, S., Shah, J., Iyer, S. N., & Hawke, L. D. (2023). Stigma as a barrier to early intervention among youth seeking mental health services in Ontario, Canada: A qualitative study. *BMC Health Services Research, 23*(1), 86. https://doi.org/10.1186/s12913-023-09075-6

102. Mayo Clinic. (2017). *Mental health: Overcoming the stigma of mental illness.* https://www.mayoclinic.org/diseases-conditions/mental-illness/in-depth/mental-health/art-20046477

103. University of Utah Health (2023). *Mental health is just as important as your physical health.* https://healthcare.utah.edu/healthfeed/2022/04/mental-health-just-important-your-physical-health

104. Bryant, E., Touyz, S., & Maguire, S. (2023). Public perceptions of people with eating disorders: Commentary on results from the 2022 Australian national survey of mental health-related stigma and discrimination. *Journal of Eating Disorders, 11*(1), 62. https://doi.org/10.1186/s40337-023-00786-z

105. Subu, M. A., Wati, D. F., Netrida, N., Priscilla, V., Dias, J. M., Abraham, M. S., Slewa-Younan, S., & Al-Yateem, N.

(2021). Types of stigma experienced by patients with mental illness and mental health nurses in Indonesia: A qualitative content analysis. *International Journal of Mental Health Systems, 15*(77). https://doi.org/10.1186/s13033-021-00502-x

106. Lannin, D. G., Vogel, D. L., Brenner, R. E., Abraham, W. T., & Heath, P. J. (2016). Does self-stigma reduce the probability of seeking mental health information? *Journal of Counseling Psychology, 63*(3), 351–358. https://doi.org/10.1037/cou0000108

107. Mayo Clinic. (2017). *Mental health: Overcoming the stigma of mental illness.* https://www.mayoclinic.org/diseases-conditions/mental-illness/in-depth/mental-health/art-20046477

108. National Alliance on Mental Health (NAMH). (n.d.). *Support group.* https://www.nami.org/Support-Education/Support-Groups

109. Ibid., National Alliance on Mental Health (NAMH).

110. DeLuca, J.S. (2020). Conceptualizing adolescent mental illness stigma: Youth stigma development and stigma reduction programs. *Adolescent Research Review 5,* 153–171. https://doi.org/10.1007/s40894-018-0106-3

111. Lockett, E. (2022). *How we can change the stigma around mental health.* https://www.healthline.com/health/mental-health/mental-health-stigma-examples

112. The American Academy of Child and Adolescent Psychiatry. (2023). *Stress management and teens.* https://www.aacap.org/AACAP/Families_and_Youth/Facts_for_Families/FFF-Guide/Helping-Teenagers-With-Stress-066.aspx

113. Scott, E. (2023). *Top 10 stress management techniques for students.* https://www.verywellmind.com/top-school-stress-relievers-for-students-3145179

114. Adolescent Psychiatry. (2021). *Teen stress: Biggest triggers & 7 ways to copy.* https://www.adolescent-psychiatry.org/teen-stress-biggest-triggers-ways-to-cope/

115. American Psychological Association. (2022). *How to help children and teens manage their stress.* https://www.apa.org/topics/children/stress

116. Sudimac, S., Sale, V. & Kühn, S. (2022). How nature nurtures: Amygdala activity decreases as the result of a one-hour walk in nature. *Molecular Psychiatry.* https://doi.org/10.1038/s41380-022-01720-6

117.   Mavrantza, A. M., Bigliassi, M., Calogiuri,G. (2023). Psychophysiological mechanisms underlying the effects of outdoor green and virtual green exercise during self-paced walking. *International Journal of Psychophysiology, 184,* 39-50. https://doi.org/10.1016/j.ijpsycho.2022.12.006

118.   Cornell University. (2020). *Spending time in nature reduces stress.* ScienceDaily. 25 https://www.science-daily.com/releases/2020/02/200225164210.htm

119.   Meredith, G. R., Rakow, D. A., Eldermire, E. R. B., Madsen, C. G., Shelley, S. P., & Sachs, N. A. (2020). Minimum time dose in nature to positively impact the mental health of college-aged students, and how to measure it: A scoping review. *Frontiers in Psychology, 10,* 2942. https://doi.org/10.3389/fpsyg.2019.02942

120.   American Academy of Sleep Medicine (AASM). (2023). *Video games and social media: Factors disrupting healthy student sleep.* https://aasm.org/video-games-and-social-media-factors-disrupting-healthy-student-sleep/

121.   Ibid., American Academy of Sleep Medicine (AASM). (2023).

122.   Lokhandwala, S., & Spencer, R. M. C. (2022). Relations between sleep patterns early in life and brain development: A review. *Developmental Cognitive Neuroscience, 56,* 101130. https://doi.org/10.1016/j.dcn.2022.101130, https://www.science-direct.com/science/article/pii/S1878929322000731

123.   Columbia University, Department of Psychiatry. (2022). *How sleep deprivation impacts mental health.* https://www.columbia-psychiatry.org/news/how-sleep-deprivation-affects-your-men-tal-health#:~:text=Sleep%20helps%20maintain%20cognitive%20skills,to%20perceive%20the%20world%20accurately.

124.   National Institute of Health. (2022). *How sleep affects your health.* https://www.nhlbi.nih.gov/health/sleep-depriva-tion/health-effects#:~:text=Studies%20also%20show%20that%20sleep,%2C%20and%20risk-taking%20behavior

125.   University of Maryland, Medical System. (2023). *The connec-tion between not getting enough sleep and mental Health.* https://health.umms.org/2023/03/15/sleep-deprivation-mental-health/

126.   National Institute of Health. (2022). *Children's sleep linked to brain development.* https://www.nih.gov/news-events/nih-research-matters/children-s-sleep-linked-brain-development

127. Lokhandwala, S., & Spencer, R. M. C. (2022). Relations between sleep patterns early in life and brain development: A review. *Developmental Cognitive Neuroscience, 56,* 101130. https://doi.org/10.1016/j.dcn.2022.101130, https://www.science-direct.com/science/article/pii/S1878929322000731

128. Alrousan, G., Hassan, A., Pillai, A. A., Atrooz, F., & Salim, S. (2022). Early life sleep deprivation and brain develop-ment: Insights from human and animal studies. *Frontiers in Neuroscience, 16,* 833786. https://doi.org/10.3389/fnins.2022.833786, https://www.ncbi.nlm.nih.gov/pmc/articles/PMC9111737/

129. Cherry, K. (2023). *Effects of lack of sleep on mental health.* https://www.verywellmind.com/how-sleep-affects-mental-health-4783067

130. Cusick, S. E., & Georgieff, M. K. (2016). The role of nutri-tion in brain development: The golden opportunity of the "first 1000 days". *The Journal of Pediatrics, 175,* 16–21. https://doi.org/10.1016/j.jpeds.2016.05.013

131. Kanellopoulos, A. K., Costello, S., Mainardi, F., Koshibu, K., Deoni, S., & Schneider, N. (2023). Dynamic interplay between social brain development and nutrient intake in young chil-dren. *Nutrients, 15*(17), 3754. https://doi.org/10.3390/nu15173754

132. Roberts, M., Tolar-Peterson, T., Reynolds, A., Wall, C., Reeder, N., & Rico Mendez, G. (2022). The effects of nutritional interventions on the cognitive development of preschool-age children: A systematic review. *Nutrients, 14*(3), 532. https://doi.org/10.3390/nu14030532

133. Danielsen, K. K., Cabral, D., & Sveaas, S. H. (2023). "Students moving together", tailored exercise for students facing mental health chal-lenges-A pilot feasibility study. *International Journal of Environmental Research and Public Health, 20*(17), 6639. https://doi.org/10.3390/ijerph20176639, https://pubmed.ncbi.nlm.nih.gov/37681779/

134. Neuroscience News. (2023). *Unleashing the mind: The neuro-science of meditation and its impact on memory.* https://neurosciencenews.com/memory-meditation-23414/

135. Luders, E., Toga, A. W., Lepore, N., & Gaser, C. (2009). The under-lying anatomical correlates of long-term meditation: larger hippo-campal and frontal volumes of gray matter. *NeuroImage, 45*(3), 672–678. https://doi.org/10.1016/j.neuroimage.2008.12.061

136. Hernández, S. E., Suero, J., Barros, A., González-Mora, J. L., & Rubia, K. (2016). Increased grey matter associated with long-term

Sahaja yoga meditation: A voxel-based morphometry study. *PloS One*, *11*(3), e0150757. https://doi.org/10.1371/journal.pone.0150757

137.   Bukar, N. K., Eberhardt, L. M., & Davidson, J. (2019). East meets west in psychiatry: Yoga as an adjunct therapy for management of anxiety. *Archives of Psychiatric Nursing*, *33*(4), 371–376. https://doi.org/10.1016/j.apnu.2019.04.007

138.   van der Kolk, B., (2014). *The body keeps score: The brain, mind, and body in the healing of trauma*. Penguin Books.

139.   Gordon, J. S., Sbarra, D., Armin, J., Pace, T. W. W., Gniady, C., & Barraza, Y. (2021). Use of a guided imagery mobile App (See Me Serene) to reduce COVID-19-related stress: Pilot feasibility study. *JMIR Formative Research*, *5*(10), e32353. https://doi.org/10.2196/32353

140.   Ash, E., Sgroi, D., Tuckwell, A., & Zhuo, S. (2023). Mindfulness reduces information avoidance. *Economics Letters*, *224*. https://doi.org/10.1016/j.econlet.2023.110997, https://www.sciencedirect.com/science/article/pii/S0165176523000228

141.   Barton, Y. A., & Miller, L. (2015). Spirituality and positive psychology go hand in hand: An investigation of multiple empirically derived profiles and related protection benefits. *Journal of Religion and Health*, *54*(3), 829–843. https://doi.org/10.1007/s10943-015-0045-2

142.   Ford, T., Lipson, J., & Miller, L. (2023). Spiritually grounded character: A latent profile analysis. *Frontiers in Psychology*, *13*, 1061416. https://doi.org/10.3389/fpsyg.2022.1061416

143.   Faulhaber, M. E., Lee, J. E., Team, P., & Gentile, D. A. (2023). The effect of self-monitoring limited social media use on psychological well-being. *Technology, Mind, and Behavior*, *4*(2: Summer 2023). https://doi.org/10.1037/tmb0000111

144.   National Institute of Mental Health (NIMH). (2023). *Child and adolescent mental health*. https://www.nimh.nih.gov/health/topics/child-and-adolescent-mental-health

145.   World Health Organization (WHO). (2020, September 28). *Adolescent mental health*. https://www.who.int/news-room/fact-sheets/detail/adolescent-mental-health

146.   Witt, K., Milner, A., Chastang, J. F., LaMontagne, A. D., & Niedhammer, I. (2019). Employment and occupational outcomes following adolescent-onset mental illness: Analysis of a nationally representative French cohort. *Journal of Public Health (Oxford, England)*, *41*(3), 618-627. https://doi.org/10.1093/pubmed/fdy160

147.   Tayfur, S. N., Prior, S., Roy, A. S., Maciver, D., Forsyth, K., &
         Fitzpatrick, L. I. (2022). Associations between adolescent psycho-
         social factors and disengagement from education and employ-
         ment in young adulthood among individuals with common
         mental health problems. *Journal of Youth and Adolescence, 51*(7),
         1397–1408. https://doi.org/10.1007/s10964-022-01592-7

Chapter 14: How not to Let Childhood Trauma Interfere Your Brain Development

1.   Centers for Disease Control and Preventions. (CDC). *Fast
        facts: Preventing adverse childhood experiences.* https://
        www.cdc.gov/violenceprevention/aces/fastfact.html

2.   National Conference of State Legislatures. (2023).
        Adverse childhood experiences. https://www.ncsl.
        org/health/adverse-childhood-experiences

3.   Giano, Z., Wheeler, D. L., & Hubach, R. D. (2020).
        The frequencies and disparities of adverse child-
        hood experiences in the U.S. *BMC Public Health, 20*(1),
        1327. https://pubmed.ncbi.nlm.nih.gov/32907569/

4.   Merrick, M. T., Ford, D. C., Ports, K. A., & Guinn, A. S. (2018).
        Prevalence of adverse childhood experiences from the
        2011-2014 behavioral risk factor surveillance system in 23
        states. *JAMA Pediatrics, 172*(11), 1038-1044. https://jamanet-
        work.com/journals/jamapediatrics/fullarticle/2702204

5.   SmithBattle, L., Loman, D. G., Yoo, J. H., Cibulka, N., & Rariden, C.
        (2022). Evidence for revising the Adverse Childhood Experiences
        Screening Tool: A scoping review. *Journal of Child & Adolescent
        Trauma, 15*(1), 89–103. https://doi.org/10.1007/s40653-021-00358-w

6.   Centers for Disease Control and Preventions. (CDC). (2022).
        Fast facts: Preventing adverse childhood experiences. https://
        www.cdc.gov/violenceprevention/aces/fastfact.html

7.   Merrick, M. T., Ford, D. C., Ports, K. A., Guinn, A. S., Chen,
        J., Klevens, J., Metzler, M., Jones, C. M., Simon, T. R., Daniel,
        V. M., Ottley, P., Mercy, J. A. (2019). Vital signs: Estimated
        proportion of adult health problems attributable to adverse
        childhood experiences and implications for prevention —
        25 States, 2015–2017. *Morbidity and Mortality Weekly Report
        (MMWR), 68*(44), 999-1005. https://www.cdc.gov/mmwr/
        volumes/68/wr/mm6844e1.htm?s_cid=mm6844e1_w

8.   Giano, Z., Wheeler, D. L., & Hubach, R. D. (2020).
     The frequencies and disparities of adverse child-
     hood experiences in the U.S. *BMC Public Health, 20*(1),
     1327. https://pubmed.ncbi.nlm.nih.gov/32907569/

9.   Merrick, M. T., Ford, D. C., Ports, K. A., & Guinn, A. S. (2018).
     Prevalence of adverse childhood experiences from the
     2011-2014 behavioral risk factor surveillance system in 23
     states. *JAMA Pediatrics, 172*(11), 1038-1044. https://jamanet-
     work.com/journals/jamapediatrics/fullarticle/2702204

10. Shonkoff, J. P., Garner, A. S., Committee on Psychosocial
     Aspects of Child and Family Health, Committee on Early
     Childhood, Adoption, and Dependent Care, & Section on
     Developmental and Behavioral Pediatrics. (2012). The lifelong
     effects of early childhood adversity and toxic stress. *Pediatrics,*
     129(1), e232–e246. https://doi.org/10.1542/peds.2011-2663

11. Hostinar, C. E., Swartz, J. R., Alen, N. V., Guyer, A. E., &
     Hastings, P. D. (2023). The role of stress phenotypes in under-
     standing childhood adversity as a transdiagnostic risk factor
     for psychopathology. *Journal of Psychopathology and Clinical*
     Science, 132(3), 277–286. https://doi.org/10.1037/abn0000619

12. Center on the Developing Child. (n.d.). *Toxic stress.*
     Harvard University. https://developingchild.harvard.
     edu/science/key-concepts/toxic-stress/

13. Fung, H. W., Chien, W. T., Lam, S. K. K., & Ross, C. A.
     (2022). The relationship between dissociation and complex
     post-traumatic stress disorder: A scoping review. *Trauma,*
     Violence & Abuse, 15248380221120835. Advance online publi-
     cation. https://doi.org/10.1177/15248380221120835

14. Herman, J. L. (2015). *Trauma and recovery: The aftermath of*
     violence--from domestic abuse to political terror. Basic Books.
     https://www.amazon.com/Trauma-Recovery-Aftermath-
     Violence-Political-ebook-dp-B00X2ZW918/dp/B00X2ZW918/
     ref=mt_other?_encoding=UTF8&me=&qid=1648609785

15. U.S. Department of Veterans Affairs. (n.d.). *Complex PTSD.* https://
     www.ptsd.va.gov/professional/treat/essentials/complex_ptsd.asp

16. Centers for Disease Control and Prevention (CDC). (2021). *Adverse*
     childhood experiences (ACEs) - Preventing early trauma to improve
     adult health. https://www.cdc.gov/vitalsigns/aces/index.html

17. Neal, E. (2021). *Trauma and brain development in children.* https://www.mercyhome.org/resources/trauma-and-brain-development-in-children/

18. Cowell, R. A., Cicchetti, D., Rogosch, F. A., & Toth, S. L. (2015). Childhood maltreatment and its effect on neurocognitive functioning: Timing and chronicity matter. *Development and Psychopathology, 27*(2), 521–533. https://doi.org/10.1017/S0954579415000139

19. D'Orazio, S. (2016). Assessing the impact of adverse childhood experiences on brain development. *Inquiries Journal. 8*(7). http://www.inquiriesjournal.com/articles/1429/2/assessing-the-impact-of-adverse-childhood-experiences-on-brain-development

20. Bick, J., & Nelson, C. A. (2016). Early adverse experiences and the developing brain. *Neuropsychopharmacology: Official Publication of the American College of Neuropsychopharmacology, 41*(1), 177–196. https://doi.org/10.1038/npp.2015.252

21. Gary Donohoe, G. (2022). *How adverse childhood experiences shape our brains.* https://www.bps.org.uk/psychologist/how-adverse-childhood-experiences-shape-our-brains

22. Berthelsen, D., Hayes, N., White, S. L. J., & Williams, K. E. (2017). Executive function in adolescence: Associations with child and family risk factors and self-regulation in early childhood. *Frontiers in Psychology, 8*, 903. https://doi.org/10.3389/fpsyg.2017.00903

23. Teicher, M. H., Anderson, C. M., & Polcari, A. (2012). Childhood maltreatment is associated with reduced volume in the hippocampal subfields CA3, dentate gyrus, and subiculum. *Proceedings of the National Academy of Sciences of the United States of America, 109*(9), E563–E572. https://doi.org/10.1073/pnas.1115396109

24. Teicher, M. H., Samson, J. A., Anderson, C. M., & Ohashi, K. (2016). The effects of childhood maltreatment on brain structure, function, and connectivity. *Nature Reviews Neuroscience, 17*(10), 652-666.

25. De Bellis, M. D., & Zisk, A. (2014). The biological effects of childhood trauma. *Child and Adolescent Psychiatric Clinics of North America, 23*(2), 185–vii. https://doi.org/10.1016/j.chc.2014.01.002

26. Ibid., Centers for Disease Control and Preventions. (CDC).

27. Mehari, K., Iyengar, S., Schneider, M., Berg, K., & Bennett, A. (2021). Adverse childhood experiences among children with neurodevelopmental delays: Relations to diagnoses, behavioral health, and

clinical Severity. *Journal of Clinical Psychology in Medical Settings,* 28(4), 808–814. https://doi.org/10.1007/s10880-021-09769-1

28. Ibid., Neal, E. (2021).

29. Ditzer, J., Wong, E. Y., Modi, R. N., Behnke, M., Gross, J. J., & Talmon, A. (2023). Child maltreatment and alexithymia: A meta-analytic review. *Psychological Bulletin,* 10.1037/bul0000391. Advance online publication. https://doi.org/10.1037/bul0000391

30. Khan, A. N., & Jaffee, S. R. (2022). Alexithymia in individuals maltreated as children and adolescents: A meta-analysis. *Journal of Child Psychology and Psychiatry, and Allied Disciplines,* 63(9), 963–972. https://doi.org/10.1111/jcpp.13616

31. Copeland, W. E., Wolke, D., Lereya, S. T., Shanahan, L., Worthman, C., & Costello, E. J. (2014). Childhood bullying involvement predicts low-grade systemic inflammation into adulthood. *Proceedings of the National Academy of Sciences of the United States of America,* 111(21), 7570–7575. https://doi.org/10.1073/pnas.1323641111

32. Anderson, A. S., Siciliano, R. E., Pillai, A., Jiang, W., & Compas, B. E. (2023). Parental drug use disorders and youth psychopathology: Meta-analytic review. *Drug and Alcohol Dependence,* 244, 109793. https://doi.org/10.1016/j.drugalcdep.2023.109793

33. Calhoun, S., Conner, E., Miller, M., & Messina, N. (2015). Improving the outcomes of children affected by parental substance abuse: A review of randomized controlled trials. *Substance Abuse and Rehabilitation,* 6, 15–24. https://doi.org/10.2147/SAR.S46439

34. Hines, L. A., Jones, H. J., Hickman, M., Lynskey, M., Howe, L. D., Zammit, S., & Heron, J. (2023). Adverse childhood experiences and adolescent cannabis use trajectories: Findings from a longitudinal UK birth cohort. *The Lancet Public Health, 8*(6). e442-e452, https://doi.org/10.1016/S2468-2667(23)00095-6

35. Afifi, T. O., Taillieu, T., Salmon, S., Davila, I. G., Stewart-Tufescu, A., Fortier, J., Struck, S., Asmundson, G., Sareen, J., & MacMillan, H. L. (2020). Adverse childhood experiences (ACEs), peer victimization, and substance use among adolescents. *Child Abuse & Neglect, 106,* 104504. https://doi.org/10.1016/j.chiabu.2020.104504

36. Mateos-Aparicio, P., & Rodríguez-Moreno, A. (2019). The impact of studying brain plasticity. *Frontiers in Cellular Neuroscience, 13,* 66. https://doi.org/10.3389/fncel.2019.00066

37.   Physiopedia. (n.d.). *Neuroplasticity.* https://www.physio-pedia. com/Neuroplasticity#cite_note-Mosby's_Medical_Dictionary-7

38.   Puderbaugh, M., & Emmady, P. D. (2022). *Neuroplasticity.* National Library of Medicine. https:// www.ncbi.nlm.nih.gov/books/NBK557811/

39.   Abrams, Z. (2022). What neuroscience tells us about the teenage brain: New research now turns an old assumption on its head, as psychologists seek to optimize social contexts and environments for developing minds. *American Psychological Association, 53*(5), 66. https://www.apa.org/ monitor/2022/07/feature-neuroscience-teen-brain

40.   National Institute on Mental Health (NIMH). (2023). *The teen brain: 7 things to know.* https://www.nimh.nih.gov/ health/publications/the-teen-brain-7-things-to-know

41.   Zimmerman, M. A., Stoddard, S. A., Eisman, A. B., Caldwell, C. H., Aiyer, S. M., & Miller, A. (2013). Adolescent resilience: Promotive factors that inform prevention. *Child Development Perspectives, 7*(4), 10.1111/cdep.12042. https://doi.org/10.1111/cdep.12042

42.   Ibid., Zimmerman, M. A., Stoddard, S. A., Eisman, A. B., Caldwell, C. H., Aiyer, S. M., & Miller, A. (2013).

43.   Mesman, E., Vreeker, A., & Hillegers, M. (2021). Resilience and mental health in children and adolescents: An update of the recent literature and future directions. *Current Opinion in Psychiatry, 34*(6), 586–592. https://doi.org/10.1097/YCO.0000000000000741

44.   Pinto, T. M., Laurence, P, G., Macedo, C, R., & Macedo, E. C. (2021). Resilience programs for children and adolescents: A systematic review and meta-analysis. *Frontiers in Psychology, 12.* https://doi.org/10.3389/fpsyg.2021.754115

45.   Fergus, S., & Zimmerman, M. A. (2005). Adolescent resilience: A framework for understanding healthy development in the face of risk. *Annual Review of Public Health, 26,* 399–419. https://doi.org/10.1146/annurev.publhealth.26.021304.144357

46.   Ibid., Zimmerman, M. A., Stoddard, S. A., Eisman, A. B., Caldwell, C. H., Aiyer, S. M., & Miller, A. (2013).

47.   Zimmerman, M.A. (2013). Resiliency theory: A strengths-based approach to research and practice for adolescent health. *Health Education and Behavior, 40*(4), 381–383.

https://doi.org/10.1177/1090198113493782 or https://jour-nals.sagepub.com/doi/10.1177/1090198113493782

48.   Zolkoski, S. M., & Bullock, L. M. (2012). Resilience in children and youth: A review. *Children and Youth Services Review, 34*(12), 2295-2303.

49.   Masten, A. S. (2018). Resilience theory and research on children and families: Past, present, and promise. *Journal of Family Theory & Review, 10*(1), 12-31. doi: 10.1111/jftr.12245

50.   Taylor, J., McLean, L., Korner, A., Stratton, E., & Glozier, N. (2020). Mindfulness and yoga for psychological trauma: Systematic review and meta-analysis. *Journal of Trauma & Dissociation: The Official Journal of the International Society for the Study of Dissociation (ISSD), 21*(5), 536–573. https://doi.org/10.1080/15299732.2020.1760167

51.   Moyes, E., Nutman, G., & Mirman, J. H. (2022). The efficacy of targeted mindfulness-based interventions for improving mental health and cognition among youth and adults with ACE histories: A systematic mixed studies review. *Journal of Child & Adolescent Trauma, 15*(4), 1165–1177. https://doi.org/10.1007/s40653-022-00454-5

52.   Leigh-Hunt, N., Bagguley, D., Bash, K., Turner, V., Turnbull, S., Valtorta, N., & Caan, W. (2017). An overview of systematic reviews on the public health consequences of social isolation and loneliness. *Public Health, 152,* 157-171.

53.   Knopf, A. (2020). Prepare for increased depression, anxiety in youth due to COVID-19 lockdown. *Brown University Child & Adolescent Psychopharmacology Update, 22*(8), 1-4. https://doi.org/10.1002/cpu.30511

54.   Orben, A., Tomova, L., & Blakemore, S. (2020). The effects of social deprivation on adolescent development and mental health. *The Lancet Child & Adolescent Health, 4*(8), 634-640. https://www.thelancet.com/pdfs/journals/lanchi/PIIS2352-4642(20)30186-3.pdf

55.   Morris, A. S., Squeglia, L. M., Jacobus, J., & Silk, J. S. (2018). Adolescent brain development: Implications for understanding risk and resilience processes through neuroimaging research. *Journal of Research on Adolescence (Wiley-Blackwell), 28*(1), 4-9.

56.   Villalta, L., Smith, P., Hickin, N., & Stringaris, A. (2018). Emotion regulation difficulties in traumatized youth: A meta-analysis and conceptual review. *European Child and Adolescent Psychiatry, 27*(4), 527-544.

57.   Ibid., Orben, A., Tomova, L., & Blakemore, S. (2020).

58.   Volunteer Match - *Find the best volunteer opportunities.*
      https://www.volunteermatch.org/search/?v=true

59.   Baumeister, R. F., & Leary, M. R. (1995). The need to belong:
      Desire for interpersonal attachments as a fundamental
      human motivation. *Psychological Bulletin, 117*(3), 497-529.

60.   Mala, J., McGarry, J., Riley, K. E., Lee, E. C., & DiStefano, L. (2020).
      The relationship between physical activity and executive functions
      among youth in low-income urban schools in the northeast and
      southwest United States. *Journal of Sport & Exercise Psychology,* 1–15.
      Advance online publication. https://doi.org/10.1123/jsep.2019-0111

61.   Contreras-Osorio, F., Guzmán-Guzmán, I. P., Cerda-Vega, E.,
      Chirosa-Ríos, L., Ramírez-Campillo, R., & Campos-Jara, C.
      (2022). Anthropometric parameters, physical activity, physical
      fitness, and executive functions among primary school chil-
      dren. *International Journal of Environmental Research and Public
      Health, 19*(5), 3045. https://doi.org/10.3390/ijerph19053045

62.   Hillman, C. H., Erickson, K. I., & Kramer, A. F. (2008). Be smart,
      exercise your heart: Exercise effects on brain and cognition. *Nature
      Reviews Neuroscience, 19*(11), 648-660.
      https://doi.org/10.1038/nrn2298
      https://www.nature.com/articles/nrn2298)

63.   Stults-Kolehmainen, M. A., & Sinha, R. (2014). The effects of
      stress on physical activity and exercise. *Sports Medicine (Auckland,
      N.Z.), 44*(1), 81–121. https://doi.org/10.1007/s40279-013-0090-5

64.   Alarcón, L. F., Castillo-Martínez, L., & Sánchez-Alcaraz, B. J.
      (2020). The relationship between physical activity and exec-
      utive function in children: A systematic review. *International
      Journal of Environmental Research and Public Health, 17*(21), 7898.

65.   Contreras-Osorio, F., Guzmán-Guzmán, I. P., Cerda-Vega, E.,
      Chirosa-Ríos, L., Ramírez-Campillo, R., & Campos-Jara, C. (2022).
      Effects of the type of sports practice on the executive functions of
      schoolchildren. *International Journal of Environmental Research and
      Public Health, 19*(7), 3886. https://doi.org/10.3390/ijerph19073886

66.   van der Kolk, B. A., Stone, L., West, J., Rhodes, A., Emerson,
      D., Suvak, M., & Spinazzola, J. (2014). Yoga as an adjunc-
      tive treatment for posttraumatic stress disorder: A random-
      ized controlled trial. *The Journal of Clinical Psychiatry, 75*(6),
      e559–e565. https://doi.org/10.4088/JCP.13m08561

67. Bruce, E. S., Lunt, L., & McDonagh, J. E. (2017). Sleep in adolescents and young adults. *Clinical Medicine (London, England)*, *17*(5), 424–428. https://doi.org/10.7861/clinmedicine.17-5-424)

68. Stavrou, N. A. M., Psychogiou, L., & Parry, E. (2019). Sleep during adolescence: The importance of a biopsychosocial approach. *Adolescent Health, Medicine and Therapeutics*, *10*, 23-35.

69. Psychology Today. (2022). *Trauma-focused cognitive behavior therapy*. https://www.psychologytoday.com/us/therapy-types/trauma-focused-cognitive-behavior-therapy

70. Brunzell, T., Waters, L., & Stokes, H. (2015). Teaching with strengths in trauma-affected students: A new approach to healing and growth in the classroom. *The American Journal of Orthopsychiatry*, *85*(1), 3–9. https://doi.org/10.1037/ort0000048

71. Lohmiller, K., Gruber, H., Harpin, S., Belansky, E. S., James, K. A., Pfeiffer, J. P., & Leiferman, J. (2022). The S.I.T.E. framework: A novel approach for sustainably integrating trauma-informed approaches in schools. *Journal of Child & Adolescent Trauma*, *15*(4), 1011–1027. https://doi.org/10.1007/s40653-022-00461-6

72. Lieneman, C. C., Brabson, L. A., Highlander, A., Wallace, N. M., & McNeil, C. B. (2017). Parent-child interaction therapy: Current perspectives. *Psychology Research and Behavior Management*, *10*, 239–256. https://doi.org/10.2147/PRBM.S91200

73. Woodfield, M. J., Merry, S., & Hetrick, S. E. (2022). Clinician adoption of parent-child interaction therapy: A systematic review of implementation interventions. *Implementation Research and Practice*, *3*, 26334895221082330. https://doi.org/10.1177/26334895221082330

74. Allen, K. (2023, September 19). *The Lahaina Banyan tree: New leaves have sprouted*. HAWAI'I Magazine. https://www.hawaiimagazine.com/a-ray-of-hope-the-lahaina-banyan-tree/

75. Suarez, G. L., Burt, S. A., Gard, A. M., Klump, K. L., & Hyde, L. W. (2024). Exposure to community violence as a mechanism linking neighborhood disadvantage to amygdala reactivity and the protective role of parental nurturance. *Developmental Psychology*, 10.1037/dev0001712. Advance online publication. https://doi.org/10.1037/dev0001712

76. The White House. (2023). *A proclamation on National Foster Care Month, 2023*. https://www.whitehouse.gov/briefing-room/presidential-actions/2023/04/28/a-proc-

lamation-on-national-foster-care-month-2023/#:~:-
text=We%20recognize%20the%20biological%20
parents,find%20temporary%20and%20permanent%20homes

77.   Fishman-Weaver, K. (2024). *Supporting students navigat-
       ing the foster care system: Teachers can provide resources and
       stability to students in foster care to help ensure that school
       feels safe and inclusive for them.* Edutopia. https://www.
       edutopia.org/article/supporting-students-foster-care

Chapter 15: Transformation through the Confidence in Yourself

1.   National Institute of Mental Health (NIMH). (2023). *The
       teen brain: 7 things to know.* https://www.nimh.nih.gov/
       health/publications/the-teen-brain-7-things-to-know

2.   Morin, A. (n.d.). *What is growth mindset?* Understood.
       https://www.understood.org/en/articles/growth-mindset

3.   Dweck, C. S. (2006). *Mindset: The new psychol-
       ogy of success.* Random House.

4.   Dweck, C. S. (2016). *What having a "growth mindset" actually
       means.* Harvard Business Review. https://hbr.org/2016/01/
       what-having-a-growth-mindset-actually-means

5.   Carrots, P. (2021). *Growth mindset: The science of failure and neuro-
       plasticity.* https://jamesegerton.wordpress.com/2021/02/27/
       growth-mindset-the-science-of-failure-and-neuroplasticity/

6.   Burns. S. (2023). *Neuroscience: You will never lack motiva-
       tion again.* https://www.newtraderu.com/2023/02/25/
       neuroscience-you-will-never-lack-motivation-again/

7.   Sutton, J. (2021). *18 best growth mindset activities, worksheets, and
       questions,* https://positivepsychology.com/growth-mindset/

8.   Sigmundsson, H., & Hauge, H. (2023). I CAN Intervention to
       Increase Grit and Self-Efficacy: A Pilot Study. *Brain Sciences,*
       14(1), 33. https://doi.org/10.3390/brainsci14010033

9.   Ibid., Sigmundsson, H., & Hauge, H. (2023).

10.   Wang, S., Dai, J., Li, J., Wang, X., Chen, T., Yang, X., He, M., &
       Gong, Q. (2018). Neuroanatomical correlates of grit: Growth
       mindset mediates the association between gray matter

structure and trait grit in late adolescence. *Human Brain Mapping, 39*(4), 1688–1699. https://doi.org/10.1002/hbm.23944

11. Ibid., Sutton, J. (2021).

12. Davis, T. (2019). *15 ways to build a growth mindset. Want to increase your chances of success? Then develop your growth mindset.* Psychology Today. https://www.psychologytoday.com/us/blog/click-here-happiness/201904/15-ways-build-growth-mindset

13. Catahan, S. (2021). *13 ways to actually build confidence in yourself, from experts.* https://www.mindbodygreen.com/articles/how-to-build-confidence

14. Robbins, T. (n.d.). *18 tips for being confident from within.* https://www.tonyrobbins.com/building-confidence/how-to-be-confident/

15. Yeager, D. S., Hanselman, P., Walton, G. M., Murray, J. S., Crosnoe, R., Muller, C., Tipton, E., Schneider, B., Hulleman, C. S., Hinojosa, C. P., Paunesku, D., Romero, C., Flint, K., Roberts, A., Trott, J., Iachan, R., Buontempo, J., Yang, S. M., Carvalho, C. M., Hahn, P. R., … Dweck, C. S. (2019). A national experiment reveals where a growth mindset improves achievement. *Nature, 573*(7774), 364–369. https://doi.org/10.1038/s41586-019-1466-y

16. Porter, T., Catalán Molina, D., Cimpian, A., Roberts, S., Fredericks, A., Blackwell, L. S., & Trzesniewski, K. (2022). Growth-mindset intervention delivered by teachers boosts achievement in early adolescence. *Psychological Science, 33*(7), 1086–1096. https://doi.org/10.1177/09567976211061109

17. Hecht, C. A., Yeager, D. S., Dweck, C. S., & Murphy, M. C. (2021). Beliefs, affordances, and adolescent development: Lessons from a decade of growth mindset interventions. *Advances in Child Development and Behavior, 61,* 169–197. https://doi.org/10.1016/bs.acdb.2021.04.004

18. Hecht, C. A., Dweck, C. S., Murphy, M. C., Kroeper, K. M., & Yeager, D. S. (2023). Efficiently exploring the causal role of contextual moderators in behavioral science. *Proceedings of the National Academy of Sciences of the United States of America, 120*(1), e2216315120. https://doi.org/10.1073/pnas.2216315120

19. Robbins, T. (n.d.). *How to show confidence.* https://www.tonyrobbins.com/building-confidence/how-to-appear-confident/

20. Sigmundsson, H., Dybendal, B., Loftesnes, J., Ólafsson, B., & Grassini, S. (2022). Passion a key for success: Exploring motivational

factors in football players. *New Ideas Psychology, 65*, 100932. https://doi.org/10.1016/j.newideapsych.2022.100932 https://neurosciencenews.com/passion-success-20446/, https://www.sciencedirect.com/science/article/pii/S0732118X22000022?via%3Dihub

21.   Martin, S. (2019). *Why it's so important to validate yourself and how to start.* https://psychcentral.com/blog/imperfect/2019/11/why-its-so-important-to-validate-yourself-and-how-to-start

22.   Chamsi, F. Z., Katir, I., Korchi, A., Belbachir, S., & Ouanass, A. (2022). The impact of social media on self-esteem. *European Psychiatry, 65*(Suppl 1), S551. https://doi.org/10.1192/j.eurpsy.2022.1410

23.   Robbins, T. (n.d.). *Visualize your goals.* https://www.tony-robbins.com/how-to-focus/goal-visualization/

ADDITIONAL REFERENCES
AND RELEVANT RESOURCES

ABC News. (2019, August 22). *Doctors believe teen's lung failure due to vaping.* https://www.youtube.com/watch?v=im4bTtQ99SY

Abraham, O., Szela, L., Brasel, K., & Hoernke, M. (2022). Engaging youth in the design of prescription opioid safety education for schools. *Journal of the American Pharmacists Association, 62*(2), 441-449. https://doi.org/10.1016/j.japh.2021.10.016

Abrams, Z. (2022). What neuroscience tells us about the teenage brain. *American Psychological Association, 53*(5), 66.

Abrams, Z. (2023). *Why young brains are especially vulnerable to social media. The science behind why apps like TikTok, Instagram, and Snapchat impact your child's brain in a different way than your adult brain.* American Psychological Association. https://www.apa.org/news/apa/2022/social-media-children-teens

Ackerman, S. (1992). *Discovering the brain. Chapter 6: The development and shaping of the brain.* Washington (DC): National Academies Press (US). https://www.ncbi.nlm.nih.gov/books/NBK234146/

Addiction Education Society. (2023). *How does addiction take hold in the brain?* https://addictioneducationsociety.org/how-does-addiction-take-hold-in-the-brain/

Addiction Policy Forum. (2019). *Addiction & the brain: For kids!* [Video]. YouTube. https://www.youtube.com/watch?v=sobqT_hxMwI

Adger, H., Jr, & Saha, S. (2013). Alcohol use disorders in adolescents. *Pediatrics in Review, 34*(3), 103–114. https://doi.org/10.1542/pir.34-3-103

Agley, J., Gassman, R., YoussefAgha, A., Jun, M., Torabi, M., & Jayawardene, W. (2015). Examining sequences of adolescent substance use initiation involving over-the-counter (OTC) drug abuse. *Journal of Child & Adolescent Substance Abuse, 24*(4), 212-219.

Ahmad, S. I., & Hinshaw, S. P. (2017). Attention-deficit/hyperactivity disorder, trait impulsivity, and externalizing behavior in a longitudinal sample. *Journal of Abnormal Child Psychology, 45*(6), 1077–1089. https://doi.org/10.1007/s10802-016-0226-9

Ahmed, S. P., Bittencourt-Hewitt, A., & Sebastian, C. L., (2015). Neurocognitive bases of emotion regulation development in adolescence. *Developmental Cognitive Neuroscience, 15.* 11-25. https://doaj.org/article/e985b98a20aa4e7eabc3a8620 dc88096 , https://doi.org/10.1016/j.dcn.2015.07.006 https://www.sciencedirect.com/science/article/pii/S1878929315000717

Al Odhayani, A., Watson, W. J., & Watson, L. (2013). Behavioural consequences of child abuse. *Canadian Family Physician, 59*(8), 831–836

Alarcón, L. F., Castillo-Martínez, L., & Sánchez-Alcaraz, B. J. (2020). The relationship between physical activity and executive function in children: A systematic review. *International Journal of Environmental Research and Public Health, 17*(21), 7898.

Alipio, J. B., Haga, C., Fox, M. E., Arakawa, K., Balaji, R., Cramer, N., Lobo, M. K., & Keller, A. (2021). Perinatal fentanyl exposure leads to long-lasting impairments in somatosensory circuit function and behavior. *The Journal of Neuroscience: The Official Journal of the Society for Neuroscience, 41*(15), 3400–3417. https://doi.org/10.1523/JNEUROSCI.2470-20.2020

Allen, B., & Waterman, H. (2019). *Stages of adolescence.* https://www.healthychildren.org/English/ages-stages/teen/pages/Stages-of-Adolescence.aspx

alpha m. (2014). *Respect! Seven steps to earn respect.* https://www.youtube.com/watch?v=8dNIXtPIiEA

alpha m. (2016). *5 Secrets to boost your confidence: How to be more confident today!* https://www.youtube.com/watch?v=Ja9Fo2qqzWg

Amato, M. S., Bottcher, M. M., Cha, S., Jacobs, M. A., Pearson, J. L., Graham, A. L. (2021). "It's really addictive and I'm trapped:" A qualitative analysis of the reasons for quitting vaping among treatment-seeking young people. *Addictive Behaviors, 112.* https://doi.org/10.1016/j.addbeh.2020.106599

American Addiction Centers. (2020). *The financial toll of addiction.* https://drugabuse.com/blog/financial-toll-addiction/

American Psychological Association (n.d.). Puberty. In *APA dictionary of psychology.* Retrieved January 7, 2022, from https://dictionary.apa.org/puberty

American Psychiatric Association. (2022). *What is a substance use disorder?* [Video]. YouTube. https://www.youtube.com/watch?v=Vrb99pSgW7I&t=74s

American Psychological Association. (n.d.). Executive functions. In *APA dictionary of psychology.* Retrieved March 4, 2022, from https://dictionary.apa.org/executive-functions

American Psychological Association. (n.d.). Neural plasticity. In *APA dictionary of psychology.* Retrieved February 20, 2022, from https://dictionary.apa.org/neural-plasticity

A&P for Health Sciences. (2020). *Brain anatomy, Part 4: White vs. gray matter* [Video]. YouTube. https://www.youtube.com/watch?v=Zf4evd-Mjps

Anderson, I. A., & Wood, W. (2023). Social motivations' limited influence on habitual behavior: Tests from social media engagement. *Motivation Science, 9*(2), 107–119. https://doi.org/10.1037/mot0000292

Ando, S., Fujimoto, T., Sudo, M., Watanuki, S., Hiraoka, K., Takeda, K., Takagi, Y., Kitajima, D., Mochizuki, K., Matsuura, K., Katagiri, Y., Nasir, F. M., Lin, Y., Fujibayashi, M., Costello, J. T., McMorris, T., Ishikawa, Y., Funaki, Y., Furumoto, S., Watabe, H., ... Tashiro, M. (2024). The neuromodulatory role of dopamine in improved reaction time by acute cardiovascular exercise. *The Journal of physiology,* 10.1113/JP285173. Advance online publication. https://doi.org/10.1113/JP285173

Anzilotti, A. (2019). *What are wet dreams?* Kids Health. https://kidshealth.org/en/teens/expert-wet-dreams.html

Arain, M., Haque, M., Johal, L., Mathur, P., Nel, W., Rais, A., Sandhu, R., & Sharma, S. (2013). Maturation of the adolescent brain. *Neuropsychiatric Disease and Treatment, 9,* 449–461. https://doi.org/10.2147/NDT.S39776 https://www.ncbi.nlm.nih.gov/pmc/articles/PMC3621648/

Arnold, E. M., Greco, E., Desmond, K., & Rotheram-Borus, M. J. (2014). When life is a drag: Depressive symptoms associated with early adolescent smoking. *Vulnerable Children and Youth Studies, 9*(1), 1-9.

Arnsten, A. F., & Wang, M. (2021). Prefrontal regulation of cognitive behavior: circuits, pathways, and genes. *Neuropsychopharmacology Reviews, 46*(1), 123-156.

AsapSCIENCE. (2014). *5 crazy ways social media is changing your brain right now* [Video]. YouTube. https://www.youtube.com/watch?v=HffWFd_6bJo

AsapSCIENCE. (2016). *Why are teens so moody?* [Video]. YouTube. https://www.youtube.com/watch?v=du8siPJ1ZKo

Ask, Listen, Learn. (2020). *How marijuana affects your developing brain* [Video]. YouTube. https://www.youtube.com/watch?v=1Luw2tiMuLk

Avert. (2022). *Sharing needles to inject drugs, and HIV.* https://www.avert.org/hiv-transmission-prevention/injecting-drugs

Baams, L., Dubas, J. S., Overbeek, G., & van Aken, M. A. (2015). Transitions in body and behavior: A meta-analytic study on the relationship between pubertal development and adolescent sexual behavior. *The Journal of Adolescent Health: Official Publication of the Society for Adolescent Medicine, 56*(6), 586–598. https://doi.org/10.1016/j.jadohealth.2014.11.019

Barko, E. B., & Moorman, S. M. (2023). Weighing in: Qualitative explorations of weight restoration as recovery in anorexia nervosa. *Journal of Eating Disorders, 11*(1), 14. https://doi.org/10.1186/s40337-023-00736-9

Basedow, L.A., Kuitunen-Paul, S., Wiedmann, M.F. Ehrlich, S., Roessner, V., & Golub, Y. (2021). Verbal learning impairment in adolescents with methamphetamine use disorder: A cross-sectional study. *BMC Psychiatry, 21*(166). https://doi. org/10.1186/s12888-021-03169-3

Bayat, B., Akbarisomar, N., Tori, N. A., & Salehiniya, H. (2019). The relation between self-confidence and risk-taking among the students. *Journal of Education and Health Promotion, 8*(27). https://doi.org/10.4103/jehp.jehp_174_18 https://www.ncbi.nlm.nih.gov/pmc/articles/PMC6432809/

Beachboard, C. (2023). *Helping teens tap into the power of the future self:*

Reminding high school students why they're in school—so they can become the people they aspire to be—can be a powerful motivator. Edutopia. https://www.edutopia.org/video/helping-teens-find-future-self-icebreaker-activity?utm_content=linkpos5&utm_source=edu-newsletter&utm_medium=email&utm_campaign=weekly-2023-08-16

Beech Acres. (2019). *Self control* [Video]. YouTube. https://www.youtube.com/watch?v=esAUQW8w1Ww

Berthelsen, D., Hayes, N., White, S. L. J., & Williams, K. E. (2017). Executive function in adolescence: Associations with child and family risk factors and self-regulation in early childhood. *Frontiers in Psychology, 8*, 903. https://doi. org/10.3389/fpsyg.2017.00903

Best, J. R., Miller, P. H., & Naglieri, J. A. (2011). Relations between executive function and academic achievement from ages 5 to 17 in a large, representative national sample. *Learning and Individual Differences, 21*(4), 327-336.

Bick, J., & Nelson, C. A. (2016). Early adverse experiences and the developing brain. *Neuropsychopharmacology: Official Publication of the American College of Neuropsychopharmacology, 41*(1), 177–196. https://doi.org/10.1038/npp.2015.252

Birnie, M. T., Short, A. K., de Carvalho, G. B., Taniguchi, L., Gunn, B. G., Pham, A. L., Itoga, C. A., Xu, X., Chen, L. Y., Mahler, S. V., Chen, Y., & Baram, T. Z. (2023). Stress-induced plasticity of a CRH/GABA projection disrupts reward behaviors in mice. *Nature Communications, 14*(1), 1088. https://doi.org/10.1038/s41467-023-36780-x

Blair, K. S., Aloi, J., Crum, K., Meffert, H., White, S. F., Taylor, B. K., Leiker, E. K., Thornton, L. C., Tyler, P. M., Shah, N., Johnson, K., Abdel-Rahim, H., Lukoff, J., Dobbertin, M., Pope, K., Pollak, S., & Blair, R. J. (2019). Association of different types of childhood maltreatment with emotional responding and response control among youths. *JAMA Network Open, 2*(5), e194604. https://doi. org/10.1001/jamanetworkopen.2019.4604

Blakemore, S. (2013). *The mysterious workings of the adolescent brain - Sarah-Jayne Blakemore* [Video]. YouTube. https://www.youtube.com/watch?v=6oKsikHollM

Bocian, K., Gonidis, L., & Everett, J. A. C. (2024). Moral conformity in a digital world: Human and nonhuman agents as a source of social pressure for judgments of moral character. *PloS one, 19*(2), e0298293. https://doi.org/10.1371/journal. pone.0298293

Bohrer, B. K., Chen, Y., Christensen, K. A., Forbush, K. T., Thomeczek, M. L., Richson, B. N., Chapa, D. A. N., Jarmolowicz, D. P., Gould, S. R., Negi, S., Perko, V. L., & Morgan, R. W. (2023). A pilot multiple-baseline study of a mobile cognitive behavioral therapy for the treatment of eating disorders in university students. *The International Journal of Eating Disorders*, 56(8), 1623–1636. https://doi.org/10.1002/eat.23987

Bold, K., Kong, G., Cavallo, D., Davis, D., Jackson, A., & Krishnan-Sarin, S. (2022). School-based E-cigarette cessation programs: What do youth want? *Addictive Behaviors*, 125, 107167. https://doi.org/10.1016/j.addbeh.2021.1071

Bonanno, G. A., & Mancini, A. D. (2012). Beyond resilience and PTSD: Mapping the heterogeneity of responses to potential trauma. *Psychological Trauma: Theory, Research, Practice, and Policy*, 4(1), 74–83. https://doi.org/10.1037/a0017829

Bone, J. K., Bu, F., Fluharty, M. E., Paul, E., Sonke, J. K., Fancourt, D. (2022). Arts and cultural engagement, reportedly antisocial or criminalized behaviors, and potential mediators in two longitudinal cohorts of adolescents. *Journal of Youth and Adolescence*. https://doi.org/10.1007/s10964-022-01591-8

Borkar, C. D., Stelly, C. E., Fu, X., Dorofeikova, M., Le, Q. E., Vutukuri, R., Vo, C., Walker, A., Basavanhalli, S., Duong, A., Bean, E., Resendez, A., Parker, J. G., Tasker, J. G., & Fadok, J. P. (2024). Top-down control of flight by a non-canonical cortico-amygdala pathway. *Nature*, 625(7996), 743–749. https://doi.org/10.1038/s41586-023-06912-w

Bosk, E. A., Anthony, W. L., Folk, J. B., & Williams-Butler, A. (2021). All in the family: Parental substance misuse, harsh parenting, and youth substance misuse among juvenile justice-involved youth. *Addictive Behaviors*, 119, 106888. https://doi.org/10.1016/j.addbeh.2021.106888

BrainFacts.org. (2018). *How neurons communicate* [Video]. YouTube. https://www.youtube.com/watch?v=hGDvvUNU-cw

BrainFacts.org. (2016). *The workings of the adolescent brain* [Video]. YouTube. https://www.youtube.com/watch?v=Y8sO4tqfUEs

Brand, S., & Kirov, R. (2011). Sleep and its importance in adolescence and in common adolescent somatic and psychiatric conditions. *International Journal of General Medicine*, 4, 425–442. https://doi.org/10.2147/IJGM.S11557

Branden, N. (2014). *How to build self-esteem – The six pillars of self-esteem* [Video]. YouTube. https://www.youtube.com/watch?v=dhuabY4DmEo

Brelet, L., Flaudias, V., Désert, M., Guillaume, S., Llorca, P. M., & Boirie, Y. (2021). Stigmatization toward people with anorexia nervosa, bulimia nervosa, and binge eating disorder: A scoping review. *Nutrients*, 13(8), 2834. https://doi.org/10.3390/nu13082834

Britannica, T. Editors of Encyclopaedia (2020, February 6). *Cerebrum*. Encyclopedia Britannica. https://www.britannica.com/science/cerebrum

Brodsky, J. E., Bergson, Z., Chen, M., Hayward, E. O., Plass, J. L., & Homer, B. D. (2023). Language, ambiguity, and executive functions in adolescents' theory of mind. *Child Development*, 94(1), 202–218. https://doi.org/10.1111/cdev.13852

Brumback, T. Y., Worley, M., Nguyen-Louie, T. T., Squeglia, L. M., Jacobus, J., & Tapert, S. F. (2016). Neural predictors of alcohol use and psychopathology symptoms in adolescents. *Development and Psychopathology*, 28(4pt1), 1209–1216. https://doi.org/10.1017/S0954579416000766

Bryant, E., Aouad, P., Hambleton, A., Touyz, S., & Maguire, S. (2022). 'In an otherwise limitless world, I was sure of my limit.' Experiencing Anorexia Nervosa: A phenomenological metasynthesis. *Frontiers in Psychiatry*, 13, 894178. https://doi.org/10.3389/fpsyt.2022.894178

Bryant, E., Spielman, K., Le, A., Marks, P., National Eating Disorder Research Consortium, Touyz, S., & Maguire, S. (2022). Screening, assessment and diagnosis in the eating disorders: Findings from a rapid review. *Journal of Eating Disorders*, 10(1), 78. https://doi.org/10.1186/s40337-022-00597-8

Bryce, E. (2018, June). *How do your hormones work?* [Video]. TED-Ed Original. https://www.ted.com/talks/emma_bryce_how_do_your_hormones_work?language=en#t-284935

Bryce, E. (n.d.). *How menstruation works* [Video]. TED-Ed. https://ed.ted.com/lessons/how-menstruation-works-emma-bryce

Buck, J. M., & Siegel, J. A. (2015). The effects of adolescent methamphetamine exposure. *Frontiers in Neuroscience*, 9(151). https://doi.org/10.3389/fnins.2015.00151

Buckloh, L. M. (2021). *5 ways to know your feelings better*. Teens Health. https://kidshealth.org/en/teens/emotional-awareness.html

Buimer, E. E. L., Brouwer, R. M., Mandl, R. C. W., Pas, P., Schnack, H. G., & Hulshoff Pol, H. E. (2022). Adverse childhood experiences and fronto-subcortical structures in the developing brain. *Frontiers in Psychiatry*, 13, 955871. https://doi.org/10.3389/fpsyt.2022.955871

Burkhouse, K. L., & Kujawa, A. (2023). Annual research review: Emotion processing in offspring of mothers with depression diagnoses - A systematic review of neural and physiological research. *Journal of Child Psychology and Psychiatry, and Allied Disciplines*, 64(4), 583–607. https://doi.org/10.1111/jcpp.13734

Bush, A. M., Cook, A. M., Schier, J. G., Steck, A. L., & Spyker, D. A. (2021). Pediatric exposures to intentional abuse of prescription medications: An analysis of the National Poison Data System, 2014–2019. *Clinical Toxicology*, 59(4), 255–265. https://doi.org/10.1080/15563650.2021.1899807

Byun, Y. G., Kim, N. S., Kim, G., Jeon, Y. S., Choi, J. B., Park, C. W., Kim, K., Jang, H., Kim, J., Kim, E., Han, Y. M., Yoon, K. J., Lee, S. H., & Chung, W. S. (2023). Stress induces behavioral abnormalities by increasing expression of phagocytic receptor, MERTK, in astrocytes to promote synapse phagocytosis. *Immunity*,

S1074-7613(23)00318-7. Advance online publication. https://doi.org/10.1016/j. immuni.2023.07.005

Caballero, A., Orozco, A., Tseng, K. Y. (2021). Developmental regulation of excitatory-inhibitory synaptic balance in the prefrontal cortex during adolescence. *Seminars in Cell & Developmental Biology, 118*, 60-63. https://doi.org/10.1016/j.semcdb.2021.02.008

Caballero, D. (2023). *UO study finds teen girls' text language is linked to mental health.* https://www.kgw.com/article/news/health/university-oregon-study-teen-girls-text-language-mental-health/283-8e5fb016-e8bd-44d4-aaad-57d6812db87c

Cabral, P., Chinn, M., Mack, J., Costarelli, M., Ross, E., Henes, E., Steck, L., Williams, A. J. K., Lee, Y. B., Fretes, S., Fernandez, G., Garcia, L., Sato, L., Patrocinio, Y., & Shah, D. (2023). Psychosocial and cultural processes underlying the epidemiological paradox within U.S. Latino sexual risk: A systematic review. *Behavioral Sciences (Basel, Switzerland), 13*(3), 226. https://doi.org/10.3390/bs13030226

Calhoun, S., Conner, E., Miller, M., & Messina, N. (2015). Improving the outcomes of children affected by parental substance abuse: A review of randomized controlled trials. *Substance Abuse and Rehabilitation, 6*, 15–24. https://doi.org/10.2147/SAR. S46439

Cano, M. Á., Castro, F. G., De La Rosa, M., Amaro, H., Vega, W. A., Sánchez, M., Rojas, P., Ramírez-Ortiz, D., Taskin, T., Prado, G., Schwartz, S. J., Córdova, D., Salas-Wright, C. P., & de Dios, M. A. (2020). Depressive symptoms and resilience among Hispanic emerging adults: Examining the moderating effects of mindfulness, distress tolerance, emotion regulation, family cohesion, and social support. *Behavioral Medicine (Washington, D.C.), 46*(3-4), 245–257. https://doi.org/ 10.1080/08964289.2020.1712646

Cárdenas, E. F., Kujawa, A., & Humphreys, K. L. (2022). Benevolent childhood experiences and childhood maltreatment history: Examining their roles in depressive symptoms across the peripartum period. *Adversity and Resilience Science, 3*(2), 169–179. https://doi.org/10.1007/s42844-022-00062-0

Career and Life Skills Lessons. (2020). *Social skills: Self-discipline lesson* [Video]. YouTube. https://www.youtube.com/watch?v=LeQ7ElbaFOg

Carlén, M. (2017). What constitutes the prefrontal cortex? *Science, 358*(6362), 478-482. https://doi.org/10.1126/science.aan8868 https://www.science.org/doi/full/10.1126/science.aan8868 https://pubmed.ncbi.nlm.nih.gov/29074767/

Carleton University. (2019). *Neuroscience: Addiction and the brain* [Video]. YouTube. https://www.youtube.com/watch?v=3ndOLoG-YRg

Carr-Gregg, M. (2012, June 3). *Episode 2 - A crash course in the developmental psychology of young people* [Video file]. YouTube. https://www.youtube.com/ watch?v=9B8Tnhq3tgQ

Carr-Gregg, M. (2012). *The 8 secrets of happy young people* [Video]. YouTube.

https://www.youtube.com/watch?v=hrMa9lıguGY

Carter, R. (2019). *The human brain book: An illustrated guide to its structure, function, and disorders (DK human body guides)*. DK.

Carter, S. (2024). *Cannabis in pregnancy linked to autism and ADHD Risk.* European Psychiatric Association. https://neurosciencenews.com/cannabis-pregnancy-autism-adhd-25881/

Case, K. R., Clendennen, S. L., Tsevat, J., Harrell, M. B. (2022). Risk of respiratory, gastrointestinal, and constitutional health symptoms: A cross-sectional study of Texas adolescent and young adult nicotine and marijuana vapers. *Preventive Medicine, 159*. https://doi.org/10.1016/j.ypmed.2022.107057

Casey, B. J., Getz, S., & Galvan, A. (2008). The adolescent brain. *Developmental Review: DR, 28*(1), 62–77. https://doi.org/10.1016/j.dr.2007.08.003

Ceary, C. D., Donahue, J. J., & Shaffer, K. (2019). The strength of pursuing your values: Valued living as a path to resilience among college students. *Stress and Health, 35*(4), 532-541. https://doi.org/10.1002/smi.2886

Ceccarelli, C., Prina, E., Muneghina, O., Jordans, M., Barker, E., Miller, K., Singh, R., Acarturk, C., Sorsdhal, K., Cuijpers, P., Lund, C., Barbui, C., & Purgato, M. (2022). Adverse childhood experiences and global mental health: Avenues to reduce the burden of child and adolescent mental disorders. *Epidemiology and Psychiatric Sciences, 31*, e75. https://doi.org/10.1017/S2045796022000580

Centers for Disease Control and Prevention (CDC). (2022). *Adolescent health:*

Data are for the U.S. https://www.cdc.gov/nchs/fastats/adolescent-health.htm

Centers for Disease Control and Prevention (CDC). (2021). *Drug overdose.* https://www.cdc.gov/drugoverdose/index.html

Centers for Disease Control and Prevention (CDC). (2023). *High School - United States 2021 Results.* https://nccd.cdc.gov/YouthOnline/App/Results.aspx?LID=XX

Centers for Disease Control and Prevention (CDC). (2021). *Marijuana and public health: Teens.* https://www.cdc.gov/marijuana/health-effects/teens.html

Centers of Disease Control and Prevention (CDC). (2022). *Provisional drug overdose death counts.* National Center for Health Statistics. https://www.cdc.gov/nchs/nvss/vsrr/drug-overdose-data.htm

Centers for Disease Control and Prevention (CDC). (2020). *Sleep in middle and high school students.* https://www.cdc.gov/healthyschools/features/students-sleep.htm

Centers for Disease Control and Prevention (CDC). (2022). *Teen drivers: Get the facts.* https://www.cdc.gov/transportationsafety/teen_drivers/teendrivers_factsheet.html

Centers for Disease Control and Prevention (CDC). (2020). *Teen substance use & risks.* https://www.cdc.gov/ncbddd/fasd/features/teen-substance-use.html

Center on the Developing Child. (n.d.) *6 playful activities for teens (13-17 years)*. Harvard University. https://harvardcenter.wpenginepowered.com/wp-content/uploads/2022/12/6-Playful-Activities-for-Teens-13-17-years.pdf

Center on the Developing Child at Harvard University (2014). *Executive function activities for adolescents*. https://46y5eh11fhgw3ve3ytpwxt9r-wpengine.netdna-ssl.com/wp-content/uploads/2015/05/Activities-for-Adolescents.pdf

Center on the Developing Child at Harvard University. (2018). *How children and adults can build core capabilities for life* [Video]. YouTube. https://www.youtube.com/watch?v=6NehuwDA45Q&t=14s

Cestnick, L. (2017). *Executive functioning* [Video]. YouTube. Mind Matters. https://www.youtube.com/watch?v=GX5DzAwFVnc

Cetin-Karayumak, S., Zhang, F., Billah, T., Zekelman, L., Makris, N., Pieper, S., O'Donnell, L. J., & Rathi, Y. (2023). Harmonized diffusion MRI data and white matter measures from the Adolescent Brain Cognitive Development Study. *BioRxiv: The Preprint Server for Biology*, 2023.04.04.535587. https://doi.org/10.1101/2023.04.04.535587

Chang, Y. H., Yang, M. H., Yao, Z. F., Tsai, M. C., & Hsieh, S. (2023). The mediating role of brain structural imaging markers in connecting adverse childhood experiences and psychological resilience. *Children (Basel, Switzerland), 10*(2), 365. https://doi.org/10.3390/children10020365

Charmaraman, L., Lynch, A. D., Richer, A. M., & Grossman, J. M. (2022). Associations of early social media initiation on digital behaviors and the moderating role of limiting use. *Computers in Human Behavior, 127,* 107053. https://doi.org/10.1016/j.chb.2021.107053

Cherry, K. (2021). *Identity vs. role confusion in psychosocial development*. VeryWell mind. https://www.verywellmind.com/identity-versus-confusion-2795735

Chick, C. F. (2015). Reward processing in the adolescent brain: Individual differences and relation to risk taking. *Journal of Neuroscience, 35*(40), 13539-13541. https://doi.org/10.1523/JNEUROSCI.2571-15.2015

Child Mind Institute. (2021). *Understanding feelings - high school* [Video]. YouTube. https://www.youtube.com/watch?v=eTeYpQ32JP8&list=PLnEQkAsadC1GIKEcY iz5EqNC2Dj2jZt9n&index=1

Child Welfare Information Gateway. (n.d.). *Trauma and adolescent development*. https://www.childwelfare.gov/topics/systemwide/youth/understanding/trauma/

Cho, S. B., Su, J., Kuo, S. I., Bucholz, K. K., Chan, G., Edenberg, H. J., McCutcheon, V. V., Schuckit, M. A., Kramer, J. R., & Dick, D. M. (2019). Positive and negative reinforcement are differentially associated with alcohol consumption as a function of alcohol dependence. *Psychology of Addictive Behaviors, 33*(1), 58-68.

Choi, J., Kang, J., Kim, T., & Nehs, C. J. (2024). Sleep, mood disorders, and the ketogenic diet: Potential therapeutic targets for bipolar disorder and schizophrenia. *Frontiers in Psychiatry, 15*, 1358578. https://doi.org/10.3389/fpsyt.2024.1358578

Choukas-Bradley, S., Roberts, S. R., Maheux, A. J., & Nesi, J. (2022). The perfect storm: A developmental-sociocultural framework for the role of social media in adolescent girls' body image concerns and mental health. *Clinical Child and Family Psychology Review, 25*(4), 681–701. https://doi.org/10.1007/s10567-022-00404-5

Chu, J., Raney, J. H., Ganson, K. T., Wu, K., Rupanagunta, A., Testa, A., Jackson, D. B., Murray, S. B., & Nagata, J. M. (2022). Adverse childhood experiences and binge-eating disorder in early adolescents. *Journal of Eating Disorders, 10*(1), 168. https://doi.org/10.1186/s40337-022-00682-y

Claypool, N., & Moore de Peralta, A. (2021). The influence of adverse childhood experiences (ACEs), including the COVID-19 pandemic, and toxic stress on development and health outcomes of Latinx children in the USA: A review of the literature. *International Journal on Child Maltreatment: Research, Policy and Practice, 4*(3), 257–278. https://doi.org/10.1007/s42448-021-00080-y

Cleveland Clinic. (n.d.). *Female reproductive system: The external and internal anatomy of the female reproductive system is discussed.* https://my.clevelandclinic.org/health/articles/9118-female-reproductive-system

Cleveland Clinic. (2020). *Male reproductive system.* https://my.clevelandclinic.org/health/articles/9117-male-reproductive-system

Committee for Children. (2016). *Self-regulation skills: Why they are fundamental* [Video]. YouTube. https://www.youtube.com/watch?v=m4UGDaCgo_s

Conrod, P. J., & Nikolaou, K. (2016). Annual research review: On the developmental neuropsychology of substance use disorders. *Journal of Child Psychology & Psychiatry, 57*(3), 371-394.

Constantinidis, C., & Luna, B. (2019). Neural substrates of inhibitory control maturation in adolescence. *Trends in Neurosciences, 42*(9), 604–616. https://doi.org/10.1016/j.tins.2019.07.004

Cooke, E. M., Connolly, E. J., Boisvert, D. L., & Hayes, B. E. (2023). A systematic review of the biological correlates and consequences of childhood maltreatment and adverse childhood experiences. *Trauma, Violence & Abuse, 24*(1), 156–173. https://doi.org/10.1177/15248380211021613

Cormier, A., Mueri, K., Pavlova, M., Hood, A., Li, Q., Thurston, I., Jordan, A., & Noel, M. (2024). The Socio-cultural context of adolescent pain: Portrayals of pain in popular adolescent media. *Pain.* DOI: 10.1097/j.pain.0000000000003216 https://neurosciencenews.com/pain-empathy-teen-netflix-25839/ https://journals.lww.com/pain/abstract/9900/the_sociocultural_context_of_adolescent_pain_.560.aspx

Corroon J. (2021). Cannabinol and sleep: Separating fact from fiction. *Cannabis and Cannabinoid Research, 6*(5), 366–371. https://doi.org/10.1089/can.2021.0006

Courtney, K. E., Li, I., & Tapert, Susan F. (2019). The effect of alcohol use on neuroimaging correlates of cognitive and emotional processing in human adolescence. *Neuropsychology, 33*(6), 781-794.

Crash Course. (2014). *Emotion, stress, and health* [Video]. YouTube. Crash Course Psychology. https://www.youtube.com/watch?v=4KbSRXPowik

Crash Course. (2014). *Meet your master - Getting to know your brain* [Video]. YouTube. https://www.youtube.com/watch?v=vHrmiy4W9Co

Crash Course. (2015). *Reproductive system, part 1 - Female reproductive system* [Video]. YouTube. https://www.youtube.com/watch?v=RFDatCchpus

Crash Course. (2015). *Reproductive system, part 2 - Male reproductive system* [Video]. YouTube. https://www.youtube.com/watch?v=-XQcnO4iX_U

Crews, F. T., Robinson, D. L., Chandler, L. J., Ehlers, C. L., Mulholland, P. J., Pandey, S. C., Rodd, Z. A., Spear, L. P., Swartzwelder, H. S., & Vetreno, R. P. (2019). Mechanisms of persistent neurobiological changes following adolescent alcohol exposure: NADIA consortium findings. *Alcoholism, Clinical and Experimental Research, 43*(9), 1806-1822.

Cruz, D., Lichten, M., Berg, K., & George, P. (2022). Developmental trauma: Conceptual framework, associated risks and comorbidities, and evaluation and treatment. *Frontiers in Psychiatry, 13*, 800687. https://doi.org/10.3389/fpsyt.2022.800687

Cuncic, A. (2022). *How to develop and practice self-regulation.* Verywell Mind. https://www.verywellmind.com/how-you-can-practice-self-regulation-4163536

Cyrus, E., Coudray, M. S., Kiplagat, S., Mariano, Y., Noel, I., Galea, J. T., Hadley, D.,

Dévieux, J. G., Wagner, E. (2021). A review investigating the relationship between cannabis use and adolescent cognitive functioning. *Current Opinion in Psychology, 38.* 38-48. https://doi.org/10.1016/j.copsyc.2020.07.006

Dan, R., Weinstock, M., & Goelman, G. (2023). Emotional states as distinct configurations of functional brain networks. *Cerebral Cortex (New York, N.Y.: 1991), 33*(9), 5727–5739. https://doi.org/10.1093/cercor/bhac455

Danese, A., & Widom, C. S. (2023). Associations between objective and subjective experiences of childhood maltreatment and the course of emotional disorders in adulthood. *JAMA Psychiatry,* 10.1001/jamapsychiatry.2023.2140. Advance online publication. https://doi.org/10.1001/jamapsychiatry.2023.2140

Davidow, J. Y., Foerde, K., Galván, A., Shohamy, D. (2016). An upside to reward sensitivity: The hippocampus supports enhanced reinforcement learning in adolescence. *Neuron, 92*(1), 93-99. https://pubmed.ncbi.nlm.nih.gov/27710793/

Davis, A. N., Carlo, G., Hardy, S. A., Olthuis, J. V., & Zamboanga, B. L. (2017).

Bidirectional relations between different forms of prosocial behaviors and substance use among female college student athletes. *The Journal of Social Psychology, 157*(6), 645–657. https://doi.org/10.1080/00224545.2016.1263596

de Sousa, M. L., Peixoto, M. M., & Cruz, S. F. (2021). The association between externalizing and internalizing problems with bullying engagement in adolescents: The mediating role of social skills. *International Journal of Environmental Research and Public Health, 18*(19), 10444. https://doi.org/10.3390/ijerph181910444

Degenhardt, L., Dierker, L., Chiu, W. T., Medina-Mora, M. E., Neumark, Y., Sampson, N., Alonso, J., Angermeyer, M., Anthony, J. C., Bruffaerts, R., de Girolamo, G., de Graaf, R., Gureje, O., Karam, A. N., Kostyuchenko, S., Lee, S., Lépine, J., Levinson, D., Nakamura, Y ...& Kessler, R. C. (2010). Evaluating the drug use "gateway" theory using cross-national data: Consistency and associations of the order of initiation of drug use among participants in the WHO World Mental Health Surveys. *Drug and Alcohol Dependence, 108*(1), 84-97. https://www.sciencedirect.com/science/article/pii/S0376871609004219?via%3Dihub https://doi.org/10.1016/j.drugalcdep.2009.12.001

Dehestani, N., Whittle, S., Vijayakumar, N., & Silk, T. J. (2023). Developmental brain changes during puberty and associations with mental health problems. *Developmental Cognitive Neuroscience, 60*, 101227. https://doi.org/10.1016/j.dcn.2023.101227

Del Palacio-Gonzalez, A., & Pedersen, M. U. (2022). Youth's personal relationships, psychological symptoms, and the use of different substances: A population-based study. *Nordisk Alkohol- & Narkotikatidskrift : NAT, 39*(3), 322–337. https://doi.org/10.1177/14550725211050768

Dellazizzo, L., Potvin, S., Giguère, S., & Dumais, A. (2022). Evidence on the acute and residual neurocognitive effects of cannabis use in adolescents and adults: A systematic meta-review of meta-analyses. *Addiction (Abingdon, England), 117*(7), 1857–1870. https://doi.org/10.1111/add.15764

Delevich, K., Klinger, M., Okada, N. j., & Wilbrecht, L. (2021). Coming of age in the frontal cortex: The role of puberty in cortical maturation. *Seminars in Cell & Developmental Biology, 118*. 64-72. https://doi.org/10.1016/j.semcdb.2021.04.021

Deng, H. (2023). The brain under the influence of substances and addictive disorders: How it differs from a healthy one? In B. Halpern-Felsher (Ed.), *Encyclopedia of Child and Adolescent Health* (1st ed., pp. 231-244). Academic Press. ISBN 9780128188736. https://doi.org/10.1016/B978-0-12-818872-9.00124-2.

DeWall, N. (2014). *Self control: Teaching students about their greatest inner strength* [Video]. YouTube. Macmillan Learning. https://www.youtube.com/watch?v=E2jYdEO18nU

Diamond, A. (2013). Executive functions. *Annual Review of Psychology, 64*, 135–168. https://doi.org/10.1146/annurev-psych-113011-143750

Diamond, A., & Ling, D. S. (2016). Conclusions about interventions, programs, and approaches for improving executive functions that appear justified and those that, despite much hype, do not. *Developmental Cognitive Neuroscience, 18*, 34–48. https://pubmed.ncbi.nlm.nih.gov/26749076/

Dick, B., & Ferguson, B. J. (2015). Health for the world's adolescents: A second chance in the second decade. *The Journal of Adolescent Health: Official Publication of the Society for Adolescent Medicine, 56*(1), 3–6. https://doi.org/10.1016/j.jadohealth.2014.10.260

Didier, N., Vena, A., Feather, A. R., Grant, J. E., & King, A. C. (2023). Holding your liquor: Comparison of alcohol-induced psychomotor impairment in drinkers with and without alcohol use disorder. *Alcohol (Hanover, York County, Pa.)*, 10.1111/acer.15080. Advance online publication. https://doi.org/10.1111/acer.15080

Dodge, N. C., Jacobson, J. L., & Jacobson, S. W. (2019). Effects of fetal substance exposure on offspring substance use. *Pediatric Clinics of North America, 66*(6), 1149–1161. https://doi.org/10.1016/j.pcl.2019.08.010

Don't Memorise. (2017, November 20). *Reaching adolescence-puberty* [Video]. YouTube. https://www.youtube.com/watch?v=Nw2yHKxrj7o

Don't Memorise. (2017, November 27). *Reaching adolescence: Changes during puberty - Part 2* [Video]. YouTube. https://www.youtube.com/watch?v=J8PyEVacaVA

Don't Memorise. (2017, November 30). *Reaching adolescence: Secondary sexual characters* [Video]. YouTube. https://www.youtube.com/watch?v=aREAIE-GyDc

Don't Memorise. (2017, December 4). *Reaching adolescence: Reproductive phase* [Video]. YouTube. https://www.youtube.com/watch?v=IIngkUwD3tE

Dorol-Beauroy-Eustache, O., & Mishara, B. L. (2021). Systematic review of risk and protective factors for suicidal and self-harm behaviors among children and adolescents involved with cyberbullying. *Preventive Medicine, 152*(Pt 1), 106684. https://doi.org/10.1016/j.ypmed.2021.106684

Dow-Edwards, D., MacMaster, F. P., Peterson, B. S., Niesink, R., Andersen, S., & Braams, B. R. (2019). Experience during adolescence shapes brain development: From synapses and networks to normal and pathological behavior. *Neurotoxicology and Teratology, 76*, 106834. https://doi.org/10.1016/j.ntt.2019.106834

Dowshen, S. (2015). *Everything you wanted to know about puberty*. KidsHealth. https://kidshealth.org/en/teens/puberty.html

Drug Aware. (n.d.) *Frequently asked questions*. https://drugaware.com.au/get-the-facts/faqs-ask-a-question/amphetamines/#what-are-the-other-names-for-amphetamines

Drug Enforcement Administration (DEA). (2020). *2020 national drug threat assessment*. https://www.dea.gov/sites/default/files/2021-02/DIR-008-21%202020%20

National%20Drug%20Threat%20Assessment_WEB.pdf

Duchowny, K. A., Marcinek, D. J., Mau, T., Diaz-Ramierz, L. G., Lui, L. Y., Toledo, F. G. S., Cawthon, P. M., Hepple, R. T., Kramer, P. A., Newman, A. B., Kritchevsky, S. B., Cummings, S. R., Coen, P. M., & Molina, A. J. A. (2024). Childhood adverse life events and skeletal muscle mitochondrial function. *Science Advances, 10*(10), eadj6411. https://doi.org/10.1126/sciadv.adj6411

Duckworth, A., & Gross, J. J. (2014). Self-control and grit: Related but separable determinants of success. *Current Directions in Psychological Science, 23*(5), 319-325.

Dudovitz, R. N., Chung, P. J., Nelson, B. B., & Wong, M. D. (2017). What do you want to be when you grow up? Career aspirations as a marker for adolescent well-being. *Academic Pediatrics, 17*(2), 153-160. https://doi.org/10.1016/j.acap.2016.08.006

Duncan, P. (2020). *Substance use disorders: A biopsychosocial perspective.* Cambridge University Press. https://doi.org/10.1017/9781139025515

Dweck, C. S. (2006). *Mindset: The new psychology of success.* Random House.

Ea, P. (2019). *10 Confidence hacks* [Video]. YouTube. https://www.youtube.com/watch?v=EGKZuVoHcVo

Ea, P. (2019). *Every teenager NEEDS to hear this!* (2020) [Video]. YouTube. https://www.youtube.com/watch?v=UB7nGT3egak

Eacret, D., Veasey, S. C., & Blendy, J. A. (2020). Bidirectional relationship between opioids and disrupted sleep: Putative mechanisms. *Molecular Pharmacology, 98*(4), 445-453. https://doi.org/10.1124/mol.119.119107

Edmonds, M. (n.d.). *Are teenage brains really different from adult brains?* Howstuffworks. https://science.howstuffworks.com/life/inside-the-mind/human-brain/teenage-brain1.htm

Edralin, L. M. (n.d.). *Understanding the three stages of adolescence.* https://www.healthparkpediatrics.com/understanding-stages-of-adolescence/

Edutopia. (2019). *Developing executive function with priority lists* [Video]. YouTube. https://www.youtube.com/watch?v=AhoXKhkQ6SE

El Damaty, S., Darcey, V. L., McQuaid, G. A., Picci, G., Stoianova, M., Mucciarone, V., Chun, Y., Laws, M. L., Campano, V., Van Hecke, K, Ryan, M., Rose, E. J., Fishbein, D. H., & VanMeter, A. S. (2022). Introducing an adolescent cognitive maturity index. *Frontiers in Psychology, 13*, 1017317. https://doi.org/10.3389/fpsyg.2022.1017317

English, A., McKibben, E., Sivaramakrishnan, D., Hart, N., Richards, J., & Kelly, P. (2022). A rapid review exploring the role of yoga in healing psychological trauma. *International Journal of Environmental Research and Public Health, 19*(23), 16180. https://doi.org/10.3390/ijerph192316180

Erford, B., & Mayorga, J. (2020). *Developmental characteristics of teens.* American

Counseling Association, 1-3. https://www.counseling.org/docs/default-source/ Communications-/developmental-characteristics-of-teens-final.pdf?sfvrsn=2

Erickson, L. (2017). *Cross cultural investigation on resiliency and protective factors in the U.S. and Guatemala* (Doctoral dissertation). ProQuest. (1961607035)

Eroglu, Y., Peker, A., & Cengiz, S. (2022). Cyber victimization and well-being in adolescents: The sequential mediation role of forgiveness and coping with cyberbullying. *Frontiers in Psychology, 13*, 819049. https://doi.org/10.3389/fpsyg.2022.819049

ExpandED Schools. (2014). *Use It or lose It: The adolescent brain* [Video]. YouTube. https://www.youtube.com/watch?v=MHs7vlcwRXY

Fabris, M. A., Longobardi, C., Morese, R., & Marengo, D. (2022). Exploring multivariate profiles of psychological distress and empathy in early adolescent victims, bullies, and bystanders involved in cyberbullying episodes. *International Journal of Environmental Research and Public Health, 19*(16), 9871. https://doi.org/10.3390/ijerph19169871

Family & Youth Services Bureau. (n.d.) *HHS bulletin: The opioid epidemic: A focus on adolescents.* https://www.rhyttac.net/hhs-bulletin--the-opioid-epidemic--a-focus-on-adolescents

Farokhnia, M., Harris, J. C., Speed, S. N., Leggio, L., & Johnson, R. M. (2023). Lifetime use of alcohol and cannabis among U.S. adolescents across age: Exploring differential patterns by sex and race/ethnicity using the 2019 NSDUH data. *Drug and Alcohol Dependence Reports, 10*, 100214. https://doi.org/10.1016/j.dadr.2023.100214

Feder, A., Fred-Torres, S., Southwick, S. M., & Charney, D. S. (2019). The biology of human resilience: Opportunities for enhancing resilience across the life span. *Biological Psychiatry, 86*(6), 443–453. https://doi.org/10.1016/j.biopsych.2019.07.012

Feldstein Ewing, S. W., Sakhardande, A., & Blakemore, S. (2014). The effect of alcohol consumption on the adolescent brain: A systematic review of MRI and fMRI studies of alcohol-using youth. *NeuroImage: Clinical, 5.* 420-437.

Ferrantella, A., Huerta, C. T., Quinn, K., Mavarez, A. C., Quiroz, H. J., Thorson, C. M., Perez, E. A., & Sola, J. E. (2022). Risk factors associated with recent opioid-related hospitalizations in children: A nationwide analysis. *Pediatric Surgery International, 38*(6), 843–851. https://doi.org/10.1007/s00383-022-05088-0

Field, J. (2016). *Steve jobs insult response - Highest quality* [Video]. YouTube. https://www.youtube.com/watch?v=oeqPrUmVz-o

Fig.1/University of California. (2017). *Why the teenage brain has an evolutionary advantage?* [Video]. YouTube. https://www.youtube.com/watch?v=P629TojpvDU

Filatova, E. V., Shadrina, M. I., & Slominsky, P. A. (2021). Major depression: One brain, one disease, one set of intertwined processes. *Cells, 10*(6), 1283.

https://doi.org/10.3390/cells10061283

Flores, L. E., Jr, Eckstrand, K. L., Silk, J. S., Allen, N. B., Ambrosia, M., Healey, K. L., & Forbes, E. E. (2018). Adolescents' neural response to social reward and real-world emotional closeness and positive affect. *Cognitive, Affective & Behavioral Neuroscience, 18*(4), 705–717. https://doi.org/10.3758/s13415-018-0598-0

Fong Yan, A., Nicholson, L. L., Ward, R. E., Hiller, C. E., Dovey, K., Parker, H. M., Low, L. F., Moyle, G., & Chan, C. (2024). The effectiveness of dance interventions on psychological and cognitive health outcomes compared with other forms of physical activity: A systematic review with meta-analysis. *Sports Medicine (Auckland, N.Z.)*, 10.1007/s40279-023-01990-2. Advance online publication. https://doi.org/10.1007/s40279-023-01990-2

Forbes, E. E., & Dahl, R. E. (2020). Altered reward and emotional processing during adolescence: What can we learn from animal models?. *Current Opinion in Behavioral Sciences, 33*, 127-134. https://doi.org/10.1016/j.cobeha.2020.05.011

Fraga, J. (2018). *Helping strangers may help teens' self-esteem.* NPR. https://www.npr.org/sections/health-shots/2018/01/13/577463475/helping-strangers-may-help-teens-self-esteem

Freeman, S. J., Rasiah, S., Cohen-Silver, J., Xu, K., Lebovic, G., & Maguire, J. (2023). Mental health trajectories of children and caregivers using school-based health centers during the COVID-19 pandemic. *Journal of Pediatric Health Care: Official Publication of National Association of Pediatric Nurse Associates & Practitioners*, S0891-5245(23)00110-4. Advance online publication. https://doi.org/10.1016/j.pedhc.2023.04.002

FreeMedEducation (2019). *Part 4: Dopamine: The molecule of addiction: Your brain on porn* [Video]. YouTube. https://www.youtube.com/watch?v=bdiMFQk_aW8

Friedman, N.P., Robbins, T.W. (2022). The role of prefrontal cortex in cognitive control and executive function. *Neuropsychopharmacology. 47*, 72–89. https://doi.org/10.1038/s41386-021-01132-0

Fujimoto, S., Leiwe, M. N., Aihara, S., Sakaguchi, R., Muroyama, Y., Kobayakawa, R., Kobayakawa, K., Saito, T., & Imai, T. (2023). Activity-dependent local protection and lateral inhibition control synaptic competition in developing mitral cells in mice. *Developmental Cell*, S1534-5807(23)00237-X. Advance online publication. https://doi.org/10.1016/j.devcel.2023.05.004

Fung, H. W., Chien, W. T., Lam, S. K. K., & Ross, C. A. (2022). Investigating post-traumatic stress disorder (PTSD) and complex PTSD among people with self-reported depressive symptoms. *Frontiers in Psychiatry, 13*, 953001. https://doi.org/10.3389/fpsyt.2022.953001

Galván, A. (2013). *Insight into the teenage brain* [Video]. TEDxYouth@Caltech https://www.youtube.com/watch?v=LWUkW4s3XxY

Ganson, K. T., Hallward, L., Cunningham, M. L., Rodgers, R. F., Murray, S. B., & Nagata, J. M. (2023). Muscle dysmorphia symptomatology among a national

sample of Canadian adolescents and young adults. *Body Image, 44*, 178–186.
https://doi.org/10.1016/j.bodyim.2023.01.001

Ganson, K. T., Pang, N., Testa, A., Jackson, D. B., & Nagata, J. M. (2023). Adverse
childhood experiences and muscle dysmorphia symptomatology: Findings from
a sample of Canadian adolescents and young adults. *Clinical Social Work Journal.*
https://doi.org/10.1007/s10615-023-00908-9
https://neurosciencenews.com/muscle-dysmorphia-child-neglect-25303/

Garfinkel, S. N., Seth, A. K., Barrett, A. B., Suzuki, K., & Critchley, H. D. (2015).
Knowing your own heart: Distinguishing interoceptive accuracy from
interoceptive awareness. *Biological Psychology, 104*, 65–74.
https://doi.org/10.1016/j.biopsycho.2014.11.004

Gaynor, K., O'Reilly, M. D., Redmond, D., Nealon, C., Twomey, C., & Hennessy,
E. (2023). A meta-analysis of targeted interventions for reducing suicide-
related behaviour and ideation in adolescents: Implications for trial
design. *Comprehensive Psychiatry, 122*, 152374.
https://doi.org/10.1016/j.comppsych.2023.152374

GBD 2019 Mental Disorders Collaborators (2022). Global, regional, and national
burden of 12 mental disorders in 204 countries and territories, 1990-2019: A
systematic analysis for the Global Burden of Disease Study 2019. *The Lancet.
Psychiatry, 9*(2), 137–150. https://doi.org/10.1016/S2215-0366(21)00395-3

Gee, D. G., & Casey, B. J. (2015). The impact of developmental timing for stress
and recovery. *Neurobiology of Stress, 1*, 184-194. https://doi.org/10.1016/j.
ynstr.2014.10.004

Gentzler, A. L., Hughes, J. L., Johnston, M., & Alderson, J. E. (2023). Which social
media platforms matter and for whom? Examining moderators of links
between adolescents' social media use and depressive symptoms. *Journal of
Adolescence, 95*(8), 1725–1748. https://doi.org/10.1002/jad.12243

Ghaemi S. N. (2020). Digital depression: A new disease of the millennium?. *Acta
Psychiatrica Scandinavica, 141*(4), 356–361. https://doi.org/10.1111/acps.13151

Gibb, B. E., Owens, M., & Brick, L. A. D. (2023). Attentional biases for sad faces in
offspring of mothers with a history of major depression: Trajectories of change
from childhood to adolescence. *Journal of Child Psychology and Psychiatry, and
Allied Disciplines, 64*(6), 859–867. https://doi.org/10.1111/jcpp.13740

Giedd, J. N. (2015). The amazing teen brain. *Scientific American, 312*(6), 32-37.
https://pubmed.ncbi.nlm.nih.gov/26336683/

Ginder, D. E., Wright, H. R., & McLaughlin, R. J. (2021). Chapter four - the stoned
age: Sex differences in the effects of adolescent cannabinoid exposure on
prefrontal cortex structure and function in animal models. *International
Review of Neurobiology, Academic Press, 161*. 121-145. https://doi.org/10.1016/
bs.irn.2021.07.005
https://www.sciencedirect.com/science/article/pii/S0074774221000520

Glamour. (2016). *This is your period in 2 minutes* [Video]. YouTube. https://www.youtube.com/watch?v=WOi2Bwvp6hw&t=40s

Goddings, A. L., Beltz, A., Peper, J. S., Crone, E. A., & Braams, B. R. (2019). Understanding the role of puberty in structural and functional development of the adolescent brain. *Journal of Research on Adolescence, 29*(1), 32-53.

Goddings, A. L., Roalf, D., Lebel, C., & Tamnes, C. K. (2021). Development of white matter microstructure and executive functions during childhood and adolescence: A review of diffusion MRI studies. *Developmental Cognitive Neuroscience, 51,* 101008. https://doi.org/10.1016/j.dcn.2021.101008

Gogtay, N., Giedd, J. N., Lusk, L., Hayashi, K. M., Greenstein, D., Vaituzis, A. C., Nugent, T. F., 3rd, Herman, D. H., Clasen, L. S., Toga, A. W., Rapoport, J. L., & Thompson, P. M. (2004). Dynamic mapping of human cortical development during childhood through early adulthood. *Proceedings of the National Academy of Sciences of the United States of America, 101*(21), 8174–8179. https://doi.org/10.1073/pnas.0402680101

Gold, R. S., & Pomietto, B. (2019). Gateway drug theory. *Encyclopedia of Public Health.* https://www.encyclopedia.com/education/encyclopedias-almanacs-transcripts-and-maps/gateway-drug-theory

Goldberg, L. R., & Gould, T. J. (2019). Multigenerational and transgenerational effects of paternal exposure to drugs of abuse on behavioral and neural function. *The European Journal of Neuroscience, 50*(3), 2453–2466. https://doi.org/10.1111/ejn.14060

Gordon-Murer, C., Stöckel, T., Sera, M., & Hughes, C. M. L. (2021). Developmental differences in the relationships between sensorimotor and executive functions. *Frontiers in Human Neuroscience, 15,* 714828. https://doi.org/10.3389/fnhum.2021.714828

Goswami, U. (Ed.). (2011). *The Wiley-Blackwell handbook of childhood cognitive development* (2nd ed.). Wiley-Blackwell.

Graber, E. G. (2023). *Adolescent development.* https://www.merckmanuals.com/professional/pediatrics/growth-and-development/adolescent-development

Gray, K. M., & Squeglia, L. M. (2018). Research review: What have we learned about adolescent substance use? *Journal of Child Psychology and Psychiatry, 59*(6), 618-627. http://dx.doi.org/10.1111/jcpp.12783

Griesler, P. C., Hu, M. C., Wall, M. M., & Kandel, D. B. (2021). Assessment of prescription opioid medical use and misuse among parents and their adolescent offspring in the US. *JAMA Network Open, 4*(1), e2031073. https://pubmed.ncbi.nlm.nih.gov/33410876/

Gu, W., Zhao, Q., Yuan, C., Yi, Z., Zhao, M., & Wang, Z. (2022). Impact of adverse childhood experiences on the symptom severity of different mental disorders: A cross-diagnostic study. *General Psychiatry, 35*(2), e100741. https://doi.org/10.1136/gpsych-2021-100741

Guerri, C., & Pascual, M. (2019). Impact of neuroimmune activation induced by alcohol or drug abuse on adolescent brain development. *International Journal of Developmental Neuroscience, 77*, 89-98. https://doi.org/10.1016/j. ijdevneu.2018.11.006. https://www.sciencedirect.com/science/article/pii/ S073657481830251X

Gupta, A. (2016). *A taboo-free way to talk about periods* [Video]. YouTube. Ted Talk. https://www.youtube.com/watch?v=OaGEM-Rms48

Guy-Evans, O. (2021, May 19). *What does the brain's cerebral cortex do?* Simply Psychology. https://www.simplypsychology.org/what-is-the-cerebral-cortex.html

Halber, D. (2018). *Motivation: Why you do the things you do.* https://www.brainfacts.org/~/link.aspx?_id=029407C12A8F4E90A24752E2B65 B09A8&_z=z

Haller, H., Mitzinger, D., & Cramer, H. (2023). The integration of yoga breathing techniques in cognitive behavioral therapy for post-traumatic stress disorder: A pragmatic randomized controlled trial. *Frontiers in Psychiatry, 14*, 1101046. https://doi.org/10.3389/fpsyt.2023.1101046

Hallgren, K. A., Jack, H. E., Oliver, M., Berger, D., Bobb, J. F., Kivlahan, D. R., & Bradley, K. A. (2023). Changes in alcohol consumption reported on routine healthcare screenings are associated with changes in depression symptoms. *Alcohol (Hanover, York County, Pa.)*, 10.1111/acer.15075. Advance online publication. https://doi.org/10.1111/acer.15075

Hammoud, R., Tognin, S., Burgess, L., Bergou, N., Smythe, M., Gibbons, J., Davidson, N., Afifi, A., Bakolis, I & Mechelli, A. (2022). Smartphone-based ecological momentary assessment reveals mental health benefits of birdlife. *Scientific Reports, 12*, 17589 https://doi.org/10.1038/s41598-022-20207-6

Hanson, J. L., Adkins, D. J., Nacewicz, B. M., & Barry, K. R. (2023). Impact of socioeconomic status on amygdala and hippocampus subdivisions in children and adolescents. *BioRxiv : The Preprint Server for Biology*, https://doi.org/10.1101/2023.03.10.532071

Hanson, J. L., Nacewicz, B. M., Sutterer, M. J., Cayo, A. A., Schaefer, S. M., Rudolph, K. D., Shirtcliff, E. A., Pollak, S. D., & Davidson, R. J. (2015). Behavioral problems after early life stress: Contributions of the hippocampus and amygdala. *Biological Psychiatry, 77*(4), 314-323. https://doi.org/10.1016/j.biopsych.2014.04.020

Hanson, J. L., O'Connor, K., Adkins, D. J., & Kahhale, I. (2023). Childhood adversity and COVID-19 outcomes in the UK Biobank. *Journal of Epidemiology and Community Health*, jech-2023-221147. Advance online publication. https://doi.org/10.1136/jech-2023-221147 https://jech.bmj.com/content/early/2023/11/01/jech-2023-221147

Harrell, M. B., Clendennen, S. L., Sumbe, A., Case, K. R., Mantey, D. S., & Swan, S. (2022). Cannabis vaping among youth and young adults: A scoping review. *Current Addiction Reports.* https://doi.org/10.1007/s40429-022-00413-y

Harrison, R. J. (2020, February 4). *Human reproductive system. Encyclopedia Britannica.* https://www.britannica.com/science/human-reproductive-system

Hathaway, W. R., & Newton, B. W. (2021, June 11). *Neuroanatomy, prefrontal cortex.* https://www.ncbi.nlm.nih.gov/books/NBK499919

Hayes, A. M. R., Lauer, L. T., Kao, A. E., Sun, S., Klug, M. E., Tsan, L., Rea, J. J., Subramanian, K. S., Gu, C., Tanios, N., Ahuja, A., Donohue, K. N., Décarie-Spain, L., Fodor, A. A., & Kanoski, S. E. (2024). Western diet consumption impairs memory function via dysregulated hippocampus acetylcholine signaling. *Brain, Behavior, and Immunity, 118,* 408–422. https://doi.org/10.1016/j.bbi.2024.03.015 https://www.sciencedirect.com/science/article/pii/S0889159124002952

Healthdirect. (2020). *Female reproductive system.* https://www.healthdirect.gov.au/female-reproductive-system

Herculano-Houzel, S. (2012). The remarkable, yet not extraordinary, human brain as a scaled-up primate brain and its associated cost. *Proceedings of the National Academy of Sciences, 109* (Supplement 1), 10661-10668. https://doi.org/10.1073/pnas.1201895109 https://pubmed.ncbi.nlm.nih.gov/22723358/

Herculano-Houzel, S. (2016). *The human advantage: A new understanding of how our brain became remarkable.* The MIT Press.

Herman, A. M. (2023). Interoception within the context of impulsivity and addiction. *Current Addiction Reports, 10*(2), 97–106. https://doi.org/10.1007/s40429-023-00482-7

Herzog, J. I., & Schmahl, C. (2018). Adverse childhood experiences and the consequences on neurobiological, psychosocial, and somatic conditions across the lifespan. *Frontiers in Psychiatry, 9,* 420. https://doi.org/10.3389/fpsyt.2018.00420

Hirsch, I. H. (2021). *Structure of the male reproductive system.* Merck Manuals. https://www.merckmanuals.com/home/men-s-health-issues/biology-of-the-male-reproductive-system/structure-of-the-male-reproductive-system#:~:text=The%20male%20reproductive%20system%20includes,the%20urinary%20and%20reproductive%20systems

Hirsch, L. (2018). *Endocrine system.* Teens Health. https://kidshealth.org/en/teens/endocrine.html

Hirsh, L. (2019). *Male reproductive system.* Teens Health. https://kidshealth.org/en/teens/male-repro.html

Ho, T. C., & King, L. S. (2021). Mechanisms of neuroplasticity linking early adversity to depression: Developmental considerations. *Translational Psychiatry, 11*(1), 517. https://doi.org/10.1038/s41398-021-01639-6

Holmes, A., Levi, P. T., Chen, Y., Chopra, S., Aquino, K. M., Pang, J. C., & Fornito, A. (2023). Disruptions of hierarchical cortical organization in early psychosis and schizophrenia. *Biological Psychiatry: Cognitive Neuroscience and Neuroimaging.* https://doi.org/10.1016/j.bpsc.2023.08.008

Hosseini, S. A., & Padhy, R. K. (2023). *Body image distortion.* In StatPearls. StatPearls Publishing. https://pubmed.ncbi.nlm.nih.gov/31536191/

Hou, Y., Benner, A., Kim, S. Y., Chen, S., Spitz, S., Shi, Y., & Beretvas, T. (2020). Discordance in parents' and adolescents' reports of parenting: A meta-analysis and qualitative review. *American Psychologist, 75*(3), 329-348.

Hughes, A. R., Grusing, S., Lin, A., Hendrickson, R. G., Sheridan, D. C., Marshall, R., & Horowitz, B. Z. (2023). Trends in intentional abuse and misuse ingestions in school-aged children and adolescents reported to US poison centers from 2000-2020. *Clinical Toxicology (Philadelphia, Pa.), 61*(1), 64-71. https://doi.org/10.1080/1 5563650.2022.2120818

Igler, E. C., Austin, J. E., Sejkora, E. K. D., & Davies, W. H. (2023). Friends' perspective: Young adults' reaction to disclosure of chronic illness. *Journal of Clinical Psychology in Medical Settings*, 1–11. Advance Online Publication. https://doi.org/10.1007/s10880-023-09956-2

Iliades, C. (2016). *8 Common behavioral addictions.* https://www.everydayhealth.com/ addiction-pictures/the-8-most-surprising-addictions.aspx

Integrity Counseling & Wellness. (2019). *How to get in touch with your emotions.* https://www.counselingintegrity.com/blog/how-to-get-in-touch-with-your-emotions/

Jackson, D. B., Jones, M. S., Semenza, D. C., & Testa, A. (2023). Adverse childhood experiences and adolescent delinquency: A theoretically informed investigation of mediators during middle childhood. *International Journal of Environmental Research and Public Health, 20*(4), 3202. https://doi.org/10.3390/ijerph20043202

Jamieson, D., Broadhouse, K. M., McLoughlin, L. T., Schwenn, P., Parker, M. J., Lagopoulos, J., & Hermens, D. F. (2020). Investigating the association between sleep quality and diffusion-derived structural integrity of white matter in early adolescence. *Journal of Adolescence, 83*, 12–21. https://doi.org/10.1016/j. adolescence.2020.06.008

Jensen, F. E. (2008). *The teenage brain; Part 1* [Video]. YouTube. https://www.youtube.com/watch?v=RpMG7vS9pfw

Jensen, F. E. (2008). *The teenage brain: Part 2* [Video]. YouTube. https://www.youtube.com/watch?v=oJRxwVpXFBo

Jernigan, T. L., Brown, S. A., & Dowling, G. J. (2018). The adolescent brain cognitive development study. *Journal of Research on Adolescence: The Official Journal of the Society for Research on Adolescence, 28*(1), 154–156. https://doi.org/10.1111/ jora.12374 https://www.ncbi.nlm.nih.gov/pmc/articles/PMC7477916/

Jiang, D. H., Kim, S., Zaidi, A., Cottrell, L., Christopher, M. C., Palacio, T. R., & Rosenfield, P. J. (2022). Insights from expanded adverse childhood experiences screening in a hospital-based outpatient psychiatry service. *The Psychiatric Quarterly*, 93(2), 677–687. https://doi.org/10.1007/s11126-022-09982-7

Johansson, A. (n.d.). *10 uplifting positive affirmation apps*. Life Hack. https://www.lifehack.org/788171/best-positive-affirmation-apps

Jones, K. A., Freijah, I., Brennan, S. E., McKenzie, J. E., Bright, T. M., Fiolet, R., Kamitsis, I., Reid, C., Davis, E., Andrews, S., Muzik, M., Segal, L., Herrman, H., & Chamberlain, C. (2023). Interventions from pregnancy to two years after birth for parents experiencing complex post-traumatic stress disorder and/or with childhood experience of maltreatment. *The Cochrane Database of Systematic Reviews*, 5(5), CD014874. https://doi.org/10.1002/14651858.CD014874.pub2

Johns Hopkins Medicine. (n.d.). *The growing child: Adolescent 13 to 18 years*. https://www.hopkinsmedicine.org/health/wellness-and-prevention/the-growing-child-adolescent-13-to-18-years

Johnson, S. B., Blum, R. W., & Giedd, J. N. (2009). Adolescent maturity and the brain: The promise and pitfalls of neuroscience research in adolescent health policy. *The Journal of Adolescent Health: Official Publication of the Society for Adolescent Medicine*, 45(3), 216–221. https://doi.org/10.1016/j.jadohealth.2009.05.016

Jolles, J., & Jolles, D. D. (2021). On neuroeducation: Why and how to improve neuroscientific literacy in educational professionals. *Frontiers in Psychology*, 12, 752151. https://doi.org/10.3389/fpsyg.2021.752151

Jones, R. M., & Somerville, L. H. (2019). Peer influence on development during adolescence: A longitudinal perspective. *Developmental Cognitive Neuroscience*, 39, 100712. https://doi.org/10.1016/j.dcn.2019.100712

Juárez Olguín, H., Calderón Guzmán, D., Hernández García, E., & Barragán Mejía, G. (2016). The role of dopamine and its dysfunction as a consequence of oxidative stress. *Oxidative Medicine and Cellular Longevity*, 9730467. https://doi.org/10.1155/2016/9730467

Kaestle, C. E., Allen, K. R., Wesche, R., & Grafsky, E. L. (2021). Adolescent sexual development: A family perspective. *Journal of Sex Research*, 58(7), 874–890. https://doi.org/10.1080/00224499.2021.1924605 https://www.tandfonline.com/doi/full/10.1080/00224499.2021.1924605

Kageyama, N., & Chen, P. (2018). *How to stay calm under pressure* [Video]. TedEd. https://www.youtube.com/watch?v=CqgmozFr_GM

Kaiser, R. (2019). *Teen brains are not broken* [Video]. YouTube. TEDxBoulder. https://www.youtube.com/watch?v=ZQUBFgenMXk

Kalina, E., Boyd-Frenkel, K., Patock-Peckham, J. A., Schneidewent, L., Broussard, M. L., & Leeman, R. F. (2023). Does relationship-contingent self-esteem play a role in the stress to impaired control pathway to alcohol-related problems in a college student sample?. *Behavioral Sciences (Basel, Switzerland)*, 13(2), 185. https://doi.

org/10.3390/bs13020185

Kandel, D. B. (2002). *Stages and pathways of drug involvement: Examining the gateway hypothesis.* Cambridge University Press.

Kaneshiro, N. K. (2021). *Adolescent development.* National Library of Medicine/ MedlinePlus. https://medlineplus.gov/ency/article/002003.htm

Kang, W., Hernández, S. P., Rahman, M. S., Voigt, K., & Malvaso, A. (2022). Inhibitory control development: A network neuroscience perspective. *Frontiers in Psychology, 13,* 651547. https://doi.org/10.3389/fpsyg.2022.651547

Keeshin, B. R., & Monson, E. (2022). Assessing and responding to the trauma of child maltreatment. *Focus (American Psychiatric Publishing), 20*(2), 176–183. https://doi.org/10.1176/appi.focus.20210033

Kelley, L. A. (2023). *Beyond addiction: Study targets rising cocaine use disorder.* https://neurosciencenews.com/addiction-research-cud-23238/

Kendall-Taylor, N and Stanley, K (2018) Seeing context through metaphor: Using communications research to bring a social determinants perspective to public thinking about child abuse and neglect. *International Journal of Environmental Research and Public Health, 15*(1): 8-14. https://doi.org/10.3390/ijerph15010152

Kerker, B. D., Zhang, J., Nadeem, E., Stein, R. E., Hurlburt, M. S., Heneghan, A., Landsverk, J., & McCue Horwitz, S. (2015). Adverse childhood experiences and mental health, chronic medical conditions, and development in young children. *Academic Pediatrics, 15*(5), 510–517. https://doi.org/10.1016/j.acap.2015.05.005

Keshavan, M. S., & DeLisi, L. E. (2021). The adolescent brain and schizophrenia. *Schizophrenia Bulletin, 47*(2), 213-219. https://doi.org/10.1093/schbul/sbaa155

Kessler, R. C., Amminger, G. P., Aguilar-Gaxiola, S., Alonso, J., Lee, S., & Üstün, T. B. (2007). Age of onset of mental disorders: A review of recent literature. *Current Opinion in Psychiatry, 20*(4), 359–364. https://doi.org/10.1097/YCO.0b013e32816ebc8c

Kesty, S., & Ploszay, M. (2023). *Encouraging teens to develop self-regulation skills:*

When students understand their individual strengths, they can advocate for themselves and meet their own needs. Edutopia. https://www.edutopia.org/article/guiding-teens-develop-self-regulation-skills?utm_content=linkpos4&utm_source=edu-newsletter&utm_medium=email&utm_campaign=weekly-2023-08-16

Keyes, K. M., Rutherford, C., Miech, R. (2019). Historical trends in the grade of onset and sequence of cigarette, alcohol, and marijuana use among adolescents from 1976-2016: Implications for "Gateway" patterns in adolescence. *Drug and Alcohol Dependence, 194,* 51-58.

Khan Academy. (2014). *Gray and white matter: Organ Systems* [Video]. YouTube.

https://www.youtube.com/watch?v=ZZQzMeFoZYo

Khan Academy. (2014). *Reward pathway in the brain: Processing the Environment* [Video]. YouTube. https://www.youtube.com/watch?v=YzCYuKX6zp8

Khan Academy. (2014. April 24). *Subcortical cerebrum* [Video]. YouTube. https://www.youtube.com/watch?v=A_2f3onF3S8

King, S. G., Gaudreault, P. O., Malaker, P., Kim, J. W., Alia-Klein, N., Xu, J., & Goldstein, R. Z. (2022). Prefrontal-habenular microstructural impairments in human cocaine and heroin addiction. *Neuron, 110*(22), 3820–3832.e4. https://doi.org/10.1016/j.neuron.2022.09.011 https://www.cell.com/neuron/fulltext/S0896-6273(22)00816-9?_returnURL=ht tps%3A%2F%2Flinkinghub.elsevier.com%2Fretrieve%2Fpii%2FS08966273220081 69%3Fshowall%3Dtrue https://neurosciencenews.com/brain-pathway-addiction-25247/

Kirschner, H., Nassar, M. R., Fischer, A. G., Frodl, T., Meyer-Lotz, G., Froböse, S., Seidenbecher, S., Klein, T. A., & Ullsperger, M. (2024). Transdiagnostic inflexible learning dynamics explain deficits in depression and schizophrenia. *Brain: A Journal of Neurology, 147*(1), 201–214. https://doi.org/10.1093/brain/awad362 https://academic.oup.com/brain/article/147/1/201/7460176

Kleeven, A. T. H., de Vries Robbé, M., Mulder, E. A., & Popma, A. (2022). Risk assessment in juvenile and young adult offenders: Predictive validity of the SAVRY and SAPROF-YV. *Assessment, 29*(2), 181–197. https://doi.org/10.1177/1073191120959740

Klobucista, C. (2022). *The U.S. opioid epidemic.* Backgrounder. https://www.cfr.org/backgrounder/us-opioid-epidemic

Knabbe, J., Protzmann, J., Schneider, N., Berger, M., Dannehl, D., Wei, S., Strahle, C., Tegtmeier, M., Jaiswal, A., Zheng, H., Krüger, M., Rohr, K., Spanagel, R., Bilbao, A., Engelhardt, M., Scholz, H., & Cambridge, S. B. (2022). Single-dose ethanol intoxication causes acute and lasting neuronal changes in the brain. *Proceedings of the National Academy of Sciences of the United States of America, 119*(25), e2122477119. https://doi.org/10.1073/pnas.2122477119

Kolk, S.M., Rakic, P. (2022). Development of prefrontal cortex. *Neuropsychopharmacol. 47*, 41–57. https://doi.org/10.1038/s41386-021-01137-9

Kolozsvári, L. R., Rekenyi, V., Garbóczy, S., Hőgye-Nagy, Á., Szemán-Nagy, A., Sayed-Ahmad, M., & Héjja-Nagy, K. (2023). Effects of health anxiety, social support, and coping on dissociation with mediating role of perceived stress during the COVID-19 pandemic. *International Journal of Environmental Research and Public Health, 20*(8), 5491. https://doi.org/10.3390/ijerph20085491

Kong, G., Bold, K. W., Cavallo, D. A., Davis, D. R., Jackson, A., & Krishnan-Sarin, S. (2021). Informing the development of adolescent e-cigarette cessation interventions: A qualitative study. *Addictive Behaviors, 114*. https://doi.org/10.1016/j.addbeh.2020.106720

Konova, A. B., Ceceli, A. O., Horga, G., Moeller, S. J., Alia-Klein, N., & Goldstein, R. Z. (2023). Reduced neural encoding of utility prediction errors in cocaine addiction. *Neuron*, S0896-6273(23)00700-6. Advance online publication. https://doi.org/10.1016/j.neuron.2023.09.015

Konrad, K., Firk, C., & Uhlhaas, P. J. (2013). Brain development during adolescence: Neuroscientific insights into this developmental period. *Deutsches Arzteblatt International*, 110(25), 425-431. https://www.ncbi.nlm.nih.gov/pmc/articles/ PMC3705203/

Koponen, A. M., Nissinen, N. M., Gissler, M., Autti-Rämö, I., Sarkola, T., & Kahila, H. (2020). Prenatal substance exposure, adverse childhood experiences and diagnosed mental and behavioral disorders - A longitudinal register-based matched cohort study in Finland. *SSM - Population Health*, 11, 100625. https://doi.org/10.1016/j.ssmph.2020.100625

Körner, R., Röseler, L., Schütz, A., & Bushman, B. J. (2022). Dominance and prestige: Meta-analytic review of experimentally induced body position effects on behavioral, self-report, and physiological dependent variables. *Psychological Bulletin*, 148(1-2), 67–85. https://doi.org/10.1037/bul0000356

Kuhlman, K. R., Antici, E., Tan, E., Tran, M. L., Rodgers-Romero, E. L., & Restrepo, N. (2023). Predictors of adolescent resilience during the COVID-19 pandemic in a community sample of Hispanic and Latinx youth: Expressive suppression and social support. *Research on Child and Adolescent Psychopathology*, 51(5), 639–651. https://doi.org/10.1007/s10802-022-01019-8

Kurkinen, K., Kärkkäinen, O., Lehto, S. M., Luoma, I., Kraav, S. L., Kivimäki, P., Nieminen, A. I., Sarnola, K., Therman, S., & Tolmunen, T. (2023). The associations between metabolic profiles and sexual and physical abuse in depressed adolescent psychiatric outpatients: An exploratory pilot study. *European Journal of Psychotraumatology*, 14(1), 2191396. https://doi.org/10.1080/20008066.2023.2191396

Kwan, L. Y., Eaton, D. L., Andersen, S. L., Dow-Edwards, D., Levin, E. D., Talpos, J., Vorhees, C. V., & Li, A. A. (2020). This is your teen brain on drugs: In search of biological factors unique to dependence toxicity in adolescence. *Neurotoxicology and Teratology*, 81, 106916 https://pubmed.ncbi.nlm.nih.gov/32698050/ https://doi.org/10.1016/j.ntt.2020.106916

Kwapong, Y. A., Boakye, E., Khan, S. S., Honigberg, M. C., Martin, S. S., Oyeka, C. P., Hays, A. G., Natarajan, P., Mamas, M. A., Blumenthal, R. S., Blaha, M. J., & Sharma, G. (2023). Association of depression and poor mental health with cardiovascular disease and suboptimal cardiovascular health among young adults in the United States. *Journal of the American Heart Association*, 12(3), e028332. https://doi.org/10.1161/JAHA.122.028332

Lam, L. T., & Lam, M. K. (2021). Sleep disorders in early childhood and the development of mental health problems in adolescents: A systematic review of longitudinal and prospective studies. *International Journal of Environmental Research and Public Health*, 18(22), 11782.

https://doi.org/10.3390/ijerph182211782

Lam, N. H., Borduqui, T., Hallak, J., Roque, A., Anticevic, A., Krystal, J. H., Wang, X. J., & Murray, J. D. (2022). Effects of altered excitation-inhibition balance on decision making in a cortical circuit model. *The Journal of Neuroscience: The Official Journal of the Society for Neuroscience, 42*(6), 1035–1053. https://doi.org/10.1523/JNEUROSCI.1371-20.2021

Landin, J. D., & Chandler, L. J. (2023). Adolescent alcohol exposure alters threat avoidance in adulthood. *Frontiers in Behavioral Neuroscience, 16*, 1098343. https://doi.org/10.3389/fnbeh.2022.1098343

Langdon, C., Genkin, M., & Engel, T. A. (2023). A unifying perspective on neural manifolds and circuits for cognition. *Nature reviews. Neuroscience, 24*(6), 363–377. https://doi.org/10.1038/s41583-023-00693-x

Langston, P. K., Sun, Y., Ryback, B. A., Mueller, A. L., Spiegelman, B. M., Benoist, C., & Mathis, D. (2023). Regulatory T cells shield muscle mitochondria from interferon-γ–mediated damage to promote the beneficial effects of exercise. *Science Immunology.* https://doi.org/adi5377

Laube, C., van den Bos, W., & Fandakova, Y. (2020). The relationship between pubertal hormones and brain plasticity: Implications for cognitive training in adolescence. *Developmental Cognitive Neuroscience, 42.* https://www.sciencedirect.com/science/article/pii/S1878929320300013?via%3Dihub

Lavertu-Jolin, M., Chattopadhyaya, B., Chehrazi, P., Carrier, D., Wünnemann, F., Leclerc, S., Dumouchel, F., Robertson, D., Affia, H., Saba, K., Gopal, V., Patel, A. B., Andelfinger, G., Pineyro, G., & Di Cristo, G. (2023). Acan downregulation in parvalbumin GABAergic cells reduces spontaneous recovery of fear memories. *Molecular Psychiatry*, 10.1038/s41380-023-02085-0. Advance online publication. https://doi.org/10.1038/s41380-023-02085-0

Laviolette, S. R. (2021). Molecular and neuronal mechanisms underlying the effects of adolescent nicotine exposure on anxiety and mood disorders. *Neuropharmacology, 184.* https://doi.org/10.1016/j.neuropharm.2020.108411

LeBlanc, J. C., Alm, S., Yocum, T., & Kim, S. (2016). Identifying and addressing executive function challenges in children and adolescents with a history of complex trauma. *Journal of Child & Adolescent trauma, 9*(1), 31-43. https://doi.org/10.1007/s40653-015-0060-y

Lee, J. K. (2022). The effects of social comparison orientation on psychological well-being in social networking sites: Serial mediation of perceived social support and self-esteem. *Current Psychology (New Brunswick, N.J.), 41*(9), 6247–6259. https://doi.org/10.1007/s12144-020-01114-3

Lee, S. (2024). *Social media fuels eating disorder echo chambers.* Neuroscience News. https://neurosciencenews.com/eating-disorders-social-media-25920/

Lees, B., Meredith, L. R., Kirkland, A. E., Bryant, B. E., & Squeglia, L. M. (2020).

Effect of alcohol use on the adolescent brain and behavior. *Pharmacology Biochemistry and Behavior, 192.* https://doi.org/10.1016/j.pbb.2020.172906 https://www.sciencedirect.com/science/article/pii/S0091305719306021

Lees, B., Stapinski, L. A., Teesson, M., Squeglia, L. M., Jacobus, J., & Mewton, L. (2021). Problems experienced by children from families with histories of substance misuse: An ABCD study®. *Drug and Alcohol Dependence, 218,* 108403. https://doi.org/10.1016/j.drugalcdep.2020.108403

LeMoult, J., Humphreys, K. L., Tracy, A., Hoffmeister, J. A., Ip, E., & Gotlib, I. H. (2020). Meta-analysis: Exposure to early life stress and risk for depression in childhood and adolescence. *Journal of the American Academy of Child and Adolescent Psychiatry, 59*(7), 842–855. https://doi.org/10.1016/j.jaac.2019.10.011

Leslie, F. M. (2020). Unique, long-term effects of nicotine on adolescent brain. *Pharmacology, Biochemistry, and Behavior, 197,* 173010. https://doi.org/10.1016/j.pbb.2020.173010

Lewis, T., & Taylor, A. P. (2021). *Human brain: Facts, functions & anatomy.* Live Science. https://www.livescience.com/29365-human-brain.html

Li, Y., Sahakian, B. J., Kang, J., Langley, C., Zhang, W., Xie, C., Xiang, S., Yu, J., Cheng, W., & Feng, J. (2022). The brain structure and genetic mechanisms underlying the nonlinear association between sleep duration, cognition and mental health. *Nature Aging, 2*(5), 425–437. https://doi.org/10.1038/s43587-022-00210-2

Lichenstein, S. D., Manco, N., Cope, L. M., Egbo, L., Garrison, K. A., Hardee, J., Hillmer, A. T., Reeder, K., Stern, E. F., Worhunsky, P., & Yip, S. W. (2022). Systematic review of structural and functional neuroimaging studies of cannabis use in adolescence and emerging adulthood: Evidence from 90 studies and 9441 participants. *Neuropsychopharmacology: Official Publication of the American College of Neuropsychopharmacology, 47*(5), 1000–1028. https://doi.org/10.1038/s41386-021-01226-9

Lim, J., & Dinges, D. F. (2010). A meta-analysis of the impact of short-term sleep deprivation on cognitive variables. *Psychological Bulletin, 136*(3), 375–389. https://doi.org/10.1037/a0018883

Linden, W., & LeMoult, J. (2022). Editorial perspective: Adverse childhood events causally contribute to mental illness - We must act now and intervene early. *Journal of Child Psychology and Psychiatry, and Allied Disciplines, 63*(6), 715–719. https://doi.org/10.1111/jcpp.13541

Livingston, J. A., Chen, C., Kwon, M., & Park, E. (2022). Physical and mental health outcomes associated with adolescent E-cigarette use. *Journal of Pediatric Nursing, 64.* https://doi.org/10.1016/j.pedn.2022.01.006

Longobardi, C., Badenes-Ribera, L., & Fabris, M. A. (2022). Adverse childhood experiences and body dysmorphic symptoms: A meta-analysis. *Body Image, 40,* 267–284. https://doi.org/10.1016/j.bodyim.2022.01.003

Louisa. (2020). *A guide on how to get in touch with your feelings.* The Actually. https://

theactually.com/get-in-touch-with-feelings/

Louis, J. M., & Reyes, M. E. S. (2023). Cognitive self- compassion (CSC) online intervention program: A pilot study to enhance the self-esteem of adolescents exposed to parental intimate partner violence. *Clinical Child Psychology and Psychiatry*, 13591045231169089. Advance online publication. https://doi.org/10.1177/13591045231169089

Lucas, D. & Fox, J. (2022). Human sexual anatomy and physiology. In R. Biswas-Diener & E. Diener (Eds), *Noba textbook series: Psychology*. DEF publishers. http://noba.to/m28zt7ds

Ludwig-Walz, H., Dannheim, I., Pfadenhauer, L. M., Fegert, J. M., & Bujard, M. (2022). Increase of depression among children and adolescents after the onset of the COVID-19 pandemic in Europe: A systematic review and meta-analysis. *Child and Adolescent Psychiatry and Mental Health*, 16(1), 109. https://doi.org/10.1186/s13034-022-00546-y

Ludwig-Walz, H., Dannheim, I., Pfadenhauer, L. M., Fegert, J. M., & Bujard, M. (2023). Anxiety among children and adolescents during the COVID-19 pandemic in Europe: A systematic review protocol. *Systematic Reviews*, 12(1), 64. https://doi.org/10.1186/s13643-023-02225-1

Lumen Candela. (n.d.). *The cerebrum*. https://courses.lumenlearning.com/boundless-ap/chapter/the-cerebrum/

Lyness, D. (n.d.). *How to live a happy life*. Teens Health. https://kidshealth.org/en/teens/happy-life.html

Lyoo, I. K., Yoon, S., Kim, T. S., Lim, S. M., Choi, Y., Kim, J. E., Hwang, J., Jeong, H. S., Cho, H. B., Chung, Y. A., & Renshaw, P. F. (2015). Predisposition to and effects of methamphetamine use on the adolescent brain. *Molecular Psychiatry*, 20(12), 1516–1524. https://doi.org/10.1038/mp.2014.191

MacSweeney, N., Allardyce, J., Edmondson-Stait, A., Shen, X., Casey, H., Chan, S. W. Y., Cullen, B., Reynolds, R. M., Frangou, S., Kwong, A. S. F., Lawrie, S. M., Romaniuk, L., & Whalley, H. C. (2023). The role of brain structure in the association between pubertal timing and depression risk in an early adolescent sample (the ABCD Study®): A registered report. *Developmental Cognitive Neuroscience*, 60, 101223. https://doi.org/10.1016/j.dcn.2023.101223

Madigan, S., Racine, N., Vaillancourt, T., Korczak, D. J., Hewitt, J. M. A., Pador, P., Park, J. L., McArthur, B. A., Holy, C., & Neville, R. D. (2023). Changes in depression and anxiety among children and adolescents from before to during the COVID-19 Pandemic: A systematic review and meta-analysis. *JAMA Pediatrics*, e230846. Advance online publication. https://doi.org/10.1001/jamapediatrics.2023.0846

Malik, F., & Marwaha, R. (2022). *Cognitive development*. https://www.ncbi.nlm.nih.gov/books/NBK537095/

Manchia, M., Gathier, A. W., Yapici-Eser, H., Schmidt, M. V., de Quervain, D., van

Amelsvoort, T., Bisson, J. I., Cryan, J. F., Howes, O. D., Pinto, L., van der Wee, N. J., Domschke, K., Branchi, I., & Vinkers, C. H. (2022). The impact of the prolonged COVID-19 pandemic on stress resilience and mental health: A critical review across waves. *European Neuropsychopharmacology : The Journal of the European College of Neuropsychopharmacology, 55*, 22–83. https://doi.org/10.1016/j.euroneuro.2021.10.864

Manza, P., Tomasi, D., Shokri-Kojori, E., Zhang, R., Kroll, D., Feldman, D., McPherson, K., Biesecker, C., Dennis, E., Johnson, A., Yuan, K., Wang, W., Yonga, M., Wang, G., & Volkow, N. D. (2023). Neural circuit selective for fast but not slow dopamine increases in drug reward. *Nature Communications, 14*, 6408. https://doi.org/10.1038/s41467-023-41972-6

Marsh, I. C., Chan, S. W. Y. & MacBeth, A. (2018). Self-compassion and psychological distress in adolescents—a Meta-analysis. *Mindfulness, 9*, 1011–1027. https://doi.org/10.1007/s12671-017-0850-7

Martin, A., Booth, J. N., Laird, Y., Sproule, J., Reilly, J. J., & Saunders, D. H. (2018). Physical activity, diet and other behavioural interventions for improving cognition and school achievement in children and adolescents with obesity or overweight. *The Cochrane Database of Systematic Reviews, 3*(3), CD009728. https://doi.org/10.1002/14651858.CD009728.pub4

Martins, I., Monsalve, J.P.P. and Martinez, A.V. (2018), Self-confidence and fear of failure among university students and their relationship with entrepreneurial orientation: Evidence from Colombia. *Academia Revista Latinoamericana de Administración, 31*(3), 471-485. https://doi.org/10.1108/ARLA-01-2018-0018

Masten, A. S. (2014). Global perspectives on resilience in children and youth. *Child Development, 85*(1), 6-20.

Mastwal, S., Li, X., Stowell, R., Manion, M., Zhang, W., Kim, N. S., Yoon, K. J., Song, H., Ming, G. L., & Wang, K. H. (2023). Adolescent neurostimulation of dopamine circuit reverses genetic deficits in frontal cortex function. *BioRxiv: The Preprint Server for Biology*, 2023.02.03.526987. https://doi.org/10.1101/2023.02.03.526987

Mateos-Aparicio, P., & Rodríguez-Moreno, A. (2019). The impact of studying brain plasticity. *Frontiers in Cellular Neuroscience*. https://www.frontiersin.org/articles/10.3389/fncel.2019.00066/full https://doi.org/10.3389/fncel.2019.00066

Matson, T. E., Hallgren, K. A., Lapham, G. T., Oliver, M., Wang, X., Williams, E. C., & Bradley, K. A. (2023). Psychometric performance of a substance use symptom checklist to help clinicians assess substance use disorder in primary care. *JAMA Network Open, 6*(5), e2316283. https://doi.org/10.1001/jamanetworkopen.2023.16283

Mauri, D. (2023). Becoming parents as mending the past: Care-experienced parents and the relationship with their birth family. *Children and Youth Services Review, 148*. https://doi.org/10.1016/j.childyouth.2023.106911

Maurya, C., Muhammad, T., Das, A., Fathah, A., & Dhillon, P. (2023). The role of self-efficacy and parental communication in the association between cyber victimization and depression among adolescents and young adults: A structural equation model. *BMC Psychiatry, 23*(1), 337. https://doi.org/10.1186/s12888-023-04841-6

May, A. C., Aupperle, R. L., & Stewart, J. L. (2020). Dark times: The role of negative reinforcement in methamphetamine addiction. *Frontiers in Psychiatry, 11.* https://www.frontiersin.org/articles/10.3389/fpsyt.2020.00114/full

May, A. C., Jacobus, J., Simmons, A. N., & Tapert, S. F. (2022). A prospective investigation of youth alcohol experimentation and reward responsivity in the ABCD study. *Frontiers in Psychiatry, 13,* 886848. https://doi.org/10.3389/fpsyt.2022.886848

Mayo Clinic Staff. (n.d.) *Self-esteem: Take steps to feel better about yourself.*

If you have low self-esteem, harness the power of your thoughts and beliefs to change how you feel about yourself. Start with these steps. https://www.mayoclinic.org/healthy-lifestyle/adult-health/in-depth/self-esteem/art-20045374

McCarthy, M. L. (2019). *An almost foolproof way to get in touch with your emotions for a more productive life.* https://www.createwritenow.com/journal-writing-blog/an-almost-foolproof-way-to-get-in-touch-with-your-emotions-for-a-more-productive-life

McIlvain, G., Schneider, J. M., Matyi, M. A., McGarry, M. D., Qi, Z., Spielberg, J. M., & Johnson, C. L. (2022). Mapping brain mechanical property maturation from childhood to adulthood. *NeuroImage, 263,* 119590. https://doi.org/10.1016/j.neuroimage.2022.119590

McLaughlin, K. A., & Lambert, H. K. (2017). Child trauma exposure and psychopathology: Mechanisms of risk and resilience. *Current Opinion in Psychology, 14,* 29–34. https://doi.org/10.1016/j.copsyc.2016.10.004

McLeod, S. A. (2020). *Jean Piaget's theory of cognitive development.* Simply Psychology. www.simplypsychology.org/piaget.html

McLeod, S. A. (2020). *Lev Vygotsky.* Simply Psychology. www.simplypsychology.org/vygotsky.html

McVeigh, J. A., Smith, A., Howie, E. K., Stamatakis, E., Ding, D., Cistulli, P. A., Eastwood, P., & Straker, L. (2021). Developmental trajectories of sleep during childhood and adolescence are related to health in young adulthood. *Acta Paediatrica (Oslo, Norway: 1992), 110*(8), 2435–2444. https://doi.org/10.1111/apa.15911

Medline Plus. (n.d.). *Male reproductive system.* National Library of Medicine. https://medlineplus.gov/malereproductivesystem.html

Mehari, K., Iyengar, S. S., Berg, K. L., Gonzales, J. M., & Bennett, A. E. (2020).

Adverse childhood experiences and obesity among young children with neurodevelopmental delays. *Maternal and Child Health Journal, 24*(8), 1057–1064. https://doi.org/10.1007/s10995-020-02940-4

Meisel, S. N., Fosco, W. D., Hawk, L. W., & Colder, C. R. (2019). Mind the gap: A review and recommendations for statistically evaluating Dual Systems models of adolescent risk behavior. *Developmental Cognitive Neuroscience, 39*. 14p. https://www.sciencedirect.com/science/article/pii/S1878929318301336?via%3Dihub

Mejia, M. H., Wade, N. E., Baca, R., Diaz, V. G., Jacobus, J. (2021). The influence of cannabis and nicotine co-use on neuromaturation: A systematic review of adolescent and young adult studies. *Biological Psychiatry, 89*(2). https://doi.org/10.1016/j.biopsych.2020.09.021

Melia, R., Francis, K., Duggan, J., Bogue, J., O'Sullivan, M., Young, K., Chambers, D., McInerney, S. J., O'Dea, E., & Bernert, R. (2023). Using a safety planning mobile App to address suicidality in young people attending community mental health services in Ireland: Protocol for a pilot randomized controlled trial. *JMIR Research Protocols, 12*, e44205. https://doi.org/10.2196/44205

Mendizabal A. (2023). Contextualizing adverse childhood experiences in patients with Parkinson disease: The beginnings of a complicated area of neurologic research. *Neurology. Clinical Practice, 13*(2), e200158. https://doi.org/10.1212/CPJ.0000000000200158

Menichetti, G., Ravandi, B., Mozaffarian, D., & Barabási, A. L. (2023). Machine learning prediction of the degree of food processing. *Nature Communications, 14*(1), 2312. https://doi.org/10.1038/s41467-023-37457-1

Menstrupedia. (2020). *Hello periods (English) - The complete guide to periods for girls* [Video]. YouTube. https://www.youtube.com/watch?v=qUNTtn1WPEw

Meredith, G. R., Rakow, D. A., Eldermire, E. R. B., Madsen, C. G., Shelley, S. P., & Sachs, N. A. (2020). Minimum time dose in nature to positively impact the mental health of college-aged students, and how to measure it: A scoping review. *Frontiers in Psychology, 10*, 2942. https://doi.org/10.3389/fpsyg.2019.02942

Merianos, A. L., King, K. A., Vidourek, R. A. & Hardee, A. M. (2016). The effect of alcohol abuse and dependence and school experiences on depression: A national study of adolescents. *Journal of Child & Adolescent Substance Abuse, 25*(6), 584-590.

Merriam-Webster. (n.d.). Secondary sex characteristic. In *Merriam-Webster.com dictionary*. https://www.merriam-webster.com/dictionary/secondary%20sex%20characteristic

Merritt, P. (2014). *Neuroscience: Subcortical structures* [Video]. YouTube. https://www.youtube.com/watch?v=I_2K62zll5M

Miech, R., Johnston, L., O'Malley, P. M., Keyes, K. M., & Heard, K. (2015). Prescription opioids in adolescence and future opioid misuse. *Pediatrics, 136*(5), e1169–e1177. https://doi.org/10.1542/peds.2015-1364

Miller, C. (n.d.). *Mental health disorders and teen substance use.* Child Mind Institute. https://childmind.org/article/mental-health-disorders-and-substance-use/

Mills, K. L., Lalonde, F., Clasen, L. S., Giedd, J. N., & Blakemore, S. J. (2014). Developmental changes in the structure of the social brain in late childhood and adolescence. *Social Cognitive and Affective Neuroscience, 9*(1), 123–131. https://doi.org/10.1093/scan/nss113

Miskovic-Wheatley, J., Bryant, E., Ong, S. H., Vatter, S., Le, A., National Eating Disorder Research Consortium, Touyz, S., & Maguire, S. (2023). Eating disorder outcomes: Findings from a rapid review of over a decade of research. *Journal of Eating Disorders, 11*(1), 85. https://doi.org/10.1186/s40337-023-00801-3

Miyake, A., & Friedman, N. P. (2012). The nature and organization of individual differences in executive functions: Four general conclusions. *Current Directions in Psychological Science, 21*(1), 8–14. https://doi.org/10.1177/0963721411429458

Moawad, H., & Gans, S. (2022). *What is executive function and how can you improve it?* Verywell heath. https://www.verywellhealth.com/executive-function-5224766

Moisala, M., Salmela, V., Carlson, S., Salmela-Aro, K., Lonka, K., Hakkarainen, K., & Alho, K. (2018). Neural activity patterns between different executive tasks are more similar in adulthood than in adolescence. *Brain and Behavior, 8*(9), e01063. https://doi.org/10.1002/brb3.1063

Mojtabai, R., Olfson, M., & Han, B. (2016). National trends in the prevalence and treatment of depression in adolescents and young adults. *Pediatrics, 138*(6). https://pubmed.ncbi.nlm.nih.gov/27940701/

Molla, H. M., & Tseng, K. Y. (2020). Neural substrates underlying the negative impact of cannabinoid exposure during adolescence. *Pharmacology Biochemistry and Behavior, 195*, 172965. https://doi.org/10.1016/j.pbb.2020.172965 https://www.sciencedirect.com/science/article/pii/S009130572030215X

Monette, S., Bigras, M., & Guay, M.-C. (2016). The role of executive functions in school achievement at the end of Grade 1. *Journal of Experimental Child Psychology, 145*, 20–35.

Montvilo, R. K. (2019). *Gateway drugs.* Salem Press Encyclopedia of Health.

Mooney-Leber, S. M., & Gould, T. J. (2018). The long-term cognitive consequences of adolescent exposure to recreational drugs of abuse. *Learning & memory (Cold Spring Harbor, N.Y.), 25*(9), 481–491. https://doi.org/10.1101/lm.046672.117

Morgan, N. (2015). *Your special teenage brain* [Video]. YouTube. https://www.youtube.com/watch?v=s9EEee1s74k

Morgart, K., Harrison, J. N., Hoon, A. H., Jr, & Wilms Floet, A. M. (2021). Adverse childhood experiences and developmental disabilities: Risks, resiliency, and policy. *Developmental Medicine and Child Neurology, 63*(10), 1149–1154. https://doi.org/10.1111/dmcn.14911

Morin, A. (2022). *How to be more confident.* Verywell Mind. https://www.verywellmind.com/how-to-boost-your-self-confidence-4163098

Morita, T., Asada, M., & Naito, E. (2016). Contribution of neuroimaging studies to understanding development of human cognitive brain functions. *Frontiers in Human Neuroscience.* https://doi.org/10.3389/fnhum.2016.00464 https://www.frontiersin.org/articles/10.3389/fnhum.2016.00464/full

Morris, A. S., Squeglia, L. M., Jacobus, J., & Silk, J. S. (2018). Adolescent brain development: Implications for understanding risk and resilience processes through neuroimaging research. *Journal of Research on Adolescence (Wiley-Blackwell), 28*(1), 4-9.

Myllylä, M. T., & Saariluoma, P. (2022). Expertise and becoming conscious of something. *New Ideas in Psychology, 64.* https://doi.org/10.1016/j.newideapsych.2021.100916

Myran, D. T., Harrison, L. D., Pugliese, M., Tanuseputro, P., Gaudreault, A., Fiedorowicz, J. G., & Solmi, M. (2024). Development of an anxiety disorder following an emergency department visit due to cannabis use: A population-based cohort study. *The Lancet,* 102455. https://doi.org/10.1016/j.eclinm.2024.102455 https://www.thelancet.com/journals/eclinm/article/PIIS2589-5370(24)00034-8/fulltext

Nagata, J. M., Smith, N., Sajjad, O. M., Zamora, G., Raney, J. H., Ganson, K. T., Testa, A., Vittinghoff, E., & Jackson, D. B. (2023). Adverse childhood experiences and sipping alcohol in U.S. children: Findings from the Adolescent Brain Cognitive Development study. *Preventive Medicine Reports, 32,* 102153. https://doi.org/10.1016/j.pmedr.2023.102153

Narayan, A. J., Lieberman, A. F., & Masten, A. S. (2021). Intergenerational transmission and prevention of adverse childhood experiences (ACEs). *Clinical Psychology Review, 85,* 101997. https://doi.org/10.1016/j.cpr.2021.101997

National Academies of Sciences, Engineering, and Medicine; Health and Medicine Division; Division of Behavioral and Social Sciences and Education; Board on Children, Youth, and Families; Committee on the Neurobiological and Socio-behavioral Science of Adolescent Development and Its Applications, Backes, E. P., & Bonnie, R. J. (Eds.). (2019). *The Promise of Adolescence: Realizing Opportunity for All Youth.* National Academies Press (US). https://pubmed.ncbi.nlm.nih.gov/31449373/

National Alliance on Mental Illness (NAMI). *Trauma.* https://www.nami.org/Support-Education/Justice-Library/Trauma?categoryname=YouthAndYoungAdults

National Center for Complementary and Integrative Health. (2016). *Meditation: In depth.* https://www.nccih.nih.gov/health/meditation-in-depth

National Center for Drug Abuse Statistics (NCDAS). (2022). *Substance abuse and addiction statistics.* https://drugabusestatistics.org/

National Centre for Mental Health. (2019). *Adverse childhood experiences and the developing brain.* https://www.ncmh.info/2019/08/22/adverse-childhood-experiences-and-the-developing-brain/

National Commission on Domestic and Sexual Violence and Multiple Disadvantage. (2019). *Breaking down the barriers.* https://avaproject.org.uk/breaking-down-the-barriers-findings-of-the-national-commission-on-domestic-and-sexual-violence-and-multiple-disadvantage/

National Geographic. (2017). *Brain 101* [Video]. YouTube. https://www.youtube.com/watch?v=pRFXSjkpKWA

National Institute on Alcohol Abuse and Alcoholism (NIAAA). (n. d.). *Alcohol's effects on the body.* https://www.niaaa.nih.gov/alcohols-effects-health

National Institute on Alcohol Abuse and Alcoholism (NIAAA). (n. d.) *Drinking levels defined.* https://www.niaaa.nih.gov/alcohol-health/overview-alcohol-consumption/moderate-binge-drinking

National Institute on Alcohol Abuse and Alcoholism (NIAAA). (2021). *Treatment for alcohol problems: Finding and getting help.* https://www.niaaa.nih.gov/publications/brochures-and-fact-sheets/treatment-alcohol-problems-finding-and-getting-help

National Institute on Alcohol Abuse and Alcoholism (NIAAA). (2021). *Understanding binge drinking.* https://www.niaaa.nih.gov/publications/brochures-and-fact-sheets/binge-drinking

National Institute on Drug Abuse (NIDA). (2014). *Drugs, brains, and behavior: The science of addiction.* https://nida.nih.gov/sites/default/files/soa_2014.pdf

National Institute on Drug Abuse (NIDA). (2020). *Drug misuse and addiction.* https://nida.nih.gov/publications/drugs-brains-behavior-science-addiction/drug-misuse-addiction

National Institute on Drug Abuse (NIDA). (2021, May 24). *Is marijuana a gateway drug?* Retrieved from https://nida.nih.gov/publications/research-reports/marijuana/marijuana-gateway-drug

National Institute on Drug Abuse (NIDA). (2021). *Mind matters: The body's response to cocaine.* https://teens.drugabuse.gov/teachers/mind-matters/cocaine

National Institute on Drug Abuse (NIDA). (n.d.). *Mind matters: The body's response to opioids.* https://teens.drugabuse.gov/teachers/mind-matters/opioids

National Institute on Drug Abuse. (2022). *Monitoring the future.* https://nida.nih.gov/research-topics/trends-statistics/monitoring-future

National Institute on Drug Abuse (NIDA). (n.d.). *Opioid facts for parents.* https://nida.nih.gov/sites/default/files/opioid_factsforparents.pdf

National Institute on Drug Abuse. (2014). *Principles of drug abuse treatment for adolescents: Summary.* https://nida.nih.gov/drug-topics/treatment/principles-drug-abuse-treatment-adolescents-summary

National Institute on Drug Abuse (NIDA). (2019, October 1). *Step by step guides to finding treatment for drug use disorders.* https://archives.drugabuse.gov/publications/step-by-step-guides-to-finding-treatment-drug-use-disorders

National Institute on Drug Abuse (NIDA). (2019). *Teen brain development* [Video]. YouTube. https://www.youtube.com/watch?v=EpfnDijz2d8

National Institute on Drug Abuse (NIDA). (2016). *The human brain: Major structures and functions* [Video]. YouTube. https://www.youtube.com/watch?v=0-8PvNOdByc

National Institute on Drug Abuse (NIDA). (2019). *Treatment approaches for drug addiction.* Drug Facts. https://nida.nih.gov/publications/drugfacts/treatment-approaches-drug-addiction

National Institute on Drug Abuse (NIDA). (2021). *What is the worst drug?* [Video]. YouTube. https://www.youtube.com/watch?v=VF-pTqFnQAw

National Institute of Mental Health. (2020). *The teen brain: 7 things to know.* https://www.nimh.nih.gov/health/publications/the-teen-brain-7-things-to-know

National Library of Medicine/MedlinePlus. (2021). *Puberty.* https://medlineplus.gov/puberty.html

National Research Council (US) and Institute of Medicine (US) Forum on Adolescence. (1999). Adolescent development and the biology of puberty: Summary of a workshop on new research. *National Academies Press (US).* https://www.ncbi.nlm.nih.gov/books/NBK224692/

NCD Alliance. (2022). *Take this to heart - there is no safe level of alcohol.* https://ncdalliance.org/news-events/news/take-this-to-this-to-heart-there-is-no-safe-level-of-alcohol

Neuroscience News. (2023). *Innocent faces of fentanyl: Opioid use linked to distinct birth anomalies.* https://neurosciencenews.com/fentanyl-birth-abnormalities-25114/ https://www.gimopen.org/article/S2949-7744(23)00843-9/fulltext

Neuroscience News. (2023). *Rewiring the brain: The neural code of traumatic memories.* https://neurosciencenews.com/trauma-brain-changes-24944/

Original research article: https://doi.org/10.1038/s41467-023-41547-5

Neuroscientifically Challenged. (2016). *2-Minute neuroscience: Amygdala* [Video]. YouTube. https://www.youtube.com/watch?v=JVvMSwsOXPw

Neuroscientifically Challenged. (2020). *2-Minute neuroscience: Cerebral cortex* [Video]. YouTube. https://www.youtube.com/watch?v=7TK1LpjV5bI

Neuroscientifically Challenged. (2018). *2-minute neuroscience: Dopamine* [Video]. YouTube. https://www.youtube.com/watch?v=Wa8_nLwQIpg

Neuroscientifically Challenged. (2015). *2-Minute neuroscience: Limbic system* [Video]. YouTube. https://www.youtube.com/watch?v=LNs9ruzoTmI

Neuroscientifically Challenged. (2016). *2-minute neuroscience: Nucleus accumbens* [Video]. YouTube. https://www.youtube.com/watch?v=3_zgB19TE-M

Neuroscientifically Challenged. (2019). *2-Minute neuroscience: Prefrontal cortex* [Video]. YouTube. https://www.youtube.com/watch?v=i47_jiCsBMs

Neuroscientifically Challenged. (2015). *2-minute neuroscience: Reward system* [Video]. YouTube. https://www.youtube.com/watch?v=f7EomTJQ2KM

Neuroscientifically Challenged. (2016). *2-minute neuroscience: Striatum* [Video]. YouTube. https://www.youtube.com/watch?v=EEUxKFmIUiI&t=1s

Nguyen, C., Mondoloni, S., Borgne, T., Centeno, I., Come, M., Jehl, J., Solié, C., Reynolds, L. M., Durand-de Cuttoli, R., Tolu, S., Valverde, S., Didienne, S., Hannesse, B., Fiancette, J., Pons, S., Maskos, U., Deroche-Gamonet, V., Dalkara, D., Hardelin, J... Faure, P. (2021). Nicotine inhibits the VTA-to-amygdala dopamine pathway to promote anxiety. *Neuron, 109*(16). 2604-2615.e9. https://doi.org/10.1016/j.neuron.2021.06.013

Nguyen, N., Peyser, N. D., Olgin, J. E., Pletcher, M. J., Beatty, A. L., Modrow, M. F., Carton, T. W., Khatib, R., Djibo, D. A., Ling, P. M., & Marcus, G. M. (2023). Associations between tobacco and cannabis use and anxiety and depression among adults in the United States: Findings from the COVID-19 citizen science study. *PLOS ONE, 18*(9), e0289058. https://doi.org/10.1371/journal.pone.0289058

Nicolelyn. (2016). *AP psychology- The human brain* [Video]. YouTube. https://www.youtube.com/watch?v=d4Hym5TekUE

Nicolucci, C., Pais, M. L., Santos, A. C., Ribeiro, F. M., Encarnação, P. M. C. C., Silva, A. L. M., Castro, I. F., Correia, P. M. M., Veloso, J. F. C. A., Reis, J., Lopes, M. Z., Botelho, M. F., Pereira, F. C., & Priolli, D. G. (2021). Single low dose of cocaine–Structural brain injury without metabolic and behavioral changes. *Frontiers in Neuroscience, 14*. https://www.frontiersin.org/article/10.3389/fnins.2020.589897 https://doi.org/10.3389/fnins.2020.589897

Nissinen, N. M., Gissler, M., Sarkola, T., Kahila, H., Autti-Rämö, I., & Koponen, A. M. (2021). Completed secondary education among youth with prenatal substance exposure: A longitudinal register-based matched cohort study. *Journal of Adolescence, 86*, 15–27. https://doi.org/10.1016/j.adolescence.2020.11.006

Nixon, C. L. (2014). Current perspectives: The impact of cyberbullying on adolescent health. *Adolescent Health, Medicine and Therapeutics, 5*, 143–158. https://doi.org/10.2147/AHMT.S36456

Norbom, L. B., Ferschmann, L., Parker, N., Agartz, I., Andreassen, O. A., Paus, T., Westlye, L. T., & Tamnes, C. K. (2021). New insights into the dynamic development of the cerebral cortex in childhood and adolescence: Integrating macro- and microstructural MRI findings. *Progress in Neurobiology, 204*, 102109. https://doi.org/10.1016/j.pneurobio.2021.102109

Nutting, R., Ofei-Dodoo, S., Rose-Borcherding, K., & Strella, G. (2022). Brief mindfulness intervention for emotional distress, resilience, and compassion in family physicians during COVID-19: A pilot study. *PRiMER, 6*, 3. https://doi.org/10.22454/PRiMER.2022.746202

Oasis Mental Health Applications. (2020). *Addiction: Types, causes, and solutions* (For Teens) [Video]. YouTube. https://www.youtube.com/watch?v=dsTwkX1cdCY

Ochoa, C., Kilgore, P. C. S. R., Korneeva, N., Clifford, E., Conrad, S. A., Trutschl, M., Bowers, J. M., Arnold, T., & Cvek, U. (2023). Trends in drug tests among Children: A 22-Year retrospective analysis. *Pathophysiology: The Official Journal of the International Society for Pathophysiology, 30*(2), 219–232. https://doi.org/10.3390/pathophysiology30020019

Odegaard, K. E., Pendyala, G., & Yelamanchili, S. V. (2021). Generational effects of opioid exposure. *Encyclopedia, 1*(1), 99–114. https://doi.org/10.3390/encyclopedia1010012

Office of Population Affairs. (n.d.). *Adolescent health.* https://opa.hhs.gov/adolescent-health?adolescent-development/substance-use/

Office of Population Affairs. (n.d.). *Cognitive development.* https://opa.hhs.gov/adolescent-health/adolescent-development-explained/cognitive-development

Office of Population Affairs. (2023). *Mental health for adolescents.* https://opa.hhs.gov/adolescent-health/mental-health-adolescents

O'Leary-Barrett, M., Mâsse, B., Pihl, R., Stewart, S., Séguin, J., & Conrod, P. (2017). A cluster-randomized controlled trial evaluating the effects of delaying onset of adolescent substance abuse on cognitive development and addiction following a selective, personality-targeted intervention programme: The Co-Venture trial. *Addiction, 112*(10), 1871-1881. http://dx.doi.org/10.1111/add.13876

Olstad, K., Sørensen, T., Lien, L., & Danbolt, L. J. (2023). Adolescents with developmental traumas in therapy in a child and adolescent mental health service, outpatient unit: Experiences of daily living and expectations for therapy - a qualitative study. *Frontiers in Psychology, 14*, 946394. https://doi.org/10.3389/fpsyg.2023.946394

Op den Kelder, R., Van den Akker, A. L., Geurts, H. M., Lindauer, R. J. L., & Overbeek, G. (2018). Executive functions in trauma-exposed youth: A meta-analysis. *European Journal of Psychotraumatology, 9*(1), 1450595. https://doi.org/10.1080/20008198.2018.1450595

Orenstein, G. A., & Lewis, L. (2020, November 22). *Erikson's stages of psychosocial development*. National Center for Biotechnology Information. https://www.ncbi.nlm.nih.gov/books/NBK556096/

OxfordSparks. (2017). *Brain development in teenagers* [Video]. YouTube. https://www.youtube.com/watch?v=dISmdb5zfiQ

Palmer, C. A., Bower, J. L., Cho, K. W., Clementi, M. A., Lau, S., Oosterhoff, B., & Alfano, C. A. (2023). Sleep loss and emotion: A systematic review and meta-analysis of over 50 years of experimental research. *Psychological Bulletin*. Advance online publication. https://doi.org/10.1037/bul0000410

Parent, A., & Carpenter, M. B. (1995). "Ch. 1". *Carpenter's human neuroanatomy*. Williams & Wilkins. ISBN 978-0-683-06752-1.

Parkhill, T. (2023). *Running parallels antidepressants in reducing depression*. Neuroscience News. Original source: European College of Neuropsychopharmacology (ECNP). https://neurosciencenews.com/running-ssri-depression-24928/

Peters, K. Z., & Naneix, F. (2022). The role of dopamine and endocannabinoid systems in prefrontal cortex development: Adolescence as a critical period. *Frontiers in Neural Circuits*, *16*, 939235. https://doi.org/10.3389/fncir.2022.939235

Petrican, R., & Fornito, A. (2023). Adolescent neurodevelopment and psychopathology: The interplay between adversity exposure and genetic risk for accelerated brain ageing. *Developmental Cognitive Neuroscience*, *60*, 101229. https://doi.org/10.1016/j.dcn.2023.101229

Paus, T. (2018). Adolescent brain development and mental health. *Nature Medicine*, *24*(8), 859-864. https://doi.org/10.1038/s41591-018-0156-0

Petrilli, K., Ofori, S., Hines, L., Taylor, G., Adams, S., & Freeman, T. P. (2022). Association of cannabis potency with mental ill health and addiction: a systematic review. *The Lancet Psychiatry*. https://doi.org/10.1016/S2215-0366(22)00161-4

Pietilä, J., Helander, E., Korhonen, I., Myllymäki, T., Kujala, U. M., & Lindholm, H. (2018). Acute effect of alcohol intake on cardiovascular autonomic regulation during the first hours of sleep in a large real-world sample of Finnish employees: Observational study. *JMIR Mental Health*, *5*(1), e23. https://doi.org/10.2196/mental.9519

Planned Parenthood. (n.d.). *What are the parts of the female sexual anatomy?* https://www.plannedparenthood.org/learn/health-and-wellness/sexual-and-reproductive-anatomy/what-are-parts-female-sexual-anatomy

Planned Parenthood. (n.d.). *What are the parts of the male sexual anatomy?* https://www.plannedparenthood.org/learn/health-and-wellness/sexual-and-reproductive-anatomy/what-are-parts-male-sexual-anatomy

Pollastri, A. R., Epstein, L. D., Heath, G. H., & Ablon, J. S. (2013). The collaborative problem solving approach: Outcomes across settings. *Harvard Review of Psychiatry, 21*(4), 188–199. https://doi.org/10.1097/HRP.0b013e3182961017

Ports, K. A., Ford, D. C., & Merrick, M. T. (2016). Adverse childhood experiences and sexual victimization in adulthood. *Child Abuse & Neglect, 51*, 313–322. https://doi.org/10.1016/j.chiabu.2015.08.017

Prada, J. (n.d.). *Executive functioning: An overview.* Smart Kids. https://www.smartkidswithld.org/first-steps/what-are-learning-disabilities/executive-function-overview-2/

Prakash, S., Gu, Y., & Previti, M. (2023). Quantitative survey on prevalence of prescription pain medications and stimulants use in young adults. *Substance Abuse: Research and Treatment, 17*, 11782218231162827. https://doi.org/10.1177/11782218231162827

Preston, J. L., Coleman, T. J., 3rd, & Shin, F. (2023). Spirituality of science: Implications for meaning, well-Being, and learning. *Personality & Social Psychology Bulletin,* 1461672231191356. Advance online publication. https://doi.org/10.1177/01461672231191356 https://journals.sagepub.com/doi/10.1177/01461672231191356

Prochnow, T., Patterson, M.S., Hartnell. L., & M., & Meyer, M. R. U. (2023). Online gaming network communication dynamics, depressive symptoms, and social support: A longitudinal network analysis. *Sociological Focus.* https://doi.org/10.1080/00380237.2023.2199171

PsychologyWriting. (2023). *Piaget's and Vygotsky's theories of cognitive development.* https://psychologywriting.com/piagets-and-vygotskys-theories-of-cognitive-development

Pysiopedia. (n.d.). *Cerebral cortex.* https://www.physio-pedia.com/Cerebral_Cortex

Qu, G., Liu, H., Han, T., Zhang, H., Ma, S., Sun, L., Qin, Q., Chen, M., Zhou, X., & Sun, Y. (2023). Association between adverse childhood experiences and sleep quality, emotional and behavioral problems and academic achievement of children and adolescents. *European Child & Adolescent Psychiatry,* 1–12. Advance online publication. https://doi.org/10.1007/s00787-023-02185-w

Quigley, J., Ryan, S. A., Camenga, D. R., Patrick, S. W., Plumb, J., Walker-Harding, L. (2019). Alcohol use by youth. *Pediatrics, 144*(1), e20191356. https://doi.org/10.1542/peds.2019-1356

Raab, D. (2018). *Being in touch with our emotions.* Psychology Today. https://www.psychologytoday.com/us/blog/the-empowerment-diary/201807/being-in-touch-our-emotions

Rapp, C., Hamilton, J., Richer, K., Sajjad, M., Yao, R., & Thanos, P. K. (2022). Alcohol binge drinking decreases brain glucose metabolism and functional connectivity in adolescent rats. *Metabolic Brain Disease.* https://doi.org/10.1007/s11011-022-00977-8

Raver, C. C. (2012). Low-income children's self-regulation in the classroom: Scientific inquiry for social change. *The American Psychologist, 67*(8), 681–689. https://doi.org/10.1037/a0030085

Reboussin, B. A., Wagoner, K. G., Ross, J. C., Suerken, C. K., & Sutfin, E. L. (2021).

Tobacco and marijuana co-use in a cohort of young adults: Patterns, correlates and reasons for co-use. *Drug and Alcohol Dependence, 227.* https://doi.org/10.1016/j.drugalcdep.2021.109000

Recovery Centers of America. (2022). *Economic cost of substance abuse disorder in the United States, 2019.* https://recoverycentersofamerica.com/resource/economic-cost-of-substance-abuse-disorder-in-united-states-2019/

Ren, M., & Lotfipour, S. (2019). Nicotine gateway effects on adolescent substance use. *The Western Journal of Emergency Medicine, 20*(5), 696–709. https://doi.org/10.5811/westjem.2019.7.41661

Retorta, R. (2018, December 13). *3 Stages of adolescence* [Video]. YouTube. https://www.youtube.com/watch?v=mDcnh_gTPzM

Richman, E. B., Ticea, N., Allen, W. E., Deisseroth, K., & Luo, L. (2023). Neural landscape diffusion resolves conflicts between needs across time. *Nature,* 10.1038/s41586-023-06715-z. Advance online publication. https://doi.org/10.1038/s41586-023-06715-z

Rishard, H. (2022). *Seeing a better world through pets* [Video]. YouTube https://www.youtube.com/watch?v=54TG8vjJ_98

Roach, J. P., Churchland, A. K., & Engel, T. A. (2023). Choice selective inhibition drives stability and competition in decision circuits. *Nature Communications, 14*(1), 147. https://doi.org/10.1038/s41467-023-35822-8

Roark, C. L., & Chandrasekaran, B. (2023). Stable, flexible, common, and distinct behaviors support rule-based and information-integration category learning. *NPJ Science of Learning, 8*(1), 14. https://doi.org/10.1038/s41539-023-00163-0

Robbins, P., & Alvear, F. (2023). Deformative experience: Explaining the effects of adversity on moral evaluation. *Social Cognition* (Forthcoming). https://ssrn.com/abstract=4500500 https://neurosciencenews.com/child-adversity-moral-juudegement-23806/

Roeser, A., Gadagkar, V., Das, A., Puzerey, P. A., Kardon, B., & Goldberg, J. H. (2023). Dopaminergic error signals retune to social feedback during courtship. *Nature,* 10.1038/s41586-023-06580-w. Advance online publication. https://doi.org/10.1038/s41586-023-06580-w

Rogers, J. M., Iudicello, J. E., Marcondes, M. C. G., Morgan, E. E., Cherner, M., Ellis, R. J., Letendre, S. L., Heaton, R. K., & Grant, I. (2023). The combined effects of cannabis, methamphetamine, and HIV on neurocognition. *Viruses, 15*(3), 674. https://doi.org/10.3390/v15030674

Romeo, R. D. (2017). The impact of stress on the structure of the adolescent brain: Implications for adolescent mental health. *Brain Research*, *1654*(Pt B), 185–191. https://doi.org/10.1016/j.brainres.2016.03.021

Rosner, J., Samardzic, T., & Sarao, M. S. (2021). *Physiology, female reproduction*. National Library of Medicine. https://www.ncbi.nlm.nih.gov/books/NBK537132/

Ross, E. J., Graham, D. L., Money, K. M., & Stanwood, G. D. (2015). Developmental consequences of fetal exposure to drugs: What we know and what we still must learn. *Neuropsychopharmacology: Official Publication of the American College of Neuropsychopharmacology*, *40*(1), 61–87. https://doi.org/10.1038/npp.2014.147

Ross, M. (2023). *Eating foods that decrease gut inflammation is an effective way to boost your mood, says a nutritional psychiatrist—Here's how*. https://www.wellandgood.com/inflammatory-foods-anxiety/

Rutter, M. (2012). Resilience as a dynamic concept. *Development and Psychopathology*, *24*(2), 335–344. https://doi.org/10.1017/S0954579412000028

Saint-André, V., Charbit, B., Biton, A., Rouilly, V., Possémé, C., Bertrand, A., Rotival, M., Bergstedt, J., Patin, E., Albert, M. L., Quintana-Murci, L., Duffy, D., & Milieu Intérieur Consortium (2024). Smoking changes adaptive immunity with persistent effects. *Nature*, 10.1038/s41586-023-06968-8. Advance online publication. https://doi.org/10.1038/s41586-023-06968-8

Salmanzadeh, H., Ahmadi-Soleimani, S. M., Pachenari, N., Azadi, M., Halliwell, R.F., Rubino, T., Azizi, H. (2020). Adolescent drug exposure: A review of evidence for the development of persistent changes in brain function. *Brain Research Bulletin*, *159*, 105-117. https://doi.org/10.1016/j.brainresbull.2020.01.007 https://www.sciencedirect.com/science/article/pii/S0361923019308809

Samaritan Neuropsychology. (2020). *How do drugs affect a baby's development during pregnancy?* https://www.samhealth.org/about-samaritan/news-search/2020/06/08/how-do-drugs-affect-babys-development-during-pregnancy

Sands, L. P., Jiang, A., Liebenow, B., DiMarco, E., Laxton, A. W., Tatter, S. B., Montague, P. R., & Kishida, K. T. (2023). Subsecond fluctuations in extracellular dopamine encode reward and punishment prediction errors in humans. *Science Advances*, *9*(48), eadi4927. https://doi.org/10.1126/sciadv.adi4927

Sawyer, S. M., Azzopardi, P. S., Wickremarathne, D., & Patton, G. C. (2018). The age of adolescence. *The Lancet. Child & Adolescent Health*, *2*(3), 223–228. https://doi.org/10.1016/S2352-4642(18)30022-1

Scheyer, A. F., Laviolette, S. R., Pelissier, A. L., & Manzoni, O. J. J. (2023). Cannabis in adolescence: lasting cognitive alterations and underlying mechanisms. *Cannabis and Cannabinoid Research*, *8*(1), 12–23. https://doi.org/10.1089/can.2022.0183

Schilling, K. G., Li, M., Rheault, F., Gao, Y., Cai, L., Zhao, Y., Xu, L., Ding, Z., Anderson, A. W., Landman, B. A., & Gore, J. C. (2023). Whole-brain, gray, and white matter time-locked functional signal changes with simple tasks and model-free analysis. Proceedings of the National Academy of Sciences of the United States of America, 120(42), e2219666120. https://doi.org/10.1073/pnas.2219666120 https://www.pnas.org/doi/10.1073/pnas.2219666120

SciShow. (2012). *The chemistry of addiction* [Video]. YouTube. https://www.youtube.com/watch?v=ukFjH9odsXw

SciShow. (2014). *The teenage brain explained* [Video]. YouTube. https://www.youtube.com/watch?v=hiduiTq1ei8

SciShow Psych. (2017). *When does your brain stop developing?* [Video]. YouTube. https://www.youtube.com/watch?v=_KxRAfXEzIQ

SciShow. (2014). *Your brain is plastic* [Video]. YouTube. https://www.youtube.com/watch?v=5KLPxDtMqe8

Seemiller, L. R., & Gould, T. J. (2020). The effects of adolescent alcohol exposure on learning and related neurobiology in humans and rodents. *Neurobiology of Learning and Memory, 172*, 107234. https://doi.org/10.1016/j.nlm.2020.107234 https://www.sciencedirect.com/science/article/pii/S1074742720300782

Segalowitz, S. J., & Davies, P. L. (2018). Charting the maturation of the frontal lobe: An electrophysiological strategy. In L. S. Wasserman, C. R. Genovese, & K. M. Kafadar (Eds.), *Handbook of Experimental Methods for Social and Behavioral Sciences* (pp. 559-579). John Wiley & Sons.

Selin, C., Rice, M. L., & Jackson, Y. (2022). Adversity exposure, syntax, and specific language impairment: An exploratory study. *Journal of Speech, Language, and Hearing Research: JSLHR, 65*(9), 3471–3490. https://doi.org/10.1044/2022_JSLHR-21-00578

Sethi, S., Wakeham, D., Ketter, T., Hooshmand, F., Bjornstad, J., Richards, B., Westman, E., Krauss, R. M., & Saslow, L. (2024). Ketogenic diet intervention on metabolic and psychiatric health in bipolar and schizophrenia: A pilot trial. *Psychiatry Research, 335*. https://doi.org/10.1016/j.psychres.2024.115866 https://www.sciencedirect.com/science/article/pii/S0165178124001513?via%3Dihub

Sharpe, S. L., Adams, M., Smith, E. K., Urban, B., & Silverstein, S. (2023). Inaccessibility of care and inequitable conceptions of suffering: A collective response to the construction of "terminal" anorexia nervosa. *Journal of Eating Disorders, 11*(1), 66. https://doi.org/10.1186/s40337-023-00791-2

Sheridan, M. A., & McLaughlin, K. A. (2014). Dimensions of early experience and neural development: Deprivation and threat. *Trends in Cognitive Sciences, 18*(11), 580-585.

Sherman, C. (2019). *A delicate balance: Risks, rewards, and the adolescent brain*. Dana Foundation. https://dana.org/article/a-delicate-balance-risks-rewards-and-the-adolescent-brain/

Sheynin, J., Lokshina, Y., Ahrari, S., Nickelsen, T., Duval, E. R., Ben-Zion, Z., Shalev, A. Y., Hendler, T., & Liberzon, I. (2023). Greater early post-trauma activation in right inferior frontal gyrus predicts recovery from posttraumatic stress disorder symptoms. *Biological Psychiatry: Cognitive Neuroscience and Neuroimaging.* https://doi.org/10.1016/j.bpsc.2023.07.002

Shohamy, D. (2018). *Teenage brains: Wired to learn* [Video]. YouTube. Columbia University's Zuckerman Institute. https://www.youtube.com/watch?v=1GSvzgrBKaM

Shonkoff, J. P., Garner, A. S., Committee on Psychosocial Aspects of Child and Family Health, Committee on Early Childhood, Adoption, and Dependent Care, & Section on Developmental and Behavioral Pediatrics (2012). The lifelong effects of early childhood adversity and toxic stress. *Pediatrics, 129*(1), e232–e246. https://doi.org/10.1542/peds.2011-2663

Shuai, R., Magner-Parsons, B., & Hogarth, L. (2023). Drinking to cope is uniquely associated with less specific and bleaker future goal generation in young hazardous drinkers. *Journal of Psychopathology and Behavioral Assessment, 45*(2), 403–414. https://doi.org/10.1007/s10862-023-10032-0

Shulman, E. P., Smith, A. R., Silva, K., Icenogle, G., Duell, N., Chein, J., & Steinberg, L., (2016). The dual systems model: Review, reappraisal, and reaffirmation, *Developmental Cognitive Neuroscience, 17*(C), 103-117. https://doaj.org/article/bcf2a35903f14e508a5b63149a144758

Siegel, D. (2018). *The adolescent brain* [Video]. YouTube. https://www.youtube.com/watch?v=oO1u5OEc5eY

Siegel, D. (2014). *The remodeling brain: Pruning and myelination* [Video]. YouTube. https://www.youtube.com/watch?v=jXnyMoZuKNU

Silke, C., Brady, B., Devaney, C., O'Brien, C., Durcan, M., Bunting, B., & Heary, C. (2023). Youth suicide and self-Harm: Latent class profiles of adversity and the moderating roles of perceived support and sense of safety. *Journal of Youth and Adolescence, 52*(6), 1255–1271. https://doi.org/10.1007/s10964-023-01762-1

Simonton, A. J., Young, C. C., & Johnson, K. E. (2018). Physical activity interventions to decrease substance use in youth: A review of the literature. *Substance Use & Misuse, 53*(12), 2052-2068.

Singh, S., & Topolnik, L. (2023). Inhibitory circuits in fear memory and fear-related disorders. *Frontiers in Neural Circuits, 17*, 1122314. https://doi.org/10.3389/fncir.2023.1122314

Sinha, R. (2018). The role of stress in addiction relapse. *Current Psychiatry Reports, 20*(10), 80.

Sithisarn, T., Granger, D. T., & Bada, H. S. (2012). Consequences of prenatal substance use. *International Journal of Adolescent Medicine and Health, 24*(2), 105–112. https://doi.org/10.1515/ijamh.2012.016

Soares, S., Santos, A. C., & Fraga, S. (2022). Adverse childhood experiences, bullying, inflammation and BMI in 10-year-old children: The biological embodiment. *PloS One*, *17*(8), e0273329. https://doi.org/10.1371/journal.pone.0273329

Society for Neuroscience. (2017). *The interactive brain model.* Brainfacts.org https://www.brainfacts.org/3d-brain#intro=false&focus=Brain

Somerville, L. H. (2016). Searching for signatures of brain maturity: What are we searching for?. *Neuron*, *92*(6), 1164–1167. https://doi.org/10.1016/j.neuron.2016.10.059

Sommer, M. (2022). *The US lacks adequate education around puberty and menstruation for young people – an expert on menstrual health explains.* The Conversation. https://theconversation.com/the-us-lacks-adequate-education-around-puberty-and-menstruation-for-young-people-an-expert-on-menstrual-health-explains-187501

Sosa, L. (2023, November 21). *Prenatal stages of brain development.* https://study.com/academy/lesson/prenatal-stages-of-brain-development.html

Spear, L. (2018). Effects of adolescent alcohol consumption on the brain and behaviour. *Nature Reviews Neuroscience*, *19*, 197-214. https://doi.org/10.1038/nrn.2018.10 https://www.nature.com/articles/nrn.2018.10

Spear, L. P. (2011). Rewards, aversions and affect in adolescence: Emerging convergences across laboratory animal and human data. *Developmental Cognitive Neuroscience*,*1*(4), 390-403. https://doi.org/10.1016/j.dcn.2011.08.001 https://www.sciencedirect.com/science/article/pii/S1878929311000818

Squeglia, L. M., Rinker, D. A., Bartsch, H., Castro, N., Chung, Y., Dale, A. M., Jernigan, T. L, & Tapert, S. F. (2014). Brain volume reductions in adolescent heavy drinkers. *Developmental Cognitive Neuroscience*, *9*, 117-125. https://doaj.org/article/cbe9cdb3f22341edb009d42bfaeee2a1 https://www.sciencedirect.com/science/article/pii/S1878929314000139?via%3Dihub

Stanford Children's Health. (n.d.). *The growing child: Teenager (13 to 18 years).* https://www.stanfordchildrens.org/en/topic/default?id=the-growing-child-adolescent-13-to-18-years-90-P02175

Steinberg, L. (2014). *Age of opportunity: Lessons from the new science of adolescence.* Houghton Mifflin Harcourt. https://psycnet.apa.org/record/2014-35308-000

Steinberg, L. (2016). *Age of opportunity: Lessons from the new science of adolescence* [Video]. YouTube. Microsoft Research. https://www.youtube.com/watch?v=MKMIKdvGsKI

Steinberg, L., Icenogle, G., Shulman, E. P., Breiner, K., Chein, J., Bacchini, D., Chang, L., Chaudhary, N., Giunta, L. D., Dodge, K. A., Fanti, K. A., Lansford, J. E., Malone, P. S., Oburu, P., Pastorelli, C., Skinner, A.T., Sorbring, E., Tapanya, S., Tirado,

L. M. U., ...Takash, H. M. S. (2018). Around the world, adolescence is a time of heightened sensation seeking and immature self-regulation, *Developmental Science, 21*(2). n/a. https://doi.org/10.1111/desc.12532

Stöppler, M. C. (2022). *Female reproductive system*. Medicine Net. https://www.medicinenet.com/female_reproductive_system/article.htm

Storz, M. A. (2020). Child abuse: A hidden crisis during Covid-19 quarantine. *Journal of Paediatric Child Health, 56*(6), 990-991.

Strike, L. T., Hansell, N. K., Chuang, K. H., Miller, J. L., de Zubicaray, G. I., Thompson, P. M., McMahon, K. L., & Wright, M. J. (2023). The Queensland Twin Adolescent Brain Project, a longitudinal study of adolescent brain development. *Scientific Data, 10*(1), 195. https://doi.org/10.1038/s41597-023-02038-w

Stringfield, S. J., & Torregrossa, M. M. (2021). Disentangling the lasting effects of adolescent cannabinoid exposure. *Progress in Neuro-Psychopharmacology and Biological Psychiatry, 104*. https://doi.org/10.1016/j.pnpbp.2020.110067 https://www.sciencedirect.com/science/article/pii/S0278584620303833

Substance Abuse and Mental Health Services Administration (SAMHSA). (2019). *Key substance use and mental health indicators in the United States: Results from the 2018 national survey on drug use and health.* https://www.samhsa.gov/data/sites/default/files/cbhsq-reports/NSDUHNationalFindingsReport2018/NSDUHNationalFindingsReport2018.pdf

Substance Abuse and Mental Health Services Administration (SAMHSA). (2023). *Mental health and substance use co-occurring disorders.* https://www.samhsa.gov/mental-health/mental-health-substance-use-co-occurring-disorders

Substance Abuse and Mental Health Services Administration (SAMHSA). (2021). *Rise in prescription drug misuse and abuse impacting teens.* https://www.samhsa.gov/homelessness-programs-resources/hpr-resources/rise-prescription-drug-misuse-abuse-impacting-teens

Substance Abuse and Mental Health Service Administration (SMHSA). (2022). *SAMHSA's national helpline.* https://www.samhsa.gov/find-help/national-helpline

Sullivan, R. M., Wade, N. E., Wallace, A. L., Tapert, S. F., Pelham, W. E., 3rd, Brown, S. A., Cloak, C. C., Feldstein Ewing, S. W., Madden, P. A. F., Martz, M. E., Ross, J. M., Kaiver, C. M., Wirtz, H. G., Heitzeg, M. M., & Lisdahl, K. M. (2022). Substance use patterns in 9 to 13-year-olds: Longitudinal findings from the Adolescent Brain Cognitive Development (ABCD) study. *Drug and Alcohol Dependence Reports, 5*, 100120. https://doi.org/10.1016/j.dadr.2022.100120

Sydnor, V. J., Larsen, B., Seidlitz, J., Adebimpe, A., Alexander-Bloch, A. F., Bassett, D. S., Bertolero, M. A., Cieslak, M., Covitz, S., Fan, Y., Gur, R. E., Gur, R. C., Mackey, A. P., Moore, T. M., Roalf, D. R., Shinohara, R. T., & Satterthwaite, T. D. (2023). Intrinsic activity development unfolds along a sensorimotor-association cortical

axis in youth. *Nature Neuroscience, 26*(4), 638–649.
https://doi.org/10.1038/s41593-023-01282-y

Tabachnick, A. R., Eiden, R. D., Labella, M. H., & Dozier, M. (2023). Effects of prenatal opioid exposure on infant sympathetic and parasympathetic nervous system acti vity. *Psychophysiology*, e14470. https://doi.org/10.1111/psyp.14470

Tamnes, C. K., Herting, M. M., Goddings, A. L., Meuwese, R., Blakemore, S. J., Dahl, R. E., Güroğlu, B., Raznahan, A., Sowell, E. R., Crone, E. A., & Mills, K. L. (2017). Development of the cerebral cortex across adolescence: A multisample study of inter-related longitudinal changes in cortical volume, surface area, and thickness. *The Journal of Neuroscience : The Official Journal of the Society for Neuroscience, 37*(12), 3402–3412.
https://doi.org/10.1523/JNEUROSCI.3302-16.2017

Tan, B., Browne, C. J., Nöbauer, T., Vaziri, A., Friedman, J. M., & Nestler, E. J. (2024). Drugs of abuse hijack a mesolimbic pathway that processes homeostatic need. *Science*. https://doi.org/10.1101/2023.09.03.556059

Tavolacci, M. P., Ladner, J., & Déchelotte, P. (2021). Sharp increase in eating disorders among university students since the COVID-19 Pandemic. *Nutrients, 13*(10), 3415. https://doi.org/10.3390/nu13103415

Teens Health. (2018). *Methamphetamine (Meth)*. Kids Health.
https://kidshealth.org/en/teens/meth.html

Telzer, E. H., Goldenberg, D., Fuligni, A. J., Lieberman, M. D., & Gálvan, A. (2015). Sleep variability in adolescence is associated with altered brain development. *Developmental Cognitive Neuroscience, 14*, 16–22. https://doi.org/10.1016/j.dcn.2015.05.007

Terry-McElrath, Y.M., O'Malley, P.M. & Johnston, L.D. (2020). Changes in the order of cigarette and marijuana initiation and associations with cigarette use, nicotine vaping, and marijuana use: U.S. 12th grade students, 2000–2019. *Prevention Science, 21*, 960-971.
https://doi.org/10.1007/s11121-020-01150-2
https://link.springer.com/article/10.1007/s11121-020-01150-2#ref-CR4

Tervo-Clemmens, B., Calabro, F. J., Parr, A. C., Fedor, J., Foran, W., & Luna, B. (2023). A canonical trajectory of executive function maturation from adolescence to adulthood. *Nature Communications, 14*. 6922. https://www.nature.com/articles/s41467-023-42540-8

Tetteh-Quarshie, S., & Risher, M. L. (2023). Adolescent brain maturation and the neuropathological effects of binge drinking: A critical review. *Frontiers in Neuroscience, 16*, 1040049. https://doi.org/10.3389/fnins.2022.1040049

Thackray, A. E., Hinton, E. C., Alanazi, T. M., Dera, A. M., Fujihara, K., Hamilton-Shield, J. P., King, J. A., Lithander, F. E., Miyashita, M., Thompson, J., Morgan, P. S., Davies, M. J., & Stensel, D. J. (2023). Exploring the acute effects of running on cerebral blood flow and food cue reactivity in healthy young men using functional magnetic resonance imaging. *Human Brain Mapping*, 10.1002/

hbm.26314. Advance online publication. https://doi.org/10.1002/hbm.26314

Thayer, R. E., Hansen, N. S., Prashad, S., Karoly, H. C., Filbey, F. M., Bryan, A. D., Ewing, S. W. F. (2020). Recent tobacco use has widespread associations with adolescent white matter microstructure. *Addictive Behaviors, 101*,106152, https://doi.org/10.1016/j.addbeh.2019.106152 https://www.sciencedirect.com/science/article/pii/S0306460319302916

The American College of Obstetricians and Gynecologists. (2018). *Your changing body: Puberty in girls (Especially for Teens).* https://www.acog.org/Patients/FAQs/Your-Changing-Body-Puberty-in-Girls-Especially-for-Teens

The Conversation. (2021). *Teenage mental health: How growing brains could explain emerging disorders.* https://theconversation.com/teenage-mental-health-how-growing-brains-could-explain-emerging-disorders-154007

The Psych Show. (2017). *How to learn major parts of the brain quickly: Learn how the brain works in 5 minutes using only your hands* [Video]. YouTube. https://www.youtube.com/watch?v=FczvTGluHKM

The Recovery Village Columbus. (2022). *Teen drug addiction and abuse resources.* https://www.columbusrecoverycenter.com/teen-addiction-resources/

The United States Drug Enforcement Administration. (2022). *DEA warns of brightly-colored fentanyl used to target young Americans.* https://www.dea.gov/press-releases/2022/08/30/dea-warns-brightly-colored-fentanyl-used-target-young-americans

Thirumoorthy, A., & Philip, M. (2023). Relationship of personality, psychological distress, and substance use with social network characteristics of college going young adults. *Indian Journal of Psychiatry, 65*(8), 832–838. https://doi.org/10.4103/indianjpsychiatry.indianjpsychiatry_182_23

Thompson, D. (2020, February 10). *Puberty starts a year earlier for girls now than in the 1970s.* HealthDay Reporter. https://www.webmd.com/children/news/20200210/puberty-starts-a-year-earlier-for-girls-now-than-in-the-1970s

Thorpe, H. A., Hamidullah, S., Jenkins, B.W., & Khokhar, J. Y. (2020). Adolescent neurodevelopment and substance use: Receptor expression and behavioral consequences. *Pharmacology & Therapeutics, 206.* https://doi.org/10.1016/j.pharmthera.2019.107431 https://www.sciencedirect.com/science/article/pii/S0163725819301834

Tobore, T. O., (2019). On the potential harmful effects of E-Cigarettes (EC) on the developing brain: The relationship between vaping-induced oxidative stress and adolescent/young adults social maladjustment. *Journal of Adolescence, 76.* 202-209. https://doi.org/10.1016/j.adolescence.2019.09.004

Todd, J., Cardellicchio, P., Swami, V., Cardini, F., & Aspell, J. E. (2021). Weaker implicit interoception is associated with more negative body image: Evidence from gastric-alpha phase amplitude coupling and the heartbeat evoked potential. *Cortex; A Journal Devoted to the Study of the Nervous System and Behavior, 143,* 254–266. https://doi.org/10.1016/j.cortex.2021.07.006

Toga, A. W., Thompson, P. M., & Sowell, E. R. (2006). Mapping brain maturation. *Trends in Neurosciences, 29*(3), 148-159.

Tran, H. G. N., Thai, T. T., Dang, N. T. T., Vo, D. K., & Duong, M. H. T. (2023). Cyber-victimization and its effect on depression in adolescents: A systematic review and meta-analysis. *Trauma, Violence & Abuse, 24*(2), 1124–1139. https://doi.org/10.1177/15248380211050597

Transforming Education. (2017). *Importance of self-efficacy* [Video]. YouTube. https://www.youtube.com/watch?v=VW5v6PQ5PEc&t=0s

Truth Initiative. (2021). *Flavored tobacco use among youth and young adults.* https://truthinitiative.org/research-resources/emerging-tobacco-products/flavored-tobacco-use-among-youth-and-young-adults

Tyler, M. (2018). *What is addiction?* https://www.healthline.com/health/addiction

Tucker, J. S., Rodriguez, A., Dunbar, M. S., Pedersen, E. R., Davis, J. P., Shih, R. A. &

D'Amico, E. J. (2019). Cannabis and tobacco use and co-use: Trajectories and correlates from early adolescence to emerging adulthood. *Drug and Alcohol Dependence, 204.* https://doi.org/10.1016/j.drugalcdep.2019.06.004

Turker, S., Kuhnke, P., Eickhoff, S. B., Caspers, S., & Hartwigsen, G. (2023). Cortical, subcortical, and cerebellar contributions to language processing: A meta-analytic review of 403 neuroimaging experiments. *Psychological Bulletin.* Advance online publication. https://doi.org/10.1037/bul0000403

Turnbridge. (2021). *5 common mental health disorders among teens.* https://www.turnbridge.com/news-events/latest-articles/common-mental-health-disorders/

Twenge, J. M. (2020). Increases in depression, self-harm, and suicide among U.S. adolescents after 2012 and links to technology use: Possible mechanisms. *Psychiatric Research and Clinical Practice, 2*(1), 19–25. https://doi.org/10.1176/appi.prcp.20190015

Uchitel, J., Hadland, S. E., Raman, S. R., McClellan, M. B., & Wong, C. A. (2019). *The opioid epidemic: A needed focus on adolescents and young adults.* Health Affairs. https://www.healthaffairs.org/do/10.1377/forefront.20191115.977344/full/

UNICEF. (2018). *The adolescent brain: A second window of opportunity.* https://www.unicef-irc.org/article/1750-the-adolescent-brain-a-second-window-of-opportunity.html

United Kingdom Drug Situation. *Summary.* (2021). at: https://www.gov.uk/government/publications/united-kingdom-drug-situation-focal-point-annual-report/uk-drug-situation-2019-summary

University of Florida Health. (n.d.). *Puberty and adolescence.* UF Health. https://ufhealth.org/puberty-and-adolescence

University of Maryland School of Medicine. (2013). *How marijuana affects the adolescent brain* [Video]. YouTube. New University of Maryland School of Medicine Research. https://www.youtube.com/watch?v=Tgp-oZ_f6Xk

University of Michigan. (2021). *Daily marijuana use among US college students reaches new 40-year high: National study also shows increases in hallucinogen use, reaching highest level among college students since early 1980s.* https://news.umich.edu/daily-marijuana-use-among-us-college-students-reaches-new-40-year-high/

University of Rochester Medical Center. (n.d.). *Executive function.* https://www.urmc.rochester.edu/encyclopedia/content.aspx?ContentTypeID=1&ContentID=3051

University of Utah Health Sciences. (2015, February 11). *Meth messes up brains of youths far more than adults.* ScienceDaily. www.sciencedaily.com/releases/2015/02/150211131854.htm

U.S. Department of Health & Human Services. (n. d.) *Alcohol use in adolescence.* https://www.hhs.gov/ash/oah/adolescent-development/substance-use/alcohol/resources/index.html

U.S. Department of Health and Human Services, National Institute of Mental Health. (2017). *Major depression.* https://www.nimh.nih.gov/health/statistics/major-depression

U.S. Department of Health and Human Services, National Institute of Mental Health. (2021). *Mental illness.* https://www.nimh.nih.gov/health/statistics/mental-illness.shtml

US Department of Health and Human Services. (2017). *What are some common signs of pregnancy?* National Institutes of Health. https://www.nichd.nih.gov/health/topics/pregnancy/conditioninfo/signs

Uytun, M. C. (2018). Development period of prefrontal cortex. *Journal of Neurology and Neuroscience, 9*(2), 1-5.

VanBronkhorst, S. B., Abraham, E., Dambreville, R., Ramos-Olazagasti, M. A., Wall, M., Saunders, D. C., Monk, C., Alegría, M., Canino, G. J., Bird, H., & Duarte, C. S. (2023). Sociocultural risk and resilience in the context of adverse childhood experiences. *JAMA Psychiatry,* e234900. Advance online publication. https://doi.org/10.1001/jamapsychiatry.2023.4900

van der Kolk, B., (2014). *The body keeps score: The brain, mind, and body in the healing of trauma.* Penguin Books.

van der Laan, S. E. I., Berkelbach van der Sprenkel, E. E., Lenters, V. C., Finkenauer, C., van der Ent, C. K., & Nijhof, S. L. (2023). Defining and measuring resilience in children with a chronic disease: A scoping review. *Adversity and Resilience Science,* 4(2), 105–123. https://doi.org/10.1007/s42844-023-00092-2

Van Dijken, H., Malti, T., & Loeber, R. (2018). Callous-unemotional traits as a predictor of severity and chronicity of child and adolescent antisocial behavior. *Aggression and Violent Behavior, 38,* 82–95.

van Drunen, L., Toenders, Y. J., Wierenga, L. M., & Crone, E. A. (2023). Effects of COVID-19 pandemic on structural brain development in early adolescence. *Scientific Reports, 13*(1), 5600. https://doi.org/10.1038/s41598-023-32754-7

van Duin, L., Bevaart, F., Zijlmans, J., Luijks, M. A., Doreleijers, T. A. H., Wierdsma, A. I., Oldehinkel, A. J., Marhe, R., & Popma, A. (2019). The role of adverse childhood experiences and mental health care use in psychological dysfunction of male multi-problem young adults. *European Child & Adolescent Psychiatry, 28*(8), 1065–1078. https://doi.org/10.1007/s00787-018-1263-4

Vannini, P. (2023). The psychological impact of the Coronavirus pandemic and the importance of resilience. *Biological Psychiatry. Cognitive Neuroscience and Neuroimaging, 8*(2), 133–134. https://doi.org/10.1016/j.bpsc.2022.12.001

Vannucci, A., Fields, A., Hansen, E., Katz, A., Kerwin, J., Tachida, A., Martin, N., & Tottenham, N. (2023). Interpersonal early adversity demonstrates dissimilarity from early socioeconomic disadvantage in the course of human brain development: A meta-analysis. *BioRxiv: The Preprint Server for Biology,* 2023.02.16.528877. https://doi.org/10.1101/2023.02.16.528877

Varodayan, F. P., Pahng, A. R., Davis, T. D., Gandhi, P., Bajo, M., Steinman, M. Q., Kiosses, W. B., Blednov, Y. A., Burkart, M. D., Edwards, S., Roberts, A. J., & Roberto, M. (2023). Chronic ethanol induces a pro-inflammatory switch in interleukin-1β regulation of GABAergic signaling in the medial prefrontal cortex of male mice. *Brain, Behavior, and Immunity, 110,* 125–139. https://doi.org/10.1016/j.bbi.2023.02.020

Vasković, J. (2021. December 21). *Subcortical structures.* Ken Hub. https://www.kenhub.com/en/library/anatomy/subcortical-structures-anatomy

Viejo, C., & Fernandez, N. T. (2022). *Teenage brains: What is happening and why it leads to more risky behaviors.* The Conversation. https://neurosciencenews.com/teenage-brains-risk-21757/

Walker, D. M., Bell, M. R., Flores, C., Gulley, J. M., Willing, J., & Paul, M. J. (2017). Adolescence and reward: Making sense of neural and behavioral changes amid the chaos. *The Journal of Neuroscience: The Official Journal of the Society for Neuroscience, 37*(45), 10855–10866. https://doi.org/10.1523/JNEUROSCI.1834-17.2017

Walter, N., Nikoleizig, L., Alfermann, D. (2019). Effects of self-talk training on competitive anxiety, self-efficacy, volitional skills, and performance: An intervention study with junior sub-elite athletes. *Sports*, 7(6):148. https://doi.org/10.3390/sports7060148

Webwise. (n.d.) *A parents' guide to Minecraft.* https://www.webwise.ie/parents/a-parents-guide-to-minecraft/

Welsh, J. W., Dennis, M. L., Funk, R., Mataczynski, M. J., & Godley, M. D. (2022). Trends and age-related disparities in opioid use disorder treatment admissions for adolescents and young adults. *Journal of Substance Abuse Treatment*, 132, 108584. https://doi.org/10.1016/j.jsat.2021.108584

Welsh, J. W., Sitar, S. I., Hunter, B. D., Godley, M. D., & Dennis, M. L. (2023). Substance use severity as a predictor for receiving medication for opioid use disorder among adolescents: An analysis of the 2019 TEDS. *Drug and Alcohol Dependence*, 246, 109850. https://doi.org/10.1016/j.drugalcdep.2023.109850

West, M. (2021). *Female reproductive organ anatomy.* Medical News Today. https://www.medicalnewstoday.com/articles/female-reproductive-organ-anatomy

Whitaker, R., Hendry, M., Aslam, R., Booth, A., Carter, B., Charles, J. M., Craine, N., Tudor Edwards, R., Noyes, J., Ives Ntambwe, L., Pasterfield, D., Rycroft-Malone, J., & Williams, N. (2016). Intervention now to eliminate repeat unintended pregnancy in teenagers (INTERUPT): A systematic review of intervention effectiveness and cost-effectiveness, and qualitative and realist synthesis of implementation factors and user engagement. *Health Technology Assessment (Winchester, England)*, 20(16), 1–214. https://doi.org/10.3310/hta20160

Williams, A. S., Park, B., & Pedersen, Z. P. (2023). The influence of music on self-paced fitness consumers' perceived motivational qualities and optimal level of emotional state and satisfaction with exercise experience. *International Journal of Sport Management and Marketing*, 23(4) 310–326. https://doi.org/10.1504/IJSMM.2023.131950

Williamson, A. A., Zendarski, N., Lange, K., Quach, J., Molloy, C., Clifford, S. A., & Mulraney, M. (2021). Sleep problems, internalizing and externalizing symptoms, and domains of health-related quality of life: bidirectional associations from early childhood to early adolescence. *Sleep*, 44(1), zsaa139. https://doi.org/10.1093/sleep/zsaa139

Willbrand, E. H., Ferrer, E., Bunge, S. A., & Weiner, K. S. (2023). Development of human lateral prefrontal sulcal morphology and its relation to reasoning performance. *The Journal of Neuroscience: The Official Journal of the Society for Neuroscience*, 43(14), 2552–2567. https://doi.org/10.1523/JNEUROSCI.1745-22.2023

Wimmer, G. E., Liu, Y., McNamee, D. C., & Dolan, R. J. (2023). Distinct replay signatures for prospective decision-making and memory preservation. *Proceedings of the National Academy of Sciences of the United States of America*, 120(6), e2205211120. https://doi.org/10.1073/pnas.2205211120

Win, E., Zainal, N. H., & Newman, M. G. (2021). Trait anger expression mediates childhood trauma predicting for adulthood anxiety, depressive, and alcohol use disorders. *Journal of Affective Disorders, 288*, 114–121. https://doi.org/10.1016/j.jad.2021.03.086

Winhusen, T., Theobald, J., Kaelber, D. C., & Lewis, D. (2019). Regular cannabis use, with and without tobacco co-use, is associated with respiratory disease. *Drug and Alcohol Dependence, 204*. https://doi.org/10.1016/j.drugalcdep.2019.107557

Wolpert, M., Görzig, A., Deighton, J., & Fugard, A. J. (2015). Young people's satisfaction with mental health services: Bridging the gap between research and practice. *The British Journal of Psychiatry, 206*(5), 383-384. https://doi.org/10.1192/bjp.bp.114.153072

Wondrium. (2017). *What does the brain's frontal cortex do? (Professor Robert Sapolsky explains)* [Video]. YouTube. https://www.youtube.com/watch?v=3RRtyV_UFJ8

World Health Organization (WHO). (2020, September 28). *Adolescent mental health.* https://www.who.int/news-room/fact-sheets/detail/adolescent-mental-health

World Health Organization (WHO). (2022). *Mental disorders, key facts.* https://www.who.int/news-room/fact-sheets/detail/mental-disorders

Yarborough, B. J. H., Stumbo, S. P., Coleman, M. J., Ling Grant, D. S., Hulsey, J., Shaw, J. L., Ahmedani, B. K., Bruschke, C., Carson, C. P. A., Cooper, R., Firemark, A., Hulst, D., Massimino, S., Miller-Matero, L. R., Swanson, J. R., Leonard, A., Westphal, J., & Coleman, K. J. (2023). Suicide-related care among patients who have experienced an opioid-involved overdose. *General Hospital Psychiatry, 85*, 8–18. https://doi.org/10.1016/j.genhosppsych.2023.09.006

Yeager, D. S., & Dweck, C. S. (2020). What can be learned from growth mindset controversies? *American Psychologist, 75*(9), 1269–1284.

Yeo J. (2023). Influence of food-derived bioactives on gut microbiota compositions and their metabolites by focusing on neurotransmitters. *Food Science and Biotechnology, 32*(8), 1019–1027. https://doi.org/10.1007/s10068-023-01293-2

Youth.Gov. (n.d.) *Opioids.* https://youth.gov/youth-topics/substance-abuse/opioids

Yu, Q., Peng, Y., Mishra, V., Ouyang, A., Li, H., Zhang, H., Chen, M., Liu, S., & Huang, H. (2014). Microstructure, length, and connection of limbic tracts in normal human brain development. *Frontiers in Aging Neuroscience, 6.* https://doaj.org/article/b035e8cf8ac1431eaed5dead2c8fd074

Zeiner, K., Dabiri, B., Burns, C., Kummer, L., & Kaniusas, E. (2023). Mental and physiological wellbeing while rowing across the North Atlantic: A single-case study of subjective versus objective data. *Frontiers in Physiology, 14*, 1244438. https://doi.org/10.3389/fphys.2023.1244438

Zelazo, P. D., Blair, C. B., & Willoughby, M. T. (2016). *Executive function: Implications for education.* NCER 2017-2000, National Center for Education Research.

Zhu, J., Anderson, C. M., Ohashi, K., Khan, A., & Teicher, M. H. (2023). Potential sensitive period effects of maltreatment on amygdala, hippocampal and cortical response to threat. *Molecular Psychiatry*, 10.1038/s41380-023-02002-5. Advance online publication. https://doi.org/10.1038/s41380-023-02002-5

Zolkoski, S. M., & Bullock, L. M. (2012). Resilience in children and youth: A review. *Children and Youth Services Review, 34*(12). 2295-2303. https://doi.org/10.1016/j.childyouth.2012.08.009 https://www.sciencedirect.com/science/article/pii/S0190740912003337

ACKNOWLEDGEMENTS

I extend my warmest appreciation to the readers who embraced Book 1 with open arms. Pouring my heart and soul into these pages, I aimed to make a difference, and your enthusiasm and support have fueled my journey to bring Book 2 to fruition. Your encouragement inspires me beyond measure.

To those who shared their thoughts and reviews of Book 1, your feedback has been invaluable in shaping the direction of this sequel. Thank you for your honesty and insight, which have enriched the experience for me and my fellow readers.

I offer my heartfelt thanks to Ms. Yvette M. Calleiro, an experienced educator and prolific young adult author, for generously giving her time to read advance copies of Books 1 and 2 and providing me with insightful feedback. Ms. Calleiro, your expertise is a treasure I hold dear.

I also want to sincerely thank Ms. Kristy Jo Volchko, a children's book writer, for her unwavering support of this series. The hours she spent reading and offering heartfelt reviews of the initial concept mean the world to me.

Moreover, I extend my eternal gratitude to Dr. Mikael Häggström, the creator and editor of Radlines (https://radlines.org), for graciously allowing me to use his "Secondary Sex Characteristics" image in Chapter 3. Dr. Häggström, your willingness to share your resources enhances the connotation of the text, and I am truly honored.

I want to express my immense gratitude to the editor, Mr. Barry L. at Reedsy. You were meticulous, responsive, and communicated well throughout the work. Your final draft's polish elevates the script's quality.

My social media followers, your unselfish support has been constant source of inspiration and motivation. I am deeply grateful for your encouragement.

Finally, my dearest family, words cannot express my gratitude for your unwavering support. As I spent countless hours crafting this series, you were my rock.

ABOUT THE AUTHOR

Dr. Chang-Lim, a multi-award-winning author with a Doctorate in Optometry, a Master of Science in Microbiology, and a Master of Arts in Psychology (focusing on developmental psychology), undertakes all the research and writing processes.

Dr. Chang-Lim's extensive experience in clinical research and over 30 years in eye-care practice uniquely position her to delve into various topics in the series. Drawing from academic and creative writing backgrounds, she ensures scientifically and clinically supported content, providing valuable insights for readers. The integration of professional and personal experiences allows Dr. Chang-Lim to address the challenges and aspirations of teens and young adults.

Passionate about mental health awareness, Dr. Chang-Lim aims to inspire resilience, foster mental well-being, and contribute to a happy and fulfilling life for all. She believes that everyone deserves a joyful existence. To learn more about Dr. Chang-Lim, please visit her website: www.EichinChangLim.com

ABOUT THE REVIEWER AND EDITOR

Dr. Lora Erickson is an international psychologist, licensed mental health clinician, and core faculty in the Master of Arts in Psychology program with The Chicago School of Professional Psychology. She earned her Bachelor of Science in Psychology from Illinois State University, her Master of Arts in Counseling from Lincoln University, and her Doctorate in International Psychology (trauma specialization) from The Chicago School of Professional Psychology. For nearly 20 years, Dr. Erickson has been teaching and providing clinical services to children, teenagers, and young adults. She is also a mother to a teen and preteen and cares deeply for young people, wanting the very best that life has to offer for them. She is also an award-winning researcher within APA (American Psychology Association) Division 52 (International Psychology) and has held multiple positions within the APA as Early Career Psychologist Chair for Division 52, and currently serves as an editor for APA Division 2 (Teaching Psychology) for the their online publication, "This is How I Teach." To learn more about Lora, see her websites, https://www.thechicagoschool.edu/academics/faculty/byname/lora_erickson/

ABOUT THIS SERIES

- How to triumphantly wade through the traps of social media
- Ways to eliminate the stigma of mental illness so any young person can be comfortable seeking support and treatment
- Key strategies to tackle self-harm, panic attacks, bullies, childhood trauma, substance abuse, neurodiversity, and much, much more!

Talking About Adolescence: Anxiety, Depression, and Adolescent Mental Health is the must-have guide to thriving during those formative years and is the first book in the *Talking About Adolescence* series. If you like life-changing knowledge, learning more about yourself, and gaining control, then you'll love this comprehensive handbook.

Buy *Talking About Adolescence* to find self-empowerment today!

Amazon and Barnes & Noble: https://mybook.to/TAA1

Apple Books https://mybook.to/TAA_Bk1

Google Play https://bit.ly/TAA1_GooglePlay

Kobo https://bit.ly/TAA1_Kobo

Others https://books2read.com/TAA1

TALKING ABOUT ADOLESCENCE

How to Navigate through Adolescence Successfully and
Have a Happy Life
Book 3: Love, Sex, Relationships and Life
(Coming Soon!)

Are you ready to take your dating and relationship game to the next level? Book 3 of the *Talking about Adolescence* series is here to guide you through the twists and turns as you navigate love and intimacy during your teenage years. From crushes to first dates and beyond, this book is packed with practical advice on building healthy relationships that can support you in feeling happy and fulfilled. Discover how to communicate effectively, set boundaries, and make decisions that are right for you. Learn how to avoid common pitfalls that can derail your dating life, and get tips on dealing with heartbreak and toxic relationships. This book is your go-to guide for developing positive and fulfilling relationships that will enhance your confidence and happiness.

Stay tuned for the release of this exciting book!

Dear Reader,

Thank you for finishing Book 2 of *Talking About Adolescence: Supercharge Your Body and Brain Power!* Your support means the world to me. Reviews are vital for helping other readers find my book, and I would greatly appreciate it if you could take a moment to leave your thoughts.

Thank you again for your time and support!

Warm regards,
Eichin Chang-Lim

Sign up for my newsletter: Please click on the link: https://eichin-changlim.com/contact/.